CW00501078

ALL IS FAIR IN LOVE
AND WAR

THE PRICE OF SILENCE 4

ELLE MAE

The Price of Silence

Cover design by Ryn Katryn Digital Art

Edits by Lilly

ISBN 978-1-7376000-8-4 (paperback)

ISBN 978-1-7376000-5-3 (ebook)

www.ellemaebooks.com

ALSO BY ELLE MAE

Stand Alone:

Contract Bound: A Lesbian Vampire Romance

Other World Series:

An Imposter in Warriors Clothing

A Coward In A Kings Crown

Winterfell Academy Series:

The Price of Silence: Winterfell Academy Book 1

The Price of Silence: Winterfell Academy Book 2

The Price of Silence: Winterfell Academy Book 3

Short and Smutty:

The Sweetest Sacrifice: An Erotic Demon Romance

Eden Rose(Contemporary Pen Name):

The Ties That Bind Us

For those who want more than a story about coming out.

NOTE

This is a work of fiction. Names, characters, business, events and incidents are the products of the author's imagination. Any resemblance to actual persons, living or dead, or actual events is purely coincidental.

Before moving forward, please note that the themes in this book can be dark and trigger some people. The themes can include but are not limited to; sexual assault, death, gore, domestic abuse, character deaths, trafficking, dubious consent, mention of CSA, mention of incest, misgendering, blood play, self harm, cannibalism, and violence.

If you need help, please reach out to the resources below.

For those who need resources:

National Suicide Prevention Lifeline

1-800-273-8255

https://suicidepreventionlifeline.org/

National Domestic Violence Hotline

1-800-799-7233

https://www.thehotline.org/

THE PRICE OF SILENCE 4

WINTERFELL ACADEMY

ELLE MAE

I
MALIK

Exhaustion weighed on me.

I no longer felt like the unbeatable demon I once had been. I was once blinded by my power, thought that I was above everyone and anything in this world. After a millennium, I finally realized that I was just as much a pawn in this game as everyone else.

I should have been upset or angry that my time in the lime-light was taken from me...but instead I was relieved. It was *tiring* to try and prove to the world that you were the one in charge and woefully unfulfilling, even with a power like mine.

I didn't want people to run and hide, or cower when they looked towards me. I wanted them to run to me. I wanted to be trusted and to trust others...and I didn't realize how much I was missing out on until I saw Rosie interact with the others.

She had a power that was undeniable, and it had nothing to do with her heritage.

She had an intenseness to her that seemed to attract people like moths to a flame. *I* wanted that. *I* wanted to not just be around her and soak up the light, but emit it as well.

It was Xena and Ezekiel who had taught me that personali-ties like Rosie's were a weakness. They taught me that you needed to grab the world by the throat and make it submit and you were permitted to do whatever you wanted to make people bend, just because you had the power to do so.

But they were so wrong.

They instead tried to say that *they* were at the top of the food chain. The Originals, the first demons and witches of this world who had single-handedly changed the course of our world for good.

But they too were blinded by their power. They were too cocky in their ways and had full faith that their plan to rule over the world would succeed. The years they had lived unharmed and surrounded by their demon-shaped armor had lulled them into a false sense of security.

But if this worked, they wouldn't live to see the end of this year, and I would make damn sure that they would never hurt my people *ever* again.

If I could attain that...this exhaustion was well worth it.

The coolness of the dark, empty room settled around us. There was a slight bite to it, warning us of colder months that lay ahead, but that wasn't all it warned of.

The air around us was charged with magic so powerful even as a demon I could feel the tingle of it run across my skin.

It was a warning that someone powerful lay ahead.

I shifted my gaze, noting the glowing eyes beside me. This time, it was no longer just Matt and his siblings. Now we had backup and that same jolt of magic could be felt through us all, binding us to our fate here.

The others, they had given up a lot to come here with me. There was no guarantee that this would work and in all honesty, the chance of us showing up dead to our next meeting with Xena and Ezekiel felt far more likely.

But I knew Marques, trusted him enough to know that if the demons next to me wanted to risk their lives, it wouldn't be him delivering the killing blow.

The others shifted and waited for a sign that we were welcome.

A pair of glowing hazel eyes met mine and even through the silence I felt the threat of their unspoken words.

We had come further than I had imagined, all of the pieces were coming together and we were just waiting on one more final piecc to settle before we could move...and end this thing once and for all.

That was the hope I was holding onto.

The once dark room lit up without warning, jolting my senses. I scanned the room, looking for a threat but all I saw was an empty foyer in front of us. A sense of relief washed through me when I saw that the group I had come with, still had all of their limbs.

Eli, Matt, Maximus...and Rae all stood next to me in various levels of discomfort.

Rae was scanning the place as well before her gaze met mine again. She was patiently waiting for directions, a move that was astonishing coming from anyone that allied themselves with Eli.

It was risky to bring Rae, but I had a feeling that she would only continue to hinder us if she was not brought into this as well. She had caught on too quickly to our actions before and we couldn't chance someone as cunning as her falling to the wrong side.

Eli was standing next to Rae, but their gaze was glued on Matt. They were...displeased to have to continue work with the redheaded hybrid and insisted that erasing Rosie's memory of the burning town had been a mistake.

Maybe it had been... I thought.

But that thought came out of my weakness for her. I knew, logically, that we were too close to the end to leave any possible stone unturned. Any liability would need to be dealt with and that came to our meeting today...

We had used Claudine's power to get us across the border into Canada where Marques's main base was kept. Deep within the woods stood an impossibly old manor that was surrounded by a blue shimmering barrier that would cut the intruders in half if they tried to force entry.

It was a strong piece of magic and one only capable by a very talented witch. The same witch that stood next to Matt with his arms crossed and a scowl on his face.

Maximus was a hidden gem that had taken years to cultivate. Without him, there would have been no way for us to accomplish such a feat as this. I would rely on him heavily for what was to come.

His brother, Matt, looked my way and sent me a triumphant smile. The one that I was starting to understand as the most dangerous expression he had.

The man we had been waiting for entered the room with long strides, from an open door to our left. His black hair hung limply at his shoulders and he was dressed in a suit and tie. With each step his aura radiated out of him and I fought to keep from flinching as his dead eyes met mine.

While I knew this man, grew up with him, I had seen him commit the types of sins that I could not stomach. He was not one to be messed with, no matter what our relationship had been.

He stopped a mere twenty feet away from us, his head turning back to watch as Claudine entered the room the same way he had come from.

Her red hair was bouncing with each step and her bright pink dress clashed against the dark interior of the manor. She smiled at Marques as if they were best friends.

Marques did not return the gesture.

"Let's cut to the chase, shall we?" Marques asked, his voice cutting through the silence and slashing us harder than the cold air had.

"I don't know what you expect from Eli and me," Rae said in a tone that aired her displeasure with ease.

I had relaxed too soon, I grumbled in my head.

Leave it up to Eli's group to mouth off to the most powerful being in this world.

"I don't *expect* you to do anything," he answered, his eyes looking over Rae carefully. I felt her shift next to me. "You are here because I require assistance and in return you get something from me. It is a mutual exchange."

"I already killed my parents," Rae said without a hint of remorse. "There is nothing else you can give me."

There was a pause between the group and my mind went into overdrive.

I may not care about the girl next to me as much as I did Eli...but Rosie would be heartbroken if Rae was taken from her so soon and even just the thought of Rosie in pain caused my chest to twist.

"We need your help," I said before Marques could speak.

Rae shot me a look as if she didn't believe my words.

"Xena and Ezekiel are at their weakest and this will be the only time that we can finally be free," I continued. "We need as many people on this as possible and I hate to say it...but you are talented when it comes to scheming."

The flash in her eyes betrayed her emotionless face.

"You have had years to plan this," Eli interrupted. "Centuries even...and you expect me to believe you have no plan? We free the people from the town, force the Originals out of their hiding spots, and then what?"

"They are going to kill them," Rae said. "No... You want us to kill them. To do your dirty work just like they asked of Rosie."

"A mutual exchange," he reminded. "Eli is willing to kill their father, or has that changed since the last time we spoke?"

Eli shoved their hands in their pants pockets and shrugged.

"That was the plan," they replied with an air of disinterest.

"What makes you think Rosie will want to kill her mom?" Rae asked. "Matt erased her memory, we have been keeping secrets from her, how are we any different from them?"

I looked down at my feet. It was a long shot to believe that Rosie would bend over for people she hardly knew.

People who wanted to turn her into a murderer.

It wasn't ideal, nor was it what I wanted personally for her. I wanted her to stay out of this as long as possible, leave the hard stuff to me and the others while she lives the life she never could.

But right now, we need to end this.

"She has a choice," I said. "Like you all do. The memory...it was necessary."

But the more I thought about it, the less I agreed. It was a split-second decision and it was made out of pure panic.

But then again Matt didn't know what we knew. I caught Claudine's gaze and she sent me a nod, confirming what I knew all along.

Leave it to the twins to save the day, I thought.

The tiredness in my bones lifted enough for me to catch my breath.

"They watch her," Matt added. "Because of her blood. She is useful because they think they can use her as a shield."

"And Eli?" Rae asked. "Daxton? He ate her father."

"Daxton's magic will be the death of him," Marques said. "They are sure, as am I, that his magic will corrode him from the inside out. His body was not made to handle this power so he is not a threat. And Eli..."

"They have lost faith in me," they answered for the Marques. "That much I know. To them I am useless, too reckless."

Rae was silent at their admission.

"She has to know," Rae insisted. "I refuse to let her go through this blind."

"It's not you—" Matt started with venom slipping through his words but I stopped him with the clearing of my throat.

"We can arrange something," I said. Any further arguing and I was not sure that we would get out of here before the others noticed. "I agree that it is wrong to have her so in the dark especially when her role is so vital." Rae's shoulders relaxed at my compromise. "But not now... They are too close to her at the moment. We need to wait until we can safely separate her from them and then we can explain the plan to her. She can decide then if she wants to continue down this path."

Rae nodded.

"And then what?" Eli asked. "When do I get to kill him?"

Marques smiled at them.

"I think it would be more satisfying to get your mother first, don't you?" he asked.

Eli tried to hide their smile but I saw the twitch of their lips. It was a troubling sign.

"What if she doesn't want to kill them?" Rae asked.

"Stop worrying about her," Matt said with a huff. "Just go with it, make your demands, and have Rosie figure it out on her own."

The ice-cold glare that Rae sent Matt was enough to start my own heart.

"In a room full of snakes, at least *one* person needs to look out for the key to this plan," Rae hissed then turned back to Marques. "Because that's what she is, right? No one is worried about Ezekiel."

Marques eyed her for a moment before speaking.

"No," he confirmed. "Not a soul is worried about Ezekiel, at the moment."

The weight of his words was felt around the room.

"So what do we do?" Rae pushed again.

"I will get Eli's mother," Marques said. "When I have secured her I will send you a message, that is when the plan starts."

"And the others?" Eli asked.

"First," Marques said. "Hide your mother's body where it cannot be found. The longer they do not know, the better. Then since they are still at Winterfell, just as school starts, we need to corner them."

"Why when school starts?" Matt asked. "Why not sooner? They are just sitting ducks."

"They will have less chance to move if the campus is overflowing with students," I murmured.

I felt Marques's power grab ahold of me and the plan unfolded in my mind, but it would only work with Rosie.

And a particularly volatile Rosie. Then when they were busy with her...we would attack alongside Marques.

It was simple, just needed to be kept from them long enough so that we could slowly tear off each of their strongest warriors, and it started with Eli's mother, and then I would take care of her handmaidens.

"Easy," I said and crossed my arms. "We target the mother first, I will put the rest of the plan in place and then we pull Rosie away from them and get her on board." I turned to Rae. "That will be your job."

"Is that enough to establish trust?" Marques asked and held out his arm to Claudine.

She conjured a bright pink dagger and held it to his skin.

"If I take the oath," Rae said. "How much access will you have to my mind?"

"More than what you are comfortable with, child," he said. "But understand I only do this for your benefit and safekeeping. With this your powers will increase and if anything were to happen, I can intervene."

Rae swallowed and did not dare to step forward.

"I am not getting on my knees," Eli said stepping forward. They sent a look to Rae. "I told them to fuck off last time they offered, but now it seems we don't have a choice."

"You do," I interjected. "You have a choice, but we are so close to ending this that we cannot do this half-assed. *Everything* is on the line here. Rosie's life, your future, they know everything and have eyes everywhere. There is no escaping."

"Will I have access to you as well?" Rae asked.

Marques smiled at her.

"To an extent," he said. "If you need me I am but a thought away."

Eli closed the space between them and Marques and nodded towards Claudine.

Marques didn't even flinch as she brought down the dagger and drew a solid line through his forearm, dark blood pulsating out of the wound.

"You should get that checked out," Eli murmured and leaned down to lick the blood from the wound.

They reeled back and began coughing immediately before falling to the ground in a heap. Their body convulsed as they clawed at their neck. Their mouth was open but no screams sounded.

"Eli!" Rae yelled and dashed forward.

"Wait," I commanded. Her eyes met mine just long enough that my power was able to hit her and she stopped in her tracks.

Eli's body stopped convulsing and the same aura that came out of Marques in waves started to flow from them. Slowly they crawled to their knees, a manic laughter filling the space. With shaky limbs they stood and reared their head back, their blue eyes wide as they looked up to the ceiling.

"It's there," they said between their giggles. "I feel it."

Rae took a step back, her eyes wide as she stared at Eli. Her hand clenched into a fist.

"What do you feel?" Marques asked.

"The power," they replied. "You and...the thoughts."

They turned to look at me and walked towards me slowly. Their hand came out, stopping mere inches from my head.

"Like I can just..." they made a plucking motion with their fingers and their eyes lit up before meeting mine. A chilling grin showed on their face. "*Take it.*"

I knew the effects would simmer down after a while but there was no way in hell I wanted to deal with this monster.

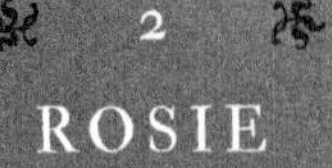

2
ROSIE

I do not remember the last time I had a full night's sleep. Before the gala I was hopeful that this summer would be the best one of my life.

Rae had offered up her family's house for us to live at and I truly believed for just a moment that we had a chance at all being happy together. No one would feel the weight of a task on their shoulders, we could just retire there and finish out our schooling in peace...but I should have known that that dream would never see the light of day.

I ran down the empty Winterfell corridor with my arms full of magical potions created by an exhausted Daxton and Amr. We had taken advantage of the empty school and ransacked the multiple science wings to use their magic gathering equipment so that we would have supplies to heal the injured.

It was hard work that left us all exhausted, and since the main ingredients in these potions were magic...we all had to donate more than our bodies could handle.

My magic was easily replenished, and I found myself less strained than the others, but Daxton and Amr were a different story. They would work themselves until they had not a drop left they could spare and then if I was able, I would share magic with them.

Though it wasn't ideal.

I burst through the double doors that led to the cafeteria and was immediately assaulted by the sheer noise of the room.

The cafeteria which was once filled with rows upon rows of tables was now emptied out to fit hundreds of cots and blankets where the injured people of Montnesse stayed. Young, old, magical, demons, we had every type of person under this roof...and all of them were in different states of dying.

Late on the night of the gala, we were hit with the news that the town had been attacked, burned from the inside out, trapping most of the people inside its barriers and cooking them alive.

When they began to pull out some of the survivors, it was worse than I imagined. I couldn't hold back the gags when I saw the state of some of the demons and witches that were wheeled into Winterfell. Because of the fires, their skin had literally begun to melt off of them and many had burns all across their bodies.

Apparently a magical barrier and fire was a hell of a combination.

Principal Winterfell, under the obvious control of Malik, had accepted the survivors with open arms...and the Originals that came with them.

I had never had any magical medical training in my life, but I was quickly put in charge of tending to the various injured people by my one and only mother, Xena.

She had insisted that I work with my *friends*, as she liked to call them, and help to heal the injured.

I refused at first but when I saw just how awful it was...I couldn't stand by and watch as they died.

Xena had a gang of witches that also volunteered to help out, but there were only a total of twenty helpers...and three hundred people.

Out of the entire town that spanned miles and housed people for centuries, only three hundred people made it out alive.

While we were short-staffed, with our magical capabilities I was hopeful that we could heal them. I had seen Daxton heal himself, I had even done it a few times on myself so I knew it was possible, but just like everything else in this world, it wasn't as easy as it seemed.

Because of the sheer amount of people with injuries, we were forced to treat only life-threatening injuries at first, but as the months went on we saw people dying of injuries that we hadn't been able to see at first. It was like one moment they were healthy and fine, and then the next day they looked as though they needed to be rolled into their grave.

I weeded through the crowd of people and to the corner where my current patient was waiting for me.

Amber, a young woman looking not much older than myself, who had been one of the people to drag the others out of the burning town. Just last week she had started sleeping more and today I found her with grey skin, and her once beautiful long brown hair had turned into a silver-grey.

She was currently in her cot and huddled under a pile of blankets that the others had donated.

I dropped to her level and carefully put the potions to the side. I unwrapped the blanket from her and was met with her pained expression. Her eyes fluttered open and her bight green eyes looked dull in the morning light.

"Rosie," she croaked.

"Hey Amber," I said in a light tone. "Can you sit up for me?"

I watched as she tried—and failed—to sit up on weak arms. I smiled at her and helped her into a sitting position. She had lost a lot of weight while I wasn't looking. It pained me to see someone so young, so like myself...dying so horribly.

"I feel like shit," she groaned.

I let out a forced laugh and grabbed the shiny blue potion that Amr had made that morning.

"This will calm you and help with some pain relief," I said and pulled the cap off with my teeth, making sure to keep one hand steady on her back.

I pushed it to her lips and watched as she downed the entire thing.

I wasn't sure what percentage Amber was, but the potions seemed to not be doing any good for her. Each day she got worse and worse and I was afraid that I would lose *another* patient.

"I think I need to sleep," Amber said in a weak voice. Her eyelids were already drooping again.

"Sure thing," I said and carefully laid her back down. "I'm sorry this is happening to you, Amber."

She let out a weak laugh and pulled the fur blanket close to her.

"It's okay, love," she said. "Anything is better than that hell hole of a town they kept us in. At least now I can feel *something* even if it is death."

"Don't say that," I hissed around the knot in my throat.

There were so many things I wanted to ask. So many things I still needed to know about the Originals and the magical town they kept. This wasn't the first time someone had uttered something about the town, but I could never get the information before they died.

If Amber didn't live through this, she would be my thirteenth patient to die under my care.

"Maybe in the next life I can have a group of lovers that dote on me like yours does," she joked, her voice trailing.

"You can get one when you get better," I promised.

She just smiled and drifted back to sleep. I let out a deep aching sigh and set to work. The other potions I brought could be applied on the skin. The issue was we couldn't tell where her injuries were coming from, so I had Amr and Daxton think of anything they could.

In the middle of work a warm hand cupped my shoulder.

I wasn't surprised to see Amr sitting next to me and Daxton

next to him. They were always here to bring me out of my spiral and I couldn't thank them enough for their support the last few months.

"Let her rest," Amr said, his deep accented voice barely above a whisper. "Xena wants to see you."

I swallowed thickly and worked on sealing the potions back up. Before we left I handed them to the witch on duty and ask that she look after Amber for the time being.

With a last look at the blanket-covered body, I left the room with both Amr and Daxton by my side.

"Are you okay?" Daxton asked as we walked.

I smiled at him and threw my hand through his. He, Amr, and I had our fair share of time together the last few months while the others were still off doing god only knows what. I got to see a side of them that I had never seen before and it only made me realize how lucky I was to have them even when I had acted so horribly the last year.

I had expected Daxton to carry a grudge for what I had to do to his parents...but if anything he seemed much happier than before. It had been helping with my guilt, though I wasn't sure it would ever go away for as long as we were together.

After I had some time to think about what I had done, and the high of it all had worn off... I came to realize just how much of a monster I was. I felt guilt because I hurt Daxton, not because I murdered someone in cold blood.

The people who had made me into such a monster were currently residing in the highest part of Winterfell, at least the one that was still standing. They had yet to remake the tower after we had destroyed it last year though I doubt someone like Xena would be caught dead in the towers. Instead, they chose something much more fitting and ironic.

A remnant of a human worship center.

It was the second-highest part of the campus and gave them the perfect view of the campus. If anyone came in or left the campus, their guards would see and be able to alert them if necessary. They stated it was the safest for them, but I knew deep down that they didn't care much about safety.

While I was in low-level school I had met with children who used to go with their human sides of the family to these worship centers and pray every week. The half breeds, as they called them, were not very welcome. But sometimes I heard stories about the humans seeing it as a sign of repent for what our kind had done to the earth.

I wondered briefly if Xena and Ezekiel were using it as a way to repent for themselves...but I doubted that was the case. They did not have a single shred of humanity in them that would make them understand the gravity of what they had done and the people they had harmed.

When we finally made it to their dwelling I had to take a moment to calm my erratic heart.

No matter how much I hated these beings, no matter how much I resented them for what they had done to my life...they still had that very life between their fingers and could at any moment snap it.

I had finished my task after all... I wouldn't put it past them to see me as a useless burden and hope to get rid of me as soon as possible.

We were treated by a few of the handmaidens that Xena kept by her side. From their brown eyes I could tell that they were witches, but the most shocking was that they looked to be no older than the age of thirteen. They were identical twins that I had seen a few times during my visits and they had a tendency to mirror each other's movements.

It sent shivers down my spine. Something about it just seemed unnatural.

They smiled at us and bowed before letting us into the renovated space.

Before the Originals had taken this spot as their home, it had been a rundown wasteland of space filled with spiders and cobwebs. I would know, because they had me scout it with her handmaidens before they even stepped foot on campus. Now, the large space had been lit up with magic lights that floated high above our heads and illuminated the entire space, and showcased the mural that was painted on the ceiling above it.

Splashes of green and blue made up the intricate ceiling and what I thought was once a depiction of some Great War between the gods and the people of this earth turned out to be the story of fallen angels. There were five that I could count, all of them bloodied and injured, and many with a portion if not all of their wings cut off. It was painted in colors that looked light and magical, but the image itself held a darker tone that hung over us with every step we took.

The once fully open space had been designed into a parlor, where they entertained guests. A few rooms on either side of the place were separated by walls that were built by magic.

It was just as extravagant as their previous house and I was annoyed that they just didn't pick a place outside of the campus. I didn't realize how much worse it was to be so close to the people that held my life in their hands. It's like it wasn't enough for them to force me to this school or commit crimes on their behalf, but now they had to be here and watch my every single step as well.

Amr's hand found my wrist and I sent him a grateful smile.

I wasn't looking forward to meeting the Originals. There had only been a handful of times that I had been summoned, though it was becoming more often as the semester neared, but each time I felt like it was another test. Like they were just checking how obedient I was, making sure I hadn't strayed.

They had refused to leave this place, even as their own people were out here dying leaving just me and a few others to help out with the dying patients. They were too busy licking their wounds and hiding from the embarrassment of finally being caught.

The walk through the makeshift home was short but felt like forever. Each time I was summoned to meet them I felt as though I was walking to my death. There was no telling with these Originals.

One minute they were welcoming me with open arms, giving me an apartment, giving me more money than I'd have in a lifetime, and the next they were forcing me to kill their prisoners as punishment.

They had set up their sitting room similar to the one in the town with floral imprints on every surface, a very large fireplace, and a table that was just big enough for the two Originals and their tea.

My mother had her long hair braided in an intricate fashion on the back of her head and even though her entire wardrobe had been burned to a crisp, she was still able to salvage some of her priciest clothing decked with gold thread that made her shine in the dim fluorescents.

Ezekiel on the other hand looked to at least have somewhat of a care about what was happening in the outside world. His normally shiny blonde hair had lost its luster and I could have sworn that there were bags under his eyes. He wore a blazer and slacks, looking as though he was off to some business venture.

He shot me a small smile as we walked in and I felt the intrusion in my mind before I heard it.

It has been a tough time for us all, child, his voice weighed heavily in my mind.

"Rosie," he said aloud. "Nice of you to join us. I know that it is out of your way."

"Yes," I said with venom laced in my tone. Amr's hand grabbed mine harshly, reminding me that there were consequences for speaking to an Original like that.

"Oh please," Xena said with a huff. When she looked over towards me her brown eyes narrowed, much like my low-level mother used to do after I had been cursed. "It's in the same campus."

The wall in my mind that I had forgotten even existed seemed to erect itself within moments, warning me not to get close. Warning me that those eyes were eyes that brought pain, not joy.

It warned me that getting too close, too vulnerable would cost more than I was willing to pay.

"How can I help you?" I asked in a tone full of mock politeness.

"We just want a status update about the patients," Ezekiel said, cutting in before my mother could.

I was in no way in charge of what went down there and couldn't help but think of this as an excuse to check on me and keep me in line.

"We have lost—"

I cut Amr off.

"They are dying," I growled. "Healthy ones, they all of a sudden get sick and die out of nowhere while you just *sit* here doing *nothing*."

"We cannot *do* anything," Xena hissed. "It is what happens when the weak stay frozen in time forever. They are *bound* to die."

It was like my body was hit with ice-cold water. They *knew?* They knew that this was going to happen and they still forced me to sit there and watch them, try to save them even when they knew it was a lost cause.

Amber's silver hair and smile flashed through my mind.

"All of them?" Daxton asked, his voice steady.

I used my grip on his arm to steady myself as my magic boiled inside of me. I couldn't be seen as weak in front of them, wouldn't dare to have what happened before happen now.

If I let them know how much this affected me, what would they do?

Kill them all at once? Make *me* kill them?

My stomach twisted and turned uncomfortably with the thought.

There were children there. People who had full lives ahead of them and deserved to have a chance of a life outside of the town and away from the Originals that controlled them.

Ezekiel's piercing blue eyes met mine.

"Most," Xena said nonchalantly. "Not all, but most. There are many in there without pure blood, and for those who find themselves unlucky, they will perish."

"You don't care about them?" I asked, unable to help myself.

Those narrowed eyes met mine once more and I knew she was trying to figure out a way to punish me for that comment. My magic welcomed the fight, growled and gnashed its teeth at Xena. I wanted her blood on my hands. I wanted to destroy her and watch as she begged for mercy.

I saw red.

I know she felt it, she had to. Because I could feel hers. It was cold and snake-like, just waiting to wrap itself around me and strangle the life out of me.

"We cannot save them, child," Ezekiel said. "They knew this when they entered the town with us. It was either that, or be hunted down by those who hated us."

I simply nodded at this, unable to find the words to fight anymore. Regardless of my unstable magic, I knew that attacking her here and now would only be the end of me.

"They are dying," I whispered. "But there are a few who have gotten better, and the rest still remain stable."

Xena nodded at this and took a sip of her tea.

"Will we keep them in the cafeteria for long?" Amr asked. "Winterfell starts its session soon."

Ezekiel's gaze shot towards Xena, his eyes wide. I wonder what thought could make the creator of demons look that scared?

"We will get them dorms," Ezekiel said, still staring at Xena, as if that gaze alone held her back from uttering anything. "For the families, we will find other accommodations."

The weight that was weighing on my shoulders dissipated

and I wanted to thank Ezekiel for his mercy, but his sharp gaze told me I was better off not saying anything.

You have more questions you can ask us, he sent to my mind. *A deal is a deal.*

Images of the mangled dead witches flashed across my mind. I even remembered how their flesh smelt after I had burned them, how their screams sometimes still haunted me in my memories. For what I did, I was given a set amount of questions that they had to answer truthfully.

A life for a single question from an Original with a track record for lying.

I am okay, I shot back.

"If that is all," Daxton said, gripping my arm. "We have a funeral to get to."

The sly smile that spread across Xena's face was one of nightmares.

"Have fun."

3

ELI

I fucking hated suits.

I tugged at the too-tight fabric that itched at my skin silently pleading that someone in the heavens would stop this event from even happening. It was a waste of time.

It was all for the image and no one was really there to mourn the fallen. And to top it off the white-haired bastard told me I had to behave.

I didn't mind most of the gatherings because neither Daxton nor Rae really cared what I chose to do while I was there.

Drugs? Totally fine.

Fucking the governor's wife in the bathroom? Have at it.

But none of that today according to Malik. Rosie would be there and I had to be on my best behavior even though it had been far too long since I last saw her.

I felt my fingers just remembering the way her skin felt against mine. All I wanted to do was be alone with her for five minutes, was that too much to ask?

Growling, I tugged at the stiff fabric trapping me. Not only did it have a death grip on my limbs, but the discarded tie that lay before me on the floor was its own death trap. I had tried, one too many times to get that stupid rope tied, but each time it looked worse than the last.

I caught my gaze in the mirror and frowned.

The high from Marques's blood had left me, but the power that now rested inside me was just as intoxicating. It swirled inside me at all times and taunted me with what was possible, but continued to stay just out of reach.

The thoughts it pulled from other people would hover at the edge of my mind like a small butterfly landing on a flower. They were innocent, delicate, and totally unaware of what I longed to do to them. I wanted so badly to grab those butterflies by their wings and tear them open, forcing them to tell me all the delicious secrets they kept.

They taunted me. Told me that if I wanted to beat Ezekiel that I could, but they remained just far enough away that I was enticed to chase them.

Catching Malik's golden gaze in the mirror, I picked up the once discarded tie at my feet and worked to try and tie it again. My eyes kept wandering to him as I felt the fuzziness of his thoughts reach me.

They were *right there.* So close that I could taste the tingle of them on my tongue.

He wanted something, but I couldn't tell what.

The normally white hair that stood on all ends was slicked back, giving me a rare look at his entire scarred face. I remember when I was young how cool I thought they looked. He fit the mold of a gangster perfectly and was everything I wished I could be.

But now I knew how his face came to look like that, and their meaning.

Thinking of what my own father did to Malik, made a sharp pain twist in my chest. I felt the same prick in my chest when I saw Rosie almost die. Albeit, it was much smaller now, but the pain was still there.

“Let me help,” he said. There was no sigh, or laugh in his tone, just a simple statement.

It made it hard to get angry at him and I gritted my teeth in anger as the thoughts kept flying at me. The closer he got the easier they were to feel, but *why* were they not coming to me yet?

I sighed and turned to face him. He didn’t hesitate, grabbing the limp tie from around my neck before tugging my collar upright and trying again.

“Now I know why you always wear your shirt unbuttoned,” he murmured. “I thought it was a fashion statement but here you just didn’t know how to tie a tie.”

“Say one more word and I cut your head off,” I grumbled.

“I have no doubt,” he said in a light tone, his eyes shifting to mine.

I stayed quiet for the rest of the time it took him to tie the stupid tie, and just watched him.

When did I stop fighting him? When did his scarred face being to make me feel warm again and not furious? Why did I suddenly want to understand the thoughts that lurked under the surface?

It couldn’t have just been Marques’s blood in me that started this change.

If anything his blood made me more restless, not the same calmness I felt when interacting with Malik.

“I don’t think I hate you anymore,” I said, my tone as indecisive as I was feeling.

He looked up at me, then back down to the tie, then stepped away before looking at my face again.

“I am glad,” he said then cocked his head. “I have always cared for you, regardless of what has happened. I hope you know that.”

Heat flashed across my face and before I even registered my actions I had backed up to the door behind me and swung it open. Leaving him alone in the room.

❦

It was unnecessarily cloudy when we arrived at the cemetery where Daxton and Rae's parents were to be buried.

Apparently this cemetery was for the best and most prominent figures in the world, and both Daxton and Rae had slots next to their parents for when they passed as well.

To the world the story was:

Both Rae and Daxton's parents left the party, never to be seen again. Rae and Daxton, with some help from prominent political figures that helped fund some money, hired a search team. The search team and police had been investigating the disappearance but after three months with zero evidence...they had to assume they had died.

Of course it wouldn't have been possible if we didn't have Malik's help to *persuade* the police force and search teams to give up...but it ended up working out well enough that the entire world now believed they somehow went missing and wound up dead.

No one even questioned the validity after Malik was done.

I mean, why would they?

If the head of the demon regulation came out and stated that there was nothing fishy going on, the world would just turn its back and focus on the next biggest thing going on in this world.

There was a crowd that surrounded the area and as expected, instead of quietly mourning there was a low chatter amongst the group. I recognized many of the faces here as those who had done dealings with *The Fallen* throughout the years and it made it all the more obvious when they blanched at Malik and me as we walked by.

Their thoughts too played at my senses, teasing me with the secrets they were keeping now that their superiors were laying cold in their caskets.

It was so tempting, but also infuriating.

"I don't even get why *I* have to be here," I grumbled to Malik and searched the crowd for my favorite hybrid.

It had been many weeks since I had alone time with Rosie and that ache was back in my chest.

I didn't much care about the secret-keeping, but I had to admit...Rae was right. She always was, but more so now than ever. The lies had to stop at some point because if not, I had no doubt our little Original would be more pissed than the time we were hiding the curse knowledge from her.

I personally wanted to see her angry. Wanted to see the murderous spitfire I had seen in Rae's memories as she slaughtered Daxton's parents. The restlessness inside me demanded a fight, demanded bloodshed, and it would be all too sweet if it was hers.

Even just thinking about it caused a warmth to flush through my body.

But...that same spitfire was carving her own path out from the prison she had been placed in.

She was no longer the shy, mute low-level that had no idea of this world. She was ready to fight, and that fight was what put me on edge.

What if this was the final straw? What if after this she finally saw what it meant to be with someone like me? People like us?

My thoughts were stirred by the brush of Malik's arm against mine. His golden eyes peered into me as if reading each thought that crossed my mind.

"They are here," he said and jutted his chin toward where the crowd was parting.

I saw Amr's long black hair that had been tied into a bun before Daxton and Rae's heads came into view. When the crowd finally parted I saw the small hybrid nestled right in between Rae and Daxton while Amr stood behind her.

Rae looked oddly calm for someone who had taken a mouthful of Original blood. Her eyes scanned the crowd, keeping close to our prized possession as if her life was at risk.

I knew the point was to protect her, and from an outsider's

perspective it looked as though they were crowding her...but it was so much more than that.

What they didn't see is with each movement Rosie took, the others would follow. If she so much as shifted her gaze, both Rae and Daxton would search to find what could possibly call her attention. And in this moment, it was me.

She met my eyes with a small smile and I soon felt the others' eyes as well, but I did not spare them any glances. Instead, I took in the woman in front of me.

Her black hair was pulled up in an intricate twist on the top of her head, showing off a shimmering pair of earrings. Her face was bare with only a hint of shine on her plump lips. She wore a long black dress that covered her from her neck to her wrists and ankles.

It was a modest dress, and that made it all the more intoxicating for me.

Here she was, acting as if she was the picture-perfect hybrid, innocent to the core, someone the people could trust...but they never got to see the look on her face as she stood over the burning bodies of her lover's parents, nor did they see the way she begged to be used by us.

The stark contrast made my mouth water because for once in my life...I had something all for myself.

She walked towards us, stopping right in front of Malik and me.

She held onto her smile but I saw the glint of anger boiling just under the surface of her perfectly crafted expression. Unable to help myself I brushed my hand across her cheek, my body on edge and begging me to take a look inside that mind of hers.

I don't like this, she said to me, her wide brown eyes meeting mine.

Her thoughts were a flurry of emotions, anger, sadness. She was tired and still thought of the townspeople that littered Winterfell. She cared for them, hurt for them.

On one hand I couldn't wait to tell her it was I who had

burned down the town, but on the other...I was *afraid.* That damn emotion had a chokehold on my being and threatened to force me to my knees so that I could beg for her forgiveness. I was afraid she would shun me, ignore me.

But I would never let that happen, I growled internally. *I will never let her try to leave even if she pleads.*

You and me both, I said in her mind and pulled her between Malik and me so that I could drop my arm around her. *So many fake bastards.*

They don't even care, she agreed in my mind. *They never did, they are all here for show.*

Rae, Daxton, and Amr stopped in front of us, each murmuring their hellos. The funeral that they had arranged was not scheduled to start for another few moments, so we were forced to wait for her under the scrutiny of the demons and witches around us.

I could feel their eyes on us, watching us intently and waiting for their moment to take Daxton and Rae away. After all, if they wanted to get in with the future leaders they would have to take advantage of when they were naive and vulnerable.

The first came up mere moments later, a balding man that I remembered as the governor of this state. They exchanged pleasantries and then dragged both Daxton and Rae away, much to Rosie's dismay, if her internal complaining held any indication of her mood.

I leaned closer to her, brushing my lips against the shell of her ear. She shivered in response.

"How does it feel to have all these people mourn those you killed?" I whispered loud enough for Malik to hear.

His hand clamped down on the arm that held Rosie and he began to squeeze.

Do not make me use my power, he threatened in my mind.

I didn't care about his anger, I only cared about the way Rosie flushed and the thoughts floating in her mind.

She thought of all of them, wondering what happened, where

they disappeared to, all while the killer lay among them. She thought about the power the secret held, the weight. But she was not upset, nor was she sad.

She was satisfied, and felt pleasure from the sickness of the secret she kept from them.

I almost couldn't hold in my groan as heat flashed through me.

If we weren't out in the open with everyone watching us, I would pull that dress up and bend her over the nearest headstone and make her recount the sick feeling her crimes left in her while I forced her to cum over and over again on my tongue.

I sent her the image and watched as her breath hitched and face flushed. She let out a small whimper and pushed back into me.

Amr watched with rapt attention as her deep breathing made her chest rise and fall rapidly.

I was tempted to show him the same dirty daydream I was showing Rosie, but I let myself enjoy it. I wanted to bathe in her moans, lock her up so that only I could hear and feel her.

I was selfish like that and I didn't care who knew.

Malik's hand gripped mine harshly. I shot him a look. He obviously wanted to fuck our little hybrid, I don't know why he suddenly got cold feet.

"Don't feel so left out," I murmured with a smirk and pushed the same image to him. His eyes clouded over and he stiffened.

I had done this once before, with Daxton and a shared witch but never with Malik.

I knew he wanted her and she him, so I wasn't surprised when his grip lightened after seeing what I was projecting into Rosie's head.

We would have to do something about this sooner or later, I mused.

"Eli," Amr growled.

I shot him a look.

"Mind your business, cat," I growled back.

"The witches can feel the spike in her magic," he explained in a hushed tone.

Looking around I saw a few select people watching us with disgust written all over their faces.

It angered me, made me want to give them an even better show...but for once I listened to the cat and pulled the scene from both Malik's and Rosie's minds.

Rosie whined and looked up at me with shining eyes. Her cheeks were flushed and her mind was telling me how wet she was underneath that dress.

"How disgusting," I murmured in her ear. "You getting off on your crimes. You almost came in front of everyone, didn't you?"

I expected her to turn away, unable to handle this talk in public, but instead she only pouted.

"Almost," she admitted. "But you stopped too soon."

This time it was I who had to grip on to Malik, to center myself.

Control yourself, Malik chided in my mind.

"Rosie," Malik growled. Rosie turned to him. "Behave yourself."

I saw the thought pop into her mind just before she took action.

I watched as her hand slipped into his pocket and she batted her eyelashes at him.

This was the Rosie I wanted to see. *This* was the one that ignited that uncontrollable fire in me.

"Only if you help me out a little," she whispered. "Tell me, Malik. Have you ever made a girl come with your power?"

The thoughts that ran through Malik's head before he distanced himself from us were sinful. Oh he *had,* and he wanted to do the same thing to Rosie. Punish her for that beautiful mouth of hers. He bent down to look her in the eyes, much like you would expect of a parent when they were scolding a child.

"I am one more word away from taking you back to Winterfell and making you regret the day you were born," he growled. "Do not test me, Rosie."

She held his gaze for a few more moments before she huffed and leaned back into my side.

"Don't worry," I said with a smirk. "I'll make it up to you later."

A small body pushed against my back and slipped under my arm. I growled aloud and was ready to break the neck of the person who separated me from Rosie, but then long red hair and brown eyes filled my vision.

The seer, I thought in a venomous tone.

"The mind reader," she said in the wistful tone that she normally spoke with.

Even though she acted as if there was a cloud over her consciousness, I knew better than to assume she wasn't paying attention. She had to see more than the average witch or demon and in all honesty, that power angered me so much because it was all-seeing and there was nothing I could hide from her.

But not for long, I thought in a smug tone as I felt the buzz of thoughts around her head.

They were frenzied, ready to burst out of her skull. I was so ready to hear them, finally.

Finally, there would be nothing she or anyone else could hide from me.

She looped her arm around Rosie's waist and held her close. Rosie shot her a shocked look before laying her hand atop the one that fell near her hip.

Since when did these two hug?

"I am sorry," Claudia whispered to Rosie. "I know it's hard."

Rosie's face dropped and I shared a look with Amr.

"Come on, ladies," Malik said and stepped forward to lay his hand upon Rosie's head. "The funeral is starting."

With that he ushered the group forward, but I caught something that would have made any heart skip a beat. Rosie looked over her shoulder at me and I could have sworn I saw a fiery glint pass her eyes, but it was gone in a second.

Interesting as always, my lovely hybrid.

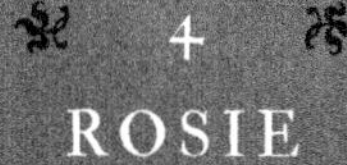

4
ROSIE

I have never been a religious person, even after the truth about our heritage came out. If anything it pushed me further away from this idea of having one omnipotent force.

But even so, I had been praying this day wouldn't come. I would sit in my bed at night, staying up after my partners were asleep and just hope that the world would show some type of mercy...but I should have known by now that wasn't how the world worked.

Even when I expected the worst, that didn't stop the pain.

It was eleven o'clock at night and I had finally convinced Daxton, Amr, and Rae to leave me with Amber for her possibly last night on this earth.

Eli and Malik were, of course, off doing god knows what so that left me all to myself for the time being. And while I could feel the loneliness that permeated my soul...I also felt a sort of relief.

I was truly alone now. The only time where I could fully indulge my thoughts, even the darkest ones that tried to hide in the recesses of my mind during the day.

There were no medic witches about, and everyone was sound

asleep except the sliver-haired girl that lay in front of me, shivering under the mountain of blankets she was wearing.

I do not know why *this* patient was the one that was threatening to break me, but it felt like claws were gripping at my throat and squeezing the life out of me as I watched over her. I couldn't move, couldn't breathe, all I could do was just sit by her side and watch as the parts of her soul wasted away.

"Amber," I croaked out and reached under the blanket to cover her cold hands.

I knew that even if I tried to ease up her pain, there would be no change. It was far too close to the end for her.

"Hey, love," she whispered, her eyes blinking open. "I am glad you are here with me."

I swallowed thickly and squeezed her limp hand, willing it to squeeze mine back.

"Of course," I said. "Anything for you."

She let out a sound that was akin to a laugh but sounded more like a rough cough as it wracked her small frame. It was painful to watch.

"It's the end, love," she said.

"I know."

"They knew this would happen," she continued. "That we would die, yet they still didn't let us leave."

"Why?" I asked finally, the questions that had been circling my head were screaming at me to get them answered.

"I thought they were trying to save us," she said. "But now I just see that they wanted to control us. They were scared we would revolt if we learned of the outside world. Learned that there was nothing to fear. *Not even them.*"

I gritted my teeth, begging the tears that were gathering not to fall. I needed to be strong for her.

"I don't get why they would do it," I said honestly.

"Because they are not royalty here," she said and let out another laugh. "But *in there,* they were gods. They were the almighty people who had saved us from the power-hungry humans that threatened our existence. Though they didn't want us to realize that it wasn't them that held the power anymore, but ordinary people like us. They didn't want them to know we *didn't need them*."

"Save your strength," I said as another coughing fit ran through her. I was so afraid she would break right then and there and I still had the foolish hope that she could live through this. That small hope hung between us like a glowing thread, but it was thin and torn... It was at the end of its life.

"There is nothing to save," she said and then with strength I didn't know she possessed she jerked me forward, our faces inches apart. "Gather the healthiest of us, love. I have a feeling something bad will happen and you need to get them out."

I shook my head.

"They are being relocated already, don't worry about this," I whispered. "I will watch over them."

The sigh that escaped her lips seemed to carry the weight of the universe with it.

"And take care of yourself too, Rosie," she whispered. "I cannot tell you how much it means for you to stay by my side all this time."

I watched in horror as her eyes closed and the light grip she had on my hand loosened.

I don't know how long I waited in that cramped space, pleading for her to take another breath, but when my form started shaking under the pressure of the awkward position I was forced to sit back up and look once more at her shell of a body.

The tears silently fell down my cheeks.

"Please," I whispered. "Please come back."

There was no answer. Her body remained still and my magic spread out, trying to feel for something, any type of vibration to indicate a life...but there was none.

My magic was threatening to tear down the entire building, it was begging for me to let it out, gnashing and snarling against the shell it was caged in. The only thing holding me together was that people, just like Amber, littered the places beside me and I couldn't bear to see them hurt.

Swallowing my sobs I put a magical barrier around her cot and with a single thought, I burned the body until there was nothing but soot in its place.

I had done this so many other times that I didn't even have to think about cleaning up the leftover debris with magic and slowly standing up to leave my spot amongst the sleeping people.

As I walked I saw a few glowing eyes peering out at me, but I couldn't hold their stare.

They saw what happened, they knew everything.

When I finally was able to force myself down the empty hallways of Winterfell, I found myself unable to catch my breath. It felt like the air had been knocked out of my chest and the sobs that I had been hiding from the sleeping bodies forced their way out of my mouth.

I was devastated about Amber, about all the others...but all I could think of was...*why?*

Why did this have to happen?

Why did they have to die in a world where anything was possible?

Why didn't I feel this way about the others I killed? The witches in the town? Daxton's parents?

Why didn't it hurt then? Why is this so different?

I leaned against the wall and let myself slowly fall to the ground; the cold tiles acted as a perfect way to calm my racing brain.

I felt his presence before I heard him. The sounds of his shoes padding across the stoned floors echoed through the hallways and his warm hands found my shoulder first. He pulled me to him and whispered in my ear.

I looked at him through my tear-filled eyes, seeing a familiar grey set of eyes and red curly hair.

Matt, what perfect fucking timing.

I threw my arms around his neck.

"I know it's hard," he whispered against me. "But you did all that you could."

"Where were you hiding?" I asked through my sobs. My hand found the side of his neck and I leaned back to look him in the eyes once more.

He sent me that famous sheepish smile of his before answering.

"Just down this hallway," he admitted. "I'm on Rosie duty tonight."

I smiled at him through my sobs. I wasn't planning to do this tonight, but this moment was too perfect. No one was in sight.

"I know."

He lifted a brow and tilted his head to the side.

He played such a good puppy, I thought.

"You know?" he asked.

I nodded and called my magic into my palm. He stiffened when he finally felt the swirling magic against his skin, the same magic that was threatening to burn a hole in the side of his neck.

He swallowed, his throat coming dangerously close to the magic in my palm. His eyes widened and then another second passed before his eyes narrowed at me. No longer did I get to see my best and only friend at Winterfell, instead I got an eyeful of the *real* person Matt was.

"What gave me away?" he asked.

His whole demeanor changed in that moment, and into a person that I didn't recognize, but one that I knew intimately. I had seen the change happen, even if I wasn't fully aware it was happening. It was in the little things, the way he fought with Eli, the way his eye would narrow when he thought no one was looking.

I knew the type of person this was because I had done the same. It was a front to keep people from knowing what was really going on.

For me it was the Originals' task... And for him...

I cannot afford to be kept in the dark any longer.

"You think that when I already was missing a day in my memory I wouldn't take precautions?" I asked.

It was a half lie. I didn't take any precautions and relied only on luck and my intuition and a single person on my side.

As the bright light blinded me I fell to the ground, acting as if I was affected by the magic that Matt threw at me. My heart was pounding and I could still hear the roaring of the flames in the background.

"I will take her back," Eli said from afar.

"I will be faster," Claudine's sweet voice said from right near me. I could already feel her hands across my back, rubbing in soothing motions. "We will meet you at the apartment."

Without another moment to waste I felt the same stomach pulling sensations and then the cool ground beneath me.

"You did good," she whispered.

I finally sat up to notice that we were not far from the ruins of Winterfell tower. The cool night breeze seeped into my body and I couldn't help the shudders.

"How did—I don't under—"

She grabbed my hand and showed me the glowing symbol she had left on me. It was smudged and barely visible to the naked eye.

"I had to act fast," she said. "I knew as soon as you grabbed onto me that most likely he would try and use his powers on you."

"You helped me," I said in a hollow voice. "Was he trying to take my memories?"

Panic rose in my chest when she nodded.

"How many times?" I asked. She gave me a pitying look.

"I know of four, but I suspect more," she answered.

"Four?" I whispered and cupped my hand over my mouth. "I thought it was only once." I felt like I was going to be sick.

Who was this person? How did I miss this?

"Listen, Rosie," she said hurriedly. "We don't have time. I need to teach you how to protect yourself."

She slipped my hand over and I watched as she drew an intricate symbol into my palm with purple glowing magic.

"Remember this symbol. I did it for you before, but remember it for

next time," she said. "If you think he will use it, draw this symbol somewhere on your body with magic and you will be fine. Better yet if you can get it tattooed. Do it."

"How did you figure out..?"

She gave me a sad smile and I couldn't help but feel pity for the little girl that had to grow up around a memory manipulator.

"Will it uncover what he has done before?" I asked.

She gave me a sad smile.

"Only he can do that," she answered.

"Thank you, Claudine," I whispered.

"It's my pleasure, though to be honest Marques was the one that suggested it," she said with a smile of her own. "Now let's take care of those pesky mind readers."

I did exactly as she had recommended and went to the same tattoo artist with Daxton and Amr and made us all get matching tattoos. They had asked many questions, but dropped it when I told them to just trust me. I had yet to bring it up to Rae and Eli as they had both been absent and would probably have a run-in or two with people that could do harm with this information.

It was sad to think about how little trust was between us now, but I had to do this to not only keep myself alive...but all the people around me as well.

Matt's jaw clenched and I watched as he thought through all of his options, his eyes scanning every inch of me.

"What do you want?" he asked after a pause.

"Take me to him," I demanded.

A smirk spread across his face.

"To who?"

I pushed the orb of magic into his neck and watched as his face flushed and pain spread across his expression. He let out a groan, but did not give in.

I pushed the orb in harder.

"Fine," he grunted. "But I have to call my sister."

"Do it," I hissed. "Now."

He patted his pockets for his phone and typed out a message to her.

I didn't know what it said, but I didn't need to. She warned me about this earlier today, it was the whole reason I was here so late anyways.

She appeared in a flash of light and looked down at us with an unamused expression.

"What a precarious—"

"Shut up and do as you are told," Matt hissed at her.

For good measure I pushed the ball further into his neck. Claudine's lips twitched and she placed a hand on us both.

This time I was prepared for the feeling of my stomach being turned inside out. When the light subsided I was hit with a chill before I saw the massive space we were in. We were in what looked to be a ballroom, but the interior seemed darker, more mysterious than those ones I had seen on TV growing up.

Claudine gave no rest; she disappeared in a flash of light.

Matt used that chance, and my moment of distraction, to push me to the ground as he straddled either side of my hips. I felt a thick rope-like object wrap around my wrists and force my arms over my head. I looked towards them to catch sight of thick vines that made their way down my arms as if they had minds of their own.

I glared at Matt and he met me with a smirk.

"Not so tough now, are you?" he asked. I felt the vines slip into my clothing and wrap around my body much like I imagined a giant snake would.

"You don't scare me," I said in a defiant tone.

"No?" he asked. "I can be very scary if given free rein."

I kept his stare down. There was no way I would be scared of him, I wouldn't allow myself to even as the vines wrapped around me and began squeezing my body.

I saw the flash of light over Matt's head and smiled before lighting the vines on fire in one burst. The ones that had snaked through my clothing fell limp and Matt frowned when he realized what happened.

He sat up and looked over at the very people we were waiting for. Right next to Claudine's form stood the man that single-handedly saved me from dying at the hands of the Originals because of my failed task.

He stood tall and dressed in a sweater that hugged his body and loose slacks. His dark hair fell in his eyes and he had scruff on his face. His dead eyes looked over the two of us without any indication of his emotions.

"I heard you took a little hostage," he said, a smirk finally spreading across his face.

"Little indeed," I scoffed and sat up only to push Matt off me. I could tell he allowed it for the second because as soon as I stood, he had my wrist in a death grip.

"Don't get too comfortable," Matt hissed behind me.

"I should say that to *you*," I hissed at him.

"Malik will hear about this," he threatened.

"What will he do, huh?" I asked and stepped closer to Matt. "Make me kneel? Bind me with his power? *Fuck off*, Matt, and don't hide behind someone else's power."

My magic was rising with each word and I had trouble controlling the shakes that traveled through my body. It dared me to treat him just like I had with the other witches in the town. I knew I could do it, it knew I could do it. The only thing holding me back was the front that Matt had shown me when I first got to Winterfell. The one that stood by me through the hard times as a friend and slowly introduced me into this world.

Turning away from him and snatching my wrist out of his hands, I walked towards Marques with my hand still throbbing.

"I wanted to first say thank you," I said. Shock ran through his face for just a moment before he composed himself. "Second I wanted to ask whose bright idea it was to kill hundreds of people by setting the fucking town on fire."

"That was Malik and Eli—"

I turned back to Matt and sent a fireball barreling towards him. He scrambled out of the way before regaining his composure and sending me a glare.

"I know it was yours," I said to Marques. "I have been trying to save them for days and they—"

"Just die," he interrupted. "I know."

I was stunned by his honesty and found myself unable to find the words to continue.

"Come, Rosie," he said and held a hand out to me. "I will explain over some tea maybe?"

I squared my shoulders and placed my hand in his.

"Some alcohol would be better," I replied.

He laughed at this and led me into the next room.

5

RAE

Tonight was the last time that we could meet with Marques before the start of the term and I hated to admit it, but I was nervous.

Nervous that the Originals would catch on. Worried that Rosie would get hurt. Worried that the world would crumble... because after killing my father, it felt like it had.

There was nothing in my control anymore. From the state of the house to the mountains of letters arriving at my door from all of my father's close colleagues, I had no idea what to do with the mountain of attention we were getting and no way to separate it from the looming threat of the Originals.

Tonight would be the night where we would plan the demise of the people who turned my world upside down. My father...was not a nice demon, but I knew that if somehow he had been able to separate himself from the clutches of the Originals, he wouldn't have been in this position and neither would Mother.

Speaking of my mother...

I stood from my place in my father's study at his desk. It had taken me far too long to comb through the condolence letters and I had to hurry if I wanted to meet Mother before I set out.

Taking a look at my phone I sighed and left the room with only ten minutes to spare.

I had moved Mother to a more comfortable space on the second floor. The room was much more vibrant than the other and I made sure it was always warm enough for her. It was the least she deserved after all the years of torture she went through.

On many nights I stayed up thinking about how awful it must have been to be confined to such a space with no one to talk to. Even the maids had forgotten about her at one point as if she was no more than a ghost.

Opening the door, my heart skipped a beat as I saw the newly hired nurse lifting my mother onto the four-poster bed. Hiring a nurse was a straightforward decision, the right one...but it was far from easy. Our finances were not in a good place and hiring her was another burden on the family.

You would think that his life insurance and the payout from the government would be enough to hold us over for years to come, but one thing I was starting to understand was Father was reckless with our money.

"Let me help you," I said in a light tone.

The nurse jumped at my sudden intrusion, her green eyes widening, but her face quickly relaxed and she sent me a soft smile. She was not much older than me but experience wasn't an issue when she had a power like hers.

"That would be wonderful," Callie replied.

I walked around the bed and helped my mother into the bed. Callie moved around me to help cover her with blankets.

I watched my mother's face for any flash of recognition...but there was still nothing.

I turned to Callie, noting her bright yellow scrubs. They had printed flowers on them that matched the ones decorating the walls of this room. There was a stark contrast against her dark brown hair and scrubs, washing out her skin tone.

"She likes them," Callie explained, probably noticing my stare. She sent me another soft smile. "Her mind has had more activity as of late and when I wear yellow...well let's just say her mind lights up."

I swallowed thickly and nodded. A sort of bitter relief washed through me.

Callie's specialty was that she could see the activity in the mind of others. She explained to me that it was like the mind was painting a picture, filled with vibrant colors and each of the colors had a meaning.

"Good," I said and straightened my clothes. "I will be leaving, see yourself out whenever. I just wanted to check on Mother before I left."

"I can leave you two for a moment," she said and without waiting for my reply turned to leave the room.

As soon as the door closed a heavy sigh escaped my chest and my shoulders caved in. Looking over to my mother I let the powerful emotions that I had been so carefully locking up fill my body.

Sadness.

Anger.

Disappointment.

Fear.

All of it swirled around my being. It had been so hard to keep up this facade around the others, especially when they were already dealing with such volatile emotions themselves. It helped that most of the summer we stayed apart. It let old wounds heal, anger die down, and everything was almost as it once was...

I don't regret killing my father.

If I had the chance to I would do it over and over again... I just wish I hadn't been so naive.

And even now, I knew what I had to do, but each step towards a normal and balanced life for me and my family seemed harder and harder.

I was torn out of my thoughts by a prick of emotion that was not mine.

It was a familiar feeling and full of pity and sadness.

My eyes trained on my mother's vacant stare.

"Was that you?" I whispered.

She gave no indication that she heard my words.

Marques's blood had indeed strengthened my powers, but not as much as I believed it would. Instead emotions just carried further, felt stronger, but I had yet to have the chance to see if I could manipulate emotions just yet.

Maybe if I could figure it out...

I rolled my shoulders and with one last lingering look, I left my mother's side and went down to the front of the house.

I smiled at Callie as I passed, not slowing my pace.

I let my emotions crowd my senses too long, and now I was late for my meeting.

"Where are you going?" Nathaniel asked as I walked through the foyer.

I stopped in my tracks and looked over at my brother. He looked pale, and worse than I had seen him before. While the demon blood in his veins healed most of his bags and dull skin, it couldn't magically make him healthy again.

He had been neglecting himself in Father's absence.

None of us liked Father, that much was apparent, but I never realized just how sheltered they had been until I asked them to take on some of the family tasks. I couldn't do it all, but I was starting to think that I may have to given their inexperience.

"I'll be back soon," I promised.

He shifted on his feet and ran his hand through his hair. He was frustrated, worried, anxious, and I could feel it packing the room enough to choke me.

"Mary was asking about repairing some of the cracked drywall in the cellar," he said. "But mentioned that it would be out of the budget they had been allowed for this quarter."

After my father's death, all of the managing of the household came down to me and my brothers, which none of us fully understood how to take care of. The maids, housekeepers, and accountants all turned to us now for any little thing that used to set my father off.

"I'm going to hire a manager to run this property at some point," I told him and straightened my jacket. "I don't know how Father managed to approve and look over all these expenses without one for so long."

He looked down at his feet.

"Are you sure we have money for that?" he asked slowly.

I could feel the anxiety rolling off his chest in waves and it surrounded the empty room, making it hard to breathe. I sent him some calming waves and his shoulders relaxed almost immediately.

"I am sure," I said confidently, even though I had had the same worry just a few days ago when I realized the cost of running all my father's properties.

I planned to sell off the properties if we had to, but until then I would pull from where we needed to and start undoing the unnecessary costs our father had put on this extravagant lifestyle.

"Don't worry about the money," I said in a softer tone. "I have already thought it through and have a plan for us."

There was a relief that washed through Nathaniel. He flashed me a grateful smile.

"Alright," he said with a sigh. "I guess don't get home too late, young lady."

I shook my head and let out a light chuckle before pushing out into the summer night.

I MET the others at the designated area only a few miles away from the apartment Malik had provided Rosie. Eli and Malik had insisted on living there as a way to escape the Originals, but Rosie didn't have a choice as she was now bound to them in a way that made it hard for her to escape them.

We gathered in a small alleyway between two large warehouses that smelled distinctly of rotting fish. My nose curled as I walked towards the group that was already waiting for me and noticed with a start that we were missing Claudine.

"Where is she?" I asked waving to the empty space between Maximus and Eli.

Maximus crossed his arms around his chest and shrugged.

"We will leave in a minute if she doesn't show," Malik said, his eyes shining in the darkness.

I looked to Eli. The way they kept flexing their fingers and the restlessness inside them was affecting me already. They had been in this group longer than I had and even if they didn't admit it, I noticed how much leaving Rosie's side affected them.

When they were finally reunited at the funeral their anxiety dropped to almost nonexistent levels. The emotions of the group at times had been almost too hard to handle, and when you pair that with the dying refugees in the campus... Let's just say there was a reason why I was avoiding that part of Winterfell.

I tried not to blame Eli and Malik for the burning of the town. I knew with or without them Marques would have found a way to do it...but it really took a toll on us all.

"Let's go check on the others first," Malik suggested. "Then if she still isn't here, we flag it."

There were a few nods and we set off down the alley and to an adjacent warehouse that unbeknownst to the public was heavily warded by Maximus.

When Maximus came no more than ten feet away from the warehouse, he began muttering something under his breath and the bright red barrier became clear for only a moment. We took our cue and rushed towards the door in silence.

Eli was too slow and I heard a hiss of pain signaling the place where the barrier singed them. Looking back I saw them send a glare to Maximus while they rubbed their arm.

"In, now," Malik hissed as he pulled the heavy door open, screeching metal filling the silent air.

We filed through the empty warehouse until we stood right in the center of it. From an outsider's perspective, it looked like a normal everyday abandoned warehouse... The secrets it held were unbelievable.

Malik knelt to the ground and rolled up his sleeve so that his forearm was bare to the world.

"You'll have to recharge later," he murmured to Maximus. "Sorry to put so much stress on you."

Maximus shrugged and opened his palm where he conjured a magical spear that lit up the dark space.

"I can handle this," he said and without hesitation dug the spear into Malik's forearm.

I could feel his pain, but he never uttered a sound. We watched silently as the blood poured from his wound and onto the hard ground. As soon as the first droplets hit the ground, a bright red light surrounded us and slowly, the real secrets of the warehouse began to show themselves.

The once dark, empty space turned light and filled with warmth. The sound always came first and tonight, that sound was laughter. Slowly the world hidden behind the veil of magic appeared.

We stood right in the middle of the makeshift dining area. Unsteady tables surrounded us and at them were the smiling faces that I came to know as refugees from the town the Originals had been hiding in.

"Eli my boy!" came a voice from behind us and just like every other time, a rugged-looking man was the first to greet us.

I felt the small spark within Eli when they heard their name being called, but made a point not to stare at them too hard. It was rare to feel that type of feeling from them, I wanted them to enjoy it as long as they could.

Eli scowled as they looked the man up and down.

"We give you a shower, a bed, free food *and* clothes, and you still can't clean up?" Eli grumbled.

The man let out a laugh and waved over to the corner where the others were watching him with apt attention.

"Come!" he yelled. "Let's have a drink!"

Eli gave him a look but followed him towards the corner anyways.

"Let's make our rounds," Malik said to Maximus and me.

I nodded and began the routine we had made for ourselves this summer.

We would go through the dining hall while Malik talked joyfully to the people there. His whole persona changed and instead of the conniving serious demon, he turned into a warm sort of caretaker for the refugees.

He would ask them how they have been, if their supplies became low or if they wanted anything special.

Many of the times they would brush him off and say that the witches here were plentiful and supplied everything they needed, but Malik would still push and Maximus would end up conjuring a handful of items the others were too weak to do on their own.

The second stop, was the infirmary.

This one always took a toll on me.

I was proficient at separating myself and blocking out the stray emotions...but the infirmary was filled to the brim with fear, anger, sadness, and all the other potent emotions that came with dying.

And now that Marques's blood was coursing through me, I had to keep my own emotions locked away or else I would be susceptive to outbursts. Though the aftereffects of keeping them in for too long wasn't ideal either, many times as I lay awake I would be shaking with the potent emotions still playing at my mind, and couldn't sleep until the last of them left my body.

From Malik's words, they had *stolen* one of the lone doctors the town had on staff and was now using them here. He was an older graying witch that had been alive for as long as Malik had, though we are still unsure how he managed that feat.

He was at the end of the infirmary, hovering over a patient.

As I passed the beds I noted the bright pink chart at the end of each.

Miller

71.33% Demon.

Power: Unknown

Status: Rapid Decay

A memory played at my mind, but I was too crowded with the emotion in here that trying to pull it to the front made my head hurt. I pulled my gaze from the glaring chart and to the rest of the bodies that littered the area. Almost every bed was filled.

Each of the sixteen beds was full with those who had a little too much human blood in them. There was no way to stop the decay; it was a sure fact that if you had human blood in you, you would age right after you left the barrier and stopping it was an impossible work of magic.

"I can sense you," the doctor said from afar, stopping Malik from getting too close to one of the patient beds where a sleeping low-level lay encased in a magic-type film that glittered in the light.

"Nice to see you Richard," Malik called back with a light tone. "What's the update? Need anything?"

The doctors stood and looked back at us with a small smile.

"I have some good news," he said and waved us over.

In front of him was another low-level encased in the same film but this time...his eyes were open and looking towards us.

"Get Eli," I said and looked toward Maximus. He nodded and left the room only to come back with an annoyed Eli a few moments later.

"Exactly what I was thinking," the doctor said smiling at me. "He has been awake but unable to talk. I need to know what he is feeling."

"Pain," I answered for him. "Though Eli can probably tell you why."

Eli gave me a look and pushed past me, towards the low-level.

"Welcome back from the dead," Eli said with a smirk and wrapped their hand around the low-level's arm.

There was a pause.

"Well?" Malik asked.

"He's mad at me," Eli explained. "And currently cursing my existence. For that I should let you stew in your injuries, would you like that?"

The low-level's eyes widened.

"Eli," Malik warned.

They rolled their eyes and removed themselves from the low-level.

"His injuries were not healed," she explained. "His leg is still hurt and he says something in his back and head hurt."

"I thought we...?" Malik trailed.

The doctor gave him a sad smile.

"I can only heal with magic what I know to be the issue and because we do not have equipment..."

There was a heavy aura settling around the room. I turned to look at the beds around us. Did this mean all of them were subjected to this pain the entire time they remained asleep? I could feel pricks of it here and there, but nothing like the man in front of me.

"Try to replicate what you did with him," Malik said. "And we will bring the mind reader and the seer next time."

"Give me a few weeks," the doctor said. "And I'll try to have an update for you."

Malik and he bid their goodbyes and we moved onto the next round.

As we were walking down the makeshift rooms, Maximus froze in his tracks.

"Claudine passed the barrier," he announced. "Something is...off."

Malik shared a look with him and without another word he dropped to the ground, preparing to take Maximus's spear.

Maximus wasted no time and stabbed the spear into his arm.

The world in front of us vanished faster than it came and we were plunged into the darkness of the warehouse.

I could feel the joy coming off of Claudine before I turned to face her.

"Marques requests you all," she said in a light voice and practically skipped her way towards us.

Eli looked at me and their emotions told me that they were suspicious of this and I couldn't help but agree.

"Why were you late?" Malik asked, his tone commanding.

"You'll see," she said in a sing-song tone. "Hands on me."

She pushed herself in the middle us of and I slowly placed my hand on her shoulder praying that nothing was burning, destroyed, or dead.

"You'll be pleasantly surprised, Rae," she said and in a flash of light, the warehouse was gone.

Again the first thing I heard was laughter. A high-pitched female laugh that rang through the warm space of Marques's mansion. The second thing I felt, even through the laughter, was a deep pain swirled with sadness.

But it was familiar, it was...

"Rosie," Malik and I growled in unison when our eyes both traveled to the couch where Rosie, dressed in her sweats and a loose t-shirt, sat laughing with a drink in hand.

Her laughter stopped and a small smile spread across her face.

"Welcome back," she said and took a sip of her drink. I spotted Matt right behind her, his eyes narrowed at her and his mouth twisted into a grotesque scowl.

His anger was almost as strong as her pain; it spread across the small sitting room and tried to seep into my bones.

"Look at you," Eli cooed and walked over to the couch, ignoring the dead-eyed Original as they sat next to Rosie and wrapped an arm around their shoulder. "How naughty."

They leaned forward to whisper something in her ear that shot a pang of arousal through her.

I looked at Marques, trying to figure out anything but he looked us over with a blank face and not a prick of emotion through him.

"How did you even get here?" Malik growled and stormed towards her, pushing Eli away and grabbing Rosie's chin.

I found myself wanting to do the same thing. I was angry, shocked, and nervous that she had been here with *him* alone.

She had risked so much to come here. Did she know this man could kill her in seconds? Did she know that without the proper precautions everything we worked for up until now would be for nothing?

I was almost as worried as I was angry.

"She cornered me," Matt spit out. "Bitch fucking fried my neck and burned my veins."

Eli was ready to pounce and Malik's head snapped over to Matt. I had never felt the two so angry before in my life and after the stint in the medical bay... I felt my head swoon.

"You're just mad you got caught," Rosie said with another laugh and pushed Malik's hand away from her so that she could down the rest of her glass.

She was tipsy, enough to affect her mood and I was worried what would come out of it. I had never seen her like this before. Not to mention her guard was down next to the most dangerous man in this world.

"So, shall we start?" Marques asked. "Rosie has quite a few topics to address it seems."

"Hell yeah I do," Rosie said and stood up. "First, you."

She pulled Malik forward by his shirt and hit the side of his face so hard the slap reverberated around the space.

"Don't ever try to erase my mind ever again. I don't care if it was Matt's power, you were the one in charge and to hear that my memory was taken from me *four* times—"

"Six," Malik interrupted. "Six times we took your memory from you."

Rosie slammed her jaw shut and I thought that she was going to slap him again but instead she smiled.

"There was the Malik I missed," she said. "Never again, got it?"

"Understood," he murmured, his eyes trailing the length of her face.

I cleared my throat and Rosie sent me a small smile.

"Right," she said. "Now I hear, you have a little refugee hide-out, is that correct?"

Her devious smile told me all that I needed to know, and man did it stir something in all of us.

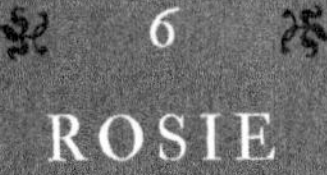

ROSIE

The honesty from the group was...refreshing.

It had taken a lot to get here and I literally had to force my way into this space, but I was grateful they finally caved. If not I would be forced to take more drastic measures and I didn't want that after we had come so far.

"The doctor there is working on a way to save them," Rae said, the first one willing to divulge more than I asked. I sent her a smile.

"We will have the results soon," Malik said and shifted on his feet. "I hope."

Only Eli, myself, and Marques dared to sit and drink on the couch. The others spread out around the room in various stages of discomfort.

It didn't get past me that Claudine, Maximus, and Malik were the closest to Marques. It spoke volumes for their true ties. Matt was standing behind us, still leaning against the wall and grumbled his opinion every now and then.

"And why are they the only ones involved?" I asked Marques. "Me, Daxton, Amr, we all want the same thing, to end this just like everyone else."

Jealous? Eli teased in my head.

Pissed, I corrected.

"Xena and Ezekiel care about them the least," Marques said and took a sip of his drink. "They were the easiest to pull away."

"We were going to tell you," Malik spoke up. "Rae wouldn't have agreed to it if we didn't have a plan to tell you."

My eyes traveled to Rae. She was standing there with her arms crossed and her head high. A warmth spread through my chest when I thought about her standing up for my right to be involved.

I had forgiven her long ago, but to know that even after we had been separated for so long, she still fought on my behalf? It almost made me tear up.

"Then what's the plan?" I asked. "Go after the Originals? They are at Winterfell now with loads of guards by their side. Not to mention they are worth at least ten of us each."

Marques's lips twitched.

"I can help with the power aspect," he said in a tone that made my skin crawl.

"We drank his blood," Eli said with a grimace. "It hurts like a motherfucker but it works. I have been able to hear some thoughts without touching people."

What? I asked in my mind. *You can hear everyone now?*

Just sometimes, they explained. *It takes practice.*

"Me too," Rae said. "Emotions are stronger, clearer than before, though I have yet to try to control them."

"Something we can rectify in training," Marques said with a smirk. I noted the way Rae's jaw clenched.

Their power got stronger through...drinking blood?

How was this possible? Was this his power?

No... It couldn't be, could it?

My mind swam with the information and possible ideas of why this was possible.

Demons' bodies reacted to other demons' blood? Or was it just Original blood?

I looked at Marques, ready to word vomit all the questions

that were running through my head...but his hard gaze stopped me.

In that moment it felt like the world had fallen away and it was just us in this room. I couldn't see his mouth move but it felt like I could hear him.

And he was warning me to not ask the questions that plagued my mind.

"I want it too," I said in a serious tone.

"Rosie," Rae chided.

Marques gave me a grin.

"I knew the daughter of Xena would outshine her one day," he said. "Come here, child."

I left Eli's comforting embrace to walk over to Marques. All eyes were on me and my steps echoed through the room. I didn't know if this was the right choice or if it would push me further into this world that I hated so much...but all I could hold onto was the hope that this would be the thing to turn the tides.

That this would finally make me the demon I was yearning to be.

Finally help me be strong enough so that never again would I be subjected to this fight.

"You think too highly of me child," Marques said with a smile as I stopped in front of his seated form. "I am merely a conduit."

"We will see, won't we?" I asked.

Claudine came over with a magical knife, grabbed his arm and without hesitation slashed his skin. His blood was like nothing I had ever seen. It was dark, and sticky. My stomach twisted but even as my mind yelled at me to run back I slowly picked up his arm and licked the blood off his wound.

Pulling away I watched his expression only to see his eyes already locked on me.

"I don't—"

Just as I was about to speak a sharp pain went through me and I was thrown to the ground. All the cells in my body felt as though they were vibrating and I couldn't stop my body from convulsing against the cold floor.

Warm arms wrapped around me and I was pulled into Rae's embrace. I held on to her and tried to breathe through my mouth as I felt the blood attacking my system.

My magic which had normally been lashing out and begging for some action quietly sat back and seemed to let the blood run through my body. Like even it was terrified of what I had just done.

"Why is it taking so long?" Rae asked from above me. "She should have been fine by now."

I let out a groan as a flash of white-hot pain radiated through my body.

"Soon," Malik spoke from somewhere near. "Claudine and Maximus had the same reaction."

Slowly as I listened to their words, my body began to relax and the pain started fading.

"I thin—*shit*," I groaned as another wave of pain shot through me. "I think it's ending."

Even as I lay there with a weakened body, Rae never let go of me and for that I was grateful. It was embarrassing and shameful to be seen like this in front of everyone but with her strong hold, I felt like I could do this.

When the last of the pain washed away I stood up with the help of both Rae and Malik.

"We are not done here," I said in a pained voice as I tried to walk back to the couch.

"You need to go back—"

I cut Malik off with a look.

"Tell me—*in detail*—the plan, and then we can go," I demanded.

I practically snuck into the couch. My body was still feeling the aftereffects of the blood.

"I'm going to kill the teacher bitch," Eli spoke up in an

excited tone. They sent me a smirk as I gave them a disbelieving look.

"Your mother?" I asked then threw my head back into the couch. "God we have issues."

I DO NOT KNOW how many hours we spent talking, but we were interrupted by the sun peeking through the dark space.

For the first time I could say that everything was out in the open and I finally knew what the fuck we were going to do next. I don't know if it made me relax or angered me because of how simple it had been.

I looked towards Marques, for some reason thinking that the sun would just destroy his frail frame but he just smiled at me. He had not moved from his chair the entire time, letting Malik do a majority of the talking while he sipped on his alcohol.

The demon with the magic blood and powers I didn't really understand looked oddly homey.

"Time to get back," he said. "Xena and Ezekiel will be worried if you are gone too long."

"Worried," Eli said with a huff next to me. I pulled myself from their embrace and stood with the rest of the group.

We were all various levels of tired, but my eyes fell on Malik, watching as he swayed. His eyes shifted to mine and he straightened as if brushing off what I had just seen.

I searched for the familiar redhead that should have been cursing my entire being in the corner but to my disappointment, he was gone. It hurt to think of how he had played me, and somehow hurt even more now that his actions lined up with the real him. I expected the Matt I knew to stick around, maybe talk about our misunderstanding...but I didn't think it was a misunderstanding to begin with. This was planned and I needed to accept that.

"Was the goal of this fight always equality?" I asked Marques as he walked us to the door. I half expected him to just shoo us away but instead, like a real host, he saw us out.

He gave me a small pitiful smile before answering.

"No, it never was," he said, his honesty stunning me for a moment. "I knew we were an abomination by the time our feet touched the ground of this plane. Others thought themselves as righteous, as saviors, as higher beings...but that is far from the truth."

I stood still, unable to pull myself from his intense stare.

"And do you remember heaven?" I asked.

He smiled at me, an all-knowing one and I couldn't help the flush of awe that rose in me. This man was the one with all the answers to everything, the Originals, our way of being, and even beyond...and here he was indulging me.

"I do, cursed one," he said. My lips twitched at his nickname.

"Is it..." I struggled to find the words to describe what I was asking.

"A word of advice," he said and paused before walking towards me. The others stepped back as if afraid of his actions. His cold hands found my shoulders and I found myself frozen in place by his eyes. "Stay alive as long as you can. You have seen the types of monsters they throw out of there... Do you really want to see what still resides there?"

"You have a point," I whispered, a smile tugging at my lips even after everything. "And hell?"

A grin slipped to his face.

"You are living it, darling."

A small bubble of laughter came out of my mouth. Though the alcohol had long been burned off by my demon blood, I still felt light and airy. Though that could just be the feeling of finally belonging somewhere.

"You are not wrong," I said. "I'll see you in practice."

A smirk played at his lips.

"I think you would prefer me to stay out of that, but I will see you soon," he said and leaned forward to place a kiss on my forehead. When he did, something like a memory zapped through my body forcing my hair to stand at all ends.

It was him alone in a chair, looking towards the forest outside. I could feel the weakness that hung over him and the tiredness that clouded his brain. Even breathing seemed like a tremendous task and with each inhale I felt the weight on his back double.

"I see," I said in a solemn tone.

I looked into his eyes, now seeing not an all-powerful man, but someone vulnerable and in pain.

He was *dying.*

How did I not see it sooner? Even his eyes had lost their shine.

"See you soon, cursed one."

❧

ELI'S HAND dug into my shoulder as we arrived at Winterfell. Claudine had used her powers to transport us here and even though she played it off well, by the sweat accumulating in her forehead, I knew she must have been straining.

Don't even think to run off to god knows where, they said in my mind. *I have plans for you.*

They sent me an image of me tied to the dorm bed, nude and writhing.

My mouth watered. It had been so long since I had had proper alone time with Eli. Let alone in an area where they had full control.

I was exhausted after the assault of information earlier this night, but it made the idea of being under Eli's control all that more enticing. I needed a break from it all, needed to get my mind away from the pain and death. For once not think about the steps I needed to take to make sure that I wouldn't die the next day.

And I couldn't think of anyone better to do the job.

I would much rather spend the time with you, I said in my mind.

Their eyes shifted to mine briefly.

"Alright," Malik said. "Disperse and don't let me see you again until next time."

The group gave a round of agreements and Eli began steering me away, but not before I caught sight of a familiar redhead walking up to our group.

Where had he gone?

I sent a glare to Matt, which he wholeheartedly returned. Malik noticed and smacked the side of his arm and Matt's glare dropped.

Unease twisted in my stomach as I watched the two.

How had Matt changed so quickly? It couldn't all be fake, could it?

Our time at Winterfell, while fake...had felt like a real friendship. Our laughs were real, the warmth I felt from him was real, the comfort...

It was never real, Rosie, Eli said in my head. *He has always been a snake, you just never knew until now.*

My last look was to Rae, who had stood silently on the side of the group. I wonder what she was thinking, feeling, during this time. Her eyes gave no indication though I could feel something simmering beneath her skin whenever I came close.

I was tempted to ask her to join us, but that was quickly shot down when I realized how little time I had spent with Eli. Rae nodded as if understanding my thoughts and turned to leave, her glowing hazel gaze lingering on us.

"Rae," Malik said in a light tone. "Can we talk?"

Rae raised a brow towards Malik but nodded anyways and followed him in the opposite direction. I wondered what the two of them could possibly talk about, but I gave them the benefit of the doubt, even though inside I wanted to turn around and demand what other secrets they were keeping. Steeling my raging magic and unsteady emotions, I tried to focus on the person that held me tight against their side.

At last, we turned away as well and set forth with Eli across the dead campus.

There was much to discuss still, but none of it safe for the prying walls of Winterfell. I have learned now that getting answers quickly was impossible, and if they came fast...well then they were probably lies.

And after the change in Matt, I had realized that there was not a person besides those I have kept around that were worth trusting, and even they sometimes had proven to break that trust.

The silence that spread across the place was eerie and held a weight to it as though we were walking in a graveyard and the dead lay right below our feet The only thing that calmed me somewhat was the undeniable thrum of magic underneath us as we walked and the traces of magical signatures left by the refugees.

"Stop being so dramatic," Eli teased, their hand moving to twist a strand of my hair. I leaned into their warmth and inhaled their familiar scent.

I had missed this much more than I thought. Eli, while brash and sometimes unhinged, had been a constant never-changing person that I could rely on to keep me grounded.

Even through everything that happened, I found them staying true to their nature in an ever-changing world.

Their strong hands continued to guide me and even as they sent explicit images of what was to come, I found myself comforted by them. I was safe in their arms and I couldn't imagine a place where I would rather be in that moment.

"I did it," they said. *The town.*

"I know," I replied.

"How did you hide it from me?" they asked.

I wondered how long the question had been gnawing at them.

"The memories?" I asked looking up at them.

They nodded.

"I just tried not to think about it when you touched me," I said truthfully.

"And how did you stop him?" they asked.

"I had help," I said and looked out at the still campus. "I will show you more later."

They nodded and dropped the conversation after that.

The rest of the way was quiet, except for the scenes in my head. Each one sent a flood of arousal through me and my magic, which had been laying low, sprung to life.

Living with my magic now, was almost like second nature.

Daxton and Amr had done wonders when it came to exploring this side of me...but it was pushy about what it was missing.

Never before had the others heard of a witch's magic being expelled with a demon's help, but mine craved a demon's touch.

Specifically, Rae's and Eli's.

Eli quickly opened the door to their dorm and the first thing that hit me was how clean the inside was. There was mostly darkness until they flipped the switch for the lights, and something I had never seen before came to life.

Winterfell dorms were all the same, to my knowledge, so I was familiar with the exposed brick and muted tones of the room, but what was out of the norm were the shelves decorating the walls and the paintings that hung on all four sides.

My mouth dropped open when I got a look at the shelves.

There were *pictures* of Eli and the others, all frowning while they seemed to be at a party not unlike the gala we had gone to together.

My mind whirled with this information.

Eli kept stuff like this?

"There is a reason I didn't want you here," they grumbled.

"I just—"

They cut me off with a tug on the back of my hair, forcing me to look up at them. Their blue eyes shimmered in the dim lights that lit the area.

"You can gawk at my dorm later," they growled and nipped at my bottom lip.

Their free hand trailed up my arm to grip onto my neck, forcing my body closer to theirs. The roughness of their skin only added fuel to the fire that was slowly burning up my insides.

I melted into their touch, submitting fully to whatever they planned for me. I trusted them enough for this, at least.

"I don't have my curse," I murmured against their soft lips.

Their lips quirked.

"I have a plan for that," they replied. "Now strip. I want you kneeling before the bed naked and ready for me."

A shiver ran through me. I thought about fighting, just for the thrill of it. Talking back, hitting, pushing away, just to see how far I could push them as I remembered the first night we ever had together and how the roughness of their touches stayed with me for weeks. But I decided against it.

Instead I stepped out of their grasp and slowly peeled my clothes off, giving them a view of my fully naked body before turning and walking towards the bed.

"Facing me, this time."

I did as they told and knelt down with the bed behind me. Even though the air was warm in the room, I couldn't stop the shivers that wracked my body. I couldn't stop the way my nipples hardened under their gaze or the way my pussy began to throb.

All it took was one pointed look from them and I was already becoming a puddle at their feet.

They walked closer towards me, the height difference causing me to shift my gaze upward. I could feel the ends of my hair brushing my bare ass. Their gaze ran up the length of my body and I found my breathing becoming quicker.

My magic was reaching out wildly trying to wrap around Eli and force them to our side, but I stayed put.

Their hand came to rest on the side of my face and I leaned into it. Their mouth quirked at my actions.

"This will be rough," they said.

I swallowed down the nervousness rising up in me.

"I know," I whispered. Their thumb traced my lower lip. "I want it rough."

Their gaze became hooded and they pushed their thumb past my lips to push down on my tongue. I closed my lips around it and sucked lightly.

"It's not like before," they said. "Back then... I didn't feel the way I do for you now."

My heart pounded so hard in my chest that the sound of it began to drown out everything else.

"I feel like I am being torn in two when I am away from you," they said. "I loathe the people that hurt you." They took a deep breath as if trying to calm themselves. Their gaze was wild now, with a smile spreading across their lips.

"I want you, no—I *need* you now," they continued. "More than ever."

"Eli," I tried to say around their thumb.

"And that means I just want to *hurt* you more."

There was a bit of fear mixed into all of this, but that only spiced up the arousal that was coursing through me. Sitting like this in front of them, so vulnerable, and waiting for them to ravish me... I was positively dripping.

And on top of it, it was *my choice.*

My choice to be here in front of them.

My choice to hand over control.

They kneeled down so they were at eye level with me.

"Hurt you because of the things you make me feel," they explained. "Because how *dare* a hybrid who grew up parading around as a dirty low-level bring me to my knees like this. How dare that same person turn and viciously murder her lover's parents, and not give a damn."

"Eli—"

"I am not done," they growled and removed their hand only to fasten it around my neck.

"I do not know if hating you," they said, "...or whatever this is, is worse. But there is no going back and I swear to you if you ever think about leaving my side I *will not* show you any mercy."

My mind exploded.

Is this...is this how they tell me they love me?

Before I could think of any other thoughts their lips crashed against mine and their rough hands forced my legs apart. Their fingers immediately found my wetness but instead of starting rough like I expected, they slowly trailed the length of my slit, only stopping to rub circles in my clit before continuing their teasing touch.

I continued to kiss them, our tongues intertwining with each other, but in my mind, I was screaming.

I love you, I sent them. *I don't care, hurt me, bind me, torture me... my heart still beats for you.*

"Good," they purred against my lips. "Because me feeling for you, does not mean I will give you a break. I am not a good person, Rosie."

"And I don't ask you to be," I said in return.

They sent me a devious smile.

"Face down on the bed, ass up."

I DIDN'T KNOW how much longer I could handle in this position. I was face down in the bed, with my ass up in the air, fully naked. I could not stop the shaking in my legs as I sobbed through the intense pleasure that was shooting through me.

Eli had brought back the toys in full force.

Not only did they get real cuffs that tied me to the opposite ends of the bed, but that damned egg was back as well. They had turned it on the highest setting, sat back on the opposite side of the room and watched to see how long it would take for me to break.

I was close to my breaking point now, three orgasms in and it was hard to find my grip on reality because as much as my magic begged to be let out, it wouldn't settle for this stupid toy. It wanted a real demon between my legs as I came.

My wetness had gathered and I could feel it leaking down my legs.

My back was aching and I tried to shift in order to get to a more comfortable position, but Eli's stern voice gave a firm warning.

"Is that all?" they teased.

I shifted, the cuffs clanking against the metal of the bed frame. I peered over to them, my hair was damp with sweat and made it hard to make out the demon's form in the dim light.

I silenced my whines when I caught sight of the toy in their hands.

I had been so caught up in my own pleasure that I didn't notice that they were fully naked, their sleek skin simmering with sweat under the light and a toy was placed between their legs.

The toy was quiet, barely noticeable over the beating of my own heart.

They looked at me with hooded eyes and pressed a button on the side of their toy. I watched in fascination as their chest puffed and their head was thrown back, a deep moan escaping their mouth.

The sight alone caused my body to heat up and I found myself falling faster over the edge than I had the entire night. My entire body was stiff and I couldn't help but thrash around in the sheets calling Eli's name.

"Please," I begged them. "Please, no more."

They took a few deep breaths before they threw the toy

across the room and stood from the seat. They silently walked over to the shelf, taking their time as if I was not just pleading for them to end me.

They rummaged through the boxes on the lower levels of the shelves before pulling out a dark purple dildo. My jaw dropped at the pure size of the toy. It was even bigger than Amr and had to be almost the size of my forearm.

"Eli, no," I said and pulled against the cuffs that were holding me against the bed.

"In that case," they murmured and reached back into the box to pull out a much smaller one. Almost *too* small...and then I watched as they fastened it above the other one with expert precision.

"Eli, I've never..."

"I know," they answered with a smirk. They fastened the harness around their waist before bending down to get a bottle of lube. I relaxed a bit and finally let my hips drop to the bed. "I didn't say you could relax yet, little Original."

I let out a whine and lifted my hips for them.

They walked over to me chuckling lightly and I felt the bed dip when they positioned themselves behind me.

"This will hurt," they warned. I flinched as they spread my cheeks and poured cold lube onto me. "But remember you asked for this."

I let out a sob and pushed myself back into them, feeling the large head of the dildo rest at my wet entrance. Their fingers pushed inside me to retrieve the toy, relieving me from the harsh vibrations for mere moments before I felt the first tip push against my entrance.

The stretch was fine at first, and it glided in easily, then I felt the prick of pain followed by a stinging sensation as I began to fill more than I ever had before.

I took a deep breath and arched into the pain, trying not to freeze when I felt the smaller dildo line up at the puckered ring of flesh that hadn't been abused by any of the others yet.

"That's right," they breathed. I let out a high-pitched whine as the second dildo pushed past the barrier. "I know. *I know.*"

Without warning their hands gripped my hips, nails digging into my flesh and forced me back to them, sheathing both toys side of me. A hot flash of pain shot through me from head to toe as I got used to the feeling of an object inside of me.

They didn't let me rest there though. I should have known this was an act. This whole time, they were prepping me for the harshness of what they were going to do to me.

They pulled out fully before they snapped our hips together once more.

"Fuck Eli," I groaned as they began to pound into me at a pace that forced the breath out of my lungs.

I had never been so full as I had in that moment and with each thrust into me I found the pain changing into something far more pleasurable, but instead of letting me get used to it, they began fucking me harder. Their hand pushed my back down into the comforter allowing them deeper access.

I could feel each thrust hit the back of my cervix and for a second, I really thought that Eli may ruin me.

I held onto the cuffs and buried my face in the pillow to conceal my sobs. No doubt if anyone heard us they would think I was being murdered with the amount of screams that had been coming out of my mouth.

Eli's hand left my hip to rub circles in my almost forgotten clit. The bundle of nerves was so sensitive that just a single touch caused the heat that had been gathering in my belly to start to explode outwards, pushing it along my entire body.

"I can't wait until the others realize that *I* was the first to fuck this tight hole of yours," they said from behind me and moved their hand from my back to push at the abused rim of flesh with their thumb, stretching me even further. "I'll take pleasure in knowing that you will not be able to sit without being reminded of who was here first."

They pushed into me and rocked their hips in a gentle

swaying motion. Their hand left my clit to pull on my hair and force my head back at an awkward angle.

"You love it, don't you?" they asked. "Being filled to the brim. Tell me."

"Fuck, Eli. I love it, so much," I groaned and pushed my hips back against their thrusts. "Harder, Eli."

They let out a laugh and pounded into me at an animalistic pace.

"I forgot how much of a slut you were," Eli laughed and pulled on my hair. "I saw in Rae's head what you looked like as Amr and Daxton tag teamed you. *So needy.* Taking their cocks like you were starving."

Their hand left my hair and came down my ass with a loud smack. Pain and pleasure vibrated through my body and left me shaking.

"Again," I gasped as I felt the sting radiate through my body.

They brought their hand back down on my ass again.

"God I missed this," they grunted from behind me. "I am not going to let you get an ounce of sleep today you hear me? You fall asleep and you will be waking up with my cunt in your mouth."

"Fuck, I can't anymore Eli," I whined as they brought their hand back down on my ass.

They pulled out without warning and flipped me over only to reenter in one swift movement. The second dildo shining with lube and juices rubbed against my clit as they fucked me.

"Your magic," they groaned and splayed their hand across my stomach. "Here."

I grabbed onto their arm, barely keeping up.

"What?" I asked.

"Here." They pointed against my lower stomach. "I want my name carved in your body, forever, but knives will heal."

I sucked in a deep breath but conjured a magical spear all the same, but instead of doing it myself I handed it to Eli.

"If you brand me, then I brand you," I said.

Their thrusts paused and without hesitation they grabbed the spear. I heard the burning of skin as they held it over my stomach. Their hungry blue eyes flitted to mine before they brought the spear down onto my stomach.

I threw my head back and fisted the sheets at my side, a groan filling the room. My chest heaved as the burning pain of the knife slicing my skin filled my being. After Eli finished carving the first letter I bit back my scream as they spread the blood from the wound across my stomach.

As the blood leaked from my body so did my magic. I felt it releasing into the air and saw through my blurry eyes that it created shimmers.

"Beautiful," they murmured. "You were always so beautiful in red."

Their bloodied hand found my clit and they rewarded me with a few shallow thrusts. The intoxicating mix of pain and pleasure made my mind swim.

"Next," I gasped.

Eli chuckled and then went to work on the next letter. It was deeper than the last and I felt blood pool on my stomach.

"*So. Fucking. Beautiful*," they bit out with three hard thrusts. Their bloodied hand gripped my thigh, their nails digging into the soft flesh, no doubt drawing blood of their own.

"Next," I commanded again.

The dot on the eye was excruciating and I almost felt my consciousness falling away if not for Eli's careful circles on my clit, bringing me back. I felt the lost orgasm start to blossom.

"Quickly," I moaned.

They finished off the letters without removing the spear from my skin. I came as soon as the last letter was finished and Eli threw the spear across the room. The magic that came with this orgasm, while less intense, sent a warmth through my body as it burst out of my skin.

Never before had I been so whole fully satisfied with my magic resting and going silent inside of me. The beast that was residing in my skin had finally had enough and my body was able to relax into the bed.

"Amr may be onto something," they murmured with shallow thrusts as they continued to spread the blood up my stomach and around my erect nipples. Each movement was ripe with pain but slowly, it mixed together providing a hum of euphoria that ran through me. "Cause right now, I wouldn't mind kneeling before you and calling you queen."

7
DAXTON

I hated mornings.

They reminded me of the shitty life I now had to live.

Every morning I would wake up and stay as still as possible as to not disturb any of my sleeping partners. This was the time when I would replay the last four years of my life and go through every single mistake I had made.

It was the only time that I had absolutely alone, with no one to snap me out of my depression spiral.

Ever since the night my parents—

I couldn't even think about it on the bad days.

On the good days I would think about what my life could be. What this freedom with the others finally meant. I could dream about the days where I could just lounge on the couch with Amr and Rosie and sleep the day away.

During those dreams, nothing was ever bothering me and it was like my parents didn't exist. It was like it was a single bad nightmare that never bothered me again.

But on the bad days... I *missed* them.

Missed the family that I wished I would have had.

Today was a day where I loathed them. I hated what they did to me and the way they made me feel all those years growing up and was relieved that I no longer had to look at their disgusting faces anymore.

In this moment, I was grateful for their deaths... But my magic only held onto the anger.

It amplified the small bit of anger that was residing in my stomach and fanned it outward and suddenly, I was angrier than I had ever been. It *loved* the darkness inside me, wanted to see how far it could take it, mold it into something more dangerous.

The magic pushed me to destroy, pushed me to destroy the peace of Winterfell and all the students that just happened to arrive early this year.

It wanted blood.

It wanted death.

It wanted to—

A familiar warmth engulfed my being, and strong hands gripped my hips. I leaned into Amr as he left lazy kisses down my throat.

"We have to get up and find Rosie," Amr murmured into my neck, but against his words his hands trailed down my stomach and teased the hem of my boxers.

This is what I needed. I needed to calm my magic and be in the company of someone I trusted.

"If she hasn't found us by now then it means she needs more time," I said and leaned back into his warmth, soaking up the feelings that flittered inside of me.

"You're right," he said and licked the length of my neck causing me to shudder. Heat had already begun to pool in my belly because of his sleepy touches.

He reached down and ran the length of his hands up my already throbbing erection. I whimpered and reached my arms around and turned my head so I could bring his mouth to mine.

"We will go in a bit," I whispered.

"In a bit," he agreed and ran his thumb over the head of my cock. "Just a taste."

I let out a groan.

I tried not to think about what my growing magic meant, though deep down, I knew it was chipping at my existence. I had been around enough witches to know that this was not normal and nothing that awaited me could be good.

I remembered the way Father and Mother used to talk about crazed witches, but I never saw them. Not until I looked in the mirror.

"Are you here with me?" Amr asked pulling his hand away.

I quickly grabbed his wrist to stop him from moving.

"Yes," I whispered. "I am here."

The words felt like a lie.

LUCKILY SCHOOL WAS NOT in because if it was, Amr and I would have been hours late.

I kept waiting for Rosie's messy hair to pop through the door, but she never came. When Amr and I both decided that she had had enough time to herself, we ventured out into Winterfell.

A handful of students had begun to arrive early and they shared looks when they caught Amr and me walking side by side. They would whisper and point but when I glared at them they just ran in the opposite direction.

"Must be the news of the funeral," Amr said. His strong hand came to massage the knots out of my shoulders.

"Or the hybrid," I murmured and watched another pair of high-level demons stare at us from a building mere twenty feet away from where we stood.

Did they think we couldn't see them?

When one of them gasped I felt my magic surge. The feeling of it rising up in me made my head swim and my body tense.

My magic roared and pushed me to go fight. With every fiber of its being it thrashed around inside of me as if it had been starving for a decade. Its bloodlust was overpowering and for once, I felt as though I had something completely separate from my magic.

As if there *really was* a beast inside of me after all.

"I feel her," Amr said, pulling me out of my red haze. I looked over at him, taking in his beautifully tanned skin and long dark hair that was pulled back into a ponytail.

He sent me an understanding smile.

I took a deep breath, closed my eyes, and sent my magic out looking for her.

"She is back with the refugees?" I whispered.

"Maybe she never left," Amr murdered. "Something feels off her magic..."

As if his words had the ability to predict the future, there was a flash of magic that spread across the campus.

It was so strong I stumbled back as it clashed against mine.

We shared a look before bolting in the direction of the cafeteria.

With each site the magic Rosie was emitting became more and more potent and instead of running to save her, my magic was pushing me forward to consume.

It was racing with me, trying to see who could have more control over this sack of flesh before the other. It was roaring, telling me to tear apart the magic user and eat the magic core raw.

Amr beat me to the doors of the cafeteria and flung them open. He stepped in front of me as we were blasted with a fresh dose of magic.

The room that was once filled with the bundled refugees was now empty, save for four people in the middle of the room.

Eli stood to the side. They were the first to look at us as we entered.

Rae was across from them and her eyes never left Rosie.

Malik was slowly approaching Rosie with his hands up.

Rosie was in the middle of the group but it was hard to make out her form through the oozing black cloud that radiated out of her body. It was thick and fell to the ground in waves before spreading out across the floor and right towards us.

The biggest attention grabber, besides the magic pouring out of Rosie...was the bright red letters that lined every surface of the place.

"Traitor," was written all along the walls and from the small pulsing from the fresh blood, I could tell it was witches they had used for the blood.

The refugees missing with the fresh blood lining the walls was enough to break the bit of sanity that was holding me to the ground below me.

The same people we had been working the entire summer to save. Pouring our magic into potion after potion... It was *their* blood that painted the walls.

"Don't," Amr growled, but I wasn't sure if it was for Malik or myself because all I could think about as I bolted forward was how sweet the magic smelt.

I could even taste it on my tongue.

That sweet old magic that was as aged and delicious as the first day I had ever tasted it. I clawed at Amr's arm as he stopped me from running forward.

"Rosie," Malik said in a voice almost too low to hear. "Look at me."

"Did you know this would happen?" she snapped at him, her voice much louder, more powerful than his.

The tone sent me into a frenzy.

"Daxton, calm," Amr's voice commanded.

I sent a kick to his leg but he easily dodged and circled his arms around me.

"Did you know?" Rosie asked when there was no reply. "*Fucking answer me, Malik!*"

There was a pause before anyone spoke. The only sound filling the room was my growls.

"We were aware of the possibility," Rae said in a dark tone. "Though we thought with the effort—"

"I don't want to hear any more *lies!*" she yelled, her magic flaring out.

The monster inside me liked the way the others shrunk at her voice. Liked the fear rolling off of them.

Half of Malik's body disappeared as he kneeled in front of Rosie.

"Open your eyes!" he growled.

"No!" she yelled. "You are just going to manipulate me and hide things from me *again.* And I can't take another minute of it!"

She swung her arm and the black magic shot out and threw Malik across the cafeteria.

Go. Run. Feast.

This was our chance.

I struggled against Amr's hold.

"You're making this worse for everyone," Eli said. "Cat, do something."

"I have my hands full!" Amr yelled from behind me.

I dove for the floor as the black magic finally reached our position, but Amr yanked me back and held me in a headlock.

The world started to dim as Amr's hold on me tightened.

"Let me go," I choked out.

"I am sorry," Amr whispered from behind me, his voice barely audible over my own growls.

The last thing I saw as I sunk into darkness was the dissipation of the black magic and Rosie's body going limp only to be caught by Malik's awaiting arms.

8

ROSIE

"They ran for it," Malik's deep voice flitted through my fuzzy brain.

My limbs were heavy with sleep and I couldn't make sense of up or down. My head swam and the world began tipping around me. Below me was soft fluffy material which I assumed was a bed, though there was an itchy material that was laid on me.

"I didn't expect anything else," Eli said with a huff.

I peeled my eyes open and was hit with a blinding light. The smell of chemicals filled my senses and burned my nose.

As my vision cleared I sat up in a flurry and pushed back until my back hit a cold wall.

The man that had been leaning over me jumped up and straightened his spine, my sudden movement taking him off guard though his surprise quickly wore off and a small smile rose to his face.

My gaze darted towards the group on the bed next to me.

Eli was sitting on the bed with their legs hanging off the side. Their arms were crossed and they were scowling at me.

Malik was standing behind them with a small smile of his

own on his lips, and Rae was behind the two. She wouldn't look at me.

"Amr, Daxton?" I asked, my throat burning as the words were forced out of my mouth.

Eli jutted their chin forward. I followed the motion and looked to the left, and just beside me was Daxton asleep on the bed next to me and Amr was sitting next to him. He sent me a smile.

"How are you feeling, love?" he asked and reached out to grab my hand. His warmth seeped into my skin and a breath escaped my tight chest.

"I just—"

My words caught in my throat.

How could they? They had said they would find a place for them...

Was this what Ezekiel was scared of? Did he know Xena would do this?

When I woke up, I ran to the cafeteria, ready to take all of the refugees out of that hell hole and to a place where I knew they would be safe. Malik had told me that there was a place for them, and as long as we could sneak them out, Xena and Ezekiel would never be the wiser.

It was a chance to save the dying group of people that never knew any better than the trapped lives they were given.

A chance to change something.

A chance to do something *good* for once.

And then I saw the blood splattered across the walls, and that message...

"How did they know?" I asked and looked towards Malik.

He was the traitor in their mind too now.

No longer could he play the manipulator for their side, now they knew the truth.

"I do not know," he answered, the smile dropping from his face.

"But you knew they would do this," I said, a small bit of venom filling my voice.

Amr squeezed my hand.

"Not in relation to defecting," Rae said, calling my attention back to her.

At the edges of my being I could feel the familiar push of her emotions. The same ones she used when we had slept in her dorm.

They were warm and caused tears to well up in my eyes...but it wasn't enough to quench the fire that was burning through my veins. The hatred for those monsters had been festering silently below my skin, waiting for its final blow...and this was it.

This was the moment it had been waiting for.

It was ready to wreak havoc. It wanted to tear them apart and make them pay for what they did to those poor people.

"In relation to what then?" I said in a softer tone, letting her powers ease over me.

The bunched muscles in my back relaxed.

"They were always going to do it," Eli said with an annoyed tone. "Don't you get it? They didn't care for them, and now that they are fleeing they don't need the extra mess."

"And they knew it would mess with you," Malik added on.

I swallowed thickly.

"A weak enemy is one they do not have to worry about," Rae continued. "They preyed on your unhinged magic. And probably Daxton's in turn, knowing yours would call to his."

I turned from them to the doctor that was watching me with interest. Or at least I assumed he was the doctor. His hair was almost fully grey except for a few strands of black. He had a pair of circular glasses that inched down his nose, giving me a good look at his brown eyes.

"I'm sorry," I said in a low voice. "I was..."

"Startled," he finished for me with a smile. "Don't worry. Does anything hurt?"

"No," I said quickly and looked over to a sleeping Daxton. "What about him?"

The doctor's face fell slightly.

"His case is...a bit different," he said and then there was a pause.

"Which is?" I asked.

"We shouldn't talk about it until he is awake," the doctor said with a forced smile.

Anger sparked deep in my belly. I deserved to know, I wanted to help him.

"His magic is killing him," Eli spoke out.

I froze, every nerve in my body on edge.

"You're lying," I spit at them.

They met me with a disbelieving stare and a raised brow.

"I am the only one telling you the truth, mutant," they growled back.

The nickname pulled a growl out of me and I felt my magic spike wildly around me.

"It's not killing him," Malik hissed and hit the back of Eli's head.

They glared at him and stood to fight but Rae cleared her throat. They both sent her a look before frowning and turning away from each other.

"The Original magic is having adverse effects on his natural magic," the doctor said with a sigh. "His life could be in danger, if he is not careful. If his magic is calmed by that of an Original then he can last longer, though I have never seen a case like this before if I am being honest."

I nodded and sent a helpless look at Amr. We couldn't lose him, not after all of this. I couldn't even think what a life without him would look like. He didn't deserve all this. He was the victim in this situation and I felt even worse that it was me who brought him into this.

If I would have just completed my task without him, maybe we would have been better off.

"We will figure it out," he whispered.

I let out a sigh, though I was anything but relieved. This

whole thing was a mess and the rage that was so carefully hidden within me came tumbling to the surface.

"Am I good to go?" I asked the doctor. "Maybe take him with me?"

"There is not anything else I can do, so feel free to leave but you are more than welcome to stay."

I gave him a small smile.

"I am not much for hospitals," I said with a grimace, remembering the last time I awoke in a hospital.

He sent me a look before looking towards Malik.

"We are not in a hospital, Rosie," Malik said.

As his words sunk in my heart picked up speed.

"The safe house," I breathed.

"The safe house," he confirmed a light twinkling in his eyes.

A spark pushed its way through my body, lighting up a once desolate darkness.

I looked around and noticed more than a few beds filled. Squinting I saw that patients laying in bed had this sort of magical film on them that shimmered in the light.

"What is wrong with them?" I asked.

"They are aging fast," the doctor responded and looked over at his patients. "The magical barrier protects them from aging while I figure out how to save them."

"There are less here now," Rae noted, her eyes snapping over the empty beds with a furrowed brow.

"Yes," the doctor said and cleared his throat. "Those who have been rapidly decaying even with the barrier have been moved to rooms where they can be more comfortable."

I swallowed thickly.

"So those ones are lost causes?" I asked, a lump forming in my throat.

Was there really no way to save them?

"I wouldn't like to call them lost causes, Ms. Miller," he said with a frown. "Though some have families and would like them to be comfortable in case they pass."

I nodded, no one else spoke and just let me stew in my own thoughts.

"Show me the rest of the safe house."

❧

AFTER CONFIRMATION FROM BOTH AMR, Rae, and the doctor that they would watch over Daxton while I was gone, I set out to explore the hideaway that Malik had built for the others.

I was almost tempted to stay with them and explain all that had happened in Marques's manor...but that would have to wait. That would be a long conversation and I couldn't wait another second to see the people who were saved.

I needed it after what I just witnessed.

The rooms were mostly empty save for a sleeping child or breastfeeding mother. The real crowd was in the "main room" as Malik liked to call it.

When we entered it my mouth dropped.

"An old warehouse served as the perfect hideout," Malik said from my side.

The space was huge and the ceiling spanned on forever. Tables littered the area and I caught a scent of delicious smelling food that made my mouth water.

People of all ages were surrounding the tables laughing, and joyfully talking as if they had not just been imprisoned for years on end. Though I could understand it.

They finally escaped the grimy fingers of the Originals and had a life where they were safe and free to live however they wanted.

The laughter and smiling faces warmed my heart, but the bitterness in my mouth didn't leave.

They were the lucky ones that still had a life to live while the others were murdered without remorse. I tried not to let my anger sour the mood; the people here deserved to be happy.

"How long do they have to stay like this?" I asked.

While I was beyond ecstatic to see them happy, this was not a life.

"Until those fuckers are dead," Eli growled next to me.

Their voice was loud enough to turn a few heads and I felt a jolt when I recognized the smiling bartender that was once in charge of the portal to the town.

"Eli!" he yelled. "Bring your lady over!"

My heart skipped a beat as Eli threw an arm over my shoulder and dragged me towards them.

"Wa—it, Eli *no*," I stuttered trying to look cool as a whole crowd of people turned to look at me. Some faces were recognizable but mostly it was just the bartender that I remembered.

"Son, what a catch," a man with a beard and long hair said. He chuckled as he lifted the drink to his lips.

"It's good to see you again," I said mostly to the bartender.

He sent me a smile and motioned for the others to pour me a drink.

I took the glass from a random witch with shaking hands and a wavering smile.

Don't be so dramatic, mutant, Eli sneered in my mind.

So this is what you meant when you said you would be worse? I egged on. *A nickname?*

They sent me an image of me tied over a school desk with that Winterfell skirt pulled up over my waist. I watched as they slapped my bare ass.

I would leave you there, they said. *For all students to see. Let them do whatever they wanted to you as I watched.*

I shuddered.

Don't test me, they warned.

"So what took you so long?" the bartender asked.

The image of "traitor" written in blood all over the cafeteria filled my mind.

"I—"

"Had a breakdown," Eli finished for me.

I sent them a glare.

"You are horrible," the bearded man muttered with a slight laugh.

"You get an extra," the witch that handed me my drink said while lifting a bottle of whiskey to my cup.

"Rosie," Malik's voice interrupted.

A wave of relief washed over me as I realized I was being saved from this hell.

As I turned I sent him a grateful smile, but it quickly turned into a look of horror as I saw the woman standing next to him.

"Oh, *it's you,*" Eli said as they turned to look at the newcomer next to Malik.

"How do you...?"

The words wouldn't come out. They dried up in my throat as did all of the assuredness and confidence I worked on in the last year. Every raging emotion in me plus my magic seemed to silence when her blue eyes met mine.

"She was next to my cell," Eli said. "Don't you remember? It was when you came to my cell—"

"This is what you took," I said, the air rushing from my lungs.

My low-level mother looked exactly the same as I left her. Her black hair still fell silkily over her shoulders and her small frame was crouched over as if she wanted to bury her existence.

The same mother that made my life hell as the curse ran rampant through my body.

The same mother that cared more about image than her daughter.

"Yes," Malik spoke. "I asked Matt to remove both yours and Amr's memory."

"Rosie," she said in a soft voice.

It was softer than I ever heard.

"You said a safe house," I accused.

He gave me a look that told me I should know better by now.

You should kill this one too, Eli said in my head. *Count it as practice.*

Oh god, I felt as though I was going to be sick. Her eyes flitted to the drink in my hand and with the only strength left I brought it to my lips and tilted my head back, drinking the entirety in one gulp.

"If this is you trying to redeem yourself, I don't want it," I growled at Malik.

"Rosie," my mother chided. I froze on spot.

I can't deal with this, I sent to Eli as I felt my skin heat to extreme levels. The once silent magic was boiling under my skin.

Why was she here? I left her—them—oh god, is my father here?

I thought Winterfell would be my ticket out, but here she was looking as healthy as I left her. Her long black hair was pulled into a low ponytail and she wore a beaded shirt and pants that looked far too expensive to be here in this safe house.

The walls felt like they were closing in on me and the noise from the people around us became louder. A layer of sweat appeared on my skin and I had to push myself into Eli in order to steady my swaying legs.

First the death of my patients and then this?

How could I even begin to explain how this happened? She had to know at least some of it right? Did she remember Xena?

I need out, please.

When they didn't answer I began to panic.

Please, Eli I beg you.

"Let's come back," Malik said with a smile to my mother. She frowned but nodded.

"Find me before you leave Rosie," she said. "We need to talk, as a *family*."

We are not family, I thought bitterly. We never were and never would be. The moment I stepped out of their life and into Winterfell was the best moment of my life and while fraught with challenges and pain...I preferred it to their company.

She eyed Eli with a scowl before turning and walking back to the hallway that kept the rooms.

"Rosie, I didn't realize—"

"Let's not talk about it?" I said quickly cutting Malik off. "Please."

He nodded before sighing and looking around.

"The clam chowder guy is around here somewhere," he muttered. "Let's get you some food."

I nodded and looked up towards Eli.

"You didn't help," I snapped.

Their eyes slowly shifted to mine and I was faced with an expression more serious than I had ever gotten from Eli before.

"I'll kill her," they said. "Will that make you satisfied since you cannot find yourself to do it?"

A cold shock ran through my body. I searched their face looking for any sign that this was a joke.

A smirk.

A twinkle in their eyes...but there was nothing.

"No-o," I said, caught off guard by their offer. "I don't want to do that."

They looked back towards where my mother had walked away to.

"I think you do want that," they murmured. "She was a horrible mother anyway and will only hold you back. The last thing we need is another loose end."

My mouth went dry and my heart went into overdrive.

"Please don't," I begged, not liking the eerie stillness in their expression. It was intense and I knew that they were weighing the decision heavily in their mind.

"I am," they said. "I just don't understand, I thought you were stronger than that." They looked back towards me. "Maybe I need to teach you."

"Let's go eat," I said quickly, trying to move away from this subject.

Whether or not I decided to forgive my mother was one thing, but there was no way that I would let Eli near her.

9
MALIK

Xena and Ezekiel fleeing was both the worst thing that has happened in my existence...and also the best.

The weight of their presence disappeared in the night with them and as I stared at the joyfully laughing demons around me, I couldn't help but think that even through all the bad...we did something good.

After all the years of death and pain, there was *finally* something I could proudly say that we did right. It took a while for us to get here, and the path here was gnarled and filled with broken glass, the people were less than honorable...but *we did it*.

And now, we had everyone right where they needed to be. The Originals were missing but we couldn't let that put a damper on our plans. If anything, it was the break we needed.

It would give us time to train those who had ingested Marques's blood, and once they were ready...it would be a piece of cake.

My chest ached and a shiver of excitement ran through me. We were so close.

I shifted uncomfortably against the wall of the makeshift dining room and searched for Rosie.

My heart melted when I saw her sitting with Eli and eating

clam chowder out of a chipped bowl. The demons around her were chatting away and she was obviously failing at trying to keep up with their tempo.

She would take a bite then smile with her mouth full and nod as if the man who was talking to her was saying the most interesting thing in the world. Then, when there was a pause she would dip back down and eat again.

I had lost count of how many times they had asked her if she was enjoying her food.

I realized in that moment, that this was the life she was supposed to live. Going forward she could be a normal college student and live her life without interference from crazed Originals.

I couldn't take this away from her, I thought. *I couldn't steal away her last hope as a real college student. The others be dammed, they had had their fair share of life, but her...*

I promised I wouldn't lie to her, and I wouldn't anymore. But I would be dammed if I let her be dragged into this plan. As much as she wanted revenge for the refugees and to get back at her birth mother...I would try and shield the weight for as long as I could.

And it started with finding where those fuckers were hiding.

The faster I found them, the faster Rosie and the other would be able to live in peace.

I caught Eli's sidelong glance and raised a brow at them.

Their lips quirked before turning back to Rosie. By the look on her face and quickly reddening cheeks I could tell that Eli was no doubt filling that mind of hers with dirty thoughts.

My curiosity for her never wavered. How could someone so young be so resilient? Someone who had magic that was far too powerful for their body sitting amongst all these people and eating clam chowder as though it was a family reunion, when not an hour ago she was bursting at the seams?

I pulled myself out from my thoughts and with a prayer that Rosie wouldn't hate me, turned back to the medical bay. With the rowdy crowd, it wasn't hard to silently slip out and in between bodies until I found myself closing in on the room.

Here goes nothing.

As I peeked in I saw that Daxton was now sitting up and talking to Amr while Rae was sitting in the bed Rosie was once occupying. They were in deep conversation and Daxton's eyebrows were pulled together. Amr had a blank expression and his arms were crossed.

Looking at Daxton, I couldn't help but feel for him.

His parents had to be the worst of them all, and even though Marques had no intention of having them fuck up Daxton's life as badly as they did...there should have been something we could do.

We weren't saints. We had killed people, lied, stolen, anything illegal you can bet that we already did it.

But we never harmed kids and Marques would never have allowed it if he could stop it.

It had been a shock when Rosie told me what they did...but somehow there was something in me that wasn't surprised at the cruelty of those people.

I was too caught up in the double life and preparing for Rosie's introduction into the world that I never thought to think about the others who were just as affected by the Originals' cruelty.

Even Eli...

Rae looked up at me through her glasses as I walked past and stopped her talk mid-conversation only to go back to her little black notebook and begin writing furiously. I tried to lean over and catch a glimpse of what she had written, but she snatched it back with a glare.

"If you are here to ask us to help you, we refuse," she hissed.

I sent her a smile.

"How did you know?" I teased. "Maybe I should have come to you all along since you are so *all knowing*."

She let out a huff and slipped the book back into her jacket pocket. The little comment seemed to upset her and she turned her head away from me.

Such children.

"Can't you just stop this?" she asked.

"Stop what?" I asked with a raised brow. "You mean trying to figure out a way to get rid of those homicidal Originals? The ones that forced you to kill your parents? Those ones?"

Her tone pissed me off more than Eli's ever had. With Eli it was like dealing with a kid, but Rae was more on Rosie's level of annoyance.

They both had that one look like they knew what they would say would get under your skin, but Rosie found entertainment out of it and Rae... She just stated it matter-of-factly.

That was much more infuriating. She acted like I hadn't been around for a millennia before her. Like I hadn't *literally* built this would with my bare hands.

"Stop creating a *bigger mess*," she said with conviction, her eyes finally meeting mine.

"A mess?" I growled. "The *only* reason you are still alive is because *I* allowed it!"

The doctor who was currently hovering over a patient cleared his throat and sent me a knowing look. I swallowed my anger and gave Rae an expectant look.

"If we are not *all* involved, we cannot help," she said in a calm voice. "You think it's not possible that Rosie will find out again? Do you realize how mad she was I kept something? *Again?* And you just want to do it again? What if next time she gets hurt because of her lack of knowledge? You said anyways we would try to get her onboarded to the plan, what changed?"

There was a sigh and I turned to see Daxton glaring at me.

"Don't act like we are not here," he growled. "You forget that we have been just as ignored as Rosie. It was *my* parents that were on the hit list. We deserve to know what's happening too."

I shrugged and sat down on the bed next to Rae. She made a noise and shifted away from me.

"The more people that know—"

"Don't pull that," Daxton interrupted. "We don't trust you for shit and we need to know going forward that we *will not* be kept in the dark any longer."

That little— Trust? He literally doesn't understand all the lashings and beatings I had to go through to keep these fuckers safe.

Rage began boiling under my skin and my hand clenched into fists, nails digging into my palms.

I was trying to keep it together not only because of the witnesses, but because I knew that brave little hybrid had a soft spot for these children and would never forgive me if I hurt them...but I was on the edge of showing them what my power could *really* do.

"I cannot trust an uncontrollable witch and a familiar—"

"Do not speak as though we are below you," Amr said with a sneer.

I hadn't been around him enough to know much about his personality but I knew enough to understand that the familiar must really hate me.

He probably only feels comfortable enough to talk back because the Originals are gone. I will never forget the way he stood in front of Rosie and bowed on her behalf as if that pitiful show would ever protect them.

"Well," I said with a slight smile. "I *am* much older than you."

Rae let out an annoyed sigh.

"It doesn't matter anymore," Rae said. "They will be involved from now on."

"You can't just make that—"

"I didn't," she said, her hazel eyes burning holes into my face. I could feel the tension between us rise sharply. We were mere inches away from each other and it would be so easy to cross this distance and force her to obey. "I asked Marques, and he approved it."

"You went behind my back," I said, grinding my teeth together in order to keep myself from yelling out.

A part of me thought that she was lying, but I knew with a simple check with Marques he would say the same. After all, he wanted the results. It was me who he left most of the groundwork to. If he thought this would guarantee a win, he would support it.

"I did," she confirmed. "Told them the whole story and then some while you were flaunting Rosie around to the others. Trying to win her over."

"I wasn't flaunting," I scoffed and looked at her.

Her sharp eyes met mine and suddenly I felt small.

It was as though her gaze alone made the world around me double in size and a spike of fear shot up my spine. The same annoyance and anger turned into something far more potent.

I began to sweat and my heart picked up pace as if I had just finished fighting hand to hand with a witch.

"*Remove* your power before I show you the strength of mine," I threatened.

Her jaw twitched and the fear that had wormed its way into my body dissipated.

"I removed it because I am tired of fighting, not because you told me to," she clarified, her eyes never leaving mine.

She knew how my power worked and so for her to meet my eyes it not only told me that she wasn't afraid of me, but that she had the audacity to think that even if I did use my power that no harm would come to her.

I swallowed my retort.

"Are you not tired, Malik?" Amr asked.

I shifted my gaze to his. His chocolate eyes bore into mine and only then could I see the years of struggle behind them. Being stuck in that cat's body must have been hell for him.

"I am," I admitted, my voice coming out more hoarse than I'd like.

"Then let's do this right," he urged. "You need our help and we refuse to do it without her."

I don't need your help, I hissed internally.

But I did.

Matt was no longer reliable. I understood that now after seeing his reaction to Rosie. I knew to an extent the act was a facade, but the coldness in his eyes...

I could not chance putting my trust in the wrong people this late in the game. And if Rosie could trust these people, then I would have to too.

"I want her to have a normal college experience," I said truthfully. Saying it out loud made me cringe. "I don't want her to fight, or fear any longer. This wasn't how it was supposed to be... I just wanted to keep her alive."

The truth. This was it. Words and sentiments I had never spoken aloud to anyone else before. An admission that I was thinking of her in a way that was not just for the better of our world.

I was no longer thinking of her as *just the hybrid*—the mindset forced upon me by Xena and Ezekiel as I got too close to each and every hybrid they created.

It had been hordes of them and while I could remember every one of their faces, I couldn't get attached. Wouldn't allow myself to because in the end it always hurt.

But with her...

From the start there was something different with her.

Amr's gaze finally slid from mine to the floor. Daxton's locked on his hands and I watched as they clutched the blanket so hard his knuckles turned white.

"While I know the others concur with your sentiment," Rae said drawing my attention back to her stoic face. "No one here has the luxury of normalcy anymore. And I for one do not want to see what happens when she finds out we kept this from her."

I too was worried about what would happen if she put this together on her own. Would the magic in her finally explode? Would she go on a rampage?

This was also a risk we needed to consider and I couldn't be blinded by my affections when it came to this.

"Fine," I said with a sigh. "We will rest, and when it is safe we will discuss the plan."

I swear I could feel Rae's satisfaction rolling off her in waves.

"Why rest?" Daxton asked, an edge to his voice.

I looked him up and down with a raised brow.

"You both ended up in the hospital," I said. "And if you want to get through the first week of school, I suggest you *both* stock up on magic."

He let out a growl.

"But the longer we wait the better they will be at hiding," he spat.

A silence filled the space between us as I tried to swallow my annoyance.

"He's right," said a voice from behind us.

God damn it, I cursed internally.

Looking over my shoulder I wasn't surprised to see Eli and Rosie standing mere feet away from us.

How much did she hear?

If she heard that I wanted to keep this from her...would she be angry?

I searched her face for a reaction but there was none. That brave face was back for all to see and I hated that face so much in that moment.

I wanted her to be angry, be scared... Just anything other than ready to face the trial that lay ahead.

Too many people have died with that same exact face and I can't let that happen to her.

"If we do not try to catch up to them, we may never find them again," she said.

Anger boiled up in me as I heard a grunt of agreement from Daxton.

"Who said the plan was to go after them, hm?" I snapped.

Her eyes widened just a fraction before her jaw twitched. Her brown eyes never wavered from mine as if just like Rae, she was challenging me to do my worst.

"They killed the refugees," she argued. "Made our lives hell and forced us to kill needlessly. We just let those demons run wild? Marques himself said that they are an abomination so why the *fuck*—"

"They are probably long gone by now," Rae spoke up, cutting Rosie off. I watched as her mouth slammed shut and she sent a glare towards Rae.

"The blood was fresh," Daxton countered. "They can't be far."

"Exactly!" Rosie chimed in.

"You really think they would do their own dirty work?" Rae asked raising an eyebrow at Rosie. "After what you went through you *really* think they would want to get their hands dirty like that? Think about it. They were long gone before you even stepped foot in the cafeteria."

The tension was rising fast and I could feel it prickling against my skin. A dull throb started near my temple.

"Finding them isn't an issue," I said finally. "We have the strongest of their team with us. We can reach them whenever we want... But the fact remains, we are not ready to fight the Originals."

Eli let out a huff of a laugh.

"When will we ever be?" they asked.

"That's why we work with Marques," Rae interjected. Suddenly I was glad to have at least someone with a rational thought by my side. "He can help us prepare. If we rush this, we die."

I noted the blood part of this deal was conventionally left out of her words.

"Let them get comfortable," I said with a small smile. "We will hit them when they are least expecting it."

Rosie's gaze fell to her feet.

"Okay," she said in a small voice.

"Okay," I said with a sigh.

I watched as she shifted uncomfortably on her feet. No

doubt wanting to retreat back into that persona I had the pleasure of knowing when we first met.

"Who is the strongest?" Amr asked stirring me from my thoughts.

A smile spread to my face.

"My favorite pair of magical siblings," I said. "When we are ready, they can help us find them."

10

ROSIE

I was less than thrilled to find myself in Winterfell—*again*. A part of me wished that I could just run away from this cursed place forever, but Winterfell had claws and each time I came back they dug deeper into my being and tied me to this place in unimaginable ways.

A place that was once so full of light and hope, had become stained with the sins of the Originals and was no more the reputable demon academy that everyone sought after.

As I walked the halls I felt a sort of acceptance wash over me. The darkness that was intertwined with the bricks of Winterfell no longer felt frightening. It felt like I was coming home. As much as I tried to reject this part of Winterfell, as much as I tried to turn a blind eye and run in the other direction...it felt like I was meant to be here no matter how much my brain told me otherwise.

My body relaxed as I felt the familiar old magic that built Winterfell brush across my senses.

The footsteps of Malik, Eli, Rae, Daxton, and Amr echoed behind me, none of them stopping me from where I felt compelled to visit.

I had planned to stay away from the cafeteria for as long as I could, but my body had a mind of its own and my feet began to guide me to the burial ground.

When I pushed open the doors to the cafeteria a rush of magic hit me and I had to grit my teeth in order to steady myself as my own magic tried to lash out. The aura of the place was dark, even though the walls were now free of blood, and settled uncomfortably in my belly.

Claudine and Maximus were in the middle of the newly cleaned cafeteria and turned to us as we entered. Claudine's bright smile sent a warmth through me and I couldn't help but return it.

She had been a surprising ally and friend that I didn't know I was lucky enough to have.

"I am sorry, Rosie," she said in a wistful tone as she walked towards me. "I know you cared for them."

I swallowed the lump in my throat. Maximus looked us over with an unreadable expression and I saw his gaze flicker when Eli's arm wrapped around my shoulders.

I don't know if Eli knew how much the simple gesture comforted me, but even something as little as this grounded me to this world.

"Thank you," I replied and leaned into Eli. A warm hand found mine and I immediately knew it was Amr's. His magic brushed against mine in a comforting manner and I felt my throat tighten.

"At least we are ready for school," Amr said from beside me. "You have a lot to handle this year."

I nodded and looked over the new cafeteria. Not much had changed from the semester before but every surface had been polished and shone lightly as the morning sun cascaded through the window. The tables and benches now covered what used to be hundreds of beds for the refugees and at the very end there was a buffet and checkout.

Last night we came back to Winterfell late and even as I

slept between Daxton and Amr, I could feel this place call to me in my sleep, begging for me to come take a look.

A part of me hoped that I was being called to this place because there was something waiting for me. Maybe a lost refugee that escaped, or a scrap of something that proved that hundreds of people lived and suffered here this summer...but there was nothing except the small barely visible traces of magic that they left.

The absence hurt more, I realized.

Because now, the lives that I tried so hard to save, just faded away into the dark history of this place, never to be seen again and leaving only a handful of people with their memory.

I wished I had asked them about their families, wished I could have found a connection to the outside for them...but I was too late. Now no one would know how they suffered.

And it was all her fucking fault.

Xena's smirk filled my mind and anger exploded inside me. She used me. Made me believe that she actually had a plan to help out the refugees.

I was so stupid.

Eli let out a snort.

Hold on to that anger, they said. *It's very sexy.*

My lips twitched at their words, but it was the reminder I needed.

I needed to hold onto this anger and mold it into something useful. Now that they had fled, we had a lot of work to do in order to bring them down, and make them pay for what they have done to not only our lives, but the countless other lives they had erased due to their own cowardice.

"Can we just take back the program?" I asked and turned to catch the white-haired demon behind us.

Since last night he had been silently following behind us. My guess was he either had nothing to do now that the Originals were gone...or was just worried that we would fuck something up while he was gone.

My bet was on the latter.

Even though the Originals were gone, that didn't mean we could stop pushing forward, and who knows what they had planned? I didn't really buy that they were just hiding away.

Xena and Ezekiel were cowards that much was for sure, but they weren't weak.

Malik gave me a sad smile. The same one he had shown me so many times before. It was a small glimpse of the demon I had become so comfortable around.

My chest tightened.

"It was already announced to the public. Going back on it would not do well for Winterfell's image," he said. "Just entertain them for a while as they get used to the school."

"It's not just entertaining," I grumbled and shifted my gaze.

In between saving the refugees and meetings with the Originals, Principal Winterfell sought me out and explained exactly what my duties entailed. Needless to say, I was horrified.

I was a mentor to all of them. I was supposed to explain the rules, show them their dorms, and help them navigate this new world full of angry high-level demons. I would have to be there at all hours and at their beck and call.

I didn't have the time, nor desire to mentor a bunch of new students after I spent so long trying to fight for my life. I didn't want to pretend anymore that this place was the magical academy it pretended to be. I knew the truth now and I would hate having to lie to innocent low-levels who had no idea what they were getting into.

They were going to come here excited, hopeful that *they* could change the world... Just like I had been. And I had to watch as their dreams were crushed right before their eyes.

I was stuck between two conflicting desires.

Retreat into a hole and never come out.

And scream at the top of my lungs at the incoming low-levels. Tell them to run. Tell them that none of this was worth it and that it was all a fraud.

"How many are there?" Amr asked, his hand squeezing my shoulder.

"Two hundred thirty-seven," Malik and I said at the same time. I turned back to look at him. The sad smile was still on his face.

"The first semester will be the worst," Rae said from beside Malik. "After that they should get the hang of it."

God I fucking hope so, I groaned internally.

If I had to hold their hands for the entire year I might as well be considered useless when it came to our plans.

"When are they coming?" Amr asked drawing my attention back to him. His voice was soft as he asked, obviously one of the only people realizing just how nervous I was.

On cue the doors behind us opened and a flustered Rhonda walked in.

I hadn't seen our lunch lady friend for a long time and my chest tugged painfully when I looked at her sweet face. She had been the first warm person that I had the pleasure to meet and I wished that I would have made more of an effort to get to know her.

Close behind her followed her staff, about fifteen low-levels all wearing aprons and looking equally as flustered as her. Rhonda didn't even look at me as she passed our group.

"Food won't be for a while!" she yelled back at us. "Go lounge somewhere else."

I tried not to feel hurt at her dismissal.

"They will be here soon," I murmured to Amr as I watched Rhonda bark orders to her staff. "Some are coming tonight actually."

Claudine turned to me with a smile.

"Have you thought of what to say to them when they come?" she asked.

I shook my head.

"The first meeting is in three days, then most if not all the students will have—"

"The cafeteria is closed!" she yelled back at us. Not a single flash of recognition spread across her face as we locked eyes and I understood now that Matt's power had to be the most sinister of them all.

"Let's go," I whispered.

As we walked out of the cafeteria Claudine, Maximus, and Malik were about to give their goodbyes but I stopped them.

"Malik, Rae," I called. Both turned to me with a questioning gaze. "Can you stay to talk?"

Eli's nails dug into my arm.

Why are you pushing me away? they asked in my mind.

I just want to question them about when we are going to Marques again, I said. *They work better in a smaller group.*

There was a pause as they weighed my words.

"Fine," they spat and pulled their arm from my side. Amr leaned down to leave a kiss on my head which was followed by Daxton's lips at my ear.

"Don't take too long," he whispered. "You heard what they said about sharing magic."

A shiver ran up my spine and I sent him a look as he left. My magic lashed around me, trying to follow him down the hall but I stayed in my spot, ignoring the two demons in front of me until everyone else had left.

"I need a date," I said to them, finally looking over to where they stood.

Malik had his arms crossed over his chest while Rae stood to the side, an arm resting on her hip.

"For?" Malik asked.

"You know what for," I growled. "Curse training and planning."

He straightened and looked back down the hallway.

"Before the first set of rankings," he said in an annoyed tone.

"A date," I hissed.

A scowl marred his scarred face and I could have sworn I heard the grinding of his teeth from across the hall.

"Three Wednesdays from now," he spit out and closed the space between us.

I stood my ground and stared at him, even as his golden eyes glared at me. His breathing was heavy and his chest almost touched my own.

His warm scent filled my senses and I had the urge to fall into him, but I kept my face blank and my feet planted. If I caved now, none of these demons would take me seriously regardless of my bloodline. I needed to show them that I was not one to bend easily, and that went for all of them.

Matt had been a sole example of that, taking advantage of my weakness and playing me like an instrument. On top of that, Malik already tried once more to keep me out of the planning, I was lucky to have someone like Rae and Daxton to push for my inclusion. Now that we had come so far, I couldn't chance any more time in the dark. It was time to take control and fight for my freedom.

"Seems perfect," I purred and let a smile tug at my lips. "Unless there is something bothering you?"

He swallowed, his eyes trailing my face before he spoke.

"We need to clarify some things," he said finally.

"We seem pretty clear," I said with an even bigger smile. "Now if you'd excuse me, I have some things to talk to Rae about."

His eyes flashed and his hand came up to grip my chin. It wasn't enough to actually hurt but he put enough pressure to remind me that he held my life literally between his hands.

"*I* am in charge here, Rosie," he spat. "Don't get cocky because you snuck into his hideout. That was Matt's fault for not being diligent. And don't think your little trick with Claudine passed right by me."

My eyes widened at the mention of Claudine's name.

"That's right," he said. "Who do you think she came to for help, hm?"

With my face still in his hands he ripped open the remaining button of his shirt. There, right under his heart, was the same symbol I had tattooed on me.

"How long have you...?" I trailed. My mind was having trouble forming coherent sentences.

My mouth went dry at the image of him half shirtless in front of me. The tattoos didn't stop at his arms and instead littered his torso as well, but there was more than that symbol that interested me; right next to it was one that I didn't recognize.

"Not long," he admitted. "I couldn't, not with *them* watching me. My mind was too open, and I couldn't risk them learning of Marques's plans. Wiping my mind was the safest way."

I swallowed thickly and nodded. I couldn't imagine what it was like to entrust Matt with erasing my memory...and *so much* of it.

"Do I need to get that one too?" I asked, my eyes still fixated on his bare torso.

I wanted to reach out so badly and run my hands up the planes of his stomach. There were scars that slashed his body spelling out his pain with the Originals and I couldn't help but think how similar he and I were.

If my mother was just a bit more careless I may have ended up looking like him.

"No," he said in a soft voice. "I think what Claudine taught you was better. Or am I wrong?"

The mind-reading, I realized. He really knew it all.

"Just a way to clean up the mind," I said with a small smile. "No magic involved at all but it does the trick."

A bit of meditation, surprisingly enough. Claudine taught me how to compartmentalize my thoughts so that it would be harder for people like Ezekiel, who read surface thoughts, to get anything out of me.

It was a work in progress, and something I was far from proficient at, but it helped enough to keep me safe.

His scowl finally broke and he let go of me.

"Don't do anything stupid while I am gone," he said and paused before continuing. "And give your all to the low-levels, Rosie. You know all too well what it was like coming into a school where everyone hated you."

I remembered it all too clearly, actually. And I remembered him helping me out, even under the guise of something completely different... He was there when I needed him.

But that wasn't the Malik I craved now, I wanted the one that threw me against the wall, the one that got angry if I talked back. That was Malik in his truest form and I loved every minute of it.

"I'll try," I said in a weak voice. He nodded to me then to Rae before leaving us.

I watched as he walked away, wishing that he could stay because unlike the others, I had no idea when he would be back. And I had no idea if he would be safe.

His and Eli's life still remained a mystery to me. I didn't know what to expect when they came home after whatever it was they did. Would they come home bloody and beaten? Would they keel over from lack of sleep?

The worries never stopped.

I heard Rae stand next to me and looked up to her with a smile.

She didn't smile back fully but I saw the corner of her lips twitch. I grabbed one of her hands and squeezed it. It had been far too long since she and I had time together and I was grateful that she even allowed this much.

We hadn't been able to talk much, but I could see she was struggling. She would leave us often and only come by every once in a while, and even when she did...she seemed distant with her mind focused on other things.

I didn't ever bring up what happened last summer. Why would I?

I understood better now. None of the others had a choice

and all thought they were doing what was best for us. And I had seen her advocate for me with my own two eyes.

"Are you okay?" I asked her. "Your siblings?"

Her eyes widened and I watched her swallow twice before she moved to answer. I waited patiently letting her gather her words.

"We are fine," she said in a voice hoarser than normal. "We did not expect the amount that Father had taken care of when he was alive."

"Work?" I asked. She shook her head and ran her thumb across my knuckles.

I recognized it as a soothing gesture but it wasn't me who needed soothing.

"The house, the finances," she admitted though her words came out slow and forced. "He was in charge of seeing to it before and now it is only my brothers and me."

"I can imagine that they would be a bit hard to work with," I whispered remembering the way Nathaniel and Benjamin had been as they accompanied me for the short time I was in Rae's house. They were mischievous and adventurous enough that I doubt menial work like housekeeping and crunching numbers would keep them entertained for long.

"Yes, well." She let out a heavy sigh, her eyes falling to our intertwined fingers. "They are doing better. Though I am very busy. I came here this morning to make sure you and the others were alright, but I will have to leave soon."

I swallowed my disappointment and sent her a smile. Standing on my tip-toes I leaned forward and planted a light kiss on her mouth. As I pulled away her hand slid into my hair and pulled my lips back to her.

She gave me a hungry kiss that stole the breath right out of me. She had packed the months of our little interaction into this kiss and kissed me like her life depended on it. It wasn't the sweet comforting kisses I had once experienced from her, these were starved and wanting.

I ate up the attention greedily and pulled at her shirt forcing us closer than we needed to be in the middle of the school hallway. I didn't care who saw us or what they thought. Rae was more important than any one person's thoughts and I wanted to show her as much.

She pulled away leaving me breathless and panting. There was a glint in her eyes.

"I'll bring you home before the end of the year," she promised. "Just let me get everything cleaned up and we can do this again."

I nodded and stepped back from her.

"Walk me to my dorm?" I asked.

She let out a small chuckle.

"I'll do you one better and walk you to Daxton's."

11

AMR

I had seen my fair share of witches growing up in a family of would-be familiars. We had to get accustomed to working with them anyways, so my parents would drag me and my siblings along wherever they could. It was normal and each time I would shake a witch's hand I would be simultaneously sizing them up and trying to see exactly what type of employer they would be. Those meetings were where I figured out all the different types of witches that littered this earth, and I got pretty good at seeing the secrets they tried to hide.

Some were openly evil. They fell deep into the darkness their unmanaged magic grew inside them and they were the easiest to pick out. Their magic was sticky and felt uncomfortable as it stretched across your skin. *Dirty*. That happened when a witch got far too consumed in the darkness their magic carried. It was easy if they were not careful, they could be changed by their magic. Those were the witches shunned by our society and it was all too obvious as soon as you came across them. They were forced underground and they had little to no chance to live a normal life, and while some hid it better than others, their path was almost certain from the moment they first lost themselves.

The more I watched Daxton, the more worried that I

became that he was on that same exact path. I had tried to watch over him, take as much of his magic as possible...but it never seemed to suffice. He seemed to come back with magic even stronger and angrier every single time.

But I would be damned if I let anyone take him away from us.

I am sure Rosie felt the same, but there was no denying that Daxton was changing and it was only a matter of time before people started to notice. Daxton was shielded somewhat by his parents because they were corrupted and wanted people to look anywhere but inwards, and now that they were gone...he was the person in the limelight. He was the last known witch of his immediate bloodline and there were already people lining up to talk to him about his future.

It was terrifying.

I watched this boy grow into a man. I watched his parents abuse him and use him however they deemed fit. Even through all that he had still remained resilient. He held onto Eli and Rae, pushing forward in hopes of a better future for himself, one away from his parents.

But now that his parents were gone...he was spiraling. There was nothing to keep him in check, no matter how much I or the others tried.

It was the little things that stood out to me the most.

The lack of sleep, the short fuse, and the insatiable magic.

He thought that I didn't know that he woke up hours before I did and just stared into space. But I did because I was awake too, just waiting there to see what he would do.

During those times I felt him reaching out his magic, draping us in it. It would stay there around us for hours sometimes and I didn't understand the point. Was he checking on us? Was he trying to get rid of excess magic? Protecting us?

I do not know why he felt the need to hide his magic as such. We knew that he had far too much to keep inside of him. I expected it...but he always pulled it back as soon as he felt us stir.

And now as I watched him with Rosie...I couldn't help the tingling sensation running up my spine and making my hair stand on end.

I was already on edge around him since Rosie had her outburst in the cafeteria and when Rae stood outside our dorm with her, I had a gut reaction to push them away and deal with Daxton's magic myself.

Daxton's normally cozy dorm room was now filled with an electric tension running through the three of us. Magic had already started accumulating in the room due to Rosie and Daxton's playing.

I couldn't bring myself to join just yet even as my cock strained against my pants.

I sat silently in the chair adjacent to the bed they were on, watching them intently.

Rosie was kneeling on the floor between Daxton's legs as he sat on the bed completely naked, as was she. His eyes shone with a glint that I had recognized a few times in the years that I had been with him. He had been rougher than was necessary with her, his hand already pulling at Rosie's hair.

From my position, I could not see her face, only her tense back and ass as she teased him. Even without a perfect view of her, I knew the moment that she took Daxton's cock into her mouth by the way he threw his head back and moaned aloud.

I watched as his chest heaved up and down as he panted. His skin was slick with sweat already and his muscles rippled as Rosie's hands began to explore his chest and stomach.

They were magnificent together.

The way their bodies and magic easily intertwined. It was like they were connected in a much deeper way than the others. They didn't even need to speak, just were somehow so in tune with each other that they knew exactly what the other needed.

Even outside of the bedroom, I noticed the way Daxton and

Rosie would orbit each other, even when Eli would lead Rosie across the room...Daxton was never far.

I should have noticed it since the first day we encountered her, but I was too wrapped up in the goddess of the woman in front of me that I completely wrote off Daxton's reaction to her.

I shifted uncomfortably in my seat as Daxton's low moans filled the room. I gritted my teeth when he pushed her down so hard on his cock that she gagged. A smirk tugged at his lips and he thrusted up into her mouth.

His eyes were hooded but I watched as they narrowed even further as Rosie took him as deep as she could. He was enjoying watching her struggle.

He used to be embarrassed when he handled her roughly, but now he was leaning into his wilder side. Even fucking her mouth wasn't enough for him and he pushed her head down even further so she couldn't move.

When I heard her choke I let out a growl. Daxton looked over towards me with hooded eyes, his smirk widening, before he thrust up into Rosie's mouth.

He was egging me on. He knew I didn't like when we were rough with her. I was furious when I saw what Eli did to her perfect skin. I was ready to blow, but I reigned myself in and waited for a time when I could show Eli what I *really* thought of their actions.

"Do that again and I'll make you sit there—*alone*—while I fuck her," I threatened.

He gripped Rosie's hair back and forced her off his cock. A line of spit followed her as he did. She gasped for air and stared up at him with wide doe-like eyes.

"He thinks I'm being too rough on you," he said with a small frown. "Do you?"

She shook her head wildly. He smirked and let go of her hair to lean back on the bed. Rosie watched as his hand ran the length of his hardened cock.

I would be lying if that gesture alone did not make my cock pulse with need, but he took it one step further.

"Come here," he said and patted his lap. She crawled up onto the bed and without instructions sunk slowly down onto Daxton's cock. She let out a whimper that filled the room. Daxton's hand came up to her throat and he pulled her to his lips.

They both fell flat to the bed and Rosie began to ride him, her ass slapping against his thighs as she fucked him. I bit back my retort and rubbed myself through my jeans, unable to help myself.

I couldn't deny how much I loved seeing them together and how much it turned me on. A dangerous and enticing dance that they did and I could watch them forever if they let me.

"Amr," Daxton called from the bed.

I watched as his hand traveled to Rosie's ass before spreading her cheeks and giving me a show of the rarely used puckered hole. He wasted no time pushing his fingers into her, pulling a moan from Rosie.

"Damn it all," I growled and stood to strip off my clothes.

I walked to the bedside drawer that held a bottle of lube that Daxton and I had used on occasion. I hesitated going to them until Rosie sat up and looked at me. Daxton's hands moved to grip her hips as he rammed into her from below.

She reached out to me, begging me to come closer even as the words came out garbled due to Daxton's ferocity.

I walked over and positioned myself with one leg between Daxton's and the other bent on the bed. Her arms lifted behind her to wrap around my neck. Her skin was sweaty against mine and her back slapped into me with each of Daxton's trusts.

I put the lube bottle on the bed next to us and wrapped my arms around her so that I could use one hand to roll her nipple between my fingers and the other to rub her clit. She gasped and threw her head back against me. Loud mewls came from out of her mouth and I could feel the magic in her spike rapidly.

"Are you sure you want this, love?" I asked and nipped at her ear.

I trailed my hand lower so I could feel where they were connected, squeezing Daxton in warning as I did. They both shuddered at my movement.

"I want *you,* Amr," she gasped against me.

I chuckled and kissed the side of her sweaty face. My cock was begging for action and each time they met Rosie would brush against me, shooting sparks through me.

"Right after you come," I promised and trailed my hand back up to her clit, putting more pressure on the forgotten nub than before.

She cried out and Daxton groaned.

"She's going to come," he forced out. "Keep going."

His eyes met mine for an instant and I got a look of the Daxton underneath it all. There with his hair sticking to his face, and his skin shiny with sweat, I saw the man I had fallen for.

"*Ah*— Faster, Amr!"

I complied and she let out a strangled sob as she came around Daxton's cock. Her magic flared around us and I felt the sweet potent magic that she had hidden inside her spill into me.

Each time I was taken aback by how addicting the feeling of her magic inside me was.

My own magic rejoiced and I could feel them swirling together until they settled inside of me. But instead of being satisfied, I wanted more.

I took the lube and spread a generous helping on both my cock and her backside. I shuddered as I rubbed my cock down the length of her. I was already so swollen and my balls were so tight with unspent release that I knew it wouldn't be long until I spilled inside of her.

"Prepare yourself love," I whispered and unwound her arms from my neck, to angle her more towards Daxton. "This may hurt a little."

"It's not my first time," she said with a mischievous glint back at me.

I looked down at Daxton with a glare.

"It wasn't me," he said defensively, pausing in his thrusts so I could line myself up at Rosie's entrance.

"Eli," she said. A small bit of anger unfurled inside of me when I realized I wasn't the first but I brushed it away.

This wasn't about me.

I pushed into her slowly at first and then with her encouragement I placed my hands over Daxton's and pulled her down on my cock as far as she would go. I groaned as I felt her squeeze around me. She engulfed me in warmth and fit me so perfectly that I couldn't fathom how I stayed away from this for so long.

She sucked in a sharp breath and I rubbed the length of her spine in a comforting manner, grinding my hips against her lightly. I was easily starting to lose myself. My magic, hers, and Daxton's played at my senses begging me to fuck her senseless.

"How does it feel?" I asked her, my voice dropping deeper. "To be filled by both of us?"

She let out a small whine as I pulled out a little just to push back into her.

"Now I know why Eli calls you a little slut," Daxton purred from underneath her. He thrust up into her once. "I always thought that was just her attitude. But you really are one aren't you? You're gripping onto me so tight that if I didn't know any better I would say you were about to come again."

Rosie sat up, pressing her back against me and pulling me further inside of her.

"Fuck me," she commanded.

With a light chuckle Daxton and I resumed our pace, albeit much slower than before. Rosie's head fell back onto my shoulder as I thrust into her.

"You take us so well," I cooed and reached over to play with her swollen clit. She let out a sob.

"It's too much," she whined as I pinched her clit.

"I know," I whispered in her ear and left kisses on the side of her face. I thrust a bit harder that time and was rewarded with a moan. "But you are doing so good. You don't want us to stop do you?"

She shook her head and tried to stifle her noises but the harder we became with her the less she was able to hide it.

Daxton and I easily found a rhythm that allowed us to pound into her with ease and as I said, she was good at taking us both. Even as her second orgasm came close she didn't shift or move in a way that would disrupt us.

"*Fuck,*" she cursed. "I'm coming."

"Me too, *shit,*" Daxton hissed.

I continued to play with Rosie's clit until she came with Daxton not far behind her. Just before he fell over the edge Daxton's hand found mine and I was hit with a dose of both of their magic.

It was so strong that my vision went white for a moment before I could regain myself.

"Be a good girl and go kiss him," I whispered to her.

She did as I asked and as soon as their lips met I pulled her hips back to mine, fucking that tight hole harder than I probably should have while I chased my own orgasm.

Her cries were muffled by Daxton's mouth and I felt a warm tingling sensation start low in my belly.

Before I knew it, my magic exploded inside of me and I came inside of her.

I pulled out of her slowly before falling back onto the bed where they both watched me with a smile.

I couldn't help but groan aloud.

These two are insatiable.

THE DAYS PASSED in a blur and suddenly on the day Rosie was supposed to welcome the low-levels…I found myself getting up in the middle of the night and watching them as they slept.

I couldn't stop thinking about how much they had suffered at the hands of this cruel world. They had changed because of it, barely holding a smidge of the people they once were. Of course, I would support them and care for them no matter what, but I was afraid.

Afraid they would lose themselves.

Afraid they would hate themselves for what they have become.

Afraid that they were in danger.

And afraid I wouldn't be able to protect them from the people who sought to destroy us.

If allowing the low-levels into Winterfell wasn't a ploy thought up by the Originals themselves, I would feel much better than I did now.

But instead, I thought of all the ways this could be a trap for us.

I mean, why else would they do this?

They spouted nonsense about her entering the government, but they knew that after the murders of both Daxton's parents and Rae's father, there would be spots for them to fill. I hadn't heard much about their positions as I stayed with mostly Daxton and Rosie, but they couldn't keep those positions long, right?

They also couldn't just wait around for them to be done with their school. They still had almost two years left.

Which made their entire plot ridiculous, unless…

The goal was to kill Marques's people, Malik had once said.

The same person that Rae had told us was on the other side of this war.

The more I thought about it the weirder it got. This was a suicide mission from the start, but if hybrids were so valuable to them, why would they chance it?

I was stirred out of my thoughts by a shuffling outside our door. I waited a moment, listening closer.

Then I heard it again.

My senses went on high alert and the hair on the back of my neck stood up. I ran towards the door and threw it open, ready to end the person that was trying to hurt us.

The dim hallway was empty and I let out a growl as I scanned the area. Just in case, I sent my magic out to feel if there was a witch nearby, but there was nothing.

As I slowly backed into the dorm I saw a flash of blue in front of me and I bust out into the hallway with my magic ready.

Two breaths went by and there was still just me in the empty hallway with only a small glimmer of magic, proving to me that I wasn't crazy.

But it was so small I couldn't determine a signature from it.

"Amr?" Rosie called.

"Coming," I muttered and looked twice over my shoulder before returning back into the dorm.

12
RAE

I had said that I would help Nathaniel figure out some stuff today, and told him I didn't have much time...but he seemed to be in a bigger mess than I originally thought. What I believed would have taken me just a few minutes had now dragged on for hours.

Nathaniel had been struggling and as much as I wanted to groan and complain about him not being able to do it himself, I couldn't bring myself to do it. He was struggling too in his own way and had been left virtually uneducated on the ways of this world due to Father's pampering.

His was messy, unorganized, but he wasn't unfeeling. Even through the mess of the papers and contracts in front of me, I could see by his notes in the margins that he put time and effort into trying to understand what was going on here.

Nathaniel had always been like this as a kid. He tried to act aloof and like he didn't care, but I could feel it and see it in his actions. He did care, he was trying... He just didn't know how to show it and even coming to me for this must have taken a lot from him.

Father had brought us up in a way that made it almost impossible to ask for help and because my younger siblings were men, they didn't have much to prove and whenever they struggled Father would just hand whatever they needed to them and that was the end of it. They never had to learn to actually ask or try to figure out their own issues.

It was me who had to fix it for everyone.

I sighed and took a sip of my father's prized aged bourbon.

I was in his office looking over the contracts with the various agencies we hired, including the maid service that Nathaniel was supposed to take care of, and found that he still had a bottle stashed in his bottom drawer. I was not a drinker usually, but today I would make an exception.

The weight of our problems weighed on me, threatening to pull me into the ground and swallow me whole. I was supposed to fix and take care of everything for my family *and* I had to think about the looming threat of Xena and Ezekiel coming back to end us all.

We knew too much. They should want us dead in order to preserve their legacy.

I thought back to the way Rosie *literally* infiltrated Marques's hideout. And how Daxton had almost lost his damn mind when it came to his magic.

And don't get me started on Eli's habit of disappearing and committing heinous murders.

Damon's murder had been all over the news and who else would have made such a mess of his death? And right on the stairs of the Demon Regulation Society nonetheless.

On top of it all we had to act like our parents *suddenly* disappeared and they were never seen again. Without Malik's power I do not know where we would be now. I hated to admit that I also hadn't thought of what we were going to tell the public. I foolishly thought that Marques would fix it all for us.

Daxton and Eli especially were all fueled by their dark need to destroy and bring havoc wherever they went. I always knew when they were planning something; it would start with a burst of curiosity that played at the edges of their emotions and would soon morph into an unquenchable hunger that would only be solved by burning or toppling something.

The Winterfell tower *just* started being repaired again in time for the new semester. A glaring reminder of just what happens when these crazed people were let loose.

My head was pounding even thinking about it.

I had a special place for them in my heart, hell I knew I cared for Rosie, maybe even *loved* her...but a demon could only take so much.

I looked up from the papers, took off my glasses, and rubbed my sore eyes. Leaning back into the old leather chair I looked towards the clock that seemed to mockingly stare down at me. The hands told me it was nearing two o'clock and almost time to leave.

I wasn't anywhere near done so I would have to come back later and figure it out.

Rosie had the orientation today for the low-levels and it was something that I couldn't miss. I wanted to be there not only to see her through it...but to watch as new people infiltrated Winterfell... It made me feel uneasy.

The low-levels themselves weren't the issue, but continuing on Xena and Ezekiel's plan even after they called us traitors and continued to threaten our lives was a risky move. Any of them could be there on the Originals' orders and we wouldn't know until they had a knife to our throat.

Pulling out my phone, I opened it to call our driver and my heart stopped when I realized it was past three o'clock. Rosie would have already been meeting the low-levels and I would be the *only* one not there.

I jumped up and stared back at the clock only to notice the minute hand stuck on something, unable to move forward.

Grumbling under my breath I sent a text to Eli letting them know I would be coming soon. They texted back immediately with a suggestive-looking emoji and my anger fumed.

I wouldn't have been stuck here if Nathaniel just did his

fucking job. Why did I always have to be the one to pick up all the pieces?

"Father couldn't even get his fucking clock fixed?" I growled and stood to take a closer look at the clock.

There was something poking out of the number "2" stopping the hand. I reached up to brush off what I suspected was some type of fuzz or part of the paint chipping, but it didn't move. I tried to grip it and to my astonishment, a small folded piece of paper came with it.

My phone buzzed again but I ignored it as I carefully unfolded the tiny paper. On it was a list of ten names that I had never heard before.

I looked back at the now unstuck clock.

Why did my father put that in there?

It was hidden and no one but me would dare come in here before this... So was this note for me?

I didn't have the choice to sit and think of all the reasons why my father would do this. Though I already had a million reasons in my head, I had to get to Winterfell. Instead of dwelling on it I carefully folded it and put it in the middle of my notebook, before leaving the room and the mess of contracts behind with it.

I WAS lucky that Rosie had planned the big speech near dinner instead of when they first arrived. It gave me enough time to not only drive the few miles from my house but also cross the school to get to the cafeteria. By the time the doors came into view, a light sweat covered my forehead and I was over two hours later than I should have been.

Pushing open the doors I couldn't help but pause as I was met with tables and tables of low-levels. Hearing the number was different than actually seeing the bodies in seats. Many were already in deep conversation but some spared curious glances at me.

Emotions attacked me from all ends and I almost regretted taking Marques's blood in that moment. All the excitement and anxiety sunk deep into my bones and I could already feel my body vibrating with anticipation that was not my own.

I searched the room and right at the front and center of the entire cafeteria, was the small woman that had nestled her way into my being, and she was *smiling*.

Like *really smiling*.

Normally, crowds like this can mess with my ability. Emotions would run together and jumble up inside me until it was too much forcing me to retreat to a quiet place...but I felt hers loud and clear. And it was comforting. As soon as I felt it the anxiety rising inside me disappeared and my body relaxed.

Nathaniel's contract and my father's note was all gone, and all that was left was the way Rosie smiled at her low-levels.

Her happiness was no longer shrouded in despair like it had been since the murder of the refuges. No longer buried so deep I was sure I would never feel it again... It was *here*, right now for everyone to see and feel.

A part of me wanted to sweep her away and lock her in a spare classroom so I could greedily eat up all this happiness. It had been so long since I had been able to feel something so pure and warm. I wanted it all to myself and felt robbed that it was here on display.

But *god*... She was radiant.

Today, she picked a light lilac dress that matched her skin tone perfectly, probably a gift from Claudine. It didn't match her usual style at all, but it fit her figure perfectly and I yearned for her to wear more clothes like this. Her hair was up in a ponytail and her skin was clear and free of dark circles.

She looked like she didn't belong in the old, chipped hallways of Winterfell and instead in some farmhouse where she could run and lounge in the grass. This Rosie was free of the worry of the Originals, and free of bloodshed and pain. *This* was the Rosie that was finally happy.

To see her so radiant again took my breath away and planted me firmly to the floor.

I was only pulled out of it when her wide brown eyes lifted to mine and she smiled then waved me over. I clenched my hands into fists, digging my fingernails into my palms, hoping the prick of pain would pull me out of my stupor.

Only then did I notice that the rest of our group, Eli, Daxton, Amr, and even Malik were sitting at the table to the far left. They were also watching her. They looked comfortable even in the room full of low-levels and it looked like they didn't even bother getting up to socialize with her.

So not only was she happily chatting with low-levels, but she was even doing it alone?

My gut twisted painfully. I wanted to help her as much as I could. She had been so nervous and scared about this moment, the least we could do was be there for her...and I was late.

I walked towards her suddenly feeling the eyes of the room on me. It wasn't bad before but after Rosie waved me over many of them looked over to see what she was waving at. I squared my shoulders and put on a small smile, not letting the sudden spike of curiosity throw me off balance.

She beamed at me as I came up and turned back to the rest of the low-levels she was talking to. It was an unremarkable group with not any one person standing out but I smiled at them anyways.

I held onto Rosie's feelings and forced myself to remain calm as a wave of nervousness fluttered through her.

Was it me that caused her to get nervous so suddenly?

My chest bloomed at the thought.

"This is Rae," Rosie said. "You'll see her a lot with me. She takes government-focused classes and is a great resource for all things Winterfell. She *literally* knows everything you could think of asking."

I tried not to grimace at the thought of low-levels coming up and talking to me as if we were friends. Even high-levels stayed away from me. I wasn't very social...but I would change for Rosie. I had changed so much already, so what's the harm in one more thing?

"*Oooh,* so we have another one Rosie-bear?" one of the guys in the front asked.

I noted his playful tone and smirk. I immediately made a mental note to jot him down in my book later. I didn't like the way his eyes lingered on Rosie and while I couldn't feel anything suggestive...his focus on her made my gut burn with jealousy.

His messy black hair curled around his head and hung into his eyes, giving him a moody look that rubbed me as more unkempt than stylish. His purple eyes were dull, not surprising given his low-level status. And his skin was slightly tanned, just covering up the freckles that lay beneath.

"What's your name?" I asked.

"Ren," he said and held out his hand, which I noted was scarred. On even closer notice I saw that he had darker freckles splattered across his hand and they almost seemed to run in some sort of a pattern, though I couldn't recognize it.

"Is that a tattoo?" I asked ignoring his outstretched hand.

He smiled shyly at me and withdrew his hand hiding it in his jacket pocket.

"Ya-a," he stuttered and tried to play it off with a sheepish laugh. "If school didn't work out I was going to become a tattoo artist for the humans, this was just a test with my machine."

I had no reason not to believe him, but for some reason I didn't. I kept quiet and nodded before I looked down at Rosie.

"Should we sit with the others?" I asked hoping she would take my offer. I still wanted to eat up all these emotions and hated the thought of being so separated from her.

"Soon," she said. There was another spike of nervousness and panic rising in her. "I have the announcement."

I nodded and sent her calming waves. *So that's what she was worried about.*

It makes sense, Rosie until now never had to really speak in front of a crowd, besides the one Xena and Ezekiel forced upon her. And this time she would be all on her own. It must have been nerve-racking.

"I will be watching from the side."

She nodded and I left to sit by the rest of the group. They watched me as I came up but didn't speak right away. I used this time to look at the low-levels surrounding us.

"I don't like the boy either," Eli grumbled from behind me after a moment.

The low-levels were spaced far from us, as if scared to get any closer. It was better this way. I had more patience than the rest of the group and Rosie would be pissed if Eli started beating up her newest arrivals before the semester even started.

"Ren?" I asked and looked back to him and Rosie talking.

She was happy again and so was Ren. He talked with her excitedly and used his hands a lot. His laughter echoed through the room and Rosie flushed, embarrassment rising in her.

"The goofy one," they corrected. "You know I'm shit with names."

"He tried to hug her and Eli got jealous," Malik said with a light chuckle.

There were a few spikes of anger from the people around us but most surprising was my own.

"Is hugging as a greeting a low-level thing?" Daxton asked.

"No," Malik and I answered at the same time.

I was too tired to glare at him. He nodded and smiled at me.

"He wants to fuck her," Eli growled.

"I don't think so," I said after deciphering the feelings around us. "I think he is just excited, happy, grateful...though he is a bit nervous."

Eli snorted.

"Sure he is," they responded.

We were interrupted by a flash of magic that flew out of Rosie's hands.

"Uhh, attention," she called.

Embarrassment was flowing out of her in waves. I sent some calm emotions to her but I couldn't help but be enamored by the whole thing.

This girl had faced high-level demons when she was still cursed and her words tore into her skin. She looked us in the eyes back then and told us to *fuck off.*

She may have been riddled with fear and pain but she still stood there in front of all of Winterfell and held her head up high even as we threatened to destroy her.

And here she was, scared, embarrassed, worried all over some low-level students.

The irony of it all was too sweet.

And then I realized that even though she never wanted any part of this...here she was doing the best she could. To help the low-levels, to help our group, all at the cost of herself.

...and now it was my turn to do the same.

I didn't realize how much of a coward I had been until I watched her in this moment talking to the low-levels as if they were her friends.

She may have been disgruntled about this, but here she was still standing tall with that pretty smile of hers and that lilac dress.

All this time I had been so focused on protecting Eli, Daxton, and myself from anything even remotely bad for our reputations, that I didn't realize the power that exuded from her was all a product of the growth she had to do in order to stay alive.

"So," she said pulling me from my thoughts. "You will all be given your schedule on orientation day. The class that you are assigned to will be your class for the next *three years* so I recommend you start off on the right foot with your classmates."

Eli let out a small snort.

"Look how that ended up for her," they snickered.

I think it ended up pretty well, I wanted to say, but I held my tongue.

A hand shot up from the back. Rosie looked taken aback but motioned for them to speak.

"Is it true that you are a witch demon hybrid?" a girl from the back yelled.

There was a silence that descended on the cafeteria as we waited for her response. A small smile spread across her face.

"Yes," she answered with conviction. "Now moving on..."

There was light laughter from some of the low-levels but nonetheless they listened with close attention as Rosie walked them through the workings of the school, the money they receive, and the dos and don'ts of this new world they were in.

"To put it bluntly, high-level demons can be jerks—*most of them.*" She sent a pointed look to our table and I heard Daxton and Malik laugh lightly. "And with a school like ours, where our rankings can be determined by the Winterfell Games... You can bet that if you even rub someone the wrong way, they will come after you during the games."

"Will they kill us?" another person asked.

"No," Rosie answered with a smile. "But it will hurt, *a lot.*"

"Is bullying a problem here?" another boy asked.

Rosie grimaced before answering.

"It won't be easy," she admitted. "But I am hoping with more and more low-levels here, the stigma behind the classes will change. Back then, it was only myself...and one other student. I am sure it will be different now."

Chatter broke out amongst the low-levels. Some panicked others disgruntled.

"Any more questions?" she asked.

"What is your power?" one called.

"Fire," Rosie answered with ease.

"How did you find out you were a hybrid?" another asked.

"I blew up the top floor of a building," she answered again with a slight smile. "Giving me this guy."

She pointed to the scar that marred her face. There were some collective gasps.

I heard a strangled laugh from Malik and sent him a glare. Eli was also glaring at him.

"I thought you said she wasn't responsible for blowing up the hideout?" they hissed under their breath.

"I lied," Malik replied with a smile.

It wasn't a very convincing lie anyways, we all suspected it.

But I wouldn't put it past Eli to want to believe their former mentor.

"How did you get the high-levels to respect you?" another called.

Rosie straightened her shoulder and a real smile spread across her face with pride rising in her.

"I beat them all in the games," she answered.

There were some claps and cheers from the low-levels and some groans from our party, but her happiness was starting to wear off on me.

"Are you happy here?" Ren asked suddenly, drawing Rosie's attention back to him.

They had an intense stare down and I felt the conflict rise in Rosie. The bit of sadness and anger was rising again in her. I wanted to make that annoying boy pay for interrupting her happiness.

"I have found happiness at Winterfell," she said in a light voice, though her eyes did not show the same light they once did. "And you all will too."

A bell chimed from behind her and the low-level lunch lady nodded to Rosie.

"Let's eat! Principal Winterfell will stop by later so get your fill now, you will need it."

I watched her as the low-levels came up to her one by one before getting their food. The others behind me had started talking amongst themselves but I couldn't pull my eyes away from Rosie as she smiled and laughed with strangers.

Was this how she would have been if the curse did not ruin her life? I wondered.

Was this what it would be like if we didn't step in?

The bench I was sitting on moved as Malik sat next to me. Even though I did not look up at him I felt his emotions swirl next to me. They were calmer, more collected than the majority of demons I had been around. Like he had compartmentalized them and only let a few slip out when he needed them.

It was impressive...though I would never admit that to him.

"This was the Rosie I saw too," he whispered next to me.

A prick of anger and jealousy played at my chest.

"When?" I asked in a low voice.

I caught Rosie's awkward laugh as she motioned for people to get in line for the food.

"I took her to the beach once," he answered. "She was different there, somewhat like this, though this version is much happier."

I nodded.

"But this isn't completely real," I said as Rosie's eyes met mine. She was struggling to keep her smile up now and the sadness and anger that Ren ignited was getting stronger by the second.

"It's real enough," Malik said. "Though the spitfire has to be my favorite version of her."

I finally tore my eyes from Rosie to look at Malik. He had a small smile on his face as he watched her. There were warm emotions unfurling inside him that caused my throat to tighten.

"I stayed away too," I told him.

He looked at me with a raised eyebrow.

"I am an empath, there is little you can hide from me," I said.

He sighed and shifted in his seat.

"Since when do you have this type of conversations with the others?" he asked.

"I don't," I admitted and looked back at Rosie. She finally got the last low-level in line and let out a heavy sigh. "I am just so tired of lying."

I let him stew in the silence for a bit longer until I dared to breach it.

"Who is Mary Langworth?" I asked in a whisper.

The folded-up paper burned in my pocket.

I felt the panic inside him but it did not show on his face, instead he kept the same facial expression with his eyes locked on Rosie.

"Where did you hear that name?" he asked, his tone low and deadly.

A sliver of fear ran up my spine.

"My father," I lied. "Was babbling about her and a few others before..."

Malik's head slowly turned and I was met with a cold stare. *This* was the face of someone ready to attack and it made me regret inviting him into my house at all. I was sure that tonight I would be woken up by that same exact face though this time, he would have a knife in his hand.

"Never speak that name again," he threatened. "You are smarter than that and smarter to think you could lie to me."

"I am not—"

His eyes narrowed.

"End of discussion," he growled and turned back to Rosie.

Maybe I wasn't the only liar after all.

13

ROSIE

Talking was proving to be exhausting.

Since I was ten I never had the chance to talk as much as I did now and every word felt like I needed to pull it out with all my strength.

My throat was sore.

My feet were killing me.

And I was starving.

Principal Winterfell showed up and spewed his bullshit to the low-levels at the welcoming feast, but didn't do much else. Like everything he did, it was all for show. Many of the low-levels ate it up, just like I had when I first joined, though now I was the one that was continuing the lie on his behalf.

I tried to catch him before he left and ask about the demon I would work with, but the low-levels ran to me as soon as we concluded the session and I had to watch as he weaved out of the crowd expertly avoiding me. I knew he was doing it on purpose too because just as he gripped the door, he turned back and smiled at me.

I bottled up my annoyance and tried to focus on the eager low-levels for the rest of the orientation.

I was happy to have been a part of this, I realized after I talked to the low-levels.

I was happy to finally talk with people who came from a similar background as me and who understood the hardships of growing up in a low-level household...but that's where it stopped.

As I stood in front of all of them telling them what Winterfell was all about, I realized that they were no longer my people.

The wide-eyed excited young people that were just coming into this academy had no idea the extent of shit I had gone through this past year...and it caused the hole in my chest to spread open.

Suddenly it felt like *I* was the imposter in this room.

Here I was a demon-witch hybrid, helping the students become like me... But they couldn't become like me, could they?

I was lying straight to their faces about the wonders here and in reality I should have been telling them that they made a huge mistake in coming here.

But how could I have done that?

How could I have told the girl who gushed to me about how excited she was to finally be able to make a living for her single mom and three siblings, that a girl that I was in charge of taking care of died right where she was sitting not days before.

How could I crush all of their hopes and dreams and feel okay about it afterwards?

Unlike me, these low-levels still had a chance in life to be the change that I was supposed to be.

"Do you ever stop thinking, and just live?" Eli asked, dropping their voice to a low whisper.

Between helping the low-levels around campus and getting them settled in their dorms, the days flew by and all of a sudden, it was time for orientation.

The high-level demons showed up the day before orientation and since then I was constantly on edge.

Many had nodded to me in the hallway even as I showed the other low-levels around, showing me that they still remembered who I was and that they would be fighting me in the games this year.

It was a relieving thought, but I knew it wouldn't last forever.

Now there were many more targets at their disposal, and none of them had a gang of demons and witches for their protection.

"I know, I know," I whispered back.

We were all seated once again in the auditorium. This time it was magically expanded to fit all of the new arrivals and the noise was deafening. Demons and witches alike were chattering and shooting glances at the new arrivals all while waiting for Principal Winterfell to make his grand entrance.

The stage remained empty as people filed in and found their seats. The low-levels navigated through Winterfell and to the orientation by themselves, but as soon as they saw me many ran to crowd the space around me, only moving when asked by a disgruntled demon or witch.

Eli was to my left and Daxton took my right while Amr Rae and Malik were forced to sit behind me.

Matt, Claudine, and Maximus had yet to show and now that the Originals were gone, I guessed that they no longer needed to pretend to be students. Though Matt did say that he was a third-year last year, so he wouldn't need to be here anyways.

I had wished for the time back when there was a buzz of excitement and nervousness around us, when we thought that it would be only us against all these high-levels for the rest of the time we were here.

It was sweet and innocent, or at least I was led to believe it was...and that only hurt more.

I wanted to have the happy-go-lucky best friend that laughed with me in the courtyard of Winterfell and gave me purple flowers when I was sad. I wanted someone there with me who knew the struggles of my upbringing and still tried to make every day the best it could be.

I tried to push those thoughts out of my mind and focus on

the way he changed. The anger and hatred I saw when his eyes narrowed at me, and the way it felt to be held down by him in Marques's manor.

"Can we tell them to leave us alone?" Daxton whispered in my ear. His hand clamped down my thigh and I felt his magic sink into my skin.

I shivered at his tone.

"They aren't even bothering us," I hissed back.

And just as I said that I caught dull purple eyes and a teasing smile from a row ahead of me.

"Rosie!" Ren whispered loudly and waved at me.

I forced a smile to my face and leaned forward.

"Yes, Ren?" I asked in a polite tone even though I had no energy to keep up this facade.

"Can you please show me my class after this?" he asked.

Swallowing my annoyance I nodded.

He beamed at me and leaned back in his seat. The girl next to him turned to look up at me as well.

"Mine too?" she asked.

Daxton let out a chuckle from behind me while Eli growled.

"Of course," I replied.

She sat back down in her seat with a wide smile.

More heads turned to me and suddenly I was in charge of showing more than twenty people their classrooms.

"They aren't even bothering us," Daxton teased as I leaned back in my chair.

"Shut up or I will make you take a group as well."

His mouth snapped shut and I heard Eli snicker.

"You too, Eli."

"You couldn't make me even if you tried, mutant," they responded.

A gasp sounded through the chatter around us and I looked around only to catch a low-level staring at Eli with wide eyes.

"It's okay," I assured them, heat crawling up the back of my neck as low-levels turned to stare.

I didn't need to explain my relationship with Eli or the others, but it wouldn't look good if they saw them walking all over me when I was supposed to be an advocate for our safety and equality.

"You have a problem, low-level?" Eli growled.

"Stop," I hissed at them. They smirked and leaned closer to me, a fresh wave of their scent filling my senses and putting me on edge.

I hated to admit how much this part of Eli affected me.

"Make me," they tested.

Slowly a smile made its way to my face and with a brush of confidence I didn't know I had I turned to the group behind us. Amr, Rae, and Malik were watching the scene play out before them, each with their own reaction. Amr was scowling at Eli while Rae looked indifferent and Malik... Well, he looked slightly amused. I batted my eyes at Malik and watched as a triumphant smile flashed across his face.

"Behave, Eli," Malik said in a low tone.

Eli frowned and squeezed my arm.

"You can't throw his power around like that," they hissed at me.

"But she can," Malik said and leaned forward. "Now, *behave* and listen to what Rosie says, hm?"

I could hear Eli's teeth grind together and they were forced back into their seat. They sent nasty words into my mind through our connection but I couldn't help but laugh at them and leaned into Daxton's side.

He shifted so that his arm was on the back of my chair and I could lean comfortably onto his warm chest. I could feel his lips hover on the top of my head and the whole moment filled me with warmth.

"Good pet," I teased, just to get an extra rise out of them.

Before they could fight back the lights dimmed and out walked Principal Winterfell. His bright purple hair and eyes were the first thing that drew my attention. The second was the disgustingly extravagant suit he wore that had millions of green flashing squiggles on them.

Even from afar they hurt my head.

"Here we go," I groaned and sunk into my chair.

❧

RIGHT AFTER THE ORIENTATION, myself and the others, plus a good majority of the low-levels, gathered in the halls of Winterfell. The other demons and witches gave us dirty looks as they pushed past us and I heard more than a few muttering about taking up space.

I was lucky enough to have dealt with this kind of sentiment with Eli and the others to keep a cool expression on my face even though I was seething inside.

Me winning the games and acclimating into this academy should have shown them by now that there was no need for those comments, and that their own ideas about bloodline and purity were conflated.

But I knew better than to expect them to change in such a short time.

It made me rethink the plan to join the government and fight for low-level and hybrid rights...but I already had too much on my plate.

"Okay so we have," I said looking at the group in front of me, "Demon History and Culture to the left." Only a handful of people moved. "Government to the right." A majority of the people moved. "And Mathematics and Science in the middle."

Many of the low-levels seemed to lean towards the government portion and while I was surprised, it made sense.

These people were here to change the course of this world, where better to start?

"I can take Government," Rae said from my side.

I jumped, not even noticing her presence until that moment. Her hazel eyes stared down at me and I felt a chill run through me. Even though we were not touching I felt a pull to her.

It had been so long since we had any alone time together and that kiss in the hallway was currently playing in my mind on repeat. I swallowed thickly and tried to find a somewhat coherent sentence.

"You want to help?" I asked in a weak voice.

The side of her lips twisted, a devious-looking smile if I had ever seen one.

"Of course," she said and looked at the group in front of us. "Each major is on a separate area of the campus, unless you refuse?"

"No, that's fine—great even," I said tripping over my words.

Why was I getting so nervous and flushed?

I cursed internally and wiped my sweaty hands on the sides of my skirt. I had known her for over a year now, seen her intimately...why would she still pull a reaction out of me.

She nodded though her eyes were alit, almost like she could see right through me.

I felt oddly naked in front of her.

"I'll take science and math people," Malik interrupted, coming to stand at my other side.

A warm feeling shot up inside me and for some reason, it made me want to burst into tears. *Finally,* I wasn't alone with these low-levels.

"Alright," I said.

"It won't get you brownie points," Eli grumbled in a low voice from behind us.

Malik gave me a smirk that told me he knew it did.

"Demon History and Culture, with me then," I said and waved people off.

Ren broke out of his government section and ran towards me.

"Can we talk after?" he asked. "I have some more questions about the games."

"Sure," I said. "I'll find you afterwards."

He gave me a smile and ran off with the group that was now being led by Rae. She had already jumped into a lecture on the hall they were going to and the history of the school. Her enthusiasm, even if obviously forced, made me smile.

"Well," Malik said and shifted next to me. "I don't know —*or care*—about the history of Winterfell but if you stick around I can tell you where each of your powers originated from."

There were a few gasps before the low-levels started rambling off about their powers.

"Um," I stalled as the low-levels eyes looked towards me. "I guess I am the boring one. Let's go to our classes."

There were a few chuckles, but they followed me nonetheless. As I walked them to the hallway I pointed out my own class and showed them to their classes as well.

Eli, Amr, and Daxton followed me silently and didn't interrupt even as the low-levels bombarded me with questions that had nothing to do with their classes.

I understood that to them, I was some sort of commodity, and of course they would take advantage of my time. I would too if I was in their position, but it made it all the harder to hold onto my energy.

Talking and interacting was something I haven't been able to do at scale for more than ten years of my life and I could already feel the soreness gathering in my throat.

To my relief none of them were in my class, though I knew soon enough many would pop in to find me at some point now that they knew where I was most of the time.

As soon as they were settled and began dispersing, Eli grabbed me by the arm and forced me to walk in the direction of the dorms. Their grip on me was powerful, and I had to swallow my whines as they dragged me.

I had almost forgot about the earlier anger because they were so quiet during the tour.

"First you use Malik's power on me, then you fucking entertain those low-levels for two hours?" Eli hissed in my ear.

"Eli," came Amr's voice. "Calm yourself."

"I *will not* listen to a dirty cat who thinks that just because Rosie takes your di—"

"Eli," I said in a serious tone, cutting off their angry rant.

My magic flared inside of me and there was a crackle between us. Eli's eyes widened and they jumped away from me, ripping their hand from my arm.

Their eyes filled with anger and hurt as if I had just done the worst thing imaginable to them.

"Did you just...?"

"Yes," I said and squared my shoulders. "I have a duty to those low-levels and why do you think it's okay to talk to Amr like that?"

Their blue eyes narrowed in my direction and they began taking deep breaths.

"Let's go get a celebration coffee," Malik's voice said and his arm wrapped around my shoulder, pulling me further from Eli.

I was caught off guard by his sudden appearance but I didn't mind, not in this moment where Eli was on the edge.

I could take the bullying, I could take the cuts and pain...but I would be dammed if *anyone* talked to Amr like he was not worthy of his place on this earth.

Amr had been trapped in his familiar body for *years* because Daxton's parents thought of him as *lower* than the other witches. He deserved far more than verbal abuse. No matter what Eli's normal temperament was, this could not be excused.

Eli glared up at Malik and their body tensed like they were ready to pounce.

"It's a nice day, Eli," he said. "Let's keep it that way."

My heart was beating in my chest like crazy because not only did I know that Eli was going to punish me later for this, but the way Malik's arm was holding me to his side was surreal.

I used to have to pull his reaction out of him through pure

anger...but here he was giving in to it without me even having to ask, though I wish it was under a better circumstance.

"Let's get the frozen one," Daxton said, appearing from behind Eli. "I bet you haven't had one of those, have you?"

I shook my head and he smiled at me while putting a hand on Eli's shoulder.

I looked towards Amr and grabbed his hand. He sent me a warm smile but by the creases near his eye, I could tell that he was unhappy with the way Eli spoke to him.

"Let's go," Malik said. "Someone text Rae."

He began to pull me towards the opposite side of campus.

"Oh wait—" I said and dug my heels into the ground. "I have to meet Ren."

"He can wait," Malik said dropping his voice low.

It caused shivers to run up my spine and his thumb began drawing patterns in my arm. I swallowed thickly and tried to reign in my magic as it fanned out, begging for me to take things further.

It wanted the white-haired demon far more than it should have.

Ever since that moment in the town where he forced me to kneel in front of him, my magic had been on the hunt. It pushed me closer to him every time, begging for me to sample him.

His hand gripped my shoulder and it was far too easy to imagine them in my hair, imagine his scarred body over mine, sweating.

Amr tensed in my grasp and I tried to reign in my magic.

"Okay-y," I stammered and let him guide me towards the parking lot.

14
ELI

I stormed down the hallways of Winterfell with anger coursing through my veins. My skin felt like with any drastic movement, it would rip in two.

Every face that passed was one I wanted to slam into the concrete until they were unrecognizable. Every laugh or whisper made me want to scream and every stray thought that brushed up across my mind made me want to rip my hair out.

Not only had all activity with *The Fallen* been canceled, but Rosie had been ignoring me for weeks forcing me to suffer this pain alone. I thought for sure with her help I could be happily distracted from the mundane life that I was forced to live now, but even that was too much to ask of her.

I tried every day through every class to get just a smidge of her attention but each day she was swept away by a series of low-level demons that demanded her time. Low-levels that she thought were apparently more important than me.

I didn't take myself as a jealous person, but how dare she treat those monstrosities as more deserving of her time?

Malik, Rae, Daxton, even the *fucking* cat would have been better than those damn low-levels.

You would think that once those useless sacks of skin finally started that their insistent yammering would stop, but no.

It just got worse.

Now Rosie was still fielding complaints and even as we reached our second full week of school it had only gotten worse.

Apparently Principal Winterfell had *forgotten* to name a demon representative and so there was no one to hold the demons back from their attacks on the low-levels. Forgotten may not be the right word—it's more like Malik didn't use his powers on him and no one here wanted to step up and name themselves as the one in charge of these rampant demons.

The attacks were well deserved in my opinion, but that didn't stop them from complaining to Rosie.

Rae and Amr had stepped in to help talk to the demons who had been bothering the low-levels but Rae was tired and Amr.... Well, Amr was not well received in the demon community as a witch.

As I rounded the corner to our classroom I found one of my current annoyance leaning against the wall, whistling as he watched others enter the classroom.

That purple-eyed kid.

Everything from his black messy hair to his wrinkled shirt, to his fucking horrible posture made me irate. It's like he was born to irritate the shit out of me. He had been by far the low-level most attached to Rosie, meaning that I saw him all the *fucking* time.

His face dropped as he caught my gaze and his whistling fell short.

"Eli, hey," he said in a nervous tone.

"Don't bother her today," I growled at him.

His thoughts were in a flurry and shot out every which way as if even they were trying to escape the shitty situation he was in. Even they could understand that they were in danger.

My breath caught as one of the thoughts became clearer. It

was useless, but it was more clear than I had ever heard it before without touching another person.

Oh shit, his thoughts whispered.

I wanted to hear more, I needed it. Because finally that bastard's blood was working. Finally, I was just a smidge closer to that useless sperm donor.

"I just have a few questions," he said with his hands raised in surrender. "I haven't been able to talk to her for weeks."

Join the club, I thought wryly. I wracked my brain trying to think of anything to say or do that would make his thoughts pop out again like that.

But just as I was about to give him a verbal beating, a hand shot out and grabbed the hair on the top of his head, forcing his head back into the concrete wall. I heard the crack of his skull and while that should have excited me I was more annoyed that the hand got to it before I did.

Because I heard another thought.

A small, *What the?*

I looked at the high-level demon with a scowl. I didn't recognize him though he seemed to recognize me, and he nodded and laughed as if I was enjoying this.

How dare they pull out a thought that I barely managed to do myself. My blood boiled and I began to see red.

How many times today did the universe need to tell me I was useless?

How many more times would I feel as though I was trapped in my own skin?

My haze fell away and I forced my jaw to unclench.

I smirked at the unsuspecting high-level and gripped their wrist.

"I was having a talk with this one," I said in a polite tone. Though I put a significant amount of strength behind my grip and they let go immediately.

His face dropped and their pained thoughts reached my mind. I scratched my neck and looked down at them through hooded eyes.

This was what I needed, I realized as the throbbing in my head began to subside.

A small calm washed through me and in an instant my mind was clearer than it had been in weeks. I understood now what this power, *his blood,* required from me.

It makes sense that Marques's blood would react better to this. React better to violence, fear, and pain because after all... that's what he was forged out of. I wouldn't pretend to know what it took to survive among his kind and then forcibly be cast out like him, but I would grasp at whatever shining string was left for me.

Yes, I thought. *I understand this now, maybe Rosie wasn't the only way to cure my boredom.*

I squeezed harder as they let out a groan, tears welled up in their eyes and I couldn't help the bubble of excitement that floated through me.

"Please, Eli I'm sorry, I thought you hated them as much as we did," he sputtered. "Please, I'm sorry."

I squeezed harder and watched as he fell to his knees. A sick pleasure shot through me.

"I was *busy* with him, or did you not see? And the more you mess with the fucking low-levels the more they interrupt me, does your puny brain understand that?" I asked. "Do you realize every single one of them runs to Rosie about this, hm? Next time tell the other dumbasses to *fuck off* or I swear I will visit you in your sleep and slit your god damn throat."

He tried to hold in his groan but as I snapped his wrist in my hands he couldn't help but cry out like the weakling he was. I reveled in the way he jerked against my hold, trying so hard to get away but still remaining just as trapped as a rat.

These types of high-level demons made me sick. They made low-levels look like god damn saints and it was disgusting that they disgraced us so horribly. *We* were the ones that were supposed to be superior. *We* were the ones that were untainted and remained as much a part of heaven as our Original ancestors.

Except you are also tainted by that blond bitch...

The thought hit me and caused me to pause.

"Get out of here," I growled and threw his limp hand back at him wishing internally that it would heal wrong. He deserved much more than the leniency I gave him, but that would be for another day, and another time.

I turned to the annoying boy still clutching his head. He looked up at me with a pitiful expression, his blue eyes wide and scared.

His thoughts were burrowed back into his head forever gone from my power.

"Don't fucking bother Rosie ever again," I warned and walked into the classroom without another word.

I wasn't surprised to see Daxton and Amr in their seats already but I scowled when Rosie's seat remained empty. She must have been busy with the low-levels again and I couldn't stop the growl that left my chest.

Tonight, I would change that. Or at least blow off some steam with her, I thought. It was the only thing that pulled me further into the classroom.

Mr. Falkner, or should I say *Original scum,* was seated at his desk, looking over some papers as students filed in. He hadn't left with the others and it made me all the more suspicious. I would have to remember to ask Malik if his inclusion with them was purely because of his mind control or if there was something deeper.

After all, he could be reading back information to the Originals.

Felling extra aggravated this morning I walked over to his desk and slammed my hand down on his shoulder.

He looked up at me, blinking a few times before he spoke.

"Yes, Eli?" he asked.

I leaned forward with a smile.

"Don't think I forgot where your ties lie," I whispered in a low voice to him.

His mind remained blank and I was tempted to cause a scene just to pull something useful out of his head...but I didn't want to chance Rosie getting mad at me.

"I don't know what you mean Eli," he said in a smooth voice and brushed my hand off his shoulder. "Now don't ever try to intimidate me ever again."

I smiled and stood back up to peer down at him.

"We will see about that," I said with a smirk and turned to walk to my seat.

Daxton's arm shot out and gripped my wrist as I walked by.

Did you get anything useful? he asked in my mind.

Nope, I replied back and looked over my shoulder at Mr. Falkner who, as was no surprise, was watching me back. *Still nothing from him.*

We should ask Malik tonight, he said.

I sighed and pulled my wrist away to sit in my seat. I didn't need to be told what to do, by Daxton no less. I had been in this far longer than him, ran back and forth from the magical town, met and killed my brother for god's sake. I knew what I needed to do.

Tonight, was the night we visited Marques's place to discuss the plan.

It was about time. I was tempted to destroy something if I didn't get any action soon. No outings with Malik, no Rosie, no talk of a way to get back at those Originals.

I gripped the side of the table when I thought of Ezekiel. He'd tried to play it as though he was the nice guy in this situation. Tried to stand back and make it seem like Xena was the crazy bloodthirsty one...but I saw inside that mind of his.

I saw the way that he thought about me and the other children.

He didn't care one bit for us.

He only saw us as players in his game and didn't mind if he lost a few pieces while he was at it.

Seeing my blood brother only confirmed it.

This family was fucking insane and had no idea the hell I was going to reign in on them when I finally got my hands around his throat.

I had a plan for him. If Rosie and Malik took too long to prepare, I was ready to seek them out and end this myself.

I saw Rosie's flustered face enter into the classroom. I could never get enough of her school uniform and I couldn't wait to rip it off of her as soon as I got her alone. Watching her stride across the room, her skirt rising with each step was almost enough to make me jump out of my seat and take her right there in front of everyone.

"Sorry," she murmured as she brushed past me.

As soon as she sat down I grabbed her stool and dragged her closer to me, not caring that it caused a loud noise to fill the room.

I could feel the stares but I knew they would be gone soon. I clamped my hand down on Rosie's bare thigh and sent her the collection of fantasies I had been feeling about her lately. It was the only thing I could do to stop my hands from wandering.

Bent over a desk, taking my strap while Daxton fucked her face.

Tying her to the bed and denying her an orgasm for hours.

Forcing her to wear a vibrator in her underwear while she attended her classes.

Her face flamed a bright red as I hit her with fantasy after fantasy.

"What has gotten into you?" she whispered under her breath.

The bell rang and I used this as a chance to duck lower and speak into her ear.

"After the meeting tonight you and I are gonna have a talk about how you have been ignoring me these last few weeks," I whispered.

Mr. Falkner called the class's attention and jumped straight into his lecture as he always did. I paid no mind to him and focused on sending Rosie mental images of all the dirty ways I wanted to violate her tonight.

"Eli, we are in class," she whispered and tried to focus on the teacher.

Feeling her unhappiness I pulled away and vowed to myself that tonight, would be a night she would never forget.

❦

THE PLAN WAS to meet at Rae's house before we set out and I arrived with Rosie early in hopes to see my plan come to fruition before we had any real work to do.

My mouth was watering at the thought and I knew Rosie would go crazy for what I had in store for her.

"We should have waited for Daxton and Amr," she grumbled as we climbed out of the car.

"I have a surprise," I said with a smirk.

She raised a brow at me and that quickly silenced her complaints. A small light of curiosity lit her eyes and I knew she was hooked.

"What kind of surprise?" she asked as we ascended the stairs to Rae's house.

I didn't knock and just opened the door without warning. No one was in the front room and this made it all the better. No one would stop us on our way to my surprise.

I hadn't fully believed it would work, but I wouldn't complain that it did.

"You'll like it," I said. "Trust me."

She would like it for sure. And it would fulfill at least one of the fantasies I had with her and hopefully tide me over until I could carve into that beautiful skin again.

I led her to the hallway to the left of the entrance and down a short corridor to the last room on the right. I was taken aback by the absence of maids, but Rae had told me a bit about their troubles with the contracts. There was no shortage of struggles now, but I wouldn't let it distract me.

She also told me another interesting little secret. A change that happened after the Originals had cast us out of their light.

I listened outside the door and when I heard nothing I pushed it open.

A flutter of warmth spread through my belly as I realized the main room was empty. Looking closer I saw that there was a light shining from the bathroom door and I could hear the water running from inside.

So perfect. Even better than I expected.

Her mind was in a frenzy as I pulled her into the room and shut the door softly behind us.

"Closet," I whispered.

She looked at me wide-eyed.

Is there someone in here? she asked in my mind.

"Closet or I leave you here to find out," I whispered.

That spurred her into action, and I followed her silently to the shuttered closet. Closing the door behind us, I peered out into the room. The slitted shutters gave us the perfect view of the bedroom without being in the open.

"Perfect," I whispered and turned to Rosie and without warning attacked her lips with my own.

She didn't hesitate to wrap her arms around my shoulders and push her breasts into me. It would seem that even the Rosie, who had all of us at her will, had been longing for some type of release. Her nails dug into me and she clung to me as if I was the only thing keeping her in this world.

Her eagerness made me absolutely feral and only exacerbated the itch I had been feeling the last few days. I *needed* this. Needed her. She was the only constant release that I could count on, and the only one that made this boring life worth it.

I gripped at her shirt and pulled it open. The buttons snapped and flew everywhere.

The closet was cramped and clothes were brushing across us,

but I didn't care. All I cared about was getting these annoying clothes off of her.

She gasped against my mouth and worked to undo her bra. When she finally threw it to the side I leaned down and brought her erect nipple into my mouth, sucking on it before biting it.

I never got tired of the taste of her. Every time it pushed me forward, pulling a ravenous state out of me that I could barely control.

She let out a soft moan and threaded her hand through my hair.

"Fuck, *Eli*," she cried as I pulled her underwear down with one hand.

I stood back up and gave her a scorching kiss before I finally decided to put my plan into action. I grabbed her and forced her in front of me, turning her so that she could look out and into the bedroom.

The closet was small, but had just enough room for me to fuck her against this door without the hindrance of the closet. I couldn't wait anymore.

I unzipped my pants and pulled out the strap. It was the same one I used on her before. It was large to use without lube, but I was sure she would be drooling all over herself in mere minutes when her gift arrived.

Plus, I knew she liked the pain that came along with it.

Kicking her legs apart I slipped two fingers into her already soaked pussy. She arched back into me and I watched in amusement as her hand came down to rub her clit.

"Where is that sweet, innocent Rosie, hm?" I teased and removed my fingers to rub the head of the strap against her lips. "The one that acts like such a good girl in front of everyone? Who knew you were so wet for me already."

"Hurry," she whispered. "We have to meet them soon."

Just then the water stopped and she froze.

"Eli?" she whispered.

I hushed her and grabbed her chin so she was looking out into the bedroom.

I couldn't see much but I could hear the familiar sound of wet feet against the wood floor and then the carpet as my surprise left the backroom.

Is that...?

An image of Malik fully nude and using a towel to dry his hair flashed through my mind.

I had noticed Malik coming and going with Rae on multiple occasions and it only took a little persuasion for both to give me all the details. Poor Malik wanted to keep an eye on Rosie, ergo coming and going with our favorite blackmailer every day to school and conveniently living in her house.

After all, we were both out of a job.

Hard times indeed, but perfect for this.

"Surprise," I whispered.

"Are you sure this is what you want?" Malik's voice from earlier flitted into my mind.

"Yes," I said with an annoyed tone. "Not like I haven't seen your dick before."

I swore Malik flushed and looked down at his feet.

"And Rosie?" he asked in a small voice.

"She will fucking love it," I said with a wicked smile. "And don't forget that you owe me."

His eyes flashed and he let out a sigh.

"As long as she will like it."

And she did. Rosie was frozen in front of me but in her mind I could see how her eyes roamed Malik's body. How they stopped at his hips before taking in his erect cock.

Rosie was not innocent. Rosie was a dirty, horny little Original and she was all *ours.*

15

ROSIE

Eli's hand covered my mouth and they thrust slowly into me.

I gripped onto the sides of the closet, trying to keep my noises to a bare minimum.

The stretch was painful but god damn was this everything I wanted and more.

I had so many questions, starting off with:

Why the fuck was Malik here?

And secondly:

How did Eli even come up with this?

But I was too distracted by the god in front of me to even care about how this worked.

Taking in every single detail of Malik's body as he dried his hair. My eyes ran down the side of his torso as I followed the trail of his tattoos and scars to his firm ass. It wasn't long until my eyes narrowed in directly on his mouthwatering cock which was already standing erect.

It looked swollen and painful like he had been denied for far too long and I couldn't help but imagine kneeling in front of him again, this time taking it all into my mouth.

I heard Eli's taunts in my head and they began slowly

pumping in and out of me. Each time their hips met mine they paused to rock our hips together, starting small sparks deep in my belly. They knew the thought of being here, watching him while Eli fucked me silently was turning me on immensely.

My pussy was so wet that even with the size of the strap, Eli moved inside of me seamlessly. They picked up their pace as I stayed quiet, rewarding me for good behavior.

That's right, Rosie, they purred in my mind. *Stay quiet so Malik doesn't catch us. We don't want this to end early do we?*

God no, I said back and moved my hand back to my clit.

Malik paused for a moment and my heart jumped into my throat. Eli was careful to not thrust into me hard enough that the slap of skin could be heard, but I was so wet that it was almost impossible to disguise the sound of them fucking me.

I bit back my whimper as Eli delivered a harder thrust, almost knocking me into the door.

Suddenly, Malik turned to sit on the edge of the bed, discarding the towel as he did so. He leaned back and looked at the ceiling and finally—*finally*—his hand came to stroke his erect cock.

Eli leaned over me to peer out of the closet and slowed their thrusts. Each time Malik's hand would travel base to tip, Eli would follow suit matching his pace.

The veins in Malik's neck stood out as he threw his head back and let out a loud groan that filled the room. I couldn't stop the whimper that escaped my mouth as both Malik and Eli sped up.

Malik started out slow and calculated in his movements but in an instant they turned harder. So hard I could hear the sound of his hand hitting the base of his cock with each pump.

His eyes were closed and his mouth remained open, small pants coming through his plump lips. I wanted—*no needed*—so badly to be on his cock. Be the one that was riding him as he made those noises. *I* wanted to be the person to draw this reaction out of him.

Jealousy suits you, Eli said in my mind with a chuckle. They slammed their hips into me harder, the sound of them fucking me becoming louder. Far too loud for Malik not to hear.

But he stayed, with his eyes remaining closed, furiously pumping his cock in his hand.

A warmth started to expand deep in my belly and I found myself falling faster towards my climax than I had before. Eli pulled me back to them, both hands over my mouth as I came around their strap.

The orgasm was so violent and sudden that I jerked against them. Quickly with one hand on Eli's wrist I brought the other down to my clit to ride out the orgasm, watching as Malik grunted and came all over his stomach and chest.

His golden eyes flashed towards us in the closet and I thought for sure he heard me and was going to come end us. But instead he simply took the towel he discarded, cleaned up and went back into the bathroom.

Eli grabbed some of the fallen clothing and something from the hangers around us before ushering me out of the room in only a skirt.

❧

THE WALK of shame through Rae's house wearing my skirt with soaked panties and a random sweater found in Malik's closet had to be the hands-down most embarrassing moment of my life.

"You should have told me!" I hissed to Eli as they steered me through the house. I was far too embarrassed to even comprehend the layout of this place, let alone think about anything else than Malik's soft pants and groan as he jacked off.

"Don't act like you didn't like it," they teased.

"Should have told him then!" I hissed. "That's a total invasion of privacy and consent."

They paused, stopping outside of a double door, and looked down at me with a playful expression.

"Don't worry about him," they replied and pushed open the doors.

Everyone was already there except me, Eli, and Malik.

Heat flamed my face as all attention was turned towards us.

"Finally," Rae muttered.

"Once Malik shows his face, I will transport us into the wards," Claudine said with a smile.

I hide my gaze from the group suddenly feeling like what we had done was all too obvious. Eli walked us over and positioned me between them and Rae.

I sent Rae a small smile and she looked me up and down with a curious look. Her brows were pulled together like she was trying to locate a missing piece of a puzzle.

"Is that...?"

The doors were pushed open by a freshly showered Malik, his hair still wet. He wore a t-shirt and jeans, similar to what I saw him in when we went to the beach.

I swallowed thickly and looked back at Rae.

She looked from me to Malik, and then Eli before looking down and pushing her glasses up. A flash of understanding crashed her eyes.

That was the missing piece, I guess.

"Of course, that's what you do with the information I gave you," she muttered and if I didn't know her any better I would have assumed she was holding in a bout of laughter.

"It was fun," Eli said with a laugh.

If my face got any hotter it would have caught flames.

"Hold on to me!" Claudine yelled impatiently.

We each stepped forward and placed an arm on her. Her warm smile filled my vision and I felt a sense of relief fill me. When the last person gripped a hold of her, which happened to be Malik, we were engulfed in a bright light.

I had to steady myself against Eli and Rae as I felt the pull of magic at my core. You would think that after all of the times of using this to travel, I would have gotten used to it, but it was still the same twist in my stomach and flash of nausea that caused me to groan aloud and lose my balance.

Unfortunately, right after I blinked the blurriness from my eyes, the first eyes I met were Malik's. There was an unreadable expression in them, and I had to look away in embarrassment, my face heating uncontrollably.

I suddenly felt far too toasty in the sweater and wanted to run for the hills at the first chance that I got.

Fucking Eli, I cursed in my mind and heard their light laughter.

Malik would be pissed when he found out and I worried if this crossed too far of a line with him. I would have liked to cross the line with him myself, but bringing Eli along made it feel all the more serious.

Looking around I noted that we were in the front hall of the manor again. A cold spread through the room and I shivered, pulling Malik's sweater closer to me. The manor, just as before, held an aged and almost creepy vibe to it that made my skin crawl.

I spotted familiar curly red hair waiting for us near the adjacent room.

Anger burned inside of me and all the unshed magic seemed to boil under my skin.

Of course, he was here... Why would I expect any different.

Though if truth be told, inside I was happy to see him again even if my magic was more angry than not.

He sent me a smirk.

"Welcome back," he said in a cocky tone. "Let's get this over with shall we?"

Eli's arm wrapped around my shoulders as I glared at Matt.

My magic was raging inside of me. Throwing itself against the confines of my skin like a wild animal in a cave.

Besides Xena, I have never wanted to hurt a single person so badly before. I imagined a thousand deaths for him, each of them more gruesome than the last.

A fresh wave of hurt slashed through me.

As I watched the low-levels interact these last few weeks, I couldn't help remembering what we used to have. The way he helped me through the first few months at Winterfell.

He stood up for me.

Pretended to be the friend when I didn't have one.

He was the single person that introduced me to this world and now he just stood there laughing down at me.

Don't mind him, Eli said in my mind. *We have bigger things to take care of.*

And just as the words were uttered the black-haired dead-eyed demon showed himself. His head peeked out from the threshold and he smiled at us. It was almost a playful act that humanized one of the strongest beings on this earth.

"I hear we have some planning to do," he said in a light voice.

"Unfortunately," I said and freed myself from Eli's arms to walk towards Marques.

"I am sorry to hear about your beloved patients," he said in all seriousness.

"Thank you," I murmured. "I can rest easy once we have a plan on how to deal with this going forward."

"That's easy, dear," he said and waved for the others to come over. "We wait."

I grimaced at him.

"I assume the familiar and rampant magic users are aware of what we do here?" Matt asked, smugness filling his tone.

Instead of giving in to my urge to smash his face into the wall, I let the others answer for me.

"As aware as anyone else here," Rae spoke on their behalf.

"Welcome," Marques said with a smile. "Get comfortable, this will be a long talk."

"We will never match up to the strength of an Original," Daxton said to Marques. "Even if they have your weird-ass blood or not, we will *die*."

We had gone in circles for hours now and finally I realized why it was better for a select group to make the plans because at this rate, we wouldn't be leaving this place until the morning.

We had found a side room complete with a fireplace that helped ward off the chilly atmosphere and had enough chairs for us all to sit, though Claudine, Maximus, Malik, and Matt unsurprisingly wanted to stand.

They acted as though they needed to be battle-ready in minutes and while it put me on edge, it also calmed me to know that they were there for us.

Eli was sitting next to me on the couch, an arm around me at all times, while Amr sat on the other side of me and Daxton by him.

Rae sat off to the side in a single love seat and I saw her shift a few times and reach to grab her notebook, but with a firm look from Malik, she would scowl and drop her hand to her lap.

Marques of course, had his own love seat as well and had been patiently answering all of our questions...though I knew he was tired by now.

Daxton was...reasonably upset at the information shared and had no problem airing those concerns.

"And you are still against giving us some of your blood?" Daxton asked, his hand clenching into fists that rested on his thighs.

"I do not know how it will affect magic users yet," Marques replied with a cool tone. "And given your already, *fragile* situation... I do not want to chance an overload on your system."

There was a silence.

"Because it's tearing me apart," Daxton muttered bitterly.

My heart squeezed painfully as I watched in real time, him coming to terms with how bad his magic was. I didn't want to think of what it meant for his magic to run rampant, I couldn't bear it.

"Rosie's will help keep it together," Marques assured. For the first time his voice softened, as if he was talking to a child.

Daxton didn't reply, just simply nodded, and relaxed back into his seat.

I wanted to reach out to him and grab ahold of his hand, but didn't want to upset him further, so I stayed seated.

"Why is it you cannot fight them?" Amr asked, his voice cautious.

"I have been trying for years," he said. "And sustained many injuries since, I am not the young demon I once was."

He sent me a knowing look. *He was dying* and no one here would know. No one could know...because if they did, he would be the first one they would go after and we would lose the only bit of protection that we had.

"How do we know when we are ready?" I asked him.

He sent me a grateful smile.

"You will never be *fully* ready for what faces you out there, but defeating me would be a good start," he said.

Rae stiffened beside me.

"Don't worry young one," he said. "I won't hurt her."

I looked between them. *Was he speaking to her?*

"What is your power?" I asked.

He just leaned back and cocked his head to the side.

"In the real world, demons will not come up to you and explain their power before they tear you to shreds," he said.

I grimaced at the imaging of Xena ripping me apart in my mind.

"We know Ezekiel's power," Daxton said. "And since Xena is a witch, it is pretty straightforward."

A slow smile spread across Marques's face.

"Is it?" he asked. "Are you sure that is the only power he holds?"

Eli let out a scoff.

"Trying to scare us?" they asked. "My power was passed down from them, I should know if they had anything else."

Marques leaned over to grab his cup of wine and brought it to his lips. His silence settled louder than any words could.

"Can demons that are not hybrids have multiple powers?" I asked Marques. Again he didn't answer. I turned to Malik with a questioning stare. "You must know."

Malik shifted uncomfortably, his actions only confirming what I was scared of. If the Originals, or any other demons for that matter, had two powers...then how could we possibly defeat them?

And how the hell did they get the second power in the first place?

For hybrids, I could understand the power in combination with the magic and how it expanded their arsenal...but regular demons too?

"That is something you'll have to figure out yourself," he said in a forced tone.

I sat back slowly and looked at the group. A sick feeling settled in my stomach and I felt a sourness rise in the back of my throat.

We weren't safe here.

The thought scared me to my core.

Even here in the place of one of the last demons still wasn't safe enough to speak such things out loud.

And if here wasn't safe, then where was?

"So we train," I said breaking the heavy silence. "And find them when we are ready."

And from Malik's previous words, in a place where we were safe, Claudine and Maximus were powerful enough to help us with that.

I looked towards Matt wondering if he had ever been to the safe house. If he had, and was not a suspect...

They are listening.

"Finally, you get it," Malik said in a teasing tone. "We train at night and on the weekends so everyone can keep up with school."

"I will take the demons," Marques said. "Maximus will take the witches."

"And I will take the hybrid," Malik said with a grin.

My face flushed when I realized how close we would have to be in order to train.

God what if he made me tell him what happened?

"So you already had this planned?" Rae asked. "What was the point of even discussing this."

"You insisted," Malik replied with narrowed eyes.

16
DAXTON

It's not that I didn't trust the others. I did. I trusted them with my life and there was no one else I would rather have by my side during this time...but that didn't mean they knew everything.

Both Malik and Rae liked to act as if they knew everything, but neither of them was a witch and I would be damned if I went to Matt with this issue.

And after the way Marques had looked at me with those haunting eyes... I couldn't chance going to him either.

I still can't believe that they all just rolled over and changed their bodies so drastically because of him. They were now connected with him for as long as they lived, and literally could not keep anything from him.

From my perspective, that didn't make him any better than Xena or Ezekiel and we were right back where we started. It was all a game of chance and we didn't truly know who had our best interest in mind, though I doubt Originals could see past their own desire to rule this earth.

Even just thinking about the Originals and how fucked up this entire thing was caused my magic to boil under my skin. I was used to the way it would lash out, but that didn't mean I just overlooked it.

It was different now...and it had been bothering me.

I could feel it at night when I was sleeping. It would wake me up with a start in the dead of night as if someone was attacking me. My heart would be beating so hard I swear my bedmates could hear it, and when I blinked the sleep from my eyes, around me would be a cloud of black billowing smoke.

It never woke up Amr or Rosie, but it would hover over them as if taunting me. Never touching, but just getting close enough to feel the vibration of magic against their skin, take wisps of it as they slept, leaving them none the wiser.

It would be so easy to take them now, it would whisper. *So easy to just rip them open and find their magical cores to eat them whole.*

It scared me. I would lay there terrified that it would act on its own and hurt them. I would stay up for as long as I could, watching its next moves as it expanded and filled the room to the brim. Sometimes it would brush across their skin and draw a reaction from them, but then slowly it would pull back inside of me and I would be left staring at the ceiling for hours until exhaustion pulled me back to sleep.

Neither of them could know. If they did, they would ask to go to Marques and the last person on earth I wanted to trust with this was a demon. They wouldn't understand the complexities of magic, or understand how it felt to be at the whim of something so bloodthirsty.

They didn't know that it was like being in the backseat of your own body and unable to say or do anything to stop it.

And while Marques had said that Rosie's magic would help me keep mine in control...that was only true to a certain extent. Right after we shared, I was fine... But the intervals between when I needed to share became increasingly shorter each time.

So that left me only one choice...

I had traveled in the dead of night to a place miles from Winterfell. A place where the buildings were crumbling and the air smelt like a sewer. It was a district that poor and disadvantaged witches often found themselves, especially if they pissed off any high-levels as of late.

The ground was wet though it had not rained recently and I made sure to keep my eyes downcast as I navigated my way through the narrow streets and alleyways.

I had heard of this place in high school from some of the witches who got caught distributing a sort of magical elixir that made demons see colors and run around as if crazed. That was when I first started to understand that there was more out there for witches than stuffy prep schools and government titles.

That was when I first started to understand that I had only called forth a smidge of my power, and this place had offered me the dream of more.

I shifted on my feet as I came to a stop at the rundown bar in front of me.

There was no signage to indicate the business that they did here, but thanks to those witches from so long ago, I knew that inside was a place where any answer you were looking for could be surfaced if you knew the right people.

It was a bar and fight club all in one, and while no one was coming in or out of the place, I could feel the magic seeping out of the ground below my feet, enticing me to come in. If I was in a different situation, I may come here to let off some steam and lose myself in the army of magical potions they offered here...but I needed to be ready to face the person that awaited me down there.

They were not patient, and I didn't want to keep them waiting and risk losing my chance for some answers.

Showing myself to the side door I flared my magic and waited. Only those who didn't belong here tried to use the obviously fake front door. That was lesson one with dealing with witches such as these: the front door was almost always fake and had some kind of a magical trap on it.

Slowly a person materialized from the brickwork and shook off their camouflage just enough so I could make out their face and eyes. They were tall and radiated powerful magic, but not as powerful as mine. They seemed to realize that as they looked me up and down with dark brown eyes before waving their hand.

The wall where they were camouflaged sunk into itself and a set of dark stairs appeared. Loud music filtered out into the silent alleyway we were in, swirling around the dead space bringing small bits of magic with it.

I nodded towards the man and headed towards the stairs. As soon as the wall shut behind me I was assaulted by sweet-smelling magic that permeated the air. It was similar to that of a sickly sweet hard candy that used to make my teeth hurt as a child, but now that I was older and had been around these types of places, I came to realize that it was a special aroma made by the various owners of these establishments to loosen up their patrons. Excite them.

My own magic shifted inside of me as if awaking from a long sleep. I inhaled deeply, enjoying the way the bursts of magic filled my being. It was addicting, that was the whole thing that kept people coming back here to spend their money.

Pushing myself forwards, I navigated down to the underground where witches of all kinds were drinking and talking loudly without a care in the world. Many had tattoos much like myself, others had scars that seemed to span their entire body.

This was a place where those with less than legal lives chose to have fun and right in the middle of the dark, wet space was a caged-off area where two magic users were already going at it. The interior was not much different than the outside. It was grimy, wet, and only smelled slightly better because of the magic in the area.

I navigated my way to the back of the place where I knew the person I was looking for would be waiting. A few people stopped to stare at me as I passed, no doubt feeling the magic that resided inside me. Their brows would furrow and they would look as though they were trying to place where exactly they had felt my magic before, but it would be lost to them.

If this was before the incident, I would feel worried that they may try to fight me, but their stunned expressions told me they were more wary of me than anything else. My magic, of course wished that they would try to fight me. Maybe drag me into the ring and give me an excuse to unleash this angry demon inside me...but no one dared.

The back of the establishment was the only place with full booths. They were made out of dark cracking red leather and the table was always sticky with some type of residue and shined in places where people spilled their precious magical elixirs after having one too many.

Normally, I had not seen too many people use these booths. When I saw them filled, I usually chalked it up to business and sex dealings.

But tonight it was me who decided to take a booth.

I stopped at the booth at the very end, the one that was shrouded in the most darkness as the lights above had long since burned out. From afar you couldn't tell that there was anyone occupying the booth, but as you got closer the unmistakable thrum of magic was there.

As I approached the figure hiding in the shadows did not even so much as look at me, but I could feel their magic stir and reach out to mine.

This was an assessment, I realized. I stayed still as their magic prodded against mine, and when it finally pulled back I slid into the booth on the opposite side of them.

"I need a contact," I said in a low voice.

They moved then, giving me a glimpse of the inside of their hood. She couldn't have been older than twelve, with bright pink hair and brown eyes that seemed to pierce my soul.

I would have assumed she was just some kid, if I hadn't seen her look exactly the same years before. She was the person who had met with me on my first visit here; for some reason she had wandered up to me as I watched the witches pummel into each other.

We talked for a short while, then she disappeared but not before leaving me with one lingering message.

Come find me if you require assistance.

I could tell by the look in her eyes that she was remembering the same moment I was.

"Daxton," she said in a polite tone. "You have got into some trouble have you?"

I swallowed thickly. Trouble was an understatement.

"Trouble found me," I said. "My magic, I mean."

She nodded with a hum.

"I can see that," she said, her eyes trailing my form.

She could visualize magic, I knew that much from our short conversation...but everything else remained a mystery and a lot of the rumors about her were chalked up to an urban legend. They called her Cumae in the rumors, as a reference to some sort of oracle, stating that her powers were nothing like anyone in the world had seen.

I was lucky she took pity on me all those years ago, or I would have never been able to find her now. It was simple, if she didn't want you to find her, you never would.

I never told anyone that I had met her in fear that she would never appear in front of me again.

"I just want my magic to go back to what it once was," I said in a whisper.

She was my last hope; I needed this to work.

She cocked her head and hummed. It was a low but musical tone that floated in the space around us and sent a shiver down my spine.

"I don't know if that's possible," she said. "The demon inside you is rather...clingy."

I shuddered at the idea of Rosie's father living inside me.

"It's not him it's his—"

"I know, boy," she said in a curt tone. "I can find you a contact that can help remove it, but I cannot guarantee what their price will be. That will be up for you to negotiate."

I shifted in my seat and looked at the witch in front of me.

I was no stranger to these deals, but now that I had Rosie in my life, I was hesitant to jump straight into this in fear of fucking up everything we had been working on up until now.

What if they asked me to deliver on something I couldn't? What if they tore me from her?

The family I had worked so hard to surround myself with was something I couldn't lose.

The alternative is being eaten alive by your magic, you feel it don't you? a small voice in the back of my mind said.

"And your price?" I asked.

"If this works out I expect to be introduced to the Original that is feeding you magic," she said in a dark tone.

I bit my tongue to stop myself from correcting her. She didn't need to know Rosie's true heritage.

"If it works," I said.

She nodded and then turned so her face was once more hidden by the light.

"You will be contacted with the next steps if they agree to meet you," she said.

I knew a dismissal when I heard one and slowly got out of the booth and hightailed it out of there before anyone else could stop me.

17

MALIK

Rosie let out a loud groan after unsuccessfully trying to mold her magic into a curse form.

To keep safe, we went to the refugee hideout and sectioned off a small part for ourselves. It was by far the best place for us to be while we prepared, even though the noise of the people seeped through the walls. This was our long-awaited training time, both of us sitting on the cold concrete ground as Rosie tried her best to curse me.

I knew little about wielding magic, but I have been around long enough to understand what was happening in her body right now.

Untamed magic ran wild and only cooperated when she was in some type of grave danger, hence the games she was subjected to in the town. Fortunately, I was not like those monsters and would never make her do something like that again...but I would need to push her.

I acted as though we had all the time in the world, but on the inside I was antsy. I was worried they would get suspicious, or even bored and come looking for their *beloved* hybrid.

Was it wrong for me to hope that there was some poor sod already pregnant with their next batch? Maybe this time they would succeed in separating them from their family.

"I wanted to talk to you about something," I said, breaking Rosie's concentration.

She looked up at me with a raised brow.

"Am I in trouble?" she asked innocently.

I bit back my suggestive retort for something more along the lines of what I wanted to say.

"You know if your mother had returned you..." I trailed, letting her soak up my words.

She dropped her hands and her shoulders slumped forward as if a weight was just put on her back and was far too heavy for her to bear.

"I know," she said softly. "I probably would have ended up dead like the others, am I right?"

I nodded solemnly.

"You are the strongest I have seen so far," I said. "But that doesn't mean that it would have ended differently. Same with Eli."

She peered up at me between her lashes.

"Why did he abandon Eli?" she asked.

I leaned back and looked up at the metal beams above us. This was a hard conversation to navigate, but one I should have had a long time ago...with both of them.

"I don't know what the main reason was," I said. "Maybe a combination of things. They were always so methodical in the things they did. There was a reason for everything. When you were born, who you were born to, your task after you were taken and even—"

"Our death if necessary," she finished for me. I gave her a sad smile.

"I have to think it was that you did not show up. The children are raised together so it would have been a hassle to do another batch so soon," I said. "It takes *some* effort from them too. Not to mention Sarah refused to let Ezekiel have other partners."

"She birthed all of them?" Rosie asked, her jaw hanging open. I let out a light laugh.

"Unfortunately, though she was never really a caretaker," I said with a smile. "She liked to hand them off to the handmaidens."

Rosie nodded thoughtfully.

"Maybe they realized their methods didn't work," she offered.

"I may have also been part of the issue," I admitted and let out a big sigh. "I was, tired of watching them die... At least at *The Fallen* I could have seen them grow away from this world but..."

I let the silence hang between us. There wasn't anything else I could say, nothing I could do to get the guilt of what I have done to Eli, to Rosie, to all the others out from my system.

"I understand," Rosie said with a small smile and looked back up to me. "How many were there?"

I shrugged.

"I lost count," I said. "Truly."

She nodded and went back to her magic.

I was grateful she didn't try to push me on it because in all honesty, while I did forget how many...if I stayed here long enough and tried to remember each of their faces I am sure I could come up with a number.

But I was already so exhausted and worn out, that I didn't think I could handle any more of the death.

I watched as her magic gathered around her, red sparkles becoming visible in the air, floating around on silent winds.

This was my favorite part, and always so mesmerizing. The way her brows pulled in concentration, the way she would pull her plump bottom lip into her mouth and bite it.

I was jealous of those teeth. *I* wanted to be the one to do that.

"How is your body reacting?" I asked unable to help myself.

She sent me a smile and the magic around her disappeared. She held up her hand and in the very middle sprouted a flame, but it was no longer red. Instead it was a pure black that sucked the light from the surrounding areas into its body.

I had seen this once before, with her father.

"The flames of hell," she said with a slight laugh to her tone. "At least that's what Marques told me to call it."

I swallowed thickly.

"Your father called it that too," I said. "Sorry for the interruption but glad your body is adjusting okay."

"Me too," she said. "I was worried about my magic, but it seems normal."

"That's good," I said with a smile.

I liked this portion of our relationship. It was easy, simple. Though I wouldn't deny the pull I felt, especially when she gave me *that look*.

I would eat up every moment of my time here, even if it was on these conversations about nothing. As long as I could get this time, I would be happy and not try to push for anything more, even though my body had been pushing me to.

I had messed up quite a few times with her and now that we were so close to the end, a part of me was worried... But after remembering Rae's words, I also couldn't get the idea of her out of my head. So much so that I let Eli talk me into something completely insane, something that would make the way I viewed Rosie change forever.

Even with her so close to me, it was easy to get lost in my daydream of what I wished to do to her. I couldn't get those wide brown eyes out of my mind, couldn't get the way she was pressed up against that closet out of my mind, her pert nipples peeking out through the slits.

"I can't do it," Rosie said with a pout after trying once again to call on her magic.

I swallowed thickly, the air suddenly feeling much heavier than it had been.

"It takes time," I said in a light tone, not trying to discourage her.

"Malik." She turned to me with a serious face. The sweat that had once been a light sheen was now pouring down her face and her hair clung to her skin. "It has been weeks."

"It takes time," I repeated and tried not to watch as a stray drop of sweat fell down her face, following the curve of her neck and into her cleavage.

She moved to sit down on the ground next to me, her arm brushing mine.

I tried not to react as it sent a course of electricity through me.

God, she was so tempting.

"Tell me about school," I said, cringing as I realized how weird the words sounded.

She sent me a shit-eating grin as if she had the same thought.

"Yes, *Dad,*" she teased. The word caused my body to heat and I had to shift my gaze away from her.

"Behave," I growled.

She let out a heavy sigh.

"The low-levels are getting better," she said. "They just went through their first ranking."

I looked towards her with a raised brow.

"How did that go?" I asked.

Her smile dropped a bit.

"Many scored really low," she said.

"But that's normal, given their status, right?" I asked.

"Ya..." she trailed. "Except this one boy..."

She surprised me by leaning her head against my shoulder. I swallowed thickly and allowed myself a short inhale of her flowery scent before turning away.

Keep it in your pants for god's sake Malik, I cursed to myself.

"The boy?" I asked.

"Forget it," she said with a sigh. "Can we go to the beach again?"

My heart ached. I would love nothing more than to go and watch the waves lap the water at her feet until the sun set, but...

"It's not safe," I said.

"Nowhere but here is safe," she grumbled.

She wasn't wrong. There really wasn't a place where we were safe so long as Xena and Ezekiel stayed alive. Though they were probably just as scared as we were.

They were cowards who left their hybrid experiment running around without a leash. She was bound to tap into her full powers sooner or later and go hunt them down.

It was the cycle, yet no one but Rosie had the drive to do it just yet.

"Let's start again," I said.

She grumbled but moved so that she was sitting in front of me. Her forehead creased as she concentrated and I waited a few moments for her to gather her magic.

"Why is Claudine not teaching me this?" she asked.

I sent her a smile.

"Stop procrastinating," I said. She sent me a look and my heart warmed.

I watched as she let out a deep breath and straightened her spine. Her face took on a calm expression and her breathing evened out.

I had seen Claudine do this on more than one occasion, though I didn't know the point. It was stupid in my opinion even as Claudine insisted it did wonders, I never fully believed her. I thought it was just new-age bullshit...

And then I felt it.

My finger twitched on my right hand.

Then my arm lifted.

Her eyes shot open and a brilliant smile spread across her face as she realized it worked finally.

We started easy.

A curse that allowed someone to control another's movements. I had seen it used in many battles, cause many deaths, but it also was the easiest to control by Claudine's expertise.

She leaned forward, crawling towards me, and looked at my raised arm.

Today she was wearing her school uniform and the top buttons were unbuttoned enough that I had a perfect view of her lacy white bra which was now dampened with sweat.

I shuddered no longer able to keep the image of Eli fucking her out of my mind. She tried so hard to make sure she wasn't caught, but I heard it, *all of it.* And loved every dirty minute of it.

I loved knowing that she was getting railed behind that door to the image of me jerking off. Knowing that she wanted me so bad in that moment that she was willing to be fucked in a closet.

It was a stupid, stupid idea, I hissed in my mind as I felt myself harden.

Rae was right about one thing, the barrier between us would not last. I had dreamed of this moment, where I would finally get this spitfire under me. I watched in jealousy as the others wasted their time with her.

All I wanted was to take that beautiful face in my hands and force her lips to mine...but I couldn't do it. Couldn't move.

I watched as her throat constricted as she swallowed.

"Try again," I whispered in a husky voice. Her hooded eyes trailed to my lips and then lower and lower. "Try again."

This time I repeated it with a bit of my power mixed in.

"Damn you," she hissed.

"*This* is why I am here," I said. "Your magic knows what to do, you just have a mental block."

She smiled at me and I felt my body lean forward, towards her.

My pulse began to quicken, and my mouth watered when I realized what she was doing.

She stayed utterly still as I leaned forward, closer to her. I could feel her breath fan across my face and smell the sweet candy she must have had before this.

I wanted so badly to *taste* it.

"Practice is over," I said when I was just a hair's breadth away.

She let out a loud growl and stood, giving me a scowl as she did so. As she turned to walk away, I was flashed with white panties that matched her bra.

She fucking came prepared, I realized and groaned internally.

I RAN to catch up to Rosie as she stormed through Winterfell campus.

It was dark and she didn't want to wait for the others to finish their training. Instead she demanded that I take her back that instant.

She was running away, putting herself at risk all because I rejected her back at the hideout.

Anger coursed through me at her idiocy.

The Originals were still out there and she had the audacity to make me chase her down. Did she not realize that they could be hiding anywhere, Winterfell included?

"Rosie," I called and followed her through the small intricate paths she took me on.

I thought I knew Winterfell pretty well but as she led me through turn after turn, I had to admit that I was completely lost.

She stopped dead in her tracks when we finally reached a small clearing where the purple rose bushes had far outgrown their normal height.

She turned to face me; her face was stone cold and her shoulders were squared.

I didn't like that look one bit, but I was too angry to think anything of it.

"You reckless demon," I growled and infused every word with

my power. "Listen to me and go back to your fucking dorm, *now.*"

With jerky movements she walked towards me and then took a sharp left.

"I fucked Eli in your closet," she yelled.

"Stop," I commanded. Her body obeyed.

All of the anger and frustration was beginning to be too much. I couldn't sit there and think about disciplining her while she brought *that* up knowing how bad I wanted to brush it from my mind, but couldn't.

That image of her would be the death of me and I felt it tearing at the seams of my control.

If I was any less of a demon I would make her submit right there where she stood and fuck her senselessly against the wall until she was screaming for mercy.

Teach her some respect.

Damnit all, I groaned internally. *Why couldn't she keep this to herself?*

It would have been much easier if she just listened, and silently went to her dorm. The consequences of her being angry at me was something I could deal with...but this went way farther than I was capable of handling.

"After you showered," she said. "I saw you—"

"I know," I admitted.

Her head whipped to the side to give me a shocked look.

"You know?" she asked.

"Rosie," I growled and walked towards her. She was still frozen in her spot and I used her stillness to trail my hand lightly on her shoulder. "I *fucking* saw you through the slits in the closet door."

Her face turned a bright red before looking at her feet. I ate up the facade in front of me knowing there was a spitfire just waiting to break free.

"Where did that fight go, hm?" I asked in a low voice and

tugged on the end of her hair. "Embarrassed that you're caught in a lie? Or embarrassed I caught you being railed by Eli?"

"Why didn't you say anything?" she asked.

I walked around her so that I could stand in front of her, our chests mere inches apart. I trailed a single finger underneath her chin and forced it up so that she had to look me in the eyes.

Watching her stew in her own shame shouldn't have been as enjoyable as it was, but sure enough I felt myself harden and this time I was so close it brushed against her stomach.

I let out a content sigh and leaned closer to her, our lips once again centimeters apart. I couldn't control myself anymore. Each moment it was like I was fighting against my own restraints but instead of chains, they felt more like flimsy strings, just willing me to give in. Begging me to take her.

"Because I wanted to see how you would react when I was around," I whispered.

Her mouth opened slightly. The tension between us was so thick it was overwhelming.

The year's worth of electricity between us was putting me on edge and I was beginning to shake just from the intensity of it.

I was so close I could taste the sweetness of her on my tongue and wondered how her pussy would taste. Wondered how she would feel as I fucked her late into the night, not letting her go until all these months of waiting had finally been accounted for.

"I wanted to see how many times you looked at me." I tilted my head and lightly licked her bottom lip which she immediately brought back into her mouth, sucking my taste off her. "And imagined being fucked by me. Even with everyone around. Acting like the innocent girl you pretend to be, but inside you are like a dog in heat panting for a good fuck."

Her eyes flashed in anger and a scandalized gasp left her mouth.

"There she is," I cooed and gripped her chin. "Do you ever get tired of pretending? You really thought that if you stormed out of there, that it would be the thing I needed to give you this?"

I pushed my swollen cock against her letting out a groan.

"You're fucking—"

"What?" I asked dangerously and pulled her lip into my mouth before tugging on it. When I let go her eyes were once again alight with the anger I loved so much. "Use your words like a big girl."

"Nothing," she said with a smirk. "I was just curious, but it seems I will be left with another disappointment."

Her eyes trailed down my body and when she reached the obvious erection pushing against my jeans she let out an exaggerated sigh.

It was all I needed to push me forward.

"You are so cocky now," I said and gripped her chin harshly. "We have to fix that don't we?"

She rolled her eyes.

"I don't want your puny dick," she hissed.

I chuckled. She wanted to act like she wasn't as affected as I was? Like she wasn't begging me to take her?

She had another thing coming and there was one thing I knew for certain... I was much more cruel than Eli.

"I'll give you one chance to take that back," I said in a low voice. "And *trust me,* you won't like what I have in store for you."

Her jaw clenched and her hands balled into fists at her side.

"*Fuck you*," she growled. "You don't get to berate me and treat me like I am lower than you. You can do whatever and I won't care. Make me kneel again, *just see* how that ends up for you."

"Oh no, I have much worse for you," I said and leaned back to look in her eyes. "You can't come until I say so."

Her mouth dropped open as she felt my power wash through her.

"You didn't," she gasped.

"Maybe when you have learned how to control your attitude," I said and took a step back. "Maybe I will forgive you."

"Malik my magic—"

"Will be fine," I growled. "Now march that bratty ass of yours back to your dorm room."

She let out a loud groan as my power worked through her.

"Come to me when you have less of an attitude," I called after her and chuckled when she flipped me off.

I would be lying if I said I didn't find this game of ours the best I ever played.

18
ELI

The familiar itch was back again.

It started from the base of my spine and trailed up to my head.

It made me want to rip my fucking skin off. Made me want to destroy everything and anything in my path. I didn't care who or what it was, but I needed *something* to get rid of this fucking feeling or I was bound to go crazy.

It made my blood boil, my teeth ache, and my legs restless.

It was pure boredom and it grated my nerves until they are overstimulated and sent jolts through my body.

"Is that all you can manage?" Matt asked me, his voice cutting through my concentration.

It was my task from Marques to try and make the images he was seeing in his head as real feeling as possible and right now we were cycling through a few of my favorite scenes, one of which involved him being torn in pieces by many horses.

This was the stupid training I had to deal with. It did nothing and was probably just an excuse to watch us and make sure we weren't off doing anything that would call unwanted attention to us.

I had foolishly thought that working with Marques would

give me more freedom, but I found myself just as confined as with the other Originals.

In times like these where I was trapped like a wild animal and had no other place to turn to get rid of my boredom...it called for drastic measures.

"Shut up," I growled and squeezed his shoulder harshly in warning.

We had tried before to do this from afar, without touching, but Marques's blood had yet to affect my power all that much yet.

Another fucking failure.

"Let's take a break," Marques said from behind me.

Marques's manor had become a hot spot for us, and we were dragged here every time they decided we needed to test the limits of our power. And instead of a nicely cleaned and comfy space for us to practice, they had put us in the ballroom, and had us sit on the dirty floor like peasants. I looked to Rae to see how she was holding up under these inhumane conditions and noted her stoic expression.

Of course she wouldn't outwardly show her disgust, not when someone like Marques was around her. She had a thing for keeping up appearances and even that was another thing that got on my nerves.

Matt stood up and pushed my hand off his shoulder with a smirk, before walking to the other side of the room. I gritted my teeth as I watched him stretch his arms and back like he had been doing all the hard work when in reality, he just sat here and made snide comments.

He knew what he was doing.

When his eyes met mine and that knowing smirk made its way to his face, I knew that he specifically was sent to torture me. I should have known it when I first met him; no one was that happy and bubbly and now that his facade was gone, he was filling with a disgusting amount of cockiness for someone of his genetic heritage.

He had made this whole training even worse than it already was with his comments and stares. For some reason, Marques wouldn't let Matt out of his sight so we were forced to interact with him.

I was ready to break out of this training. It was useless. I didn't *need* any training to strangle that bastard of a demon. All I needed was alone time and enough of a window to tear his head off.

Much like how I wanted to do to Matt.

I let him sit for a few minutes while I listened to Marques's teachings.

"Your mother had this ability," he said to Rae. "And I have seen it in you too."

"No one in my family inherited her power," Rae said with conviction.

"Don't be so sure," he said.

There was a pause before Rae went back to her training.

"Don't see them as your own emotions, child," he said in a softer tone than I had heard him use before. "You feel mine, use those instead. Bend them to your will. You are not trying to push your own emotions onto me but change the ones I already have."

Not being able to stand the dullness anymore I walked over to the space Matt was currently occupying.

His brow lifted.

"I may have something interesting for you to see if you meet me at Winterfell tomorrow," I said in a low voice and leaned against the wall, my gaze shifting to his.

He looked to Marques with a blank expression.

"What are you playing?" he asked.

"Nothing," I lied. "I have just...come to some terms with some things."

He looked me up and down, taking his time to answer.

"Why would I trust you?" he asked.

"You don't trust *me*," I said and smirked. "Trust that I am bored."

His eyes lit up and I knew I had already caught my prey.

"5 a.m. inside the new tower," he said.

"Deal," I said and pushed off the wall.

Marques gave me a look as I passed him and I felt the intrusion of him in my mind before I heard it.

You are playing a dangerous game, he warned. *Actions like these have consequences, ones that can hurt you and your loved ones.*

I scoffed aloud before continuing across the room and sitting back down next to Rae for the remainder of my training.

❧

I DIDN'T EVEN SLEEP that night in preparation for this meeting.

I was too excited about what awaited me to even attempt to, and of course I needed to be wide awake for this.

When I finally snuck into the tower I leaned against the cool brick and lit up a cigarette.

This tower had finally been erected with barely any time to spare before the semester started, and now it was as if Rosie and Daxton never went on their rampage to begin with.

Learning about their own boredom never failed to amuse me. They were more like me than they wanted to admit, but I saw through them. I read their minds and knew that just like me, they wanted something more from this world. They couldn't stand the boring Winterfell Academy life. They didn't want to sit in class with a fake teacher and learn about things that would never benefit them after they graduated.

They wanted to explore. Test the boundaries. And fight against the world that damned them.

Which is exactly what I planned to do.

The morning air was cool and the sun hadn't even begun to rise. There was a silence that fell across Winterfell as everyone slept soundly in their beds, dead to the world and unknowingly sleeping through what was about to be the greatest experiment I have ever run.

A shiver of excitement ran up my spine and I couldn't wait to find Rosie after this. She would see the real monster after this. I had nothing to hold back anymore, she accepted this part of me and tonight... I planned to show her in detail what it was really like to pair with a monster like me.

I felt the flurry of his mind before he showed up. I could just barely hear his thoughts and smiled when I found out he was just as excited as he was suspicious of my motives.

He too was bored and hoping for something to move along his plans. Though I was not privy to what those plans entailed, I reveled in his thoughts nonetheless.

"I feel you," I said aloud.

His curly head popped into the opening of Winterfell tower, mostly shrouded in darkness except for the red light of the torch that was placed above the door.

"You came prepared," he said noting the light.

"Of course," I replied.

He stepped in fully and looked around the place with his hands in the pockets of his hoodie. When his eyes finally landed on me I couldn't help but smirk.

"So, what is it you wanted to show me?" he asked.

His thoughts became clearer then, cutting through the night.

He was hoping I had some secret... A secret he could use against Marques and Malik.

"Malik has been on my nerves recently," I said with a sigh. His face lit up as I played into his little fantasy. "Marques too, I just don't want to follow old senile men anymore."

I wondered if said old senile man was listening to my thoughts now. Wondering if he was panicking while listening to what I was going to do.

Matt let out a small chuckle.

"Is this the boredom you were talking about?" he asked.

"Something like that," I muttered and inhaled my cigarette.

I held out my free hand to him; he did not move from his spot.

"You think I'm stupid?" he asked. "Don't think for a second I trust you."

"And you shouldn't think for a second that I trust you," I growled. "I just want to be aware of eavesdroppers."

He shifted on his feet, taking far too long to decide whether or not he was going to go through with it.

"And what about Marques?" he asked. "He can hear you can't he?"

But not you, I thought in a smug tone. *Because he refused you, didn't he?*

"What can he do?" I asked with a small chuckle. "Come kill me?"

I heard his indecisiveness. Heard how worried he was that this was a trap and that he should turn and leave right this second before things got out of hand.

But it was the curiosity that pulled him back to me. After all, what could Eli possibly want to tell Matt? The one person I seemed to hate the most.

I ate all the thoughts up hungrily.

"What the hell," he muttered and walked towards me.

At least if worst comes to worst, I can erase her memory, he thought.

I smiled at his idiocy.

Just a few nights before, Rosie had a wonderful surprise for us that involved a tattoo parlor and a bit of magic. There would be no memory loss even if he tried.

His slimy hand clasped mine and I immediately used all my strength to crush the bones in his hands before that pesky power of his could start to work.

He fell to the ground with a yell, his face twisting into an ugly snarl.

I took the cigarette and forced it into his open mouth and let go of his hand to send a punch to his jaw.

I had to be quick or else those *stupid* plants would come after me in a moment.

When he hit the ground I was surprised he didn't get back up.

I hesitated for a moment, listening for thoughts...but there were none.

I let out a laugh and stalked to the dark corner of the tower where all my supplies were stocked.

I made quick work of gathering them before turning back to the unconscious hybrid.

"Too easy," I said with a laugh.

I regretted those words as soon as a body slammed me to the ground and a fist connected with my cheek.

I flailed to catch the fists flying at me.

"I knew you were full of shit," Matt hissed at me.

I felt the vines of his power trail around my torso and up my chest. I panicked and shot my hand out to grab hold of his neck and flip us.

The sun was just starting to slip through the cracks of the tower and I caught a full look at his anger-filled face.

Fucking bitch, I am going to bring her to Xena and Ezekiel and watch as they skin her alive, his thoughts rang out loud and clear in my mind.

I tightened my hold on his neck, his mouth gasped open as he was trying to pull air into his lungs, but it was useless. His vines fought to reach my neck but they slowed as his consciousness was ripped from him.

When at last, his lids fluttered closed, I rolled off his body and dove for my ropes.

I made quick work of hog-tying him.

When I successfully tied him together I rummaged around in my bag and a crazed laugh left my mouth as I brought out my favorite new human gadget.

I didn't even wait until he had a chance to wake up. I shifted the plastic box in my hand and aimed it right at his back. Two strings shot out and embedded into his back. I watched in fascination as they lit up as if infused with magic and his body jerked to life.

His scream echoed through the tower and after a few seconds I turned it off and listened carefully.

His curses were hard to drown out but once I did I smiled as his thoughts began to push to the surface. They were clearer than I had ever heard before.

They were trying to escape, as if they wanted me to hear them... They just needed a little help.

A little push.

I turned it on again, the flashing magical lights hitting him in the back. His body went stiff, his screams silenced by the intensity.

When I turned it off next, his entire body fell limp.

With a scowl I discarded that toy and moved on to my favorite.

With a knife in hand I bent down near Matt and ran the dull side up his arm, making sure not to touch him with my hands. He was unresponsive.

"Come on, Matt," I provoked. "Where is that fight of yours?"

When he didn't answer I dug the tip into his arm.

His eyes shot open and I felt the vines of his magic weakly prod at my sides.

If I don't get out of here soo—

"You will die, yes," I cooed. "That's the point."

"I thought you said his blood—"

"Didn't work, right well," I interrupted and dragged the knife down his arm. "I found pain." I twisted the knife, enjoying the way his screams filled the empty air. "And fear, helps a bit."

His thoughts were so vivid in the moment a sick satisfaction filled my body.

I needed to signal them quickly, he thought. I saw the image of him sending out a shot of magic to signal his precious Originals and without hesitation I dug the knife into his skin deeper than before.

"Well, I guess I got my answer," I said with a sigh of disappointment. I wanted to play with him longer. Make him scream just like I had with Damon...but I guess I just had to wait for Rosie.

I removed the knife and threw my leg over his back. One had threaded through his hair pulling his head back so his neck was bare and ready for me. The other held the knife.

"Any last words?" I asked and prepped the knife at his throat.

"We are going to make you pay," he spat. "There are people on our side just waiting for a chance to scoop Rosie up and I swear to you we will skin her and send her bones back to you in a box but not before we test that tight—"

The rest became garbled as I ran the knife across his throat, his skin splitting open as easy as cutting butter.

I let go of his hair and he fell face-first into the ground.

It wasn't long before he drowned in his own blood. I sat next to him enjoying the images that were pouring out of his mind. They were mostly memories and now I understood when people talked about their last moments flashing before their eyes as their life slipped from their body.

I did see pictures of him and his siblings but I was surprised to see Rosie as well, during the time when they first came to Winterfell.

He had been happy then as well, oddly enough.

He liked the carefree version of himself. Free from burden and able to enjoy a life that he never had before. He felt like a real college student with her and wished that he could have stayed her friend just a bit longer before the whole thing blew up in his face.

Pulling out my phone I called Malik.

"It's too early to be hearing from you," Malik groaned from the other line. His voice was heavy with sleep.

"The spy was Matt," I told him and threw the bloodied knife into my bag of tools.

"How did you—*tell me you fucking didn't Eli.*" Malik's voice rose in pitch and I couldn't help but laugh.

"Someone had to," I said playfully. "Now come be useful and clean up for me, will ya? Winterfell Tower."

I heard a few curses from the other end.

"I will go wake Rae," he said with a groan. "Stay there, I will need your clothes."

"No," I growled. "I am going to visit Rosie."

"You most certainly *will not!*" Malik yelled. "Stay there or I swear to you I will lock you in Winterfell's jail myself."

"I didn't know Winterfell had a jail," I mused.

"Shut the fuck up Eli," he growled. "You fucked up, real bad and you better hope Claudine doesn't come after your ass."

"The seer?" I asked. "She can't do shit to me."

"God damnit Eli," Malik groaned. I heard a door slam. "Stay there, I will be there in ten."

❧

I DIDN'T STAY, obviously.

Right after I hung up the phone I waltzed out of the tower.

It was still too early for the students to be out so I was able to freely walk around campus, even with the hybrid's blood staining my clothes.

I walked back to my dorm, showered, and changed clothes, discarding the other ones in the trash can before leaving to find Rosie.

An unbearable heat had settled deep in my belly. I wasn't anywhere near satisfied with killing Matt.

He had been but a small annoyance in the grand scheme of things... The person I really wanted?

Sarah.

That fucking disgrace of a demon was next on my list and I couldn't wait until my present was delivered to me, and if

Marques took any longer, then I would be forced to take it into my own hands.

On my way to Rosie's dorm I was stopped in my tracks as Daxton left his dorm. He gave me a shocked look.

"You're up early," he noted.

I simply nodded and ran my eyes down his form.

He was dressed in a hoodie and jeans, obviously not ready to go to school.

"Are you sneaking out?" I asked.

He gave me a sheepish look and ran a hand through his hair.

"I wanted to see Rosie," he admitted. I let a smile form on my face.

"Me too, though I was thinking..." I trailed and his eyes lit up. "Maybe we can spice it up a little?"

His excited thoughts buzzed around me.

"Fuck ya we can spice it up," he said.

With a laugh I led him down the empty hallway.

My blood was already pumping but instead of the crazed feeling taking over me, I felt a sort of calm wash over me.

My head was clear, my rage had subsided, and I felt invincible.

When we reached Rosie's dorm I didn't hesitate to break the lock for the second time.

"Maybe she will just finally stay with us after this," Daxton joked. "I don't even know why she even tried to have her own place. She spends most of the time in our dorm anyways."

I let out a noise of agreement and stepped into the dark room.

As my eyes adjusted I noted a lone figure sitting up on the bed.

The anger that was a mere shadow of itself came back with a roar when golden eyes met mine.

"You are far too predictable, Eli," Malik chided.

He stood to his full height and looked both of us over with obvious distaste.

"Where is Rosie?" Daxton asked, anger and a bit of panic seeping into his voice.

Malik cocked his head.

"Ask Eli," he said. "They were the ones that fucked this up."

I felt Daxton's eyes on me.

"What do you mean?" he asked. "Just tell me where Rosie is, you fuck. I don't trust you and I am not above calling for the others."

Malik let out a laugh and shook his head, his white curls bouncing with each shake.

Daxton's thoughts were worried. He thought Malik had taken her, done something horrible to her. His mind went in a spiral...

All while Malik's thoughts stayed on me.

His were far clearer than they ever have been, giving me a rare look at the inside of his mind.

He saw me as a coward. As unhinged. He was angry...but also disappointed.

"*I* did good work," I growled. "He was a rat and was obviously going to hurt Rosie. And I *know* he was the one who caused the refugees' death. You should be thankful that I did the job you couldn't bring yourself to do."

There was a pause as Malik looked me over.

"I knew," he said.

"You knew what?" Daxton asked. "Eli? What happened?"

I ignored him even as his hand cupped my shoulder.

"You knew and you let him put us in danger?" I asked.

Why a hypocrite, I thought angrily. *These people act like I am the bad one here when they were putting our lives in danger the entire time!*

"It's not that simple, Eli," he said in a soft tone that only made me angrier. "There is more to this than you think. You can't just go murdering people. Especially those who have ties to Xena and Ezekiel, we told you we were going to give you Sarah, why couldn't you jus—"

"Why can't you just tell us the truth?" I growled. "If you knew he was a traitor why didn't you say anything?"

"Eli—" Daxton started but was interrupted by a voice coming from the hallways behind us.

"What is going on here?" Amr's deep sleep-ridden voice came. "Students will wake soon and I can hear you from down the hall."

"God damn it," Malik growled and ran and hand through his hair. "Rosie will be staying with me and Rae from now on, and Eli..."

"Don't you act like you're in charge here," I hissed and stepped towards him.

"Stop and stay there until I am out of range," he said, his voice threaded with power. My feet froze to the ground, stopping me in my tracks. "You will not be allowed near the house until you can control yourself. Rosie will be escorted by me when she is in school and if you kill another person—"

"I am going to fucking kill you," I growled and tried to grab him but he was just far enough out of reach that my fingers brushed the fabric of his shirt.

"If you kill another person I will see to it to have you punished," he said. "And not by me."

By me, Marques's voice warned in my head. *I told you this action would have consequences, child.*

Malik took a long look at me before passing me, his shoulder bumping into mine on purpose.

I turned to catch Daxton's hand grabbing the front of Malik's shirt. Malik's hand slammed into the side of Daxton's head and pushed him away.

Amr let out a growl and stood up to him next.

"Regardless of what Eli has done you cannot—"

"I can," Malik interrupted in a low, dangerous tone. A chill fell over the room, one that I hadn't felt in a long, long time. Malik was angry, but not in the explosive type way that we had seen since working with him, but in a cold calculated way.

This was that Malik that scared me when I was younger, this was the Malik that earned my respect. Grown demons would cower in fear when Malik's stone-cold face was shown, and this time I knew he was not joking around.

"You better hope this issue ends here, Eli," Malik threatened. "Because if it doesn't... I am not sure we have a chance of winning this war."

There was no other push to stop him from leaving. Both Daxton and Amr were silent and finally after what seemed like forever my muscles relaxed and I could move.

"Eli..." Amr said in a low voice. "Who did you kill?"

I turned to face his accusing stare.

"The fucking rat," I hissed. "Matt."

Amr's eyes widened and his gaze shot to Daxton whose gaze was currently fixed on me.

"He was for sure on their side?" Daxton asked.

Anger and betrayal flooded my senses.

"How long have you known me?" I growled. "Why are you acting like I fucked up? *I* eliminated a threat, he was thinking of signaling them to come to Winterfell—"

"Did he ever say that he was on their side?" Amr asked. "Did he ever tell you why?"

Swallowing my urge to fight I pushed past both of them and left the dorms without a look back.

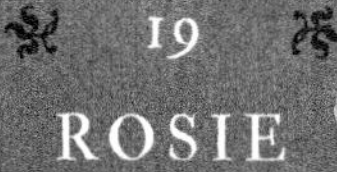

19
ROSIE

Being woken up by shaking hands was not the best way to welcome the day...

Nor was being magically transported to Rae's house at an ungodly hour, with everyone panicking around me.

It was Malik who had awoken me from my slumber and it was a shock to see him in my bedroom. The last time I had spoken to him was almost a week before, when we had an explosive argument that led to him rejecting me—*again.*

So to see those golden eyes over me in the middle of the night, I was sure it was a wet dream.

But he quickly shot that down when he forced me to get up, explaining that I needed to leave Winterfell right this instant and Claudine would be taking me to Rae's house.

I had mere minutes to come to my senses before Claudine appeared and in a flash of light I was pulled in all different directions only to land right in the middle of Rae's foyer.

She had sweats and a hoodie on, her hair was a mess around her head, and she was missing her glasses. I was shocked to see the missing glasses but was quickly pulled out of my awe by their conversation.

"Malik will be back soon," Claudine said. "Maximus and I will clean up and…" Her voice became thick. "Hold a funeral." Her eyes lingered on my face before she disappeared in a flash of light.

"Rae, what is—"

"We are not going to school today," she said in a grave tone. Her hazel eyes searched my frame and with a small frown her arm wrapped around my shoulders and she steered me to the stairs.

Panic and fear clawed my throat. A funeral? Clean up? Who died?

"Rae, please," I said and gripped her hoodie forcing us to a stop. "Please tell me it wasn't one of the others. Amr, Daxton, Eli? Are they okay?"

She paused, and my mind went to the worst.

"It's not them, just…" She let out a heavy sigh. "Please, let's get you warm and back into bed. I will explain in a bit."

"I don't want to go to bed!" I yelled. "No more secrets remember?"

She swallowed and her tongue shot out to wet her lips.

She was stalling.

Rae didn't stall. Rae always knew what to do and what to say. She was the one who had everything together and helped us through this shit show of life… What could make her change so drastically?

"I don't want to chance your magic going crazy," she said and started pulling me up the stairs. "You can rest easy knowing that Amr, Daxton, and Eli are not hurt and are fine at Winterfell."

A part of me did calm at the thought of them being safe, or it could have been Rae's power worming its way into me. But that still didn't answer the question and knowing that, my magic may go crazy.

Anger boiled under the surface. They were secret-keeping again, though this time it was important enough to drag me from Winterfell in the middle of the night and hide me miles away.

"I need to know, Rae," I growled, though I didn't stop her from leading me to her room.

I knew it was hers by the decoration. Everything was in dark greens and satins. It smelled fresh, like the shampoos she had back at the dorm.

"I know," she said in a slightly annoyed tone. "I don't know much either if I am being honest. I just know the bare minimum, I am still awaiting details. Let me get you some clothes."

I had to bite my lip to keep from fighting with her. She left my side and disappeared into her closet to come out with a large sweatshirt and some sweats that would have to be tied at the waist.

"The bathroom is over there," she said and motioned to the other side of the room but I had already started undressing, taking my tank top off in one motion.

"Nothing you haven't seen before," I said with a smirk and grabbed the sweatshirt from her hands first. The cold air had hit my upper body and I could feel my nipples harden. By the look on Rae's face she had noted it too.

"What are you trying to do?" she asked.

"Change," I said and pulled the sweatshirt over my head. Next I dropped my shorts and hurried to put pants on my freezing legs.

"Rosie, I thin—"

The door to her room burst open and I saw Malik standing there in all his glory, a cold expression on his face.

That expression caused the blood to pump harder in my veins and I felt the already chilly room drop a few degrees.

"Did you know?" Malik asked and crossed the room towards us.

I turned and stepped back only to run into Rae's front. Her hands grasped my shoulders and pulled me closer to her.

"You're scaring her, stop," Rae growled as Malik came to a stop in front of us. He looked down at me with more anger than I had ever seen. "Of course she didn't know."

"What happened?" I asked. "Why did you guys—"

He cut off my words by grabbing my face with one hand.

"Rosie, you better not be lying to me because if you knew this was going to happen, I cannot go lenient on you," he warned.

Fear settled in my belly, but also something else. Something darker. My neglected magic thrashed inside me, unable to get out.

It was angry, it was tired, it was panicked, and most of all...it was *famished.*

"Stop, this isn't the time Malik," Rae said. "Her magic cannot handle this and I am afraid..."

"That she'll blow up the god damn house again?" Malik asked, his eyes traveling above my head, presumably to meet Rae's gaze.

"You know the situation," she said. "We don't have the liberty to afford these repairs right now."

Repairs on Rae's house? What, they were having issues with money?

My thoughts were shaken as Malik's molten gaze met mine and his hand squeezed my face harder.

"When was the last time you shared magic?" he asked.

I used all my strength to smack his hand off my face, enjoying the way his eyes lit up with anger.

"Not since before you fucking took away my ability to come," I growled. "I tried to blood let but it only made me weak and my magic angry. I tried with Amr's help but I *can't do it* and it's your *fucking fault.*"

"Are you kidding me?" Rae growled.

Malik's face twitched and I saw a glimpse of what looked like regret.

"Are you sure bloodletting didn't work?" he asked.

"This is my magic, you really think I am that fucking stupid?" I hissed.

I wanted so badly to pounce on him but my magic was stopping me; it was waiting politely to see what Malik would do. It was excited at the prospect of being so close to these two and wanted so badly to take things further.

It had lost all the panic and fear and was now raging and clouded by lust.

"You let her go a week without sharing magic?" Rae asked. "I thought you were smart but you are just as reckless as the others."

Malik's gaze shifted to hers and there was a pause between the two.

"I think I am going to do something she won't like," Malik said.

"I highly advise you don't," Rae said, her hands wrapping around my front and pulling me closer into her. "Give me some time, I can help her with her magic."

Yes, my magic purred.

"No time," he said. "We need to do this fast and now before it becomes bigger."

His hand gripped my face once more and I saw his eyes light up with something dark.

"Malik," Rae warned.

"Rosie," he said his voice dropping low and I could feel the power radiating from his chest. "Come."

I couldn't even look away if I tried. My entire body froze and in an instant an intense heat filled my body, gathering deep in my belly. I couldn't stop the whine as I felt my pussy throb with a sudden orgasm. It was intense, and I had to grip onto Malik's arm to steady myself.

Even without being touched it had felt just the same as any other orgasm and I found myself beginning to shake as my neglected magic began swirling inside me.

But...it didn't escape.

Even as I shook against Rae's hold, my orgasm drawing out moans from my mouth, it stayed put...but boy was it hungry.

Shame and embarrassment filled me as Malik watched me

come down off of the orgasm. I wanted him, badly, but never thought it would be like this. I imagined us hate fucking against a wall after I pushed him one too many times, or on my knees as he fucked my face...but not this.

"It didn't work," Rae muttered from above me.

"Fuck you," I hissed.

Malik growled at me, his eyes flashing.

"*Again,*" he commanded.

"I swear to god Mal—" My protests were cut off by a sharp spike of pleasure running through me. My hips began bucking wildly as the heat rose in me and just like before I found myself falling over the edge without a single touch from the two.

I could feel the wetness that was accumulating between my thighs and I rubbed them together as the aftershocks of the orgasm rocked my body.

"Useless," Rae muttered and removed Malik's hand from my face so she could force me to look up at her. Shame filled me violently and I felt awfully exposed.

I didn't want Rae to think I wasn't trying, and I wouldn't want to cause her any more trouble. I didn't know much about her situation, but from the simple sentence I could glean that it wasn't ideal.

"I'm sorry I—"

"Not you," she whispered in a soothing tone. "I feel you, understand you. You just need a little help. Will you let me help you?"

If I wasn't wet before her words definitely had an effect on my body.

"Yes," I whispered. "Please help me."

"I am not much for group things," she whispered and leaned down to nip at my bottom lip. "But I will make an exception for you."

"Rae, I—"

"Let's teach Malik how you liked to be touched, hm?" she asked.

"I don't need to be taught how to touch a woman," Malik growled. His hands grabbed my hips and pulled them to his.

I let out a strangled moan when I felt his erection grind into me. My magic was going positively feral no matter how mad I was at him.

"You can't rush things," Rae said and then planted another kiss on my lips before removing her hands and lifting my sweater, exposing my bare chest to Malik.

I flushed and closed my eyes, not liking the attention on me.

Rae's two fingers pushed past my lips and I began to suck on them, heat filling my body as I felt Malik's hands trail from my hips to my stomach.

I was shivering between the two now, and it had nothing to do with the cold.

Rae may have been onto something about taking it slow, but I have never yearned more for their hands on me than right in this moment.

"Take her pants off," Rae commanded.

"You're lucky I have been waiting a lifetime for this, because if I hadn't I would have kicked you out by now," he growled, but his hands slipped into the waistband of my pants and began pulling them down. Only then did I peek and look at him through my lashes.

My stomach clenched when his golden eyes met mine. He started to kneel down with the pants and didn't stop until he was eye level with my swollen pussy.

The air hit my wetness and I shivered when he gave me a predatory look before ripping my pants off and throwing them across the room. Rae's wet fingers traveled from my mouth to my nipple where she pinched one lightly between her fingers.

A light moan came from my mouth but I couldn't take my eyes away from Malik, especially not as he took one of my legs and picked it over his shoulder and stared at my throbbing pussy. His stare darkened and I felt myself get wetter under it. Rae's hand traveled down my stomach and to my lips where she pulled them apart, giving Malik a perfect view of my sopping wet hole.

I threw my head back as those same fingers came to circle my clit.

"Now," Rae commanded, her free hand forcing me to look at Malik.

His golden eyes met mine while he leaned closer to my folds.

"Come," he whispered, his hot breath fanning across my wetness.

I couldn't keep his stare as the violent orgasm ripped through me. I threw my head back against Rae's chest and shook as a tingling heat spread through me.

My magic exploded around me, filling the room with red sparkles. It was a weight off my chest and I felt like *finally* I was no longer being held hostage by my magic...but I was far from done.

"God," Malik moaned, his tongue licking up my inner thigh. "Please let me taste."

I shuddered at the hunger in his voice. Rae's hand moved from my pussy and she grabbed my hand only to thread it through Malik's messy white hair.

"Do you want him to taste you, Rosie?" she asked. "It would be cruel to deny him at this point."

I gripped Malik's hair and pulled him closer to where I was aching for him.

"Please," I whispered.

He wasted no time, his tongue licking up the length of my folds slowly before pulling my clit into his mouth and sucking.

"That's it," Rae coaxed, her voice in a low whisper. She left kisses down the side of my face. "Do you like this, Rosie?"

"I do, I do," I gasped as he sucked once more on my clit. He let out a groan that vibrated against my lips.

"Tell him," she whispered. "Tell him how much you have wanted him to do this to you."

"Fuck I—" Malik cut me off by inserting two fingers into me

while still sucking on my clit. I bucked against his hand and Rae's hands fastened around my hips to stop my movements. "I wanted you so bad, Malik."

I was rewarded with a groan and he began to thrust his fingers into me.

"Say you wanted to come on his mouth," Rae commanded. Her tone was strong yet soft at the same time. I had no choice but to comply.

"I wanted to—*ah god.*" Malik sucked on my clit in hard intervals pulling sobs out of my shaking mouth. "Come on your mouth."

"Seems like you are almost there," Rae said and ground my hips against Malik's face causing sharp bolts of pleasure to run through me.

"I am, *I am,*" I moaned as once more magic rose up inside me. "Harder, Malik, *please.*"

His fingers pounded into me harder and with each suck on my clit I found myself hurdling faster towards my orgasm. A bright red light flashed through the room and I shuddered against Rae as I came.

Malik dropped my leg and stood, his lips crashing to mine. As his tongue sunk into my mouth I could taste my own release.

His free hand began to undo the button of his pants, then he paused and pulled away. There was an unreadable expression on his face.

"*Shit,* I am sorry Rosie," he said his tone heavy. "I took this too far. It's not..."

"Appropriate," Rae finished for him.

My stomach dropped. Did this mean he didn't want me? That he didn't want to touch me that way?

"We need to talk about—"

"I will tell her while we clean up," Rae said. "Just...go get a hold of yourself, and be ready because we will both have questions."

I watched as Malik's throat bobbed. Wordlessly he leaned

down and stole another kiss from me, leaving Rae and me alone in the room.

"Let's go take a bath shall we?" she asked in a light voice.

I swallowed thickly and looked up at her.

"It's bad, isn't it?" I asked.

She gave me a pitiful look.

"I really hope you don't blow up this house," she said. "But yes, it is bad."

"Are you...having problems with money?" I ask.

She sent me a strained smile.

"A topic for another time," she said and ushered me into the bathroom. "Your magic feels better, though I do wish we had a witch to take more of it."

Her bathroom was even bigger than in the other house and had a big jacuzzi tub.

"Are Amr and Daxton not able to come?" I asked.

She left my side to turn on the tub. I watched as she meticulously poured in shimmering powders and swirled it around.

"It's magical," she explained, avoiding my question. "It has healing properties and the person who I got it from told me it helps curb magic, though I don't know how true that is."

My chest felt tight.

"You got this for me?" I asked.

Another unanswered question. She motioned for me to get in and slowly started undressing, joining me in the tub as well.

"You know if my magic goes crazy, this is a horrible place to be," I said.

"That's why I will tell you after we get out," she replied and stepped into the tub only to pull me against her.

Her hand came to massage my scalp and I relaxed into her.

"Listen Rosie," she said her voice trailing. "You're going to have to stay here for a while."

I nodded into her chest and let out a sigh.

"I don't mind," I said. "The others will come soon right? It would be nice if they could all have their own rooms. They deserve better than Winterfell dorms."

As I sunk further into the bath I could feel the light vibrations of the magical powder start to sink into my skin. My already somewhat satiated magic began to calm further and I felt my body get heavy.

"Daxton and Amr may be able to come soon once we gather the facts," she said. "But Eli..."

I shot up and turned to her. Her face was expressionless and my stomach filled with lead.

Hold a funeral... Claudine's voice rang through my head.

"Eli is fine though you said," I said, my heart beating faster. "Why would Claudine mention... *Oh god.*"

Murder was not something new to this group but...who exactly did Eli murder?

"For your safety we removed you because Eli wasn't in the right—"

"Eli wouldn't hurt me," I interrupted.

How could they think they would ever hurt me? Eli wasn't a good person, nor did I try to kid myself into thinking they were, but I knew they wouldn't hurt me *like that.*

Rae's lips turned down.

"You don't know that," Rae said. "They compromised us all by their actions and even though they were warned not to do it, they still went and did it anyways."

"Just tell me," I begged. "Please Rae."

She studied me carefully.

"They killed Matt," she said in a voice barely above a whisper.

20
RAE

I expected rage. Blinding fury that threatened to destroy not only the structure we were in but the whole world if allowed.

It was what had been hiding deep inside her, coming up to the surface in bouts while the rest had stayed carefully concealed until the right moment.

I thought this would be the moment, but the more I watched Rosie as she digested the news, the more I came to understand that I don't know her well enough at all.

Matt had been a liar, someone we couldn't trust...but I knew Rosie had forgiven him just as she did everyone else. He was no exception to her kindness even if he didn't deserve it, so I assumed when she was told that the person who had been with her all through her beginning at Winterfell, had been murdered by someone she loved... I expected chaos.

But instead she simply leaned back and stared at me, the water coming up just below her breasts as she digested my words. Her lips were pressed together firmly and her breathing was erratic. It was building up; I could feel it gathering under the surface.

There was a sharp anger and then in an instant...it was gone and instead I was left with a hollow feeling. It was as if Rosie's emotions were swallowed by a black hole and there was nothing left for her to feel.

"Eli killed Matt," she repeated. The words came out slow and felt odd as she spoke them, as if speaking an unknown language.

I nodded slowly, cataloging her reaction. Then I felt the prick of sadness and guilt, but nothing else. It was too fast for even her facial expression to change.

"We were worried the shock—"

"I understand now," she said. "I—"

She took a deep breath, sinking further into the bathtub, her legs brushing against mine. I didn't let my own emotions, the lust, cloud my judgment.

Like I said to Malik in the room mere moments ago, it was inappropriate.

Rosie deserved time to feel like a normal being with emotion and pain, instead of just this toy that was passed around between us. We all cared, that much was obvious, but that didn't make the actions and lack of grace any better.

If we cared for her as we said we did, we should learn how to be with her.

"It was the right choice," she said in a voice that was far too calm. "I just don't—"

"Malik will explain later," I said in a soft voice and reached for her. I grabbed her hand in mine. "It's a lot, I know. And we still don't understand Eli's motive so it's okay to feel angry, even hurt."

"No, I mean." She paused, looking for her words. "I don't understand why my memories haven't come back."

Her response stunned me to my core and for the first time I found myself without a response. I sat back and stared at her as her neck tilted and her head leaned against the back of the bathtub. She acted as though this was just a way to unwind after a long day, instead of like someone who had just heard that her best friend was murdered.

"Also, the games are soon," she continued and lifted her leg, watching as the water droplets fell off and back into the water. "I have to be back for those."

I nodded again. She was not wrong, though that wouldn't be my first thought.

Mine was more along the lines of...*what will Xena and Ezekiel do now?*

"How about we finish up here and go talk to Malik about what happened, hm?" I asked her.

She nodded and without another word stood from the bath.

❦

A SILENCE SPREAD over us as we listened to Malik explain every detail of the crime. Both of us kept looking to Rosie to make sure she was handling it well...but her face never changed. She just sat and stared at Malik as he spoke, eyes never wavering as if she was worried she would miss an important detail.

After the bath I had taken my time to help her dry her long hair and apply the creams she liked so much, just in case the emotions would explode out of her. But even as I watched her intently in the mirror, her expression never changed and her emotions stayed level. She would just stare at us in the mirror and sometimes I even saw the tilt of her lips when she met my eyes.

It must be shock.

Now we talked in a sitting room not too far from my room. I was hesitant to go into this spare room because of how close it was to my mother and Callie, but I trusted Rosie enough now to know that when she looked me in the eyes and told me she was okay, that she was okay.

"So we knew—or suspected that he was the rat?" Rosie asked. "I am not surprised given his sudden change when I outed him."

Maliks gaze met mine and worry was practically spilling out of his pores.

"Ya, well." Malik shifted and cleared his throat. "We don't know how Claudine and Maximus feel, not to mention if there will be any revenge—"

"Matt was horrible to them," Rosie said in a firm tone that told us we could not refute her. "They may hurt for a moment but from what Claudine mentioned, I would have trouble believing this would push them over to the other side."

Neither Malik nor I dared to speak.

I knew Rosie and Claudine had to be closer than meets the eye when I saw how she talked about her to Malik, and the random hugs they gave one another. Not to mention how she all dragged us to get tattoos that Claudine designed to protect us from Matt.

It was my first tattoo, and I was against getting something that marred my skin so permanently...but I knew the consequences of not getting it outweighed the inconvenience of getting it. I didn't fully understand just to what extent his power worked and how on earth Claudine figured out that *this* was the answer, but I was thankful it was over now...

Even if it hurt Rosie.

I didn't approve of Eli's ways and was angry that they didn't come to me first. If they did, I would have thought of a better plan than this. One with more tact, something that wouldn't involve us separating them from Rosie...but Eli was unstable. They always had been, though since Marques shared his blood it felt worse. Their anger and restlessness just continued to build and I guess this was the result of it exploding.

...though I would be the first to admit that they did good.

"As far as revenge from the Originals..." she trailed. "If he was important to their plan, maybe, but I have a hard time believing that they would give up their comfy hiding space for a single hybrid."

"You are..." I didn't know what I wanted to say. "Are you okay?"

Her brown eyes met mine and I couldn't help but flinch at the sharpness of them.

"I am hurt," she said. "I thought maybe he could redeem himself but..." She let out a heavy sigh. "I don't think Eli is wrong to do this, though I do want to understand their motives. I have a hard time thinking that Matt accidentally outed himself to Eli but none of us."

Malik shifted in his chair and grimaced.

"From what Marques told me, Eli had been planning it because they were bored," Malik said slowly. "In training he heard their thoughts and—"

"So, he knew but he didn't stop it?" Rosie said, her tone sharpening. She was glaring at Malik but even I felt her words cut me.

"He warned them," Malik said his eyes shifting to mine as if I could help him out of this mess.

"He's being awfully quiet now," Rosie noted and cocked her head. "Why are we so worried about this when he obviously couldn't care less?"

Malik's rage spiked sharply and I shot him a look.

"She's not wrong," I said, even though I didn't want to fight the Original either.

I would choose my battles and one with someone like Marques was not at the top of my to-do list.

Malik narrowed his eyes at me before turning to Rosie.

"Marques has his reasons—"

"Or does he just want us to do the dirty work?" Rosie asked. "From my perspective he doesn't seem much different than the other Originals. Sitting comfy in his home while we do the hard work."

"Rosie," Malik warned, his voice low and his anger rising steadily with each word out of his mouth. His hands balled into fists on his thighs and his jaw was clenched.

Such a short fuse, I thought wryly.

"Sounds like this was his plan actually," Rosie said and leaned forward, a smile pulling at her lips.

I could feel the satisfaction flowing off of her. She *liked* this type of reaction from him.

Malik stood so abruptly the chair behind him rocked. He crossed the space between them and placed his hands on the armrests trapping Rosie.

"You forget who you are talking about," Malik growled. "Do you have no sense of self-preservation?"

Their emotions were far too powerful for this room and made my head ache. The anger and lust swirling around them began to choke me.

Just as I felt myself sway the door was pushed open and I was met with a panting and panicked Callie. Her brown hair was in a messy bun on top of her hair that threatened to topple over and today her scrubs were bright pink with yellow ducks.

"Rae, I am so sorry—"

"It's okay," I said quickly and stood. "What's the problem?"

I was just glad to have something break up the emotions in this room.

Malik and Rosie were both watching, curiosity filling them.

"Your mother, her eyes moved," she panted out.

I froze, unable to think of what to do next.

There wasn't supposed to be a chance for Mother's recovery, she had been all but a lost cause...and I didn't want to fool myself with hope only to have it crushed.

"Let's go see her," I said and turned to the others. "Work out your problems yourself. It doesn't seem like the issue here is Eli's actions."

Malik stood up and cleared his throat, pulling his gaze from Rosie.

Rosie looked like she wanted to say something but I left them to their own devices.

CALLIE HAD STAYED with me an extra hour, but Mother's eyes did not move again.

Even as she left with a soft goodbye I stayed planted to my mother's side and tried to pay attention to the black hole of emotions surrounding her. Hoping that I could feel something different for once.

Sighing I looked up to the ceiling and tried to enjoy the lack of emotions in the space.

Marques's blood had only continued to develop my power and the emotions were starting to get to be too overwhelming. I found myself visiting my mother's room more often than I used to, just to get away and decompress.

His training had helped a bit with emotional control as well, but not enough for me to do anything real with it.

A prick of nervousness, sadness, and guilt played at my mind as Rosie walked down the hallway. Malik was nowhere near her and I was glad that I only had to deal with one of them at a time.

...but I still wasn't sure if I wanted Rosie to see this part of me.

None of the others had seen my mother and even when they asked about her, I always deflected. It was not something you talked about.

Having a mother that was so abused by your father that she turned comatose and now was bedridden for the rest of her life.

Though it was only speculation, I knew Father had something to do with her state now.

Rosie knocked on the door and I quickly decided that it was time to stop hiding this part of my life.

"Come in," I called and turned my head to watch Rosie's head peek through the doorway.

Her eyes met mine before falling onto my mother's form and her brows furrowed.

“Is it okay if I am in here with you?” she asked, her voice barely above a whisper.

I nodded and held out my arm for her. She closed the door behind her and came closer. Her movements were slow and hesitant. She was also unsure what it meant for her to share this with me.

I pulled her into my lap and buried my face in her hair, inhaling her scent deeply. Warmness enveloped me and I realized that I enjoyed her company here over the thought of sitting alone in this room with no one by me.

Even though she had received the news of Matt and had been holding in her anger the entire day, I still found the familiarity of her comforting.

“She has been like this for a long time,” I said against her hair. “Without the proper care I never understood exactly what was wrong with her, still don’t.”

Rosie leaned into me and her fingers threaded through mine.

“The girl that came in, she was her caretaker?” Rosie asked. “She said something about eye movement?”

I nodded and left a kiss on her head, not really having the words to respond at the moment.

“She looked like a demon though,” Rosie continued and twisted to look at me.

“She is,” I confirmed. “Her power to see brain activity is to help my mom. I have never used witches for her care before.”

Rosie’s brows pulled together and she looked back at Mother.

“She has magic on her,” Rosie said.

My insides froze over and I felt a chill run up my spine.

“What do you mean?” I asked, panicked.

Rosie stood and walked closer to Mother’s bed, leaning over her.

“I can feel just a tiny bit,” she murmured. “But it’s a very small amount, too small to recognize a signature.”

I stood and moved to her side.

"That's not possible," I said, my breath getting caught in my throat. "We don't have any witches in the house."

Rosie stood straight and gave me a look that told me she was almost pained to say so.

"I think I need to call Claudine," she said.

I shifted and tore my gaze from her to my mother.

Even allowing Rosie in here was a big step, now inviting others in?

But she said there was magic on her...

"She is probably busy," I said quickly. "With Matt's funeral preparations... Let's wait a few days and see if maybe the magic wears off by then."

Rosie's warm hand found my face and forced me to look at her. She met me with a small smile.

"It must have been hard for you, all these years," she said in a soft voice. Her eyes searched my face before she leaned in and planted a chaste kiss on my lips. "Let me know when you are ready and we can see about having her come over."

I nodded and swallowed thickly, trying to push down the sudden tsunami of emotions that filled me.

Even without a power like mine, Rosie had read me better than anyone had my entire life.

21
DAXTON

I do not know how I got here. But I know why.

After the talk with Marques and the trainings with Claudine and Maximus I just...

With a sigh I grabbed the glass cup in front of me and threw the burning magical liquid back. It singed as it went down, but it barely fazed me anymore. I had had my fair share of drunken nights as I tried to deal with my parents' abuse, so even though I had been here for hours I knew that I could continue.

Not like I wanted to go back anyways. Rosie was still gone and I had to suffer through school with a pissy Eli and overly depressed Amr.

My body relaxed in my chair as a warmth spread throughout my body.

This club, while not in the main magical area that I liked to frequent, had proven to be a welcome surprise. They had plenty of witches in here and even a few low-levels, all looking to waste their night on something better than their reality.

The music was loud and wisps of magic swirled around me, dancing along with the music. Every time it brushed over my skin a jolt of magic passed through me. Bodies were packed in the place sweating and grinding against each other as they moved to the music, leaving little to no room for anything else.

Only I and a few other depressed losers sat on the stools, probably wallowing in their self-pity as well. I didn't pay attention to them much, just continued to throw back drink after drink, trying to get away from my own demons.

Cumae had yet to get back to me and it wore on my patience because now that Rosie was not with us, I could feel my magic getting restless. So here I was, stuck relying on someone other than myself to make sure that I could live to see the next day.

Useless, useless boy, my mind hissed. *Couldn't kill your bastard parents, now you can't even help the others with—*

"Another," I commanded and tapped my glass against the bar. Purple swirling liquid filled the empty cup and I wasted no time bringing it to my lips.

Magical bars will always far surpass demon ones. They know that if you are there to drink your life away, you don't want to have to talk to a fucking bartender each time. They would have probably cut me off by now, anyways.

Images of my father's eyes begging me not to move forward with ending his life flashed through my mind on repeat. The dreams have gotten worse, even though they are long gone. Some of them were completely real scenarios like before he died, others were images of him coming back from his grave to ruin me.

Often I remembered when they would share magic with me, but I would be on the outside looking down at the whole thing.

That made it worse.

Because I could see the fear in my eyes...it was the same fear I saw on his face when he finally realized he was going to die.

I wondered if he saw that too before the died? Did he realize it finally?

He always had a smile when he did it. The lines on his face would deepen and his brown eyes became so dark I thought they would turn black.

He deserved it.

But Mother...

She would sit there on the sidelines watching while he committed the heinous act. I would see her grimace sometimes but, she never stopped anything and after a while it just became the norm.

If the other witch organizations knew that their biggest spokespeople were doing the unthinkable…there would be a revolt.

That's why they kept everything hidden and used mounds of cash to pay off all the employees. Only after I saw the transactions on the bank account after they died, did I understand how much they tried to cover it up.

"Who are you going to vote for?" a witch with slurred words asked to my right, his loud voice breaking through my thoughts.

"I don't know…" the other trailed. "I am thinking to move out west, actually. I heard that witches have an easier time there getting into science and tech-based industries."

"The least you can do is vote for Perkins before you leave," he grunted. "At least then the people left here have a smidge of their dignity."

Christa Perkins, the next witch to take over my father's work, and the one that was supposed to work alongside Rae's father… Though they have yet to vote someone into office for that position either.

Perkins was by far the youngest and most qualified candidate I had seen take the stage. She believed in uniting demons and witches, getting rid of the stereotypes of crazed witches which my parents had worked so hard to push…

And she wanted to bring awareness to sexual abuse that was abundant in the magical community.

I was not the only one who had dealt with this, that much I knew. But from her statistics she stated that one in every *ten* had experienced some type of magical abuse and over half of that was sexual in nature.

Still…I could not shake the hold my father's eye had on me.

Could not get away from the constant screaming of uselessness in my head.

And it made it all the worse that Rosie wasn't here as a distraction.

I drank the rest of the liquid in one gulp and slammed the glass down on the table. I must have hit it too hard because the glass cracked into my hand.

The two drunkards who had been gossiping silenced their conversation and I felt their gaze on me. I was tempted to fight them, but the sane part of me held me back. I would be too powerful for them anyways and I didn't want to go on a rampage.

Before they made themselves known, I felt Eli's presence.

Ever since Marques had given them their blood I had begun to notice when they tried to invade my brain. It felt like a small push and then pressure. After that, my brain felt more crowded than usual.

It only enraged me more on top of everything else.

They stood to my right and slid a wad of cash on the table. In a flash of shimmering light the money was taken and stored in the bar's underground bank.

"I don't need your money," I growled.

"It's not mine," they answered. "It's Original scum."

It didn't make it any better who it came from, just that it was another dig at my uselessness.

"What are you doing here?" I asked not trying to hide my distaste.

"The cat is worried," they explained. "Thinks you're on a rampage."

I snorted at Amr's mother-hen-like attitude. Ever since we fucked he hadn't removed himself from my side. Always fussing, always making sure I was taken care of...

It made me feel even more *useless.*

"I for one thought you were out of money and being held somewhere to work off your debt," they continued. Their voice had a teasing edge to it. "I hoped it was a strip club but thought

I would try this place first. It wasn't hard to find you, just asked a few people if they saw a huge tattooed witch that looked like their cat just drowned."

Their joking fueled my rage and I had to clench my fist, nails biting into my palms in order to calm myself.

They spoke as if they didn't *murder* someone. Someone that was important to the people who wanted us dead. Who was important to the only people who had the ability to save us.

Who knows what Matt's death will bring us? The Originals were unpredictable and I didn't want to chance their wrath anymore.

...but they were right about the money.

I was lucky my parents had paid for this education up front because if not, I couldn't afford this year or next.

Ever since they had died, I didn't have the balls to withdraw any of their money. It felt gross. They had a fund for me, I knew about it. And they had been hoarding their wealth for years giving us no shortage of money but I just couldn't...

"Do you still have the house?" Eli asked.

I let out a sigh.

"What will it take for you to leave me alone?" I complained. I was too tired and fed up for this. I came here to lose myself, not to be reminded of the shit world that waited outside for me.

"Let's go do some stress release, hm?" they offered. "The cat can wait a bit longer."

I stared at the broken glass in front of me. Parts of it shone under the dim light and I saw my dull eyes being reflected on the surface, right next to Eli's bright blue ones.

"What do you have in mind?" I wondered, my curiosity getting the better of me.

"Well..." They trailed and put a hand on my shoulder. "If you still have the house..."

An image of the house ablaze lit up my mind.

You can get rid of it once and for all, they said in my mind. *And then move on with your life.*

"Why are you doing this?" I asked and turned to meet their eyes.

For once, Eli looked tired. Their hair was a mess on top of their head, blonde hair once combed back neatly fell limply around their head. Dark circles seemed to be permanently etched under their eyes and their cheeks seemed a bit more hollow than normal.

I know I didn't look much better, but I was a witch. Demons could heal on their own so for Eli to look like this...

"I want you to stop acting like a limp dick," they growled, their eyes coming to light. "And I'm *fucking bored* okay?"

Were they bored? Or were they going crazy that the one thing that they cared for was taken away from them?

From the beginning Eli had a tie to Rosie that went beyond their normal actions. Eli was a person who refused to form ties with anyone, and did not trust a single soul. It took years for them to even trust me fully and here they were, killing themselves over a girl they had known for just a year.

"Fine," I said and got up from my chair, stopping to stare Eli in the eyes. "But don't think I forgive you for taking her from us."

Eli's jaw clenched and I could feel the tension vibrate between us.

"She will be back soon," they spit out behind clenched teeth.

"Not soon enough," I said. "I am *dying* Eli. You think I don't understand how this works? I have lived with this magic for *years* and here it is eating away at me, leaving no crumbs in its trail. Without her I am dying and I know you know it too. Rae was kind enough to spill all the gossip while none of you were looking, while none of you *care*—"

I took a deep breath to stop the shaking in my voice.

"While none of you cared to tell me," I finished. "You just looked right past it and forgot about it, but I can't okay?"

Eli's stone-cold expression dropped and on their face was a rarely seen frown.

I hated that face. I knew it was pity. What else could make Eli make a face like that?

"Let's see what we can do to make those feelings go away, hm?" they asked in the softest voice I ever heard from them and wrapped their arm around my shoulder, then guided me out of the magical bar.

In that moment, no matter how mad I had been at Eli…I was grateful to have them by my side because *finally* someone could see my struggles.

I SAT in front of the cold structure that had been empty for months now.

All of the magic that my parents had fused into the ground, the plants, the structure…had gone cold.

The places used to be intertwined with my magic and I remember the feeling of running through it when I was a child. The feeling of it tickling my senses.

I was in awe of magic and what it could do. Back then the feeling of being surrounded by magic was comforting. It was like a warm blanket was placed over the area. It felt like it was protecting me.

I only learned much later that it was there to trap me, not protect me like I had once thought.

Now all that magic was gone, and the ground was cold.

It was as if it never existed. As if *we* never existed.

My parents were gone.

Their hold on me was gone.

This empty house that spanned far too large and desolate ground were proof that they were no longer here…

Now it was just me here left to deal with the ruins.

"I hope you don't need anything in there," Eli muttered by my side.

"The accounts are under my name now, Amr had it dealt with for me..." I said. "I just haven't touched them.

Guilt weighed heavy in my gut when I thoughts about how caring Amr had been the last few months...all while I left him back at Winterfell to worry his poor head off.

"Any prized family heirlooms we should sell?" they asked. "Anything black market worthy?"

I shook my head.

"I don't think I want anything to come out of there," I said in a weak voice.

"Do you want to go in?"

I shook my head.

I allowed myself two more deep inhales before I held out my hand and created a perimeter around the house.

It wasn't hard to set the house alight, but it did take a lot of magic.

I watched as in one flash the house was engulfed by flames.

It was an old house with dried bushes and splintering wood. It didn't take long for it to start to crumble.

The fire licked at the bright blue perimeter but never went beyond it.

The magic inside me turned hungry. It liked the act of destroying and it wanted *more.* It didn't want to stop until every last thing in its path was destroyed.

It took me more than a few moments to reel myself out of the magic haze and pull my gaze to Eli.

They were watching me intently.

"The cat will be worried," they said.

I nodded.

"Just a few more minutes," I said and turned to watch the structure collapse, and along with it every painful memory my parents scarred me with.

22

ROSIE

I had gone to sleep the night before with a head full of worries and an empty, unfeeling chest. I only wished it would stay that way; maybe if the universe looked more highly upon me they would have allowed me to stay in that state.

But given my parents, I knew that the universe wouldn't give me a break. Who else would pay for their sins?

I was awoken by my magic in the early morning. A restlessness filled my being and practically flung me from the comfort of Rae's bed.

Even as my magic woke up inside of me and started to ignite a path of fire, the only thing I could think of was how dangerous it would be if I was stuck inside with Rae and her mom.

The others would live, but I worried for those who were too close and could not defend themselves.

I blindly ran down the hallway and bolted down the stairs, pushing my clumsy legs faster as my magic clawed at me.

I found myself barging through the side door and out into some sort of garden area. Everything passed by me in a blur as I tried to get as far away from the house as possible before I fell to my knees into the damp ground.

A cold passed over my overheated skin and without a second

to rest I conjured a magic knife and ran it down my forearm. Thick blood started to leak from the wound but it was slow-moving and inside my magic was building up faster than the blood fell.

Rae's shirt stuck to me as I panted and sweat poured down my back. Holding in the blast of the magic was painful; it was stretching against my skin and threatening to take down everything near us.

I lifted the shirt away from my thighs, never more grateful to have not worn pants to bed, and began leaving deep cuts as I hurried to get the magic out. Each cut burned less than the last, the pain from the magic overtaking it all.

Tears clouded my eyes as I slashed at any naked skin I could get to.

Please, please, please come out, I begged my magic.

"Please," I cried and lifted the knife above my head with both hands and brought it down to my stomach.

A pale hand shot out from the darkness and caught it just as the tip bit into my skin.

I let out a cry and flung my head against the attacker only for them to grab my head and bring it close to their chest.

"Get away," I moaned against them. My body was shaking now. "*Leave!*"

I felt the first wave of magic roll off of me and out of my cuts, but it didn't do much to stop the crazed magic inside me.

I pounced on the person, throwing us both into the dirt. I raised my hands ready to bring them down on my target but froze when Malik's golden eyes shone in the darkness.

He sat up suddenly, his hand coming to grab my wrists and force them to my side.

"What the fuck do you think you are doing?" he growled at me.

I struggled against him and threw myself backwards, trying to get away. He was in the line of destruction now and even though he had survived last time, I doubted that he would be able to survive this time.

"Get off me!"

Malik pushed us back so that he was now straddling me and forcing me into the dirt below us. He overpowered me and left not an inch for me to fight him off.

I bucked, kicked, tried to fling my arms about but there was no escaping him.

"Rosie if you do not stop this right now I will have to use my power on you," Malik warned. "And this time you will not like it."

I knew by his tone that he was serious, that I would not like anything he was about to do to me...but my magic wanted more.

"My magic," I choked out through my sobs. "It's too much. It woke me—hurts—I don't know—"

"Then do some magic or something!" he yelled. "Conjure those birds or some shit. We need to get you inside, where it is safe."

I shook my head violently, my vision swimming to keep up.

"Too slow!"

I felt the thick blood trickle down my body and into the ground beneath us, the magic swimming around us. The ground below me heated to a point where it felt like it was burning.

And then finally like a sigh of relief, the next wave of magic washed out of me and I could feel the open cuts ache as blood started to pour from them.

Malik's eyes trailed my form and he sat up slowly, noting every single new cut on my body.

"The bloodletting," he murmured as if the thought just occurred to him.

Exhaustion fell over me and I felt myself sink further into the ground.

"It didn't want to come out," I whispered, my voice hoarse as if I had been screaming.

Had I been? Was that how Malik found me?

"It's coming out normally now," he said and lifted my wrist, inspecting the deep wound that now marred my beautiful raven. It would be disgusting and gnarled after this, even if I did heal it with magic...but I wasn't done yet.

Just because I made it in time to not blow up Rae's house, didn't mean that it wouldn't happen again.

And now that I knew how bad the effects of magic could be, I refused to put the others in danger.

"It was dark, thick," I said. His gaze stayed planted on my arm and blood started to flow towards my face, dripping and staining Rae's shirt even more. "Like *his.*"

Malik slowly dropped my arm back to the ground and looked down at me. His mouth was turned downwards and there was an air around him that displeased my magic.

He's unhappy, I noted.

My skin heated as I thought about his obvious disappointment. He didn't have a right to judge me on what I needed to do to keep the others safe. I did what I needed to do and there should be no shame in how I dealt with my magic.

"Heal it," he said in a low tone.

"No," I hissed. "I need to let more magic out before I go back."

Malik's eyes narrowed and his hand gripped my chin, forcing me to look into his eyes.

"Do it," he commanded with his power. "You can go expend magic another way, wake Rae for god's sake."

Blinding fury was all I felt as my arms raised by themselves and began magically healing my wounds. It was slow and painful as my mind was torn between remembering the way to stitch my own flesh together and how to get back at Malik for this.

He moved off me so that I could sit and heal the slashes on my legs. I grimaced as I saw the amount of damage I had done. My legs, which were already littered with scars from the bloodbath in the town, now had fresh scars running up them, ruining my once smooth skin.

Dirt was caked onto every surface and I felt it dry and crack as I healed myself. Once the last cut was healed and I felt Malik's power leave me, I turned as fast as I could and launched myself at him.

I was far from proficient in my curses but I trained enough with him to be able to focus my power on his hands and force them over his head.

I straddled him and gripped his chin much like he had done to me moments ago. His eyes widened and his expression was a mix of shock and anger as he realized that his hands were now stuck.

"Fine," I said in a sickly sweet voice. I ran my hand down his throat and grabbed it tightly, enjoying the way his Adam's apple nodded as he swallowed. "Let's burn some magic, shall we?"

I moved down so that I was directly straddling his half-erect cock and began grinding against him. With even such a little move magic burst through me and I found my hands flailing to come tear off the fabric that separated us.

My concentration must have slipped because Malik sat us up and threaded his hands in my hair, pulling it back hard enough to pull a yelp from my mouth.

His hot breath fanned over my face and our chests were brushing together with each pant.

I smirked down at him, noting the dark look on his face. He tried to play it off in the room, acting as if he regretted his actions, but I saw the look he gave me.

He was just as hungry as I was.

"Do you still taste me?" I asked and let out a gasp as he stood, throwing me to the ground.

"Get your ass inside or I will have you sit out here making magic birds for the rest of the morning," he threatened.

I looked up at him with a glare only to see that his back was to me.

"You wouldn't," I dared.

He turned, his golden eyes flashing under the moonlight. An excited tremor ran through me.

"I would," he said. "And if Xena and Ezekiel come to finish their job? I would let them."

I was left with my own shock as Malik walked towards the house.

"Don't tell Rae!" I yelled after him.

MALIK WAS BECOMING AN EVEN BIGGER dick than usual since the incident the other night, though I was glad that he didn't tell Rae about my almost tantrum.

Today was a prime example.

I was sitting with Nathaniel and Benjamin as they asked me question after question about my hybrid status and life at Winterfell. It wasn't what I wanted to be doing with my free time. I would much rather be with the others at Winterfell...but I was stuck here until it was *deemed safe.*

My anger had not simmered down quite as easily as I would have liked. Instead I found myself dreaming of how to get back at Malik, about finally bringing down Xena...and of course about Eli.

"I'm not saying I don't *believe* you..." Nathaniel trailed, a smirk spreading across his face.

Benjamin visibly paled as he sensed the tension between us rise.

The brothers were interesting and I still couldn't get over how similar to Rae they were. In looks anyways—their personalities were totally different.

"I am just saying it is not very likely," Nathaniel continued. "All studies showed that the fetus miscarried. So how is it that you flew under the radar for so long?"

I sighed and leaned back in my chair, my eyes floating to Malik. I had come here for him, and when I heard he was in the family's library I thought it would be the perfect time to talk to him.

I had planned to ask him to bring Daxton and Amr here so I could get rid of some of my magic, but to my surprise both Nathaniel and Benjamin were already here with him.

Malik was settled across a bench right underneath a floor-to-ceiling window that overlooked the property. His eyes were skimming a very old book in front of him, seemingly stuck inside a world of his own.

His aloof attitude annoyed me and made me only want to push him further, demand that he pay attention to me. His disregard...hurt after all.

I had been attracted to him for a while but beyond that, he had been the first one to show me some care and treat me like I mattered for the first time in my life. And then all of a sudden, after taunting me with his words and advances, he puts a hold on it and acts like I am nothing once more.

"Because I didn't know," I said with my gaze still planted on Malik. "But Malik did, didn't you?"

His hand froze as it was about to turn a page and his head cocked to the side.

"I found out when you did," he lied.

I huffed and rolled my eyes. When I turned back to Nathaniel I saw a devious look spread across his face.

"Malik," Nathaniel said in a mock astonished tone. "I never took you for a liar."

I raised an eyebrow at Nathaniel.

"I am not lying," Malik said from behind me. "Anyways, it's not your business."

Nathaniel leaned back in his chair and threw me a grin.

"You should know better to lie to someone whose whole power revolves around it," Nathaniel said.

What I would do to have his power, I mused. *It sure would have helped with Xena in the early days.*

"Whatever," Malik grumbled.

"Anything you want to ask him Rosie?" Nathaniel asked. "Maybe his bank PIN, or maybe why he has suddenly found the library very interesting even though he has never been here before three days ago?"

"I can add a dash of persuasion," Benjamin chimed in shyly.

I opened my mouth to decline but Malik's voice cut through the silence.

"Out," he commanded.

I sat in my seat refusing to leave as both Nathaniel and Benjamin left with heavy sighs. When the door closed I turned back to Malik. I jumped when I was met with his torso.

He had come much closer as I was watching Nathaniel and Benjamin leave and his sudden closeness caused me to jump in my seat.

"I need Daxton and Amr," I said quickly before I chickened out.

Leaning back to look at his face my breath caught in my throat as finally after days of ignoring me, he looked me straight in the eyes.

"You need to use what you have," he growled.

"But you said—"

"Eli is *not* in the right headspace to be around you," Malik cut me off. "And I don't think for a second that Daxton will listen to me, so he has to stay away too."

Heat engulfed my body and I wanted so badly to tackle him, just like I did the other night.

"Eli *would never* hurt me," I growled.

Malik leaned down and put a hand on my shoulder, stretching me out against the couch. With his free hand he ripped up my shirt to showcase my bare belly and jagged scars that spelled out Eli's name.

"They already have," Malik said. "They were on a rampage and ready to do more damage. Just because you get off on their abuse doesn't mean that we can chance you getting killed by them."

My mouth flopped open like a fish and I was left without words.

"I don't—"

"Rosie," Malik said in a tone so soft it made my chest feel tight. "Stop being so *selfish* and go ask Rae for some help."

Embarrassment flooded through me.

"I have been," I growled. "But it's not enough if you would just listen to me—"

"No," Malik growled. "*You* listen to *me*." His grip tightened on my shoulder. "You need to understand that just because the Originals are not here with us, does not mean life is back to normal. I am in charge for a reason and you do not get to disobey me just because you feel like being a brat."

My eyes trailed down to his lips, remembering how he kissed me in Rae's room. It was feral, needy...and I wanted to feel it again. I wanted to turn the man in front of me into nothing more than a beast that couldn't control himself.

"Then you help me," I said, a warmth pooling in my belly. "You haven't touched me since that night, but I know you want to. Why can't you just get over yourself already?"

I knew I fucked up by the way his face hardened. He stood abruptly and stared down at me for a moment, as if deciding if I was worth a response.

It hurt and angered me at the same time.

I guess he found me unworthy because he just turned and stormed out the door of the library.

DAYS HAD PASSED since the library incident and I found myself angrier than ever.

I had explored the place from basement to ceiling. Spent time with Rae's brothers, and mother. I even tried to read in the library to pass the time but it did nothing for me and just started to bore me.

That boredom turned very quickly into something much hotter and soon I was seething.

It wasn't all because I was cooped up in the house, though a lot of it had to do with my magic.

I was still mad at Eli. Mad that they decided to take Matt's life and consequently tear me from them, Daxton, and Amr.

I was mad at Matt for being a traitor and lying to me about who he really was when all I wanted was a *real* friend.

And most of all I was pissed at Malik.

Ever since the incident in the garden, followed by the library, he became even more distant and now it was like trying to find a ghost. The only reason I knew he was still in the house was because I saw him in passing, though it wasn't the same as before.

We would have breakfast with everyone in the house and he would be there, eating breakfast and chatting with Rae. Sometimes I saw him talking outside with Claudine and Maximus, but they never came in and would disappear soon after I caught them.

Never again did I see the way he looked at me as he kneeled between my legs. All that passion and need was gone and I was left with only a shell of the person I once knew.

And that *fucking* infuriated me even more.

You keep me here, away from the others but don't have the audacity to finish what you started?

That was the thought that spurred me in my decision tonight. I needed to get this magic out and since he was the one that put me in this position, he would be the one that finished it.

It was well past midnight when I slowly unwrapped myself from Rae's arms. She had fallen asleep over an hour and a half ago but I wanted to make sure that she didn't awake when I left so I waited until she was deep asleep.

As I slid out I listened for any sign that she would wake, but she still remained peacefully asleep and unaware of what was about to transpire. I tiptoed across the room, the uncarpeted parts of the floor sending shivers through me as my bare feet made contact with them.

The house was silent, so silent I could hear each hinge strain as I slowly pushed open the door and slipped out of the room.

The outside hallway was even colder than the room and I had to hug myself to create some warmth, as being in nothing but Rae's shirt, did shit for warmth.

Walking down the hallway as silently as I could, I peeked around the corner and tried to peer down into the foyer and make sure that Malik wasn't having one of his late-night meetings with the witches.

I let out a sigh when I saw that it was still empty and made quick work of descending the steps. As my feet touched the cold marble of the front room a chill fell over me and the back of my neck itched. I searched around the dark space, but found nothing alarming.

Ignoring the lingering feeling I hurried towards the other side of the house and to where I knew Malik's room was. Thankfully, the excursion with Eli prepared me to find his room and an excited rush rose in me as his door came into view.

Just as I was about to take another step further, my body was slammed into the wall by a hard force. I let out a pained groan as a hand came to crush my face against the wall.

"*Shit,*" Malik cursed from behind me, his hands loosening just a bit. "Rosie I thought you were an intruder."

"Would an intruder really be walking around in just a shirt in the middle of the fucking night, Malik?" I hissed at him and tried to push him off but his grip tightened after my quip.

Warmth radiated from his body, fighting off the shivers that spread across my cold skin.

"Watch the attitude Rosie," he threatened, his breath fanning across my face. "Now why don't you tell me why you are sneaking out in the middle of the night?"

"I am not sneaking out," I growled back and struggled against his hold.

I suddenly regretted my decision tonight. I could have chosen any way to get back at him but instead I let my body choose for me.

"Right, so if I search the perimeter right now I will not find Eli waiting for a fuck?" he hissed.

I gritted my teeth and gathered magic in my hand. Suddenly Malik's golden eyes entered my field of vision.

"No magic use for you," he said. "Not until you tell me the truth."

His power was warm as it washed over me and even as it bound my powers, I let out a sigh in relief.

I could feel the hard planes of his stomach against my back and I arched my back, gasping as my ass brushed across his front.

His erection told me he was just as affected as I was.

Fucking liar.

The truth was that I wanted him to fuck the living shit out of me since he had been such a bastard as of late. Leading me on with no intention to actually go any further with me than he had while Rae was with us.

"I was not meeting anyone," I insisted.

He raised a brow and spun me around so that we faced each other. He grabbed both my wrists and pinned them above my head using his free hand to grip my chin and force me to look in his eyes.

The movement caused a fire to spread throughout and I found myself spreading my legs, but he did not come any closer.

"What were you doing then?" he asked. "Midnight snack with no underwear on?"

My face flamed and humiliation burned inside of me.

"Do you really want the truth?" I asked and glared at him.

"That's why I ask," he replied, his words laced with venom.

I shifted against the uncomfortable wall and glared daggers at him, all of my confidence burning away into anger. This was *not* how it was supposed to go.

I wanted to sneak into his room and surprise him while he was half asleep; I didn't expect him to attack me in the fucking hallway.

"Your silence tells me I am right," he said with a dangerous tone. "I thought you were better than this Rosie. I thought you would listen to orders for once in your life and just sit back while Eli calms down. You know we planned to bring you ba—"

"I was coming to fuck *you*," I said with a confidence I didn't know I had. His eyes narrowed in my direction before trailing the rest of my body. Fueled by the desire in his eyes, I continued. "I was going to wake you with your cock in my mouth and suck you off until you found the balls enough to *fuck me*—"

He launched himself at me. The once omnipotent and controlled demon was gone and in his place was a wild and famished beast. His mouth claimed mine brutally, his teeth biting into my lower lip, forcing my mouth open for his tongue to explore.

The hand on my chin moved in between us and I felt him pull his cock out before grabbing both my thighs and hiking them up around his waist.

Whatever thread he had been holding onto had snapped and *finally* I was met with the Malik that I wanted to meet. The one that took what he wanted with no remorse.

With my now free hands I swung them around his shoulders and pulled our bodies closer together. I positively melted under his attention and found the raging magic in me exploding as his hands gripped my thighs so hard I knew they left bruises.

His rough touches anchored me and allowed me to fully melt into his kiss. In my anger I pulled at his hair as if I was trying to rip it from his head, but he only pushed harder into me. Even as I nipped at his lips and scratched at his arms, he continued to devour me. When he let out a pained groan as I scratched at the bare skin of his neck, I tried to buck my hips against him, looking for some sort of friction to release the pent-up energy inside of me.

He was not a sweet or attentive kisser. Malik liked to claim with his mouth, liked to bruise. Through his kisses and touches I could tell that he wanted me to remember this moment, remember how he controlled my body, remember who it was I was about to fuck.

He ran the tip of his cock from my entrance to my clit and then back down, sliding through my wet folds with ease. From the time he forced me against this wall, I had been ready for him, my body begging for him to touch me, and *finally* it was happening.

He pushed me hard against the wall and lined himself up at my aching core before entering into me with one thrust. It was a brutal, powerful thrust that I wasn't prepared for, but nonetheless I took it and enjoyed finally feeling Malik inside me.

The sudden stretch was only slightly uncomfortable but as soon as he reared back and began snapping his hips into mine, I forgot all the pain.

I threw my head back, not caring about the pain of my head hitting the wall and let out a silent scream as he fucked me relentlessly.

"You look at me as I fuck you," Malik growled as his hips met mine. I peeled my eyes open to catch his snarling face.

The position was uncomfortable, but I couldn't find myself to care as the feeling of being filled by him was far more addicting than I ever imagined. I was used to the brutal ways of Eli and even some of Daxton's rougher times...but this was different.

Malik acted wild and positively feral.

"You're going to come on my cock right now and then I am going to take you into my room and fuck you until you can't walk straight do you understand?" he asked, his power bursting through me like a raging fire.

His hand clamped over my mouth as I screamed through my orgasm. His thrusts never paused as my orgasm rolled through me, each thrust feeling deeper than the last and pulling scream after scream out of me and I clenched down on his cock.

Without warning his arms wrapped around me and he walked us down to his room, while I still rode him, each step jolting me against him causing bursts of pleasure to go through me.

He opened his door with ease, shut it behind us and laid me on the bed.

"Safe word is red," he groaned and he pushed me into the bed with one hand, using it as leverage to pound into me. "Tell me you understand."

I tried to respond but I couldn't as the ferocity of his movements stole my words from me. I nodded and gripped at his arm, nails digging into his skin. I wanted to hurt him, wanted to make him groan in pain as I squeezed the life out of his cock.

His hand gripped my face, forcing me to look into his golden eyes. There was nothing but the small bit of moonlight seeping in through the windows to light his face. It caused his scars to shimmer in the light.

He gave me no moment of rest.

"I have wanted to be inside this cunt of yours for so long," he groaned and leaned down to capture my lips. His free hand came to rub circles in my clit. "I dreamed about it. Fucked my hand and imagined it was this tight pussy."

He left a trail of kisses from my lips to my chest and caught a nipple through my shirt, sucking on it before biting. I let out a moan and tangled my hands in his soft hair.

"You. Were. Just. Too. *Fucking. Tempting.*"

With each word he thrust into me harder and harder pushing us up until we were in the middle of the bed.

No words escaped my mouth no matter how badly I wanted to tell him I had waited for this moment as well. I yearned to feel his mouth on mine, to feel his touch.

"I knew you were doing it on purpose," he said pausing his thrusts to grab a pillow and place it under my ass.

He did an experimental thrust that caused my eyes to roll back into my head. The head of his cock rubbed exactly right against the place that made my body shudder with pleasure. His large hand came to push down on my lower belly right above my pelvic bone.

My hands flew to my mouth to stop the loud sobs being pulled from my mouth. The pressure from the outside combined with his slowly calculated thrusts right against my walls was going to tear me apart.

"Testing me," he said his eyes trained on me. "Pushing me." He pushed my legs apart and his eyes narrowed in on where we were connected. I leaned up to watch as well and felt myself clench as I watched his cock, coated with my release, disappear inside of me in one slow thrust only to be pulled back out again.

"Did this this cunt get what she wanted? Hm?" he asked. My body froze as the words sent a shiver through me.

Malik chuckled and picked up the pace of his thrusts, the wet slopping sounds obscenely filling the air.

"Tell me Rosie," he demanded, pinching my clit.

"Yes!" I cried out.

Malik smirked.

"Now you are going to sit there," he trailed. "And every time I make you come you are going to have to apologize for being a brat. You got that?"

I glared up at him.

"Like hell I wi—"

"Come," he commanded, stopping my protests in their tracks.

My body jerked as the orgasm ripped through me with the help of his thrusts and firm thumb on my clit. Magic burst out of me in waves as I clenched around him.

"Say it Rosie," he commanded pinching my clit. "Apologize to me."

I glared up at him.

"I don't have anything to—"

"Come."

I flailed, my hand coming to grip onto the comforter looking for something, anything to ground me as my world was blinded by red lights right before my eyes.

"It's not that hard Rosie," he said teasingly. "I mean, isn't this want you wanted? You have been pushing me for days to give this needy pussy what it wants. Just say sorry and I'll let you catch your breath."

"You're worse than Eli," I sobbed.

Malik clicked his tongue and shook his head slowly.

"You're not listening to me Rosie," he said in a low tone. "Maybe I have been too easy on you. After all, I bet the others have raised your tolerance. I could always stop you from orgasming instead..."

"Please don't," I said panicked.

He slammed his hips against mine.

"Then are you going to say sorry Rosie?" he asked in a mock sad tone, a smirk spreading across his face.

"I don't have—"

"Taking orgasms away is too cruel, I agree," he mused ignoring me completely. His thumb was rubbing lazy circles in my clit. "What's your record with the others, in one session?"

I sent him a look.

"I don't count," I answered.

"Hmm, pity," he said. "Let's start with five, shall we?"

He leaned down to plant a small kiss on my lips.

"Now you are going to come five times with five second intervals in between, each orgasm stronger than the last," he whispered. "Starting...now."

A cry was torn out of me as the first orgasm was torn out of my body.

"Count the time between the intervals," he said resuming his thrusts. The thumb on my clit in time with his thrusts sent a frenzy through me that was almost too much to handle. Tears leaked from my eyes.

As soon as the waves of the orgasm subsided I did as he commanded.

"One, t-two, three four—*Ah!*"

My back bowed as the next one ran through me, my magic exploding around me. My sobs were silenced as my body shook violently from the orgasms.

"Ohhh," Malik chuckled. "That was a nice one wasn't it?"

"Please Malik," I begged. "That's enough make it—"

"Count," he commanded his tone serious. "You know the safe word."

I did know the safe word...but even as I cried out and begged him to give me a break, I didn't want this to end. I wanted him to give me his worst. Wanted him to destroy me if he dared.

"O-one, Two—"

I was too late. The next one came sooner than I could finish counting. A scream pulled itself from my lips.

"*That's right*," he moaned looking down at me through hooded eyes. "Let everyone hear how well I am fucking you."

I grabbed his hand to stop his attack on my clit.

"I'm sorry Malik, I'm so sorry for not listening to you I swear—"

His hand came down on my mouth as the next orgasm ripped through me. Tears were falling down my face and I swore my vision went white for a second before his golden eyes found mine again.

"Last one, baby," he cooed. "I'm coming with you this time and I want to hear you scream my name at the top of your lungs as you come, you got it?"

I couldn't answer him as he slammed his hips into mine and the last orgasm seized my body. I tried my best to scream his name from behind his hand but it came out muffled and more like a beg than a cry from an orgasm.

Malik let out a deep growl and froze inside me as he released his seed. He was breathing heavily and he leaned over me, his arms resting on either side of my head, the sweat from his forehead dripping down onto my shirt and my face. His once curly crazed locks were sticking to his face, damp from sweat.

"We are not done here," he warned me, his eyes locking me in place. "I promised you I am going to be fucking you well into the night and I keep my damn promises."

❧

When I awoke next my head was pushed into a naked chest and strong arms were wrapped on either side of me. Not wanting to get rid of the warm body, I snuggled further into Malik and let out a content sigh.

All the fighting, the pushback, if it was worth this I would do it ten times over.

Malik had been...a dream.

A calm experienced hand that watched me fall over the edge time and time again giving me little to no rest in between. He wouldn't give in to my pleas no matter how many times I begged him.

Malik let out a low groan and his hand rubbed down my spine, eliciting shivers from me.

"Don't think this changes anything. We both have jobs to do and the safety of this group comes first," he growled and planted a kiss on my head.

"I know," I whispered.

I understood, I really did. It was the same with the others, regardless of what was going on between us, we had to remain safe with our heads clear.

It made me understand a bit more why Malik took the actions he did, when it came to Eli.

I didn't want to be separated from the group, and even though I knew Eli wouldn't hurt me, it would be best to have them cool down before we meet.

Though I knew that wasn't the complete reasoning as to why

they tore us apart. Now that my head was clear and my magic had subsided, I could see the situation more clearly.

This is a punishment. Eli's punishment.

His hand trailed down and cupped my ass lifting my leg over his. I felt his erection slide against my folds.

"*Fuck,* why did I stay away from this for so long?"

"I tried to tell you," I teased and lifted my head to kiss him.

He lazily thrusted against me, his length rubbing against my clit and pulling small whimpers from my mouth.

"That didn't take long," he mumbled against my lips as wetness pooled between my legs. With help from his hand he guided his cock to my entrance and entered me slowly, pulling the breath out of my lungs. "Heads up, we are going back today."

"We are?" I asked staring up at him. He gave me a small smile.

"We are," he confirmed.

"Then we have to go, we wi—" He cut me off with a thrust. I was still sore from the frenzied fucking last night, but as he slowly moved against me the pain started to dissipate.

"Rae will wait for us," he said. "Probably glad someone can take this needy cunt off her hands for a night."

My gasp was quickly muffled by his mouth.

Needless to say, we were not going to get out of this bed anytime soon.

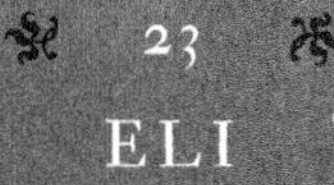

23
ELI

My whole body was on edge after Rae texted me and told me to skip class with Daxton and Amr today. Not like I had planned to go anyways; I had taken to skipping most of them because it was too hard to concentrate.

And it's not like I needed them anyways. After I finally killed that bastard I would spend my time doing whatever I wanted.

I hadn't taken much time to think about what I would do after school—if I even finished it, that is.

I thought maybe reviving *The Fallen* would be a fun endeavor. I knew the workers didn't just disappear off the face of the planet once Malik told them to disperse. They were also likely to be hurting for cash, so as long as I could provide *that*...

I kicked at the gravel on the ground, unable to keep my body still. A buzz of anticipation ran through me as we waited in the old worship center the Originals once occupied.

All the decorations and walls were destroyed, leaving this place in shambles. One look at it told you that a raging Original had been the one to tear down the interior, but surprisingly they kept the structure intact.

Amr and Daxton stood by my side, seemingly better off than

I was but I knew inside they were just as anxious to be reunited with our hybrid.

I wanted to laugh, but the sound didn't come out of my tight chest.

We were so obsessed with her.

It was funny how a little hybrid, who was once no better than the dirt under our shoes, had come in and changed our lives so suddenly.

Demons of this school cowered when we walked by and refused to associate with us if they knew there was even a smidge of their being that we would deem unworthy.

They didn't want to chance it. They saw how easy it was for us—*for me*—to snap.

Not to mention the rumors of what Daxton did to that witch previously were still embedded into the minds of every witch in this school.

Yet Rosie, a *weak* annoying low-level turned Original offspring didn't fear us, nor care about the rumors.

I doubt she even heard them. She was too busy with us that she didn't even glance at the other students.

Maybe that's why we were so drawn to her.

"They are taking for-fucking-ever," I growled and turned to pace beside Daxton and Amr.

I knew they were bringing Rosie back. I mean how obvious could you be? Rae wouldn't tell us to skip class for nothing. She had a high standard and moral compass of a saint, like hell she would actually *ask* us to leave class.

She did murder her own father though.

A hypocrite, like they all were.

Rae and Malik thought they were being smart, thought this would finally get me to obey them. They saw my weakness for her and preyed on it like vultures.

They knew it would fuck me up yet they used the action as a guise for her *protection*.

Them taking her from me only left me with built-up tension

and I would fucking *destroy* Rosie as soon as I got my hands on her just to prove a point. I had thought of all the ways I could have her while she was gone and I was forced into a dark empty dorm room with nothing but my own thoughts to occupy me.

They thought it would make me realize my actions were wrong, but it was *them* who were wrong.

And I planned to pay Malik and Rae back in full when the time was right. It would have to be *big*, make them realize that they couldn't leash me like a dog. I had a few ideas, but would have to tread carefully as my mind was unsafe.

Amr and Daxton were also still mad, though they blamed everything on me, instead of the people who actually took her. Luckily, they had come around slightly when they realized I wasn't going on a murder spree, though I still caught the cat glaring at me on occasion.

But the best thing?

Matt did help with one thing...

Pain, panic, and fear make it easier for me to read thoughts, and I planned to test the extent of that theory in time. And you bet I would make it Malik's and Rae's problem.

"Watch yourself," Amr muttered as I shifted yet again.

I sent him a glare. There he goes again on his self-righteous act he puts on. Does he really not get how annoying his entitlement is. Does he really think that just because he doesn't have his hands stained like the rest of us that he is *somehow* better?

"I only let you live because of Rosie." I paused and then jerked my head towards Daxton. "And this guy. Don't get comfortable."

Amr let out a low growl.

"Don't think you were the only one suffering because of this," he growled.

I was about to respond but finally the doors were pushed open and Malik and Rae showed up. Right in the middle, was a very angry Rosie.

A jolt of excitement ran through me as she fumed. She tried

to be scary, tried to intimidate us, but it was obvious she was no more than an angry kitten with her guard dogs beside her that did all the work.

As soon as Rosie's eyes met mine a frown marred her perfect face and she stomped over to me. Her brown uniform skirt bounced with each step, pulling my eyes from her face.

When did she get those scars?

I had seen the others before, but there were obvious new ones that littered her skin. They looked deep and painful.

Both Rae and Malik called out to her but they did not dare follow as a wave of red magic exploded in front of them, keeping them frozen in place.

"Eli!"

I stayed in my spot as she came to a stop in front of me and connected the palm of her hand with the side of my face.

The force was enough to turn my head and spread a small bit of pain through me, but not much else.

I couldn't help the smirk that formed on my face at the action and the heat that coursed through me from the feistiness of her. It would be so satisfying to watch her break down later.

Her chest was rising and falling with each inhale, her face starting to flush, and there were tears behind her eyes.

I paused when I saw them.

Why was she crying? She hit me so she must be mad at me... But the death of Matt, a man who hurt her...would make her sad?

I didn't pretend to understand the emotions of the people around me. Sometimes I got lucky, but others, like now, seemed to be lost to me.

A part of me felt like I should comfort her...but the other part felt angry.

I wanted to make her cry, make her beg...scream even, but not *like this.*

This was a face I had seen only a few times from her but this one was the most painful.

And I wanted to stop it...but I was the one who caused it.

"You shouldn't have done that," she whispered. "We should have probed him for information at least before the killing, but I hear we didn't get anything useful? Did you even question where Xena and Ezekiel are?"

I cocked my head to the side, stunned at her words.

Was she mad I killed him? Or mad I didn't do a good enough job at killing him?

"You're not sad about—"

"I am *mad*," she interrupted. "Furious, that you would endanger us like that without even thinking through the consequences. Thinking about how it would affect our plan."

Her voice cracked towards the end and I felt the same pain rip through my chest. I didn't like this, not one bit.

"I apologize for making you mad," I said.

She straightened and let out a sigh, a small smile forming on her face as she wiped away a few of her tears.

"Promise you'll let us know before you try to kill anyone again," she demanded.

"I will," I lied.

Sorry, Rosie...after this one. After my payback for them taking you from me, I will tell you everything.

Rosie looked from me to Daxton and Amr with a sad smile.

"I missed you all," she said. "It wasn't that long but, it was still—"

There was a ringing that filled the still air, and everyone turned to look at each other.

Rosie waved away the wall of magic separating Rae and Malik from us then stepped back looking for the noise.

I caught Rae's glance; we didn't need to check where it was coming from. I heard it last year and I wouldn't forget it again.

"Is that...?"

"The games," Rae and I finished at the same time.

"They are early," Rosie said, a hint of worry in her tone.

Her thoughts reached out to me without any prompt. They were frantic and swirled around me as if needing my comfort

It has to be Xena and Ezekiel's work.

"Tread with caution," Malik warned and began to back away towards the entrance. "I will call the others and search the perimeter."

"We will go," Rae said and reached out to grab Rosie's arm, who in turn gave her a worried look. "You're last year's winner, and have to show your face. We will watch you from the crowd."

"Take me," Amr insisted and without warning shifted into his cat form running full speed towards Rosie's open arms. She caught him with ease and pulled him to her chest, planting a kiss on his nose.

"But the games, he is in the top twenty," Daxton said from beside me.

"This will be fine, if he doesn't show up, they will just forfeit him," she said to Daxton then her eyes shifted upwards, taking everyone in. "For those on the sidelines... We need to be on the look out for anything they have planned *and* we are dealing with the low-levels' first game. I suspect that we are going to see the worst of the high-level cruelty."

The sudden change in her confidence took me even more by surprise than her acceptance of me killing her once best friend. Now her shoulders were back, her chin high, and eyes narrowed at us. No longer was she the enraged kitten but a grown woman who had a plan and was trying to lead us into the unknown.

"Sure," I said with a shrug and tried to walk forward and pull her into my arms but Rae walked over and pushed me away with a glare.

"Don't think I don't know you, Eli," she growled. "I can feel what is building on the surface and until that goes away, you have to keep your distance."

I looked down towards Rosie and she just shrugged.

"We don't have time to discuss this," she said and turned towards the open door. "Let's go."

All the students began filing into the bleachers, with varying levels of excitement and interest. There were far more students than those that made it into the top one hundred so it was like a free tournament for them, instead of a brawl.

The idea of the games excited me, but the execution was subpar.

You couldn't kill anyone.

People relied too heavily on their powers.

And of course I had to watch Rosie get pummeled into.

She only made it by sheer luck and I doubt it would happen a second time.

There were no seats available in the front, but that didn't stop me from walking over to the laughing high-levels that occupied the seat I wanted and glaring down at them.

"Move," I demanded.

The stunned demon looked up at me with wide yellow eyes.

"I'm sorry?" he asked, his voice cracking.

I felt Rae stand beside me and his friends turned to look at us, their eyes widening as well. Their faces got noticeably paler and they scrambled to leave.

I tilted my head to catch Rae's glance.

"Laid it on a little heavy, didn't you?" I asked and plopped down into the now empty chair. The uncomfortable plastic dug into my skin through the thin Winterfell slacks.

Rae and Daxton sat on either side of me, all of us focused on the mess of a PR sent in front of us.

There was a stage set in the back center of the field, leaving just enough room for the students to fight without worrying about stray powers or magic. On the stage sat the principal, Mr. Falkner, and Rosie along with at least five or six cameras stationed behind her. I couldn't see Rosie's expression that clearly from how far away we were, but I noticed her jerky moments and the way she shifted under the gaze of all the students and countless people.

There were more cameras to either side of us and a hoard of

news people who were trying to grab students to interview before the games started.

"For such an abrupt start, they sure were prepared," Daxton muttered next to me, eying the cameraman that was currently making a beeline towards us.

"Mr. Reid, Ms. Ashwell!" he called. "Care to talk about your first games with your parents gone? Any plans to take over your parents' roles after you graduate?"

Rae glared daggers at the cameraman and I watched as his face twisted and he took a shaky step back.

"We don't feel like speaking now," she said in a low voice. "Thank you though."

Even before the words left her mouth the man was turning and running back in the direction he came from.

I let out a small laugh and looked towards Rae.

"What's with your power? Seems like your blood is working better than mine," I said.

Her eyes shifted towards mine and I caught something there that made me pause.

"It hasn't changed much," she muttered.

I hope you are hearing this, but find me after this. I need help.

Curiosity burned at my senses and I found myself unable to wait for this shit show to be over.

24
ROSIE

Last year's games did not even hold a candle to these ones. In comparison, last year's was a low budget version of a pathetic underground fighting ring while these were some sort of shiny televised event broadcasted to the entire world.

Everything about this caught me off guard.

Mere hours earlier I was cocooned in Malik's embrace, excited to finally see the others after being separated again and the games were not even on my mind.

The games weren't supposed to be scheduled for another week and none of the low-levels were thoroughly prepared for what they would have to face.

I wasn't prepared either, truth be told.

Not to have to fight someone again.

Not to have to watch the low-levels get beat by people way stronger than them.

And I definitely wasn't prepared to be showcased to the entire school like a medal, nicely polished and put behind glass to be viewed at their pleasure.

Only in this case it wasn't glass, but a magical barrier and instead of casual viewing, the cameras all around me zeroed in on me like hungry dogs, just waiting for the moment I messed up.

I was lucky Rae insisted I wore a proper uniform and get ready as if I was actually going to school, or else I was tempted to show up in Malik's shirt and Rae's oversized sweats.

I shifted uncomfortably as Mr. Falkner moved to sit next to me with a smile. I still didn't know what his deal was or why he was even still in this school to begin with. His employers left, so he should have too.

Unless he was here for something else.

"Are you ready for the games Rosie?" he asked.

I looked at him critically, as he faced me. He had been here standing next to me for each game and event that Winterfell had held, like he was some sort of chaperone though he made no effort to talk to me when the others were around. All of it just added to my list of growing suspicions.

Amr gave a clear warning growl pulling Mr. Falkner's gaze from mine.

"Hello, Amr," he said pleasantly. "I see you have changed into something more comfortable."

I froze at his words. His eyes slowly met mine and I saw a glint of something sharp pass through them.

I sat back in my chair with a smile. I knew his act was bullshit.

Probe him about Sarah, child, Marques's voice said, filling my mind.

I almost jumped at the intrusion but forced my face to stay neutral.

"You know, Mr. Falkner..." I trailed. "I haven't seen that Sarah teacher around. You know, blonde hair blue eyes? I was really interested to hear about her theories last year, is she coming back?"

Mr. Falkner's smile dropped and his eyes searched my face carefully.

"No unfortunately," he replied and turned to look back at the field. "She has been quite busy recently and doesn't have time to teach."

Fourteen-fifty.

Telekinesis.

Margret.

Repeat them to him, Marques ordered me.

I did as he said and watched as Mr. Falkner became rigid. His eyes stayed in front but I watched as they darted back and forth, searching for something I suspected would never come. A small bead of sweat trickled down the side of his face.

Then he relaxed in his chair, and crossed his legs at the ankle.

"This semester we will be focusing on the path the Originals took and the settlements they created along the way," he said in a strained voice. "The ones of particular interest are the ones all along the east coast of this continent as based on our previous assumptions about wings, we are to assume they flew there and landed somewhere in Nova Scotia. So there is no need to look at hypothetical fossils anymore." His eyes shifted towards mine. "Because we already know they are there."

Noted, Marques said in my mind.

I didn't relay anything else to Mr. Falkner and was just happy to watch him wallow in his own panic.

I already knew what Marques's plans were with Sarah, and was excited that I could finally lend some help, no matter how small it may be.

Malik does not sense the Originals there, child, Marques said in my mind. *But be careful, I doubt this was caused for nothing.*

Understood, I relayed back.

Also, Marques trailed, sounding uncertain. *Watch your lovers, they are scheming.*

My eyes shot towards the group closest to the field. While I couldn't see their faces, I knew those three figures from anywhere. I caught Eli and Rae looking at each other while Daxton's eyes were focused on Amr and me.

Scheming indeed, I thought to myself.

"Welcome everyone!" Principal Winterfell called causing me to jump in my seat. I sent an apologetic look to Amr as he was jostled but he just cuddled up to me purring loudly against my chest. "This is the second annual Winterfell games!"

There were cheers that erupted from the crowd.

"To note this is also our first year that we are going to televise the games, all to welcome our newest addition to Winterfell academy," he continued, his voice echoing across the field. "The low-level demons have been proven to be one of our most successful integrations yet. With zeros dropouts and with many of the new low-levels scoring in the top six percent of all grades, we cannot believe our success rate."

There were more cheers, but not as much as before, showing that a majority of the demons in the crowd did not feel the same way as the principal.

"Now, how this will work is two stages will go at once until the final battle with our beloved Rosie Miller." The crazed purple-haired maniac smiled and motioned towards me. I sat up straight and looked into the crowd, not smiling or waving.

In my peripheral I could see my face being broadcasted on magic screens that floated in the air.

"Now there is a representative that will watch over each field and declare a winner, and please remember *no killing,* that is something Winterfell will not be held liable for!" His cheerful voice was starting to annoy me. "Now let's begin!"

Two floating numbers appeared on either side of the field and I had to squint to see the names on either side.

I sat up straight when I saw a shy low-level descend from the bleachers and stand across from what I assumed was a high-level. I remembered the girl from orientation; she had come up to me and shyly asked questions, because raising her hand in front of everyone else scared her.

I hadn't heard from her since and I had to watch her now fight someone.

Please forfeit, please forfeit, I chanted in my head over and over again. Praying that someone was out there listening.

As the numbers counted down on the one side, my eyes were pulled to the other side where another low-level I recognized made it to the field.

My heart started racing as I tried to keep the two in sight.

The girl, to my dismay, did not forfeit and instead lifted her fists as if she really wanted to fight the man. The laugh from the high-level could be heard even from where I was sitting and I watched in horror as he readied himself and lunged forward just as the numbers disappeared.

The girl had no chance, his ability was speed and he tackled her to the ground. Without hesitation he threaded his fists and brought them down onto the girl's face.

I stood abruptly and moved forward. I didn't know what I was going to do, but I couldn't watch as this girl was being so brutally pounded into. My head snapped to the other direction as the other boy screamed.

I gasped as the high-level was trying to pull off the low-level's arm.

Mr. Falkner's hand wrapped around my wrists and tugged me back down to my seat.

"They can forfeit if it's too much," he said. "But you cannot stop this."

I looked up at him in shock. Amr growled aloud letting me know his own displeasure.

"This is not a game anymore," I argued. "They are using this as an excuse to torture the students."

"This is the way it is Rose," he said. "Now sit back and wait your turn."

With a heavy heart and a sadness I watched as both the low-levels in front of me forfeited, leaving the two demons to now fight amongst themselves.

As I watched another low-level descend I felt my stomach twist.

This was going to be painful.

❧

I WATCHED every single match with barely so much as a blink in between.

The results were the same. Each time the high-level would use whatever means necessary to get them to forfeit, but not until they were done having their fun.

I felt like I had failed them and on many occasions I watched as their hands reached out to me, as if pleading for me to save them from this brutality.

I wanted to so badly, wanted to go down there and put a stop to this but Mr. Falkner's stare stopped me from moving.

I wanted to tell them that I knew all about what they were feeling, that I had been there as well before but as more and more low-levels were tortured in front of me I realized...our experiences were not the same at all.

I was protected by the monsters that found me. I somehow successfully turned the most vile and bloodthirsty of the high-levels into people who now protected me and watched my every move...the others didn't have this opportunity.

They were stuck fighting on their own as the people who hated them laughed at their tears.

"Here," Mr. Falkner said. In his hand was a water bottle. "You look like you're going to throw up."

I was in no state of mind to reject him. Instead, I just opened it and gulped it down as fast as I could.

In the middle of the water bottle I paused and tore it from my lips. The effect was almost unnoticeable at first but the familiar vibration of magic as it passed through me was unmistakable.

My magic went stone-cold inside of me before lashing out wildly. Luckily it was still not visible to the eye, but I could feel it fanning out, searching for other magic users, intent on consuming everything in its path.

"What was in that?" I growled and pulled Amr closer to me, hoping he could take the magic.

I felt him start to pull magic into him...but my magic was growing far faster than he could handle.

"A stimulant," he answered in a low tone.

His eyes glanced over to mine and a small smirk played at his lips.

"Good luck, Rosie," he said. "Your turn is soon."

I looked towards the field and watched in horror as Ren and Eli faced each other. From Eli's stance I could tell that they were ready to fight the low-level. I wanted to scream to them, tell them they had caused enough damage, but the words wouldn't come out of my mouth. All my energy went into making sure that the magic would stay tucked inside me.

With great relief I watched as Eli called out a forfeit as soon as the numbers disappeared.

Rae and Daxton followed their lead and quickly left the field one by one. Rae glanced at me and held my stare for a moment too long before turning back and walking to her seat.

It was supposed to be Malik's turn now...but after a few minutes passed Principal Winterfell stepped up to the mic.

"Now we have our champion, Rosie going against our newest low-level recruit, Ren!"

There were cheers and with stiff limbs I walked down the stage steps and across the field.

"Go to them," I whispered through clenched teeth to Amr. "Tell Eli."

Amr meowed in protest but did as I said when I came to stand across the floating number.

I could see only half of Ren's face but what I did see caused me to pause.

No longer did I see the smiling face of the low-level that had greeted me on the first day. Instead his purple eyes were narrowed and his mouth set into a deep frown.

When the numbers gave way I lifted my hand to forfeit only to have to dodge a black ball of...fire?

Did he just shoot fire at me?

I stared at him with wide eyes.

As if to prove I wasn't just seeing things he did it again, causing me to dive to the ground. The fire just brushed past me and I could feel the heat of it singing the back of my uniform.

My magic angrily thrashed inside me, pushing to get out of my skin, begging to rip the boy in front of me in half. It acted as though in front of me was not the harmless low-level, but a witch with a core that I needed to consume.

It saw him as an enemy, one that threatened the existence of myself and the people I loved.

I jumped to my feet and lifted my arm again but this time I found myself knocked over by a bright purple light of magic that singed my cheek.

Magic?

The air was knocked out of my chest and the world came to a screeching halt as I looked up at Ren. I could feel it now, why couldn't I feel it before?

The thrum of magic was vibrating next to mine as he walked towards me. With each step I felt a flare of magic spread out and rock my being. *I was scared.*

Scared of this magic.

Scared that this was the person who was going to end it all for me.

The crowd's screams and chants were muffled as he came to stand over me, his shadow blocking out the blinding sun. A crazed grin spread across his face, much like the one I had seen spread across Daxton's when he was lost to his magic.

"Hybrid," I breathed.

He let out a small chuckle.

"Say hi to Father, would you?" he asked and with a snap of his fingers blackness engulfed me.

I was too stunned to get my barrier up in time and felt the fire burn into my skin. Using my magic I built a barrier around myself and watched as the flames fought to pry open the magic.

The ground below me started to melt against the heat the fire was emitting and a slick sweat covered my skin. With shaky arms I pushed myself into a sitting position and tried to think of a way out of this.

My skin healed itself but I didn't even pay it any attention as my mind whirled.

Black hair, purple eyes, freckles... He was my brother? But I was told there were no others from Xena and my father.

A memory from when I was training with Malik hit me like a train.

"How many were there?"

Malik shrugged, a dark look overcoming his face.

"I lost count," he said. "Truly."

Was it possible one survived? Even after they tried to erase their sins, one still persevered?

If he escaped, then why is he trying to hurt me?

The flames disappeared and I used the surprise to my advantage and quickly tried to pull my magic together, concentrating on covering his form and then snapping my magic as close to his skin as I could.

I watched as his eyes widened and he struggled against my magic.

I made quick work of my magic and forced his body to the ground. He howled as he bucked wildly against my hold like an animal caught in a trap. Fear and panic were slapped across his face and my heart began to ache.

He was working with them...he was afraid I would end him, or they would on my behalf.

I had been there, I knew the pressure that came with

working with them. At least Marques had never tried to hold that power over us.

Luckily for Ren, my magic wasn't as matured as it should have been and the more he struggled, the weaker my hold got.

He broke out of my hold and I felt wisps of magic wrap around my ankle, pulling me closer to him. I flailed my arms out to the side and dug my nails into the ground, trying to hold onto anything that would keep me as far away from him as possible.

"Why are you working with them?" I yelled.

"Why are you *not?*" he asked and readied another fireball.

I quickly turned and shot one of my own at him before pushing myself up to my feet and tackling him head-first.

I did not wait for a second and created a bubble of magic around his head and sucked the air out of it. A trick that I learned from the cruelty of Xena and Ezekiel's test on the town.

I couldn't watch as he struggled and instead just focused on holding him down as his hands grasped at me and tried to pull me down with him. By mistake my eyes wandered and I caught sight of his purple face. His eyes were wide with tears tracking down them and his mouth was open in a silent scream.

When his body stopped moving I removed the bubble and looked directly towards Mr. Falkner. Displeasure was evident on his face even from so far away.

My magic was still roaring inside me, ready to kill the hybrid below me. It didn't care that this was Xena and Ezekiel's doing, all it saw was that we were in danger and the danger was still very much alive and breathing underneath me.

But my mind was the one to tell me that Mr. Falkner needed to be taken care of. If I had not let out some magic beforehand, I wouldn't have been able to stop myself. They thought that I would turn into a rampaging beast, hell-bent on destroying my own blood.

But what I couldn't figure out was...was this supposed to be my disposal or his?

Cheers echoed the field as I was announced the winner, but I didn't pay them any mind. Instead I motioned for Eli to come help me pick up Ren and waved the nurses away as they gathered around us.

"They wanted us to kill each other," I whispered as Rae came up to my side. "If you didn't notice he has the same power as me."

"I noticed," she answered. "I made the connection."

"Come with me," Daxton said, his hands full with Amr. "Malik will wait for us in a classroom."

"Here take this guy," Eli said passing off the unconscious hybrid to Daxton. Amr yowled and launched himself at me. I gladly opened my arms for him. "Rae and I will be busy."

"Where are you going?" I asked.

"We will tell you when we get back," Rae said.

I eyed her suspiciously but chose to trust them.

"I need to share soon," I told Amr and Daxton.

Daxton nodded and without another second to waste we walked off the field trying to dodge both news anchors and students alike. I heard my name being called by the principal but I paid no mind. I had bigger things to do now.

25

RAE

I knew that I was really pushing the boundaries of Rosie's trust when I refused to tell her what Eli and I were up to, but I didn't want to give anyone false hope.

There were still many unknowns and I had to put my effort into the biggest one. The names hidden in my father's clock meant something. I had suspected that he knew he was going to die, he wasn't stupid after all, and used his last chance as a way to blackmail yet another person.

If I ask you about Mary Langworth, would you tell me the truth? I asked in my head hoping it would somehow make its way to Marques.

No, he answered back right away. *Though feel free to snoop, not like I could stop you.*

I sent Eli a look, and they merely raised a brow at me, indicating they heard nothing of this conversation.

Why was Malik worried? I asked.

There was a pause before he spoke. The only thing breaking the silence was our steps against the concrete halls of Winterfell as we rushed to the office. Cheers and music were still playing at the field but given our abrupt exit, I doubted the crowd would stay there much longer.

After all, their star was gone.

Malik wants to protect me, he answered. *This information could be dangerous if it falls into the wrong hands.*

Protect Marques. Malik wants to *protect* the oldest known being on this planet. The same one who could end all of us in an instant.

But you won't stop me, I shot back.

We turned down the hallway and the Winterfell Office was in sight. I paused with my hand on the cool metal door, waiting for his answer.

You can say that you have earned my trust, he replied, his voice holding a slight bit of amusement. As if he knew that I was the last person on the earth he could entrust this secret to, but he would anyways because this option was better than anyone else finding out.

I paused to look at Eli. Their face was blank and their posture and jerky movements told me I was wearing on their patience. It would have been better for me to bring someone else given how pissed they still were at me. The anger fanned out around them and hung over us like a dark cloud. I don't even understand how they kept it all in.

...but there was no one else that I trusted more. They would have my back regardless of what happened in there.

Without a word to them, I threw open the Winterfell door and stepped into the dimly lit space. The dry air hit my skin and the first thing I saw was Tammy's flushed face. A smile spread to her face.

"Not enjoying the games, ladies?" she asked.

I felt Eli's spike of anger next to me.

"No," I said in a polite tone. "Just waiting for Principal Winterfell to get back so we can talk to him about some stuff."

Tammy visibly cringed when she met Eli's glare.

"Well, his calendar is booked so unfortunately—"

"Listen here, lady," Eli growled and took a step forward.

I made the snap decision to send as much exhaustion to

Tammy as possible and jumped when that panicked face of hers thumped right into the desk, knocking her out cold.

Eli paused and there was a silence that fell over us. The clock on the wall behind Tammy clicked a few times before either of us stirred. Carefully they eyed Tammy, stepping forward just a bit but not too much, like they were scared of getting too close. Their eyes met mine and they stood straight, casting one last glance at Tammy.

"You saw that wasn't me, right?" they asked.

"That was me actually," I said feeling my face flush, and cleared my throat. "Let's wait in his office."

Eli looked at me with a shocked face before a smirk pulled at their lips. Amusement exploded inside them. With a huff I turned around and walked towards Principal Winterfell's office, which was to our luck, unlocked.

There was nothing special about his office, just a desk, a file cabinet, and a few bookshelves, but I knew that the principal of the most prestigious demon academy had to have something valuable in here.

Eli wasted no time making themselves at home on the office chair and propped their feet on the desk, scattering some of the loose papers.

I pushed their chair to the side earning a glare from them, then bent to look through the drawers. By the third one, I had found nothing but an obscene amount of chapstick and hair ties.

With a heavy sigh I moved to the file cabinet adjacent to the desk.

I came across the student files and quickly sought out the section labeled "low-levels." There were not many low-levels as of yet so this made the search much quicker.

I was actually surprised to find Ren's folder, thinking that Xena and Ezekiel were being careless. After all neither Matt nor his siblings had one, but I am sure that they had to do what they could when they lost Malik's power for good.

"To what do I owe the pleasure?" Principal Winterfell called from the door. I didn't even look at him as I flipped through Ren's file. As promised, everything from past school records to address and more were listed, but I would need Malik to check if they were legit.

"Sit," I said and moved to stand behind Eli, only then glancing up at the principal.

He watched me with careful eyes, and I could feel anger and fear rolling off of him and clouding the small room. Principal Winterfell was a disappointment of a demon and really only used his place here to get his dick sucked by underage students.

While the trick with Emma was a good piece of blackmail, she no longer came close to our group after the gala last summer, so that leverage was as good as gone.

When he didn't move I sent more fear towards him and watched as his face lost all color. He looked back towards the door, his hands wringing his jacket before he stiffly sat down opposite us.

Now he was in the student chair and I couldn't help the low thrum of satisfaction that ran through me when I peered down at him. He looked so minimal and powerless from this perspective and I found I rather quite liked being on the other side of this desk.

"You seem comfy behind there," he said in a light tone, though his chuckle afterwards was forced. "Don't tell me you are vying for my job?"

"Maybe I am," I said in a noncommittal tone.

Eli stayed silent next to me and I handed the file to them without a word.

"Are you going to tell me why you are here?" he asked.

I looked down at him, noticing the way he squirmed in his seat.

"I am going to give you some names and you are going to tell me what you know about them," I said and threw a little more fear his way to ensure I got what I wanted.

His Adam's apple bobbed and he nodded his head, the thoughts of denying us seemingly having vanished in thin air.

"Mary Langworth," I said.

He paused; his knee started to shake. His sudden spike of panic and recognition told me what I needed to know.

"Jon Abbot," I said.

Same reaction.

I continued to list off each of the names that I found on the list my father was hiding. By the time I was finished, sweat dripped down his face and his color had turned sickly.

"They were, not people I knew personally," he said quickly.

A sour taste filled my mouth. *A lie.*

"Eli," I called.

Without needing to say anything Eli lunged over the table and grabbed Principal Winterfell's hand, crushing it without hesitation.

Principal Winterfell's screams echoed the room and I quickly moved to shut the door, hoping Tammy would stay asleep.

"Try again, James," I said and walked up behind him. I didn't dare touch his slimy skin but I let my hand brush over the chair he was sitting on.

"S-ssorry," he sputtered. "I knew them. But they were much older than I was when we met. I hadn't even started the school yet—"

"You met all of them?" I asked.

He shuddered as he felt my hands grip the chair he was sitting on. Eli sent him a devious smile.

"Yes," he answered.

"What was their relationship with my father?" I asked.

"Your father?" he echoed. "None, I don't think."

Then why did my father have their name on a piece of paper hidden in his study?

I hummed and sent a look to Eli. They reached over and Principal Winterfell let out a shout.

"I don't know anything about your father and them I swear!" he cried.

"Then how are they all related?" I asked.

"They um..." He let out a shudder. "They were *very* old. Much older than me. They migrated here from up north but I don't know much else."

"Their powers?" I asked.

Principal Winterfell paused and Eli lifted a brow.

"I'm thinking, okay? I am old now it takes me a—"

Eli grabbed his hand.

"Okay!" he cried. "I think one could search your memories or something like that, and uhh, one could put you under hypnosis, he used it to get people to tell him the truth, I think... But I don't remember the others I swear!"

My whole body froze and suddenly, I was back in the study between Marques and my father, unable to move. A sweet voice trailed in my head, persuading me to give up my secrets.

These were powers that Marques had, or at least what I think he had. But how did that work? How could a demon have powers another demon had?

"Where are they now?" I asked.

"They disappeared a long time ago," he said with a quiver in his voice. "That's all I know, and I have never seen them again. I swear."

It still doesn't make any sense...

"That's a secret that will cost you at least ten Originals."

I stood straight and stepped back from the chair.

Is it true? I asked Marques, but there was no response. I didn't need one. The world became clearer and now I understood why Marques's blood had so much effect on us.

But if the world found out demons could eat other demons and take their powers?

We'd be fucked.

"Let's go," I commanded Eli.

They threw Principal Winterfell's hand away like a piece of garbage and stood, knocking the desk as they passed.

We walked out of the office without another word.

"I heard what happened," Eli said as we walked down the hallway. "About the Original."

"Good," I grunted and pulled out my phone. There was a text from Daxton that told me the room number they were in.

I let out a sigh of relief when I realized it wasn't too far away.

When I opened the door the last thing I expected to see was Rosie standing in front of Ren with a knife in her hand.

He was bound to a desk with glowing ropes that burned into his skin, the sound and smell of his smoking flesh filling the room. His pain was immense, though no sound left his mouth.

I shot a look to Malik and he just held my gaze, giving me no indication if he had allowed these events to transpire. Daxton and Amr watched from the corner. The magic was building up inside Daxton and for a moment I thought we may have another situation like the cafeteria on our hands.

"Fuck you," Ren spit at Rosie, anger flaming his eyes, though I could feel the panic and fear settling underneath his skin.

He was also sad. A sadness so heavy I could barely stand in the room.

It was the same sadness Rosie was trying so hard to keep in right this moment.

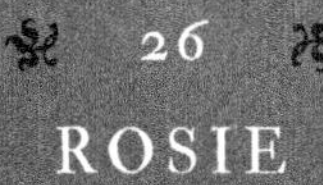

26
ROSIE

I turned to Rae and Eli as they walked into the classroom. They both looked me over, Rae with a tense expression while Eli's was of obvious enjoyment. In their hand was a thick manila envelope that looked to be of particular interest.

Even though we had been waiting for them for a while, Ren had just barely woken up, and was already proving to be difficult. He refused to answer even the simplest of questions and seemed hell-bent on dying in this very classroom.

And if my magic had its way, he would.

"Welcome," I said in a calm tone. "Malik, let's finish this."

Malik, who was standing against the wall on the opposite side of the door, walked slowly towards Ren. Said hybrid jerked against the chair, trying to get as far away from the man as possible.

He obviously knew the power the man held and knew that his fighting now, was useless.

I wanted to give Ren a chance to answer for himself before we went down this route. I didn't plan to actually hurt him, nor did I want to cause him any discomfort, I just wanted him to come clean because he *wanted* to, instead of being forced to do it.

I for one, knew how it felt to have all of your will taken from you and used against you horribly. Being in the backseat of your own body in this situation was horrifying and if he could just gather himself and tell us the truth without us having to force him, *maybe* there was a way to build trust between us.

We were apparently blood-related, after all. Shouldn't I want to trust him?

But there was another reason that had nothing to do with Ren. It was Malik.

Even as he walked the short distance to the small desk that held Ren, I could tell that he was exhausted.

He used his powers a lot last night, and I don't fully understand the extent he had gone to search Winterfell before the games.

He was important, to me and this mission so I needed him in his best state if we were to continue.

Malik grabbed Ren's chin and forced him to look in his eyes.

"Where are Xena and Ezekiel?" he asked.

Even from afar I could feel his power swirl around us and while it was woefully inappropriate...it kinda turned me on. Seeing the way he commanded his attention, the way his power brushed against me as if reminding me of its presence.

I shivered along with the magic inside me.

"I don't know," he said, trying his hardest to fight Malik's power.

"Where did you meet them last?" Malik asked.

"Montnesse."

"How do you contact them?" I asked.

He sent me a glare.

"Answer her question," Malik growled.

"I wait for their signal," he spat out. "A witch comes to find me."

"When is your next meeting?" Malik asked.

Ren's face turned bright red as he struggled against the power.

"Six weeks from now."

"Where?"

"My dorm room," he said. "If I wasn't taken by the demon regulation society before then."

His tone held some bitterness in it and all I could think of was how alone he had been in all this. They expected him to either die, or get taken to jail because he killed a student.

He was just another pawn in their game, and they really didn't care how much they lost.

I was lucky to have those around me by my side through it all, but he was all alone and had no protection against Xena and Ezekiel... If I were in the same position as him, I might have ended up the same.

"Did you grow up with low-levels?" I asked.

His eyes widened and he forcefully ripped his chin from Malik's grip to lock eyes with me.

"Why don't you just end me already, hm?" he growled. "Isn't that what your people do anyways? I know about what you did to the people of Montnesse after you didn't get your way."

"What are you talking about?" I asked through gritted teeth.

My already raging magic spiked sharply and I felt lightheaded from the sheer intensity. I reached back to steady myself on the teacher's desk.

"*You killed them*," he hissed. "You slit all their throats, and painted the walls with their blood."

His words swirled around me, invading my mind and repeating themselves over and over again.

You killed them.

And...maybe I did.

It was my fault anyways, I was the one who decided to corner Matt and force my way into Marques's hideout.

A warm hand gripped my shoulder.

Looking up I caught Amr's gentle smile.

"Is that what Xena and Ezekiel told you?" I asked, taking the strength Amr was giving me.

"No, I saw you leave the cafeteria in a rush and when I entered everyone in there was already dead," he said.

My body froze.

"When did you arrive at Winterfell?" Malik asked.

"A month before the orientation," he said with a struggle.

"Were you watching me?" I asked shocked.

"Yes and when I saw you run out I knew it was bad news so I flagged to Xena and what would you know, they were all dead when I—"

His words faded into the background and I couldn't hear them over the rush of my own blood running through my ears.

It was never Matt, a pitiful voice spoke in my head.

I couldn't even bring myself to look over at Eli even though the only thing I wanted to do was tell them how hurt I was they lied.

They told me he was the rat, but now that seemed less likely.

"Why did they move the games up?" I forced out.

There was a pause before he answered.

"They said your magic would be vulnerable," Ren answered.

"How would they—"

I was cut off by my own realization.

Because Eli killed Matt.

I looked up to meet Malik's eyes, realization dawning on him as well and he cast his eyes downward.

They knew him better than we thought.

"Keep him somewhere he cannot be found by the Originals," I said in a hollow voice. Malik's eyes drifted back to me. His face was set in a deep frown. "Do not tell any one of us where he is kept."

Malik nodded. There was no need to speak about why we couldn't know. We both understood that there were too many unstable people here and one slip up would end in his death.

Whether that be by our hands, or the Originals.

"We should think abou—"

I raised my hand to stop Rae from speaking.

"We are changing things, a little," I said. To my surprise no one fought me.

"In six weeks' time we will bring Ren back to here and meet the witch," I said. "Before then we will all take shelter in Rae's house. Malik, get Claudine and Maximus to build us a barrier. I do not think we should be here until we—*I*— recuperate. Ren is one in a million and since we have just welcomed hundreds of low-levels into this school, all with complete access to my time—"

"We cannot chance it," Rae added on.

I nodded and looked around the room.

"Any objections?"

There were none.

Good job child, Marques said in my mind. *You take after your father.*

I couldn't help the way my eyes snapped to Daxton. His eyes burrowed into me and his magic brushed up against me.

"Alright," Malik said and pulled out his phone. "Let me call for reinforcements."

Amr pulled me against his chest as Ren glared at us with so much hatred it made my heart feel like it was shriveling up. I wanted to help him, I wanted him to be on our side and get free of those psychos...but it would take time.

"You're growing into your crown, my queen," Amr whispered in my ear.

"Thank you," I whispered, tearing my eyes away from Ren to look at Amr.

He had a small, encouraging smile on his face that lifted a weight off my chest. He was here still, after everything, just like he had promised.

"Do not burden yourself with this worry, let's get you taken care of," he said.

In a flash Claudine was in front of us, and she met me with a pitiful look. I longed to reach out to her, to confide in her like I once had...but now wasn't the time.

Now was the time to stand strong. We were the closest we had ever been and if I had not been as prepared as I was today... the cycle would start over again but this time it would be Ren, and he would be alone.

"Thank you for your help," I said to her.

She sent me a wide smile, her eyes sparkling in the light.

"Anything for you," she said with a wink then turned to face Ren. "It's a pity things didn't turn out differently for you."

Malik walked over to her and placed a hand on her shoulder, his dark gaze meeting mine.

"I will be back," he declared.

"We will be busy," Daxton said and pushed off the wall to come to my side. "Take your time and don't interrupt us."

Malik's eyes shifted to Daxton and he smiled.

"Be gentle with her," Malik said in a dark tone. "I was rather hard on her last night."

Claudine let out a giggle before taking both Ren and Malik away in a flash of light.

Daxton's hand gripped my shoulder and he moved to cover my line of sight. I had to tilt my head up to meet his gaze.

"You let him put his hands on you?" Daxton growled.

"Daxton," Amr warned, his grip on me tightening. "Rosie is free to care for who she wants. You said so yourself."

Daxton's eyes flashed towards him before gripping my chin, a warning gesture. My magic reached out to him, trying to pull him closer.

Take, now, my magic seemed to say.

I had already waited long enough, and with the elixir I was handed my magic was barely keeping itself together. I had wished that maybe we could have done this under better circumstances, when my heart wasn't as beat up as it was now, but I couldn't chance an incident again.

"I can share," he said in a dark tone, his head dipping to mine. "In fact I love watching you with the others...but that *bastard*—"

"Come on Dax," Eli said from the door away and moved to stand next to Daxton, throwing an arm over his shoulder. "We knew this was bound to happen, you're just angry she was taken from us."

Eli's tongue came out to lick their lips and I shivered under their stare.

"And who's fault is that?" Rae said stepping closer.

My heart started pounding in my chest and my magic stirred inside me.

Never had they been as close as this. Never had they all been here when I needed to share magic. My mouth began to water and I rubbed my thighs together, heat flashing through me.

"I know," Eli said with a huff. "But doesn't mean we didn't miss her. Isn't that right Dax?"

As Eli spoke their rough fingers traced my collarbone and began to unbutton my top.

Amr's hands began to wander down my back, to my hips and then dipped under my skirt. I gasped when his warm hands played with the straps of my underwear.

"We did," Daxton said and moved his hand from my chin to my throat.

"Is this okay, Rosie?" Amr asked, his hot breath fanning my face.

Heat pooled low in my belly and my knees felt weak. If I was not leaning against him I would have fallen to the ground.

It was more than okay, this was everything I dreamed about. The way their hands tugged at my clothes and brushed across my skin left bolts of electricity running through me.

I shot a look towards Rae. Her eyes were hooded and there was a slight quirk to their lips. They sent me a sharp nod.

"We can take turns," she suggested. "I am sure with your...*condition,* it will take more than normal to settle you. Am I wrong?"

Eli finally unbuttoned my shirt and spread it open, their

hands coming to cup my breasts. Even through my bra, by the smirk on their face I knew they felt my hardening nipples.

"As long as I can go first," Daxton muttered, removing his hand from my neck to pull my skirt up, giving them a view of my soaked pink panties.

"Is this what you want, my love?" Amr asked and slowly pulled down my panties, exposing my swollen pussy to Eli and Daxton.

I let out a whimper.

"You'll let them take care of you like a good girl, hm?" he asked.

Eli let out a dark chuckle and in one motion ripped my bra painfully off.

"I prefer it much more when she's bad," they said.

"Good girls don't let people like us have their way with them," Daxton said and without warning kicked my legs apart and forced two fingers inside my wet folds.

I leaned back into Amr with a loud moan which came out strangled as Eli twisted my nipples.

"Good girls also don't like to get punished," Eli chuckled.

Daxton began pumping his fingers inside of me, all while his eyes never left my face. Both him and Eli were watching me intently as if they enjoyed watching their destruction.

"Cat, switch with me," Eli commanded.

To my surprise Amr just let go of me with a small kiss to my temple and moved to stand by Rae.

I felt embarrassment flood through me as I realized they were all watching me. It felt oddly vulnerable and safe all at once, knowing that with all of them here they were safe.

We were safe.

Eli clicked their tongue and took Amr's place but didn't stop there.

"We are getting on the desk," they commanded.

Daxton gave them a smirk and pulled his fingers out of me, the sudden loss of them pulling a whimper from my lips. I felt

Eli hoist me up with ease and place us on the desk, with me between their legs. They scooted to the far back of the desk and Daxton wasted no time perching himself between my legs.

"This should be a good enough view," Daxton said and pulled me closer to the edge of the desk by my thighs.

"Unzip his pants Rosie," Eli whispered in my ear.

I did as they said and quickly undid his pants before reaching in and grabbing his stiff cock. I fingered the metal of the piercing, tugging on it slightly.

He groaned and helped me push his pants down.

"Are you sore?" Daxton asked as the head of his pierced cock ran through my folds.

I winched at the stretch as he pushed into me. There was a slight burning but nothing I couldn't handle.

"A little," I admitted

At my words Daxton used my hips as leverage to slam into me. Eli covered my mouth with their hand and pulled me back to them. I wrapped my hands around Eli's arms as anchors.

"Good," they said in my ear with a throaty chuckle. "Do your worst Dax."

Daxton grunted and began slamming our hips together, each time eliciting a new pained moan from my mouth as the soreness increased.

"That's it," Eli cooed and grabbed my left thigh only to place it over theirs, giving Daxton deeper access and giving our audience a better view.

"Oh god," I groaned as Daxton fucked me harder than before.

He was ravenous, angry. I could feel his magic clinging to me in almost a cruel fashion, as if they were sinking their claws into my entire being and getting deeper with each thrust.

Eli's hand came to rub small circles in my clit.

"You can't leave like that ever again," Daxton hissed. "*You. Hear. Me?*"

With each word Daxton snapped his hips to mine so hard

the desk we were on began screeching as it was forced across the floor.

"I feel left out of this party," Eli said. "Flip her."

Daxton pulled out of me abruptly and pulled me off the desk and turned me around.

"Hands," he commanded. I was out of breath and disorientated but did as he said anyways and put my hands behind my back. With a single hand he grabbed both wrists and with the other bent me forward so he could enter me from behind.

He used my hands to force me back into him, my whole body jolting as he did so.

Eli chuckled and climbed off the desk to remove their pants.

"Look at these tits," Eli said and slapped one before climbing back on the desk.

They wasted no time grabbing a fistful of my hair and pushing me down into their wet pussy. Daxton's animalistic thrusts made it hard to stay still but I tried as hard as I could to lick the length of their slit while meeting their blue eyes.

They tasted just as sweet as I remembered and suddenly I couldn't get enough of them.

"You're not coming until I do," they growled. "So you better put some work into it."

"She already feels like she going to come," Daxton chuckled from behind. "Looks like Malik left her wanting."

"Or she's just that much of a slut," Eli chuckled and pushed my head further into her wet lips.

I latched on to their clit and began sucking. Their hand pulled roughly on my hair, telling me that they liked what I was doing.

Daxton's zipper bit into my ass as he slammed into me. I could tell he was going to come soon by his frantic patterns.

Please let me come, I begged to Eli in my mind and sucked on their clit. Their eyes narrowed at me and I felt a thrill go through me as I pulled a moan out of their mouth.

"Not yet," they groaned and their hips bucked against me.

My hands were behind my back so I couldn't indulge them as much as I wished but from the looks of it...Eli liked it better when I was restrained and they were in full control of what I was doing.

"I'm gonna come," Daxton groaned from behind me.

"Then we switch you out," Eli said with a grin, which fell off as I gave their clit a hard suck.

Daxton let my hands go and instead grabbed my hips as he pumped his release into me. The magic that snapped between us made me groan. It overtook us and I was momentarily blinded as it rushed into me and mine rushed into him.

The magic felt familiar, felt soothing, like I had been missing him this entire time and didn't even really know it until now.

I used my free hands to spread Eli's lips as I attacked their wetness.

"Amr," Rae commanded.

I felt Daxton pull out of me and felt familiar warm hands knead my ass cheeks then slowly trail down and pinch my clit.

"Are you ready, my love?" Amr asked from behind me.

I tried to nod but Eli's hand stopped me.

"She says yes," Eli grunted back.

Instead of going straight to fucking I was surprised to feel Amr's tongue swipe my wet folds, not doubt licking up Daxton's release.

Heat rushed through me as he paid extra attention to my clit. My legs began to shake and I didn't know how much longer I could hold on.

"A little more," Eli said, their head falling back.

I worked on their clit like a hungry woman, giving them no break. I felt their thighs clench around my head and was surprised by their sudden release on my tongue.

Eli cursed and pulled my head back, Amr held onto my thighs not allowing me to move from his mouth as I began shaking violently in his grip.

"Good slut," they whispered. "You can come now."

I did exactly as they asked and kept their gaze as Amr pushed me over the edge.

The magic sharing was different with Amr. It was calming, more comforting and less abrupt than with Daxton. The magic slowly rolled me into another orgasm as I held onto Eli, engulfing me in a pool of warmth.

"Rae," they called. "Do you want in on this?"

Amr stood back up and pulled me to him. I turned and caught his lips in mine.

"Yes," she said. "Go entertain yourself with Daxton."

I felt Eli's presence leave and heard some shuffling and the scrape of a chair.

Amr let me go as Rae came close. She leaned against the desk and looked at me critically, her hand coming to feel my jaw. I winced as she touched a sore spot.

"Barbarians," she said with a soft voice.

"But we aren't like that," Amr said and left kisses down my neck finally pulling off the rest of my shirt while Rae tugged off my skirt.

"No," Rae whispered, her eyes trailing to my lips. "We aren't."

When her lips met mine I melted into her body, enjoying the shift from rough to sweet. Amr ran his hands down my body and began massaging my abused pussy lips.

"Are you sure you want to continue?" he asked against me, though I do not know if it was to me or Rae.

I pulled away and looked up at Rae, giving her the choice.

"You spoil me," she said and reached down to massage my clit. "Always giving me that look. Having me decide on everything. It would be a lie if I said I didn't love it. The power you give me."

Her words caused butterflies to fly free in my stomach.

"I am ready when you are," I gasped as Amr's fingers entered me.

"No need to rush," Amr murmured.

Rae leaned down and captured my lips once more. As our

tongues intertwined I couldn't stop thinking about how lucky I was to have her, *everyone,* here with me.

My magic, while still swirling around restlessly in my body, would have been so much worse if I wasn't surrounded by people like this.

I was the spoiled one.

With Rae's and Amr's ministrations it wasn't long until I felt myself on the cusp of another orgasm.

"It's okay," Rae whispered against my lips. "Let go."

I shuddered and pushed back into Amr, wanting more than the gentle orgasm I was receiving right now. I loved the way they touched me but I felt far too empty and my magic was begging for more.

Amr lined his cock up at my entrance and left scorching kisses up my back as he entered me. Rae left kisses down my chest and bent to pull a nipple into her mouth.

I moved to undo her pants but her hands stopped me.

"This is about you," she said and lightly bit my nipple.

Amr gave his first experimental thrust then gently pushed my back forward.

Rae stood straight and pulled me closer so my hands could rest on the edge of the desk on either side of her.

"You're so perfect love," Amr growled and thrust into me again.

A strangled moan left me and Rae's eyes lit up. She reached down and started to circle my clit once more.

"I think you can go faster now," Rae said.

Amr didn't have to be told twice and began fucking me in earnest, each thrust hard yet not too fast as to overwhelm me.

I wanted to pull my gaze away from Rae as Amr fucked me. It was intimate, almost too much and reminded me of the first time Rae and I were ever together.

We were different now though, and I tried to embrace the feeling I got as her hooded eyes stared down at me.

"You handle your magic so well," she cooed and brought her

free hand to trace my open lips. "Asking for help when needed, letting us take care of you."

I let out a whine and gripped onto the desk.

"Keep going," Amr said from behind me, his thrusts picking up speed. "She likes it."

Rae's eyes lit up.

"Were the others too mean to you?" she asked.

I heard a protest from Daxton and Eli but she waved them off.

"Did they not tell you how in love they are with this pussy?" she asked and pinched my clit. Tears welled in my eyes. "Or how good you feel? *Taste?*"

Rae paused her ministrations on my clit to drag her fingers across my bottom lip. Without hesitation I pulled it into my mouth and moaned at the taste of me on my own lips.

"You're so beautiful like this," she cooed. "When you let us use you. The way you silently plead for more. This face is one I cannot forget."

"*Fuck,*" I cried as she moved her hand back to my clit.

"Yes, my love," Amr moaned. "You feel so good, come on my cock."

Rae's lips crashed to mine as the orgasm ripped through me.

Amr gave a few more thrusts before I felt his hot release inside of me and we both shuddered as our magic fluttered between us.

"Damn I missed a party," Malik said from the door.

Shocked, I looked up to see him slipping in and closing the door quickly behind him. Rae leaned forward and her arms circled around me, shielding me as I came down from my high.

"You had enough time with her," Daxton growled.

I turned to see both him and Eli close together, glaring at Malik.

"I am here to take you back to Rae's house," he said. "We have work to do."

27
MALIK

It was a horrible day to die.

Even as we were hurdling closer and closer towards the warmer months, there was a chill in the air and clouds had covered the sky all day. I had thought it would rain, but it didn't. The clouds just loomed overhead as if taunting us with what was to come. Like it knew that nothing good could come from this day and moved in just to set the atmosphere.

I stood in front of the man I had entrusted with my life over and over again, with unsteady legs. It hadn't been the first time that I had to face him with my nerves eating me alive, but I was saddened to think that it would be the last.

The last time his dulling golden eyes stared into my soul.

The last time he and I would share a consciousness.

A frown pulled at my lips, even as he smiled up at me. He was relaxed in his chair, hands on the armrests and his chest moved with each shallow breath. While he had come to terms with this, I for one, had not.

I knew this day was coming soon, but somehow through our years together I had lost track of time. He told me long ago, and never seemed to *fucking* let me forget, but now that it was actually here...

I felt like the young untamed demon I once was, though at least this time I could keep my tears inside me. They fought hard to spill over, but I didn't want his last image of me to be sobbing at his feet, begging him to find another way.

I couldn't help but remember our times before, when he had first hinted at the idea and how different our roles were now.

I didn't know how long I had been sitting out here, looking over at the clueless town below me. The people in there going along with their day, happy as could be, thinking they were safe from the impending doom that the humans brought onto us.

I had sat on this hill many times before, when the world seemed too much. I would contemplate if the life in this bubble was worth it, or if I would just be better off defending myself against the humans.

They had calmed down in recent years and every time I went out, I was attacked less often, but that didn't stop the fear of another fight breaking out...though at this point, I wasn't really sure who started it in the first place.

They took my father and mother, fed them to other humans...but why? Why would they come up with a measure so cruel?

I doubted they thought of it on their own after witnessing the cruelty of the ones that came before me.

I leaned back on the damp grass, knowing my pants would be stained but didn't care. This was the time when I needed to be alone with my thoughts or else they would threaten to tear my insides up.

I couldn't do it anymore.

I couldn't lie. Couldn't repeat the cycle. And for god's sake I couldn't keep sending those children to their deaths over and over again.

Guilt clawed at my throat and made it hard for me to breathe.

Ann—

I couldn't even let myself think of her name. A child barely over the age of eight, and already deemed a failure.

She was number eight, and I had sentenced her to her death because she could not use her magic as well as Xena had requested. Too much diluted blood in her, we needed something purer.

I wanted to take her and run away from this cursed place. I had no idea what it meant to raise a child, but I wanted to do it for her.

It was my own cowardice and self-preservation that stopped me from following my heart on this one and I knew that it would stay with me for as long as I roamed this earth. This wasn't why I stuck with them. This wasn't what I wanted to do with my time on this earth.

I would much rather spend the rest of my time in exile, fighting off everyone outside of this hell hole. While my chances were slim, at least I wouldn't have to murder children.

I felt Marques's power before he sat down next to me on the dirty ground. I hadn't expected him to follow me. He was always the stoic voice of reason, never getting too involved but making sure to speak up when he saw an issue.

...but this time he just stood there.

For some reason, him being here made the invisible claw on my hand tighter and my eyes began to water. I was far beyond the age of crying but with him by me I was reminded of everything he had done for me since my parents were taken.

Xena and Ezekiel couldn't care less about me, but he saw through my mask. Saw the immature, hurt demon within and made sure I was taken care of.

If he was a man that hugged, I would dive right into his arms this instant.

"I am going to do something that will change the way we do things around here," he said, his voice cutting through the cloud of emotion surrounding me.

"What?" I asked with a scoff. "Xena getting too much for you, or is it the experimentation and murdering of children?"

When he didn't answer I shifted my gaze to him, taking in his tired expression. Marques was always quiet and reserved, but never had I seen his face look so tired before. His whole body bowed as if carrying some type of invisible weight.

His glowing golden eyes met mine. Little did I know that after this, those eyes would slowly begin to lose their luster.

"You are old enough to know that the threat to the survival of this

world is not the humans," he said. "We have been hidden in this bubble for over a thousand years; if humans were a threat, we would have been extinct by now."

I swallowed thickly and looked out into the city.

This spot was my favorite, because it was one of the only places that you could see the entirety of the town we were stuck in. At times, when I missed the outside the most, I would squint and pretend that the magical barrier that lay right over the horizon was the ocean.

I used to love visiting the ocean. Having the sand run through my toes, jumping into the freezing water...

And most of all I loved to spread my wings and fly over the waves, swooping down to get close and pulling away just before they crashed into me. It was a thrill and comfort all at once.

Thrilling because the waves threatened to take me under, deep below the surface where no one had ventured.

A comfort because I knew what to expect from the ocean. It was deep, angry and misunderstood. I found solace in something so powerful yet delicate because it proved that it was real and had a life as much as anyone else did here.

But now the barrier seemed too prominent, and I began to feel claustrophobic.

He was right, of course he was right...but that didn't mean we could change it as easily as he imagined.

"Why are you telling me this?" I asked.

Marques had been the one to raise me in the absence of my father and mother. He had a firm hand, and rarely talked about emotions...but I knew deep down if he didn't care that I would have ended up at the whim of Xena's short fuse.

"I want you to be prepared," he said seriously, a wistful smile forming on his face. "For when you come to hate me. For when I do things that are unforgivable. For when you come to believe that I am the worst evil this world has ever known."

I paused, unable to find my words.

"What are you going to do?" I asked. My stomach felt heavy and sourness spread across my tongue.

"I am going to save the world, by watching our people burn," he said in a joking tone, though I did not think he was joking one bit.

I shifted on my feet as Marques's hacking cough filled the room. It sounded painful and I kicked myself internally for not noticing his rapid decline.

Since the last I had seen him, he was a mere shell of himself. His skin was ghastly pale and sunken in like he hadn't eaten in weeks. He couldn't move without help from Claudine, who patiently stood by his side with a solemn expression.

"Is this when we finally save the world?" I asked.

The sides of his lips curled at the old joke.

"That was a silly dream," he said and let out a huff, something I came to realize was actually laughter. "But I will do my part."

I didn't want to think about what was next, didn't want to believe that we had finally reached this stage.

...but I also couldn't let myself think of the world that awaited us if we *did not* take these steps.

Rosie, Eli...they wouldn't be safe, none of us would. We needed a push to help us defeat the Originals that awaited us.

"We will keep the barrier up around the house," Claudine said. "But it will not fool them for long, Malik. We have to work fast. Once they figure it out..."

"I know," I said in a soft tone and sent her a smile.

The poor girl, not only did she have to suffer the loss of her brother but now...

"Ensure that Rosie doesn't fight this, hm?" Marques asked. "That girl is too much like her father."

"With a healthy dose of Xena," I said in a dry tone. Even though we were joking, it did nothing to lift the weight on my heart.

"Will Rosie experience the issues you do?" Claudine asked, her brow furrowed.

"I am not sure, child," Marques spoke. "Though I would like to think that I took the punishment of all ten of my sins and she, well..."

"Will take just the one," I finished for him.

Marques nodded.

"I should be mad that you are shortening her life," I said.

Marques smiled.

"If she is lucky, she can live as long as that blond bastard," he said. "And with her track record, I would say she's pretty damn lucky."

"Or unlucky," I muttered and shifted on my feet.

"Well," Marques trailed. "Shall we get on with it?"

I froze, every single point in my body on edge, but nodded anyways.

"Do you...want me to tell her anything?" I asked. "She's your last of kin."

Marques merely shook his head and smiled.

"Rosie has heard enough from me to last a lifetime," he answered. "Though I only wish I could have learned more about her. Give her the family she deserved."

I nodded, my throat constricting. I would fight to give her the same thing, even if it killed me.

I took stiff steps towards him until I stood directly in front of his chair.

I didn't even have to tell him to look into my eyes, he met me straight on and didn't waver. He had been waiting for this moment for lifetimes.

"Thank you," I whispered. "For giving this reckless demon a chance."

Light caught his dead eyes and I saw tears begin to well in them.

"Thank you," he said. "For trusting me, and please don't hold onto this. Go home, hug your loved ones and know that *you* are making it possible for them to continue to live happy, healthy lives."

I let out a shaky breath.

"Anything else?" I asked.

"Just can't wait to see you on the other side," he said.

"Though don't hurry, enjoy yourself. You deserve it after everything."

I wanted to look away. Wanted to run and hide and never look back, but I stood my ground. He had built me up for this and now I had a job to complete.

"Sleep, have the best dream you could possibly imagine," I said, sadness ebbing into my words. "And then stop your heart."

His eyes fluttered closed and a smile spread across his face.

His body was so weak that it just sunk into the chair. I didn't dare move to touch him, I couldn't pull my eyes away.

A hand clasped my shoulder.

"Claudine and I will—"

I cut Maximus off with a wave of my hand.

"This is my burden too," I said. "Let me."

28
ELI

The cold air seeped into my clothing, pulling a light shiver from me.

I leaned back against the side of Rae's house and shoved my free hand into the pocket of my hoodie. The other hand held my half-smoked lit cigarette, and I brought it back to my lips to take another drag.

I had tried to stop, but since we had been laying low...I was getting bored again and needed *something* to tide me over.

The night was quiet, and there was no sign of any life just outside of the magical barrier Maximus had put up around us. Sometimes a stray bird or squirrel would try and get close to the barrier but it had been a few hours since I had seen any other life form.

I was starting to think that we had overestimated Xena and Ezekiel's capabilities. They were supposed to be the strongest beings of this world, the ones that started everything. Couldn't they just take what they wanted? Were they *that* scared of a bunch of college students getting the upper hand?

Maybe we were the cowards.

But on the other hand, Rosie had made the right call. I may

be itching for action, but I would stay put if it meant ensuring her safety. I was reckless, not stupid.

I exhaled the smoke into the cool air, watching as it dissipated, wishing many problems could just float away with it.

Rosie was still mad at me... Well, I wouldn't say mad.

She would give me this look sometimes. There would be a frown on her face and her eyebrows would be raised, usually followed by a sigh.

She was *that.* Whatever *that* was, was beyond me...but I didn't like it. I had thought to punish her when she first gave me that look, so that I would never have to see it again...but the constant presence of the others warned me not to.

They had continued to keep their distance, with only Daxton daring to seek me out. But even he was occupied with the cat and Rosie.

I didn't like how it made my chest feel cold; after all, I know I did the right thing. Matt was trouble, and he would have pulled some shit, even if he wasn't the one to snitch on Rosie.

The first thought in my mind after we found out that purple-eyed low-level was actually spying on us and planning to kill Rosie, was to tear him to pieces and give his corpse to Rosie as a gift.

But then when he was hidden, that ruined my plans.

So fucking boring.

"I didn't know you took guard duty so seriously," Malik said, his voice cutting through the silence.

I turned to see him materialize, stepping out of the darkness of the back entrance as if my bitter thoughts about him called his presence to me. Even in the dim light of the moon I could tell that his skin had dulled considerably. When I tried to reach out to his mind, none of his thoughts were clear enough for me to understand, but I could hear them swirling around.

He was thinking something heavy, something he didn't like to think about. It was dark and I couldn't help but wonder what would pull that type of emotion out of him.

"I don't," I answered simply and took another drag of my cigarette.

"I don't believe you," Malik said with a teasing tone. It was one he used to get on my nerves, but this time it didn't hold the weight it once did.

I looked at him critically.

Malik, who used to act all-powerful and all-knowing, seemed much more solid now and less of a god-like figure that always seemed out of my reach. I knew him almost as well as I knew myself by now and if I had to put my money on it, he was probably bored out of his mind too.

"Believe what you want," I said and shrugged. "Are you taking over?"

A twig snapped and my head snapped to the intruder.

Maximus appeared just outside the light blue barrier that separated us from the rest of the world. He was wearing surprisingly casual clothes and his long hair was pulled into a bun on top of his head.

"I will be," he said and slipped past the barrier with ease. The same barrier that I had seen shock a bird to its death mere hours earlier.

"And you are coming with me," Malik said drawing my attention back to him. "Your present has arrived."

An excited thrill ran through me causing all of my hair to stand up on end. I threw my cigarette down and stomped on it with my foot before practically running to Malik's side.

Finally, some action.

"So that dusty bastard finally kept his promise?" I asked with a laugh.

A sort of buzz overtook my senses and I couldn't wait until I actually got to indulge myself.

Malik's eyes shifted from mine to Maximus's then back to me.

"Yes," he said in a thick tone. "He kept his promise."

Without waiting for my reply he turned and walked out past the barrier and into the night.

Without looking at Maximus I followed after Malik with a growing excitement tingling my limbs.

❧

Kept his promise indeed, I thought with a smug tone.

Malik had brought me to a secluded warehouse not far from where we kept the refugees, and presented me with the person I had been waiting to tear apart.

I couldn't help but think it was all kind of fitting, somehow.

The blonde-haired blue-eyed teacher was chained and sat in the middle of the cold dirty warehouse. The space was empty except for her and a few scraps of metal. Underneath her was a large plastic tarp. A long black fabric was wrapped around her eyes, but her head turned as soon as our steps sounded in the warehouse.

I could hear her fear. It was so clear, I could almost *taste* it.

Malik stood aside silently and let me walk to her.

She struggled against the chains.

I have to get out of here, her mind screamed. *I can't die like this.*

"How does it feel?" I asked and brought my booted foot to her chest. "To be trapped against your will?"

I kicked the center of her chest and laughed as she hit the ground with a thud.

"Eliza!" she yelled.

I bent down and removed the blindfold from her face and was met with wide blue eyes. I had seen that look in the mirror more times than I would like to admit, though that was with Damon... Now this was something I controlled.

How could my own daughter do this?

I growled and grabbed her face roughly.

"Don't call me that you *cunt,*" I hissed.

Her body began shaking in my hold. Gone were the dark

stares and sinister smiles, now all that was left of the woman that ruined my life was a whimpering sack of useless skin.

"Eliza, please, you don't have to do this," she begged me.

"What do you think I am going to do?" I asked and threw her head to the side.

I stared straight and looked down at her with disgust. The tears and snot were running down her face, making a mess of a once perfectly respectable demon.

Why wasn't she angry? Why wasn't she fighting.

I didn't want to hear her beg for mercy, I wanted her to yell at me. I wanted to see that cunt of a woman that I saw when Ezekiel was still backing her.

That was the woman I wanted to end.

This was supposed to be the moment I was waiting for. I was supposed to love the idea of toying with her. Love ripping her apart as she cursed for mercy...but I found myself disgusted by her and wished that Marques would have done the dirty work himself.

There was something different about this one, as opposed to Matt or Damon. With them, I found myself getting high off of watching the life bleed from their eyes. I wanted to hear them beg and then just when they thought I was going to give them mercy, take it away right before their eyes.

I didn't even want to touch her.

"Please, Eliza," she sobbed.

"Did you like my present?" I asked. "You breed annoying children did you know that? I didn't even have to strain to tear that head of his right off."

Her sobs increased and I felt an uncomfortable pressure in my chest.

I didn't like how they bounced off the walls. They grated on my nerves and I found myself flinching as her volume raised, practically screaming for mercy.

Malik's hand clasped my shoulder and I jumped at the suddenness. I didn't even hear him come up. Normally I would shrug him off right away, but his hand felt like it was cemented to my shoulder, forcing him closer than I would allow.

A part of me wanted to move closer to him.

"Is there an issue?" he asked.

I gritted my teeth not wanting to explain the mixed emotions tearing apart my psyche.

I wanted to kill her, *god* I fucking hated this bitch and had been waiting for this moment for a lifetime.

But...

"Malik, please," she pleaded, eyes wide.

I couldn't stop my face from twisting.

"Not so tough after all, hm?" Malik asked, though while his words were meant to be joking, there was no humor in his tone.

His eyes were curious and his tone not as condescending as I needed it to be in order to see this task through.

"It's not the same," I said in a thick voice.

"Let's hope you don't think the same when we face your father," he muttered and sunk down to her height. "Stop breathing."

I watched with disgust at the woman on the floor as she struggled to gasp for breath. Her face turned a bright red and then she stopped moving entirely.

It was quick and easy, but it left an uncomfortable weight in my chest.

"Disgusting," I muttered.

Malik stood and faced me with a frown.

"I'm glad," he said in a low voice. He spared another glance at the woman on the floor before meeting my eyes again.

"You don't seem like it," I noted.

"Just surprised—confused," he said, his eyes burrowing into mine. "Though I am glad you haven't lost yourself completely, yet."

Yet.

The word hung between us uncomfortably.

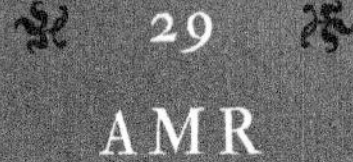

29

AMR

Even though I had spent many years in my cat form, I still found it to be comforting, especially in Rosie's hold.

I was comfortable enough with myself to admit when I needed some love and attention. I thrived on physical contact and couldn't get enough of the way Rosie's nails scratched under my chin *just right.*

Today we were in Rae's office as Rosie helped her brothers pour over their finances. It was a move that even I didn't expect.

Rosie had made it clear that she was not an expert, but then went to Rae and insisted that she become of some use to their situation... Rae reluctantly handed her over to Nathaniel and Benjamin with the instructions, *just help them figure out why we are spending so much.*

That had been an hour ago and I spent the whole time on Rosie's lap.

"You're wasting money because you were hiring witches and high-levels," Rosie grumbled as she looked over the stack of papers on the desk she was sitting on.

Rae had scowled when she saw her disregarding the chairs in the room to sit on the desk, but left soon after that with a small smile on her face. Benjamin and Nathaniel sat next to each other in a pair of office chairs, each with stacks of papers that they were combing through.

Though Nathaniel didn't seem to be much interested in doing any work. I caught him multiple times stifling a yawn and leaning back to watch as Rosie sifted through her own stack.

"Are you saying we hire *low-levels*?" Nathaniel asked, the disgust evident in his voice.

I didn't have to look at Rosie to feel the death glare she gave him. His and Benjamin's reaction was enough. They both cringed and looked to each other for an answer.

"They can do the same job, if not better," she said. "And they would absolutely foam at the mouth when they realize they could work for such a prestigious family."

Benjamin shifted uncomfortably.

"Well, it would be better than the witches," he mumbled.

Nathaniel reached back and slapped the back of Benjamin's head.

My gaze shifted as Rae's form slowly came into view as she leaned against the door frame watching Rosie interact with her brothers. A small smile played at her lips.

"Hire them," Rosie said. "And you should start auctioning off the furniture in the empty rooms."

"Wait I think that's a bit—"

"It's fine," Rae spoke from the doorway. Rosie jumped, obviously not noticing Rae's intrusion. "We don't need it anyways."

"Next you are going to say we need to get rid of the summer property," Nathaniel said with a forced laugh.

When no one responded his eyes widened.

"Really?" Benjamin asked. "I mean I knew it was a possibility...but really? Now?"

"Already sold," Rae confirmed. "Three properties have been sold and the money is deposited into the savings while the other is being prepared as a rental property."

Rae's eyes glanced towards us when Benjamin and Nathaniel failed to form coherent responses.

"Are you done here?"

"Yep," Rosie said and scooped me up before jumping off the table.

I cuddled into her and began purring as she walked towards Rae. I was addicted to this woman and I couldn't find it in myself to be bothered by it.

When I told her I would stay with her regardless of the circumstance, I meant it. I would follow her to the ends of the earth and was prepared to take any bullet for her. I would be her shield if she needed it, but after seeing her slow and ever-evolving sense of confidence, I had a feeling she may not need me as a shield.

Which was fine by me.

Guard cat. Assistant. Familiar.

I would be anything for her.

Her magic spiked as Rae's hand came to rest on her shoulder and I ate it up greedily. It had been a few days since I was able to share magic with Rosie and it felt like I was missing her far too much.

But I had to admit, everyone together under one roof for the last few weeks had been a godsend for Rosie's magic. No longer were Daxton and I the sole people to take all of her magic and it gave us a much-needed break.

"Are you prepared?" Rae asked, her words weighing heavily on us both.

"I don't know," Rosie muttered in a soft voice. "Many of the students will be there and I am just worried..."

Tonight was a gala hosted by the governor to welcome the low-levels into Winterfell. Another complication we did not expect. We would have to tread carefully as just tomorrow night, we would have to stake out in Ren's dorm and hope that Xena and Ezekiel would send the witch as planned.

"We will be on the lookout," Rae said. "Malik, Claudine, and Maximus will be there for backup."

It had been quiet since the games. Six full weeks had gone by and there was not a peep or stir from the Originals, Marques included. The older demon had not reached out to us once since we arrived and even when Malik went to go check on the refugees, there was no news of him.

"Does Marques know about this?" she asked.

Rae frowned lightly.

"I tried to reach out to him but he has not responded," Rae said. "Malik and Claudine told me he knows, but is just taking the time to adjust his plans accordingly. They assure me he is fine."

There was a pause.

"They are hiding something again," Rosie said with conviction.

"Let's confront them tonight," Rae offered. "But we have to get ready first."

❧

SUITS WERE uncomfortable and itched terribly. They were a complete waste of fabric and I didn't understand why we had to dress up so formally for a simple trip to the museum. It's not like it was the clothes that impressed people, but rather that magic and power embedded inside you.

I stared down at Rosie as she fixed the stiff collar near my neck with delicate hands.

"My love," I whispered.

A small smile spread across her face and she peered up at me through her dark lashes. Gold glitter was brushed across her eyelids and made the lighter tone of her brown eyes come forward. Her hair was pulled up into an intricate updo with a few strands falling into her face and curling around her neck. I preferred her natural face, but she had done a beautiful job at decorating herself today.

I looked down at the deep red dress she was wearing, my magic stirring inside me as I took in her figure. It hugged her body well and left a lot of her skin open. My eyes lingered on the scars on her arms, particularly the one that slashed through the raven tattoo. I hadn't asked about the scar, I wanted to give her some sort of privacy, but I noticed it along with the ones on her legs.

The slit in the dress showed a bit of her leg, showing me the deep scars that tugged at my heart. Just a year ago her skin was smooth, but because of the selfishness of the people around her, her body began to pay the price.

I bottled up my hurt and locked it inside me because I knew that to Rosie, it was a sign of her strength, her journey in this world. She should get to show it off to the people that doubted her.

Some may not understand, like the low-levels she oversaw... They would whisper when she wasn't looking and stare at her body with fear. Afraid that they would end up like her, but they didn't know what she had to go through to live up until now.

"Yes?" she asked, her sweet voice spreading warmth across my chest.

I trailed my fingers up her arm and cupped her cheek, careful not to smudge the paint she worked so hard to apply. When she leaned into my palm my heart jumped in my chest.

"Promise me, if you see anything wrong, you will let me take care of it," I said in a serious tone. Her eyes widened.

She may have wanted to lead, take charge of what was going on here...but I was not sure she was ready and tonight, I wanted to make sure that I protected her in any way that I could.

"What do you mean?" she asked.

"I have a bad feeling about this," I admitted.

The bad feeling had started ever since the start of this semester and looking back I believed it was foreshadowing the murder of the refugees and fled...but it started again ever since we moved into Rae's house.

It started at night, when I would wake up in a cold sweat thinking that someone was in the room watching us. When I searched for the culprit, I found nothing but empty hallways. Still the feeling never left me. It became like a dark cloud that hung over us at all times...ever since then I have never let Rosie without one of us by her side.

"Me too," she said softly. "But we won't know until we find out hm?"

"Just stay with me okay?" I said and leaned down to capture her lips in mine. "I can't lose you."

She smiled against me then pulled away.

"I love you Amr," she said.

"I love you too," I said and leaned in again but was interrupted by a throat clearing.

Malik and Eli were watching us from the doorway, both with different levels of amusement on their face. Eli was wearing a suit similar to mine though they forwent the jacket and of course had a majority of their chest showing, no doubt trying to piss off the stuffy demons we were about to meet.

Malik on the other hand at least tried to look prepared. He even had his hair slicked back, showing us a rare look at his entire scarred face.

I couldn't help but think how perfectly he matched Rosie and while she may have been okay with her scars, it would do well if she wasn't the only person whose body showed her struggle.

"I knew the cat would be taking all her time," Eli said with a smirk.

My eyes lingered on Malik, thinking back to the conversation Rosie and Rae had earlier.

What would he have to hide any longer? We have been through hell and back only to end up right here with one another... Why keep secrets?

Rosie followed my gaze and I felt her stiffen.

"Is it time already?" she asked and turned to them.

"It is time," Malik spoke.

Like Rosie and Rae had noted, there was something off.

Malik's usual cockiness was gone and he sort of deflated into himself.

It could be the exhaustion of it all, but my gut told me it was something different.

My gut told me to beware.

30
ROSIE

Ideally, I wanted to ask Malik what was going on before the gala because he deserved the benefit of the doubt after everything we had been through...but I never got the chance. We were always surrounded by people and the last thing I wanted to do was question him in front of the others.

It was enough for me to have this feeling of doubt, but I didn't want to corner him and throw the group into chaos.

I wanted to trust him and deep down I did, I trusted him more than anything. But his behavior had led me to believe something was wrong and I was scared of falling into another trap.

Quiet chatter filled the limo as I stared out the windows. While it was getting warmer, the leather seats sent a chill across my skin and I shifted uncomfortably in my seat.

The dress I was wearing was jaw-dropping, but it wasn't very practical.

I had planned to go a bit more casual but when Rae walked into my room with this beautiful dress in her arms...I couldn't deny her.

The limo slowed as we rounded the corner and drove into the city. We had to pass parts of downtown in order to get to the venue where the gala was being held, and it gave us a perfect view of the protests.

Normally, I would have been excited to explore parts of the city and come face to face with parts of this state that I hadn't been able to in the past; after all I had been stuck in either Winterfell or Rae's house for a majority of the school year.

But looking at the people that crowded the streets with signs and angry faces, yelling at cars to pay attention to them, made me want to turn right back and hide.

I wasn't following the election as well as I should have been, but the low-levels and witches were very unhappy with the prospects. The last time I had seen them so riled up was when my status was announced.

They blocked the sidewalks and the cars in front of us started honking at them. I heard a few shouts but couldn't tell if it was from the drivers or the protesters as all the noise outside the car started to jumble together. I wondered if I had never been introduced into this life, or been cursed to begin with, if I would have somehow found myself in line with them, fighting for the future of our dreams.

Would I be brave enough to yell in the face of the demons who shunned me? I grew up timid and scared because of my power and curse. I never wanted to hurt anyone and always found myself hanging on the sidelines, so how could I stand up like them?

Though maybe in a different life I could be like them.

I envied them, I realized. Envied their drive and passion and ability to scream at the top of their lungs for their rights. Even if I was reserved, I couldn't help but feel enraged on their behalf.

I wanted to be there with them, change the world in a way that mattered.

Instead I became the worst version of myself...one that thrives on pain—my own and others'—and murdered multiple people for no reason at all.

A rough hand squeezed mine and my gaze was drawn to Eli.

They had stolen the seat next to me while Malik sat next to them and Daxton, Amr, and Rae sat further down in the limo.

They were wearing a button-up and dress pants that matched the others, leaving only me in a dress. I didn't mind though. They were all positively mouthwatering.

Every time I looked toward Eli, I had to take a breath in order to continue because no matter how many times I saw them, I still found them breathtaking.

It wasn't just their looks that caused my heart to pound in my chest though. It was the way their eyes never left me and how a hand always rested somewhere on my body. It was comforting and maddening at the same time.

"Don't tell me you regret coming to Winterfell," they teased.

Malik leaned forward to watch my response, his expression curious if not a little hurt. The chatter was silenced.

"No," I said truthfully. "Though I will be happy when this is all over."

"This?" Malik asked with a raised brow.

"Originals," Rae answered for me.

I sent her a small smile. For the first time in a while, her glasses were off and I was given an unobstructed view of her chiseled face. Her features seemed sharper under the limo's light and her eyes darker.

"That's not a tonight problem," Malik said in a light tone and smiled, though it didn't reach his eyes.

"Are you sure about that?" I shot back without thinking.

His face fell before he quickly plastered the smile back on his face. I watched as Eli's eyes shifted towards Malik then back to me.

"As far as I am aware of," he said.

The car slowed, halting the conversation. Peering back outside I realized that we had arrived at our destination. New reporters and other media personnel noticed our car and began waving for their partners to catch up to us.

I swallowed my nervousness and squeezed Eli's hand for reassurance.

I still wasn't a fan of the attention, no matter how common it had become. I wished for them to just get bored and move on. I didn't have much to offer and their constant pestering only made me feel even more alienated than I already was.

Relax, Rosie, Eli said in my mind, their voice oddly soft.

I took a few seconds to pull myself together and then without prompting, the limo door was opened for us.

Amr was the first to exit, his eyes lingering on mine as if he was reminding me of his words. He was acting as the protector tonight...and for now I would let him, but I knew soon I would have to stop hiding behind everyone and take charge for myself.

I followed after him but froze as I was met with a scene I didn't expect.

Tonight's gala was in a museum that the governor had recently opened, stating that this had been ongoing for years. The guise was that this would be the first-ever museum to hold all of the demon and witch historical artifacts known to our kind and the first thing he wanted to do when it opened?

...bring the school's newest low-levels in as a way to "promote a healthy and prosperous future together."

It was huge with white columns holding up the main portions, causing it to look like something that came out of Rome instead of the United States. On the stairs was a fancy black carpet that high-level demons were walking up and on the sidewalk, were the press...and protesters.

The press I expected, they were always around...but why were the protesters here?

As the rest of the group filed out of the car, I reached my hand out for Malik's. With a stunned expression he came to my side and wrapped his arm in mine. I leaned into his warmth and inhaled his spicy cologne.

I gave Eli a look and they rolled their eyes.

Trying to be sneaky? I heard their voice in my mind, though it sounded distant.

What did you hear? I asked.

Pulling Malik to the stairs I tried to keep a smile as people yelled at us left and right.

I couldn't make it out, but he was worried about something, Eli said. *If you are worried about him starting something, come here. We will keep you safe.*

I didn't reply right away, focusing on the stairs underneath me.

It wasn't that I was worried he would hurt me, I trusted him more than that. But I was worried there was something I should know.

"Rosie! I heard you won the Winterfell Games again!"

"Rae, how have you been handling your Father's death?"

"Rosie, is that your spokesperson?"

I tuned them out and sent one last sentence out to Eli.

If there is something he knows about, I said. *I am the one that needs to be by his side. I cannot hide behind you all forever...plus Malik couldn't scare me if he tried.*

"You are far too silent to be up to anything good," Malik whispered in my ear as we reached the top of the stairs. His deep voice sent shivers down my spine.

He unwrapped his arm from mine to rest his hand on my lower back, his light touch sending waves of heat through me.

With my head held high I sent him a smile.

"I have a soft spot for you Malik," I said and leaned in close to him. "But I said I was done with lies and I meant it, so if you have anything to tell me, you should do it now."

His jaw twitched and I swore I could feel the anger rise up in him, then the tension between us becoming thick.

"Not here," he said simply. "But we will have a talk before tomorrow's meeting."

"Malik," I trailed in a disappointed tone.

"It's not bad it's just..." He sighed and shook his head. "You will understand when I explain."

I looked at him then nodded.

Turning to the others I switched to Daxton's arm and led him through the museum.

"I am honored," he whispered with a smile.

His smile warmed my heart as it had been a while since I had seen it. He seemed much better in the last few weeks. His skin was clear and soft and his eyes were almost glowing. My eyes trailed his face noting the growing length of his hair that now covered the tattoo on his temple.

"Let's get wasted," I whispered, a thrill running through me.

He gave me a mischievous smile.

The museum was packed with both students and non-students, each dressed in their fanciest clothing. You could tell the difference between the low-levels and the high-levels by the quality of their clothes...and how they stopped what they were doing to wave at me.

I weaved us through the crowds trying to avoid heavy conversation until I got at least one drink in my hand.

I stopped at the bar and let Daxton order for us. I knew nothing about alcohol so would defer to him for what to choose. My mouth dropped when the bartender grabbed two empty glasses and placed them on the counter, purple swirling liquid rising from the bottom of the cups.

When I lifted it I tried to look for a spout or anything that would show me where the alcohol came from, but there was nothing except the smooth countertop and the now full drink in my hand.

"I don't think they will look kindly on underage drinking," Rae muttered as we turned back to the group.

Eli watched us with a smirk while Malik and Amr seemed to have the same sentiment as Rae.

"It's not like I am trying to impress them anyways," I said with a smirk and took a sip of the glowing liquid.

As soon as the liquid hit my tongue a fruity flavor burst into my mouth and sent tingles down my body. It danced with my magic and left dull electric tingles throughout my body.

Rae's head snapped to the side and she cursed under her breath before grabbing the drink from my hand and turning around, while keeping the drink behind her back.

Peering to the side I saw a soft-faced, gray-haired man walk over to us with a blonde woman on his arm. The woman was staring at Eli as they approached.

Jealousy burned in my stomach and I caught Eli's smug gaze.

"Rae, Daxton, glad you could make it!" His booming voice caused others near us to turn and I caught a few of them whispering behind their hands.

"We couldn't miss it," Rae replied with a smile.

"Oh my, is that...?" The woman on his arm leaned over and met my gaze. "The hybrid!"

I felt a dull ache in my head form and was two seconds away from taking the drink from Rae's hand and finishing it in one gulp.

"Hello," I said in a polite voice. "I am not sure we have had a formal introduction yet."

"I am Clara," she said in an excited tone. "And this is my husband, Governor Bennett."

I gave the man a once over, confusion filling me. He was a low-level from the looks of it, how did someone like him get his position?

I guess for the image of collaboration.

"Rosie Miller," I said though I doubted I needed to. "Nice to meet you both."

"I am sure we have more time to chat later," she said with a smile and sent a pleading look to her husband. "Let's make rounds and before we know it, it will be time to eat."

They said their goodbyes and as soon as they were out of sight I grabbed the drink from Rae who sent me a glare.

Ignoring her, I turned to Daxton. I smiled at him and pulled him along with me into the museum.

"Let's have some fun," Daxton whispered as we came to look at a painting.

He nudged me to look at a couple not too far away from us. I watched as he sent a little wave and the guy was pushed into the girl next to him who gave him an annoyed look in return.

I let out a small laugh and focused my magic on the boy.

"Watch this," I whispered and tried to grab hold of the man's motor functions.

Sure enough, his hand slowly started to creep towards the woman's ass, who saw his hand and slapped it away.

"Enough," Malik's voice came from beside me. His hand gripped onto my shoulder leaving a flash of heat where his skin touched mine.

I turned to look at him and shrunk under his dark gaze.

"How annoying," Daxton mumbled from beside me.

"We aren't causing any harm," I said and tried to push his hand off, but he stayed strong.

I felt the magic buzz near us before I felt the shake of the museum. It was old, potent enough...and unmistakably Original. It crept along the floor of the museum and lapped at my feet.

Looking around I noticed the other demons in this hall looking for the culprit. We were all thrown back as another wave rocked the museum. This time the magic blew into the hallway. It was so thick it began choking me.

I held onto Daxton as we were thrown again into Malik who wrapped his arms around us to stop our tumble.

"An earthquake?" Rae asked.

"Magic," I, Amr, and Daxton replied in unison.

I met Malik's panicked eyes.

"Original," I said.

It was all Malik needed to jump into action.

"We need to get you all in a room," he said in a hushed tone. "And call Claudine."

People around us were panicking and trying to push towards the front of the museum. They were yelling and screaming. I heard some talk about this being from the protesters but now I was sure that it was all one death trap.

Xena and Ezekiel had to be close.

And then another wave hit us.

"This way," Rae said and pushed past us.

We all followed her without complaint. Everyone was running past us, going the opposite way that we were, but I knew in my heart to trust Rae and whatever was making the museum quake, was probably out there waiting for us.

We dipped into an unfinished exhibit and Amr and Daxton worked to secure the door.

Malik was on the phone and before he even finished Claudine appeared right next to me in a flash of light.

"Grab on," she commanded.

Without thinking I reached towards her, then paused just before our skin touched.

"What about the low-levels?" I asked.

Eli's growl sounded from behind me and they forced my hand to touch Claudine.

"They don't deserve your worry," they grumbled.

Just as the others were gathering around us a violent crash sounded just beyond the room and was so powerful it caused us to jerk forward, falling on top of Claudine in a mess.

"It's okay, it's okay," she gasped. "Just make sure everyone is touching me!"

She lifted her arm and Malik, Rae, Amr, and Daxton touched her skin. I felt the magic shimmer around us and the pull at my stomach.

Then, a claw-like grip tangled in my hair and pulled me away from Claudine. Pain burst across my skull and my hands went up to try and pry the claws from me.

When I realized that they were pulling me away from the group I flung my arms out, trying to reach for whichever body was the closest to me. Eli's shirt was the first thing that my fingers made contact with but I was dragged across the floor, causing my fingers to slip.

I let out a scream and started kicking and clawing against the person. Their grip loosened just enough for me to launch forward and grab the hem of Malik's jacket.

Slim hands wrapped around my ankle and pulled both Malik and me away from the group. I had no choice but to gape at the group, horror filling my body as light engulfed them and when it was gone, no one remained in place.

Malik and I were stuck.

Original magic slowly crept across my skin like a thick slime. It slowed my movements and blurred my vision. Malik's eyes narrowed above me and he bent down swiftly to hold onto my arms.

"You have been hard to get close to, my dear," Xena's voice rang out from behind me. It was her hand that had the death grip on my ankle.

When I turned to meet her brown eyes, all the rage and hate that I had pushed down so deep came bubbling up to the surface. I wanted to attack her right then and there. I wanted to make her feel the pain that she caused others.

I knew that if I let my powers go that I could blow up the entire place, Xena along with it.

But if the low-levels didn't get out...then there was a chance that they would be caught in the blast too.

...and so would Malik.

But what other time would I get so close to ending it all?

Another pair of hands shot out and gripped my arm and Malik's leg and in a flash of light the museum around us was gone and replaced with a dark sky.

I recognized the surrounding area... We were back at Winterfell, specifically the grass of the quad where the tower had once fallen. The environment was a shocking silence; the loud noises and screams from the museums were still ringing in my head.

The world tipped around me as I was pulled into a standing position.

"We have to go," I croaked out and turned to look at Claudine, whose hand was still fastened around me.

Sweat fell from her forehead and she was breathing heavily. The trip must have cost her a lot of magic.

"They will be here soon," Malik spoke in a hurried voice. Then looked towards Claudine. "We have to skip the next phase, do you still have enough magic to get Maximus here?"

"She already thought ahead," Maximus's voice sounded.

My head whipped towards him and I saw him kneeling down on the ground with Rae and Eli sitting next to him. Amr and Daxton were off to the side giving him a suspicious look.

That's when I felt it. A thrum of Original magic...but this was different than what I felt from the museum. It was fading.

All eyes were on me.

"What's going on?" I asked Malik, panicked.

Claudine's cool hands found the side of my face and forced me to look into her eyes. She was scared and panicked, just as I was, but she was taking deep breaths and asking me to do the same with her eyes.

"Marques had once entrusted you with his secret, do you remember?" she asked slowly.

I nodded and felt my blood run cold.

"He's dying," I croaked out. Claudine nodded.

"And his last wish was to ensure you could kill Xena and Ezekiel," she said speaking each word slowly.

"Last w-wish?" I asked, unable to find my words. "He's not—he didn't—"

"He's dead, Rosie," Claudine spoke in a harsh tone. "Xena and Ezekiel figured it out, that is why they are coming now."

"I *can't.*"

"Hurry up," Malik growled from beside me. "We don't have time, she is probably already on her way here."

"If he is dead how can we win?" I cried.

Claudine gave me a pitiful smile, her eyes softening as if she understood me. But how could she?

How could she understand me if *I* was the one that had to kill the Originals. I didn't even think it was possible. I didn't have the amount of control over my magic to go up against my mother let alone Ezekiel. And their powers far surpassed mine, they had millennia of experience and I didn't even have two full years.

Maximus's hand holding a small bag invaded my vision. The bag was an originally black one, but I could feel the Original magic radiating from inside of it.

"Eat this," Maximus said.

I grabbed the baggy and felt bile rise in my throat. I already knew what was in here.

"Are you stupid?" Eli asked. "We are demons, this should go to the witches."

"No!" Malik growled.

I jolted at the noise and looked up to Malik. His eyes were narrowed at Eli.

"It doesn't work on witches," Maximus explained. "Like Daxton their magic will just go haywire."

"But demons can absorb his power," Rae spoke, her tone low and barely reaching my ears.

I stood on shaky legs with Claudine's help and stared at Rae. Her expression told me she was dead serious.

"I shouldn't be surprised," Malik muttered.

"Ten powers," Rae muttered. "Anything else I should be aware of?"

There was a pause before Maximus cleared his throat.

"The blood sharing should have prepared you for some," he said. "But the worst is yet to come."

I watched in mute horror as Rae opened her bag and without hesitation lifted it to her mouth and threw her head back.

Eli took one look at her, and then did the same thing.

Was I the only one who thought this was crazy? Consuming

the flesh of a demon was no small feat, and who was to say we would even absorb these powers.

Rae was the first to start convulsing on the grass, her body becoming rigid after some time. I could feel the aura surrounding her. It was much like Marques, one that overpowered everything and hung over us like a threat.

I tried to run to her but Claudine held me back, and soon Eli was doing the same.

"Your turn," Malik said and grabbed my bag for me.

"Wait," I said panicked. "What about you?" I then gestured to Claudine and Maximus. "Them? How do we know this will even work?"

"We don't want to chance it," Claudine said. "We have too much magic in us."

"I already took mine," Malik grunted and opened the bag with a wince. "I wanted to try it out on myself before you guys."

"That's why you have been distant," I gasped.

"Yes," he answered. "Hold her."

I tried to fight as Claudine held my arms but once Malik's hand gripped my face and pried my jaw open, I quickly lost the battle.

I tried not to think about the flesh that fell into my mouth or how it felt to chew. Malik's strong hand gripped my mouth and then pinched my nose, forcing me to swallow.

He watched over me and lifted his hands. I pulled in a deep breath, sickly sweet air rushing through my lungs before my body began to convulse. Inside it felt as though every cell in my body was vibrating intensely.

My knees were the first to buckle and I fell right into Malik's open arms.

I whimpered as my magic rose sharply and my head was assaulted with memories, thoughts, and feelings that were not my own. My head felt like it would explode from the sheer size of the memories.

Images flashed through my mind, almost too fast to catch. I

saw the world when it was still young, when demons, humans and witches all existed together... And then I saw the downfall.

I saw the war, the killings, and I saw the demons and witches who once looked over the humans become twisted and start attacking them.

Were these Marques's memories?

I could feel his exhaustion weigh on me. I couldn't comprehend how many years he lived and suffered through. I saw his grief, saw his pain. I saw when he murdered, saw when he loved... but at the end all that was left was exhaustion.

...and then I saw Malik crying over me as Marques died.

Take care of them, he had whispered in his mind, but it never reached Malik's ears.

With a loud gasp I pushed Malik off of me and fell to the damp grass.

The magic and power was shooting through me like shots of electricity. They couldn't meld together and instead focused on attacking each other, fighting over the little amount of space I had left for them in my body. The pain became worse than anything I could imagine, but even as I tried to scream nothing came out of my mouth.

I clawed at the damp grass, trying to put out the sudden heat that spread across my skin. My back arched and my limbs twisted painfully.

Tears were already pouring down my face, so much that I felt like I would drown in them. I couldn't breathe, I couldn't think...

I wanted it to end.

Then it was over.

"They are here," Malik said as he lifted me from the grass and rushed me over to the group.

Eli and Rae had already composed themselves and reached out to me. Their power and the magic that surrounded us was a shock to my abused system and pain radiated through me as Daxton and Amr's magic tangled around me.

"I don't know what to do with this power," I said through chattering teeth, phantom pain still jolting through my body.

The power, it was living and breathing inside me, much like my magic. It wasn't a part of my being like my fire that belonged to me fully. It was almost like these powers knew that they did not belong inside me and just settled to swirl around inside me, carefully avoiding my magic.

"Just let it guide you," Malik said looking back at where we just came from.

I peered over my shoulder and saw a small army of witches heading towards us, all with their magic already lighting up their hands.

They were far too young to be fighting for the Originals. Many seemed to be my age or younger and had fear written all over their faces. My heart ached for them because I knew that there was no way they would come out of this alive.

"I only know something about memories, and hypnosis," Rae said. "But that is not enough to tap into the power."

"Use your own for now," Malik said through bared teeth. "On the signal pump them with as much fear as you can, and for once please *do not* look me in the eyes."

I signaled for Amr and Daxton to come to my side. Without hesitation they dove for us.

Claudine and Maximus stood in front of us. The noises from the witches got louder as they prepared their magic.

"Don't look at him," I said to Daxton and Amr.

Malik took one step forward and I could feel his power whip around us, a strong wind pushing us around.

Rae's hands covered my ears from behind and pulled me to her chest.

"Combust!" I heard Malik's voice yell, and I could feel the magic whoosh past us. It was unlike any power I had felt before.

The loud explosions sounded immediately. I couldn't count how many because of the abrupt suddenness of it all.

When I pushed away from Rae and peered around Malik I

saw at least a third of the army was wiped out, leaving a clear path to the two people that stood in the middle.

Xena and Ezekiel.

There they stood, as if above the rest. Xena was wearing her fancy brand-name clothing and looked at us with a sneer while Ezekiel had his face cast downward to the grass. I could make out some type of blazer and slacks.

"Rest," Claudine commanded.

I put my hand on Malik's arm and peered up at him. His face was paler than I'd ever seen and there was sweat pouring down his face.

"We need to attack," he said.

Blood trailed from his nose.

"Witches next," I said and didn't wait for his confirmation before turning to the rest of the group. "Magic users, take out as many as you can and Rae, Eli and I will push forward. I will try to take out as many as I can with fire."

"They need to stay in front," Rae spoke. "Long-range attacks will create a hole for us, but we will not be able to get them unless we are closer."

"You need to save your magic until we get close," Malik said.

"Two people cannot defeat—"

"Someone has to kill them!" Malik yelled. "And if I do not have the power to do it you must, so you have to save your magic. Get back."

"No Malik—"

"Back!"

That was the only warning I got before he sent out another wave of power. I shut my eyes as tight as I could and only opened when the explosions stopped, but this time they already caught on to the trick and not nearly as many were taken out.

At least half still remained.

"It will work," Claudine said in an airy voice. "Maxi."

Maximus let out a noise and I watched in fascination as he set up a magical parameter around us just as a few beams of magic came pummeling towards us. They burst in the air as they came into contact with the barrier.

"Move as a group," Claudine said.

I felt Eli's hand find my shoulder and push us forward.

As we got closer the army began attacking us with magic.

Claudine was throwing magic at them left and right but there were far too many. Calling my magic to me I peered around Malik and set my sights on the biggest group of witches and without hesitancy called forth black flames that engulfed them.

They didn't even have time to scream.

"I told you—"

"It's okay," I said to hush Malik. "It wasn't a lot."

"Rae," Claudine spoke. "Immobilize them. Daxton, Amr, some help would be nice."

I could feel Daxton and Amr's magic fly past me and see when they hit their targets, clearing a space for us, but my eyes were locked on the figures that awaited us.

It was bold of them to come alone.

"Take the hybrids alive!" Xena yelled.

Blinding fury lit up my entire body and I focused on Xena's snarling face. She was still yards away from where I was comfortable using magic, but my rage pushed me forward and my magic begged for a chance at her.

So I let it free.

Magic burst from me so strong that I was thrown against Eli. It had been waiting for this moment, begging me to let it out, and now that I finally did, it easily narrowed in on its target. Xena's face dropped as she felt the burst of magic rush towards her, but her reaction was too delayed.

Black flames engulfed her body.

The fool in me thought this was it, I had done enough, but for once I didn't listen to that voice and continued to pump magic towards her. I could feel us moving forward, but I didn't register it, all I could see was her flailing inside of my flames.

All I could think about was what she had done to us up until now. How she had brutally murdered the refugees after they escaped her clutches. How she had forced me to take the lives of so many without even blinking.

It was all a game to her. *I* was a game to her.

She pretended to want to be my mother. Lied to get close to me and turned her back on me when I started to question her motives.

She deserved this. She deserved to burn for her sins and deserved the most painful death possible. If this was what she had accomplished in two years, what had she done her entire life?

I thought of Ren...what about the others? Where was their justice.

This was for them.

It was for every single person that was affected by their cruelty and hatred. I kept the flame lit for them and them only because they deserved this as much as I did.

Warm hands covered my eyes.

"That's enough, Rosie," Amr said.

With the connection lost I felt my magic shut off abruptly. He waited for me to catch my breath but with each inhale I felt more and more power escape me. I was burning my magic and newly acquired power too quickly and my body was starting to feel the effects. When he removed his hands, I saw the utter destruction we had left on Winterfell.

The grass below us was charred, the trees that lined the outer edge of the quads were still on fire, and there were charred dead bodies all over the place.

My fire did not stop at Xena.

No, I was lucky Amr stopped me when he did because *we* would have been the next targets.

I looked to the spot where my mother should have been, but saw nothing but charred ash, and next to it a petrified and shaking Ezekiel.

We were close enough now that I could see the pain that etched his face as he slowly knelt to the ground.

Eli pushed past us, leaving the safety of the barrier. I was too exhausted to call for them. All thoughts and words escaped me as I sagged against Amr.

The fire from my father, the gift I had hated for my entire existence, was the one thing that I could do to end this battle. It enraged me and satisfied me all at once. All the pain and fear that went into this power, my curse...was suddenly gone.

Xena was gone.

My biological mother who had forced me into this life of pain and suffering...was gone.

Eli stopped walking when they reached Ezekiel and as much as I tried to hold on, my eyes began to flutter shut. I couldn't hear what they were saying, or if they were talking at all, but I could just barely make out Eli grabbing their father's head and violently ripping it off with all their might.

They then turned and lifted the head, their hungry blue eyes meeting mine. Then they threw the head up into the air and my last and final effort for this fight, was engulfing Ezekiel's twisted face in black fire.

I let my eyes close to the image of Eli's bone-chilling smile, and then tearing off the arm of Ezekiel's headless body and tearing the flesh off with their teeth.

Their laugh followed me into the darkness.

31
ROSIE

Screaming echoed in my mind. Bloodcurdling painful screams that made your bones ache and your ears ring. Images of black burning fire filled my mind along with the melted faces of the hundreds of witches I killed.

Xena's eyes as she was consumed by my flames flashed through my mind. They were horrible, painful. Those eyes followed me through my dreams and my day-to-day life...but I wasn't upset.

No...I *liked* seeing her in pain. I liked seeing her realize that her last moments on this earth would be the worst she had ever experienced.

And I found joy when it was I who brought her to her demise. I liked how she silently begged for me to let her go. The power and control I had was nothing like I experienced before. It settled deep within me, and for once my magic was quiet because finally it was satisfied with my kill.

A hand coming down on my head pulled me out of my thoughts.

I peered up to Billy's warm smile.

"You seemed lost there for a moment," he said in a light tone, but I could hear the worry underneath it. "Would you like to take a break? I am sure we can manage."

I shook my head and sent him a strained smile.

"I am good," I said quickly and pushed his hand off me. "*Fine.* And we barely got through the pile."

I looked out at the warehouse in front of me. People, papers, and random items were everywhere. It was moving day for the refugees and there was a buzz of excitement and laughter that filled the once empty space.

Demons and witches alike loaded up their belongings and were ready to start their new life.

We had them in groups, people who they were the closest with or friends they had made here, all got a place to live together. We supplied them with fake IDs courtesy of Malik and his new—*and improved if he was to be believed*—section of The Fallen.

We had used the last of Rae's properties as a place for the doctor and his remaining patients while the others all got stipends from Malik.

Apparently after years of running an illegal gang, he had quite a lot of it stashed.

The refugees were still gathering all their stuff with the help of Eli, Rae, and Malik while Daxton and Amr helped stabilize the patients. I wished I could stay to listen in on what they found out about the rapid decay of the patients, but they assured me that they still needed a few more months of testing and that I was more needed in other places.

Which left me, Claudine, and Maximus in charge of the paperwork. The folding table in front of me held everyone's passports, IDs and log-ins to bank accounts and other documents that they would need to live a normal life. Looking down at the mess of bags and folders in front of me I felt anxiety itch at my skin.

There is no way we will finish by the time the sun sets.

"We won't," Claudine said from beside me.

I looked over to her and watched as she smiled and sifted through the piles of paperwork, a mother and child waiting for her with a blinding smile. The small child peeked out from under the mom's dark hair, their large hazel eyes meeting mine.

"She will get a new lease on life thanks to you all," Billy said from beside me.

I watched Claudine intently; Maximus was beside her and I could feel his gaze boring into me, though I didn't pay him any mind. Claudine was wearing a light blue dress that fell to her knees. It covered her shoulders and had virtually no shape, but still, she made it look so pretty, so clean...so unburdened.

But how could she be like this after everything?

I didn't understand after what we saw, and did, how she would be able to move on like nothing happened while I got attacked daily by Marques's memories.

Sometimes I got lucky, and saw a happy one...but other times I got flashes of death and violence. Some so bad it made my stomach twist.

What will you do now? I wanted to ask her. *How will you live after this?*

...but the words didn't escape my mouth.

I felt someone come up to my table and I looked towards them. When blue eyes met mine, my heart skipped a beat, but unlike before I didn't feel glued to my spot.

My low-level mother was wearing a flowy shirt with a lace collar in front. Her long hair was pulled back and she was looking towards me with a sad smile.

She was pushing a wheelchair, and seated in it looking worse than ever...was my father.

His scarred face was the only thing that stayed the same, but somehow in the years I was gone he had aged considerably. His once firm hands were now shaking as he gripped onto the side of the wheelchair and his hair had turned fully grey.

I knew where their file was, I had seen it when I first shifted through them.

I could feel the stare on me as I found theirs and held it out to my mother. She took it in hand and gave me an expectant look.

"Inside is everything you need and directions to your new place," I said. "Since you'll probably need help with transportation you can wait over there until someone is free to take you."

I gestured to the area where most of the others waited. Malik had rounded a few of his ex-gang members to act as chauffeurs for the day and drop people off at their new locations.

My mother's was too close to Winterfell, in the same building I had occupied not long ago coincidentally. Though now that the Originals were dead, we didn't have to fear going back to that place and in turn all of the refugees could now use the space.

It was far better than what I had grown up with and I knew that they would be comfortable there.

"Your new surnames are Moore," I said. "With this money and housing you will be able to live for a long time without having to work."

"Will you come with us?" my mother asked, her voice hesitant.

Father's eyes watched me carefully.

"No," I answered without hesitation.

My mother's face dropped and she gripped the pile of folders in her hands so hard the plastic folder creased.

"Rosie here has to finish school, don't you?" Billy asked, his tone light. I had almost forgotten he was here.

"Rosie if you could just—"

My father cut my mother off with a growl.

"Why do you refuse to help your parents?" he asked, his voice gruff and far too loud.

I heard the conversation around us lull and I could feel the eyes weighing on me. Normally, I would have been embarrassed. My cheeks would have flamed and I would have bucked my head to hide my shame. I would have tried anything to make sure my father wasn't mad. Tried to make sure that I wouldn't get punished.

But that was then, and now...I was different.

Marque's years of knowledge and power lived inside me, strengthening my previously weak resolve. My experience with the Originals had shown me that dealing with my parents, was nothing more than a minor inconvenience and *for me,* one of the last Original hybrids still alive on this earth, to feel *shame* and *embarrassment* because of the people in front of me...well that would just be laughable.

"What other assistance do you require?" I asked and cocked my head to the side. My eyes trailed up to my mother. "There is nothing in that pile that needs my help."

"You said yourself, the money will not last," my father huffed. My mother looked away, blush coating her cheeks. "And I am not as healthy as I used to be—"

"The demon regulation society can help with disability," I said, cutting him off. "With these files you are new demons, with full lives ahead of you. They wouldn—"

"Rosie!" my father exclaimed. His face reddened and soon he was taken over by a coughing fit. Mother rushed to pat his back, but I just stood there, staring down at them. "We have done *so much* for you. Provided for you. Sent you to school. And not to mention dealing with that curse after you burned down our—"

"Are you done?" I asked in a calm tone.

I felt Billy shift beside me and Claudine placed a hand on my shoulder. Only when her hand made contact and her magic brushed up against mine did I realize how much my magic had spread out around me.

The witches in the room would be able to feel it, but if you looked closely you could see the way the air rippled around me.

My father puffed up and was ready to retort but I lifted my hand to stop him.

"I am no longer under your care," I explained. "I do not *owe* you anything for taking care of me. As someone who wants to help people affected by the Originals' cruelty I am here helping you get back on your feet, but that is where my relationship with you stops."

I caught my mother's sad gaze.

If she returned you to Xena, you would have ended up like the others.

There was something to be grateful for, but I wouldn't force a relationship with them if they continued to treat me like property and something to make money off of.

"There should be room in the next car," Billy said with an awkward laugh. "Why don't you guys go wait in line?"

My father sent him a glare.

"I wouldn't be dying if it wasn't for you," my father spat at me, his words filled with hatred. "So much for *helping us.*"

My eyes flitted to behind them where Eli towered over my mother. Their glare was burning into me and a dangerous smile passed their face.

"If I had my choice," Eli spoke, causing my parents to jump and stare back at them. "I wouldn't have dragged you from that cell."

"But you don't," I reminded, not liking the way Eli's eyes roamed my parents. They met my gaze with a smile, calling me out on my bullshit. It's not like I would be able to stop them anyways.

"It's mine," I continued, looking down at them. "It's *my* choice to decide what happens from here on out and *I* chose to help you out. Now please leave so I can get the others their papers."

Eli leaned down near my mom's ear and said, "You know she killed her blood mom, burned her to a crisp. Not even bone fragments were found. *That* was her choice too."

My mother paled and her eyes widened.

After the threat they ran to the side and refused to make eye contact with me.

"Don't go scaring people," I said to Eli as they walked up to the table, their hands brushing over the piles of sensitive documents. I could feel the thoughts of destruction behind them.

Can you? they asked in my head. The side of their mouth turned upward into a smirk. *Do I have another mind reader on my hands?*

I rolled my eyes and looked up to Billy with a small smile.

"Can you please take over from here?"

He nodded though his smile was gone. I turned to Claudine to apologize but her sweet smile stopped me.

"Go rest, Rosie," she said. "You deserve it."

32

ROSIE

Where are you going?

I jumped as Eli's voice entered my mind suddenly. I turned around, my hand still resting on the cold metal doorknob as I peered up at the stairs. Claudine shifted beside me, but did not make any noise, no doubt also sensing that we had been caught.

It was early in the morning, at a time when everyone else in Rae's house was deep asleep. The morning was silent and the barest hints of the sun rising spilled through the many windows that littered this place. The cool morning air brushed across my skin as I locked eyes with Eli who stood just on top of the stairs leading down to the foyer.

They were dressed in a hoodie and sweats, indicating that they may have just crawled out of bed, but their slicked-back hair told me differently. Their blue eyes shone in the dim light and they crossed their arms while they stared down at me. A tension rose between us and I could feel the argument that was about to break out.

"You already know, don't you?" I asked, though did not raise my voice, worried that the others in the house might hear and wake up to see what was going on.

Eli cocked their head and let out a huff. They stayed silent as if contemplating their next move. The brash Eli that I once knew was no more after they had eaten both Marques and Ezekiel's flesh; they wouldn't get as angry as they once had. It was like a switch had flipped and now they were calmer and more calculated than ever.

I knew what Marques had passed on, and while I had yet to really try out the new powers, the memories and knowledge that came with it were enough to change a person. And on top of that, I had no idea what they had taken from Ezekiel.

What did Ezekiel know about this world and its demons? What were his plans before he died? What did he tell Eli right before he was torn to pieces?

"I do," they said. "And I want you to take me."

"I refuse," I said without a moment of hesitation.

Their eyes flashed and they took one step down and paused.

"It won't be like Matt," they said. "I just have some questions for him."

I paused and stared at them. I had planned to do this with only Claudine by my side, not wanting to risk any more deaths, but having Eli there to read their mind was...enticing.

"Get Malik," I whispered to Claudine. "If Eli comes we need reinforcements."

Eli's face twisted and they walked down the rest of the stairs. Claudine disappeared in a flash of light leaving just the two of us in the space. Slowly, Eli crossed the space, their sneakers against the floor the only thing that broke the silence.

I stood tall, with my shoulders back as they came to a stop in front of me, the heat of their skin brushing across mine.

"You know he cannot stop me from doing what I want," they said in a low voice.

"I know," I said back, my eyes trailing the length of their face.

"And if I kill him?" they asked, their voice dropping to a whisper.

I didn't know if they meant Ren or Malik, but I didn't want either to die.

"I cannot forgive you forever, Eli," I said in a firm tone and took a step back to put some space between us.

They merely smirked and we waited in silence for Claudine to come back.

Another five minutes passed in silence before Claudine came back in a flash of light, an angry Malik by her side.

"Rosie just because they are dead now doesn't mean—"

I sent Malik a look that stopped his complaining in its tracks. I wasn't in the mood to fight. Any other time I would love to push his patience until he exploded, but now was the time where I needed to be listened to.

Malik's golden gaze searched my face and when he finally relaxed I grabbed onto Claudine's arm and nodded towards her.

"You know the drill," Claudine said in a tone far too light for the amount of tension in this room.

Eli smirked and complied but made sure to step close to me, their front brushing across mine as they reached out to grab a hold of Claudine's arm. I locked eyes with them and refused to back down.

I like this version of you, they cooed in my mind. I could feel the satisfaction rolling off of them.

Without warning Claudine transported us in a flash of light and the world around us tipped. Even as the power exploded around us and twisted my stomach, I held Eli's gaze.

Watch yourself, Eli, I growled in my mind.

Feisty, they teased back. *But I will let you have this...for now.*

I was the first to look away as the world came back together around us.

I was surprised to note that we were in a *very* familiar apartment. The sound of a door opening came from behind me and I turned to catch Ren looking at us with wide eyes in nothing but his boxers and a t-shirt.

"So this is where he was," Eli murmured.

"He was here the whole time," Claudine said. "We moved in right underneath him and we were none the wiser. I just merely gave him his apartment back."

"With a fucking magical tracker that tries to kill me every time I leave," Ren grumbled and ran a hand through his messy black hair. "What the fuck are y'all doing here?"

I swallowed my nerves and turned to him.

"Come back to Winterfell with me," I said.

Shock flashed across his face which he immediately tried to hide with annoyance. He ran his thumb across the small tattoos on his hand and paused, taking in my offer.

"Why invite him?" Eli asked. "He has no intention of complying with what we ask of him, I can hear it."

Ren shot Eli a glare, but his face softened when his eyes met mine.

"I am not asking him anything," I said. "I just want to give you a chance at a normal life. Malik can help get you situated and you wouldn't have to worry about—"

"Where is our mother?" he asked, cutting me off. His voice was hesitant and had a weight to it that sat uncomfortably in my chest.

"Dead," I answered. "I killed her. Now that she is gone you can live your life however you want."

Ren deflated and his mouth dropped into a frown.

"And if I choose to go back to my father's house?" he asked. I assumed he meant his low-level father and nodded.

"You can do whatever you wish," I said. "Though I wished that the offer to attend Winterfell was real, for me at least. And I wanted to give you the chance to make it real for you too."

Malik shifted, causing Ren's eyes to dart to him. I stepped forward and reached my hand out to him.

"No ties," I said. "I wish to know you and to understand what you went through, that is all. From experience I know it must have been difficult. I want to be there for you. But if you want to run as far away from me as you can, I will accept that."

Ren remained silent and his eyes fell to the floor.

"He's quiet because they treated him well," Eli spoke from behind me. "They didn't force him to kill prisoners, or ask him to take down government officials. All they asked of him was to watch you and then end it during the games. That is all."

I swallowed and a sour pit appeared in my stomach. Bitterness filled me and I wanted nothing more than to destroy this entire floor...but a part of me inside realized that I couldn't hold my own jealousy against the boy in front of me.

"One kill is still something," I said, though my voice sounded forced. "Regardless I just came to tell you this. I planned to come with less people but..."

I let my sentence trail and sent Ren a small smile. He shifted on his feet and stepped forward to take my hand in his. I felt our magic connect. It was warm, comforting, and familiar. His eyes looked up at me hesitantly.

"I would like to know more about what happened," he said. "If you would like to stay for breakfast that is."

A warm bubble filled my chest and I couldn't stop the real smile from spreading across my face.

"I would love that."

33

DAXTON

I had suspected for it to be hard to sneak away from the group after the battle between us and the Originals, but everyone seemed too distracted about the consequences of eating some of Marques's flesh to even pay attention to anything beyond themselves.

A more sane and put-together version of myself would have been bitter that I was being ignored, or maybe I would have wanted to help...but I couldn't help it as my own panic began to take hold of me.

My magic was getting worse by the day.

Instead of hanging over me like a dark could in the middle of the night, I felt it take form. I felt it leave my side and wander about the house.

It never got far, but the idea of my magic working autonomously sacred the living hell out of me.

It was violent and angry. It wanted death and destruction and nothing else.

And it was free to roam around,

Cumae had finally reached out to me through a magical carrier pigeon with nothing more than an address and instructions on what to do when I got there.

I didn't know if I could trust her fully, but now that the Originals were gone, I knew there wasn't much else out there to be afraid of.

If anything, the witches of this world should be afraid of me next. Who knows what my magic would do once it got enough strength to interact with the world on its own.

I was hopeful though, that finally I would get some answers.

I found it hard to believe that no one had run into my situation before this. The demon and witch history spanned on for years and years; there had to be a mess up somewhere. The people of this world were greedy and craved power like a drug, of course they would try and experiment much like my parents did.

Cumac had given me the address of another bar, though this one I had never been to before.

It was just a few miles away from the one where I had met her and this one spanned multiple stories. The place was cleaner as well and had a well-lit front entrance that showed the patrons inside, but I ignored it and rounded the bar for the hidden one.

The street beside it was wider, but smelled just as sour as the place before it. When I felt a flash of magic by my side I paused and called my own.

A door opened for me, this time no bouncer appeared out from the wall and I walked straight into the place.

It was much like any other magical bar I had seen, though this one was full of people who gave me death glares, even as they felt the powerful magic inside me.

I scoffed at the immature reactions and walked to the back of the bar like the note had told me. The stairs creaked under my weight and I was sure I would fall straight through the wood, but even so, I made it up the stairs in one piece.

There was a long, dimly lit hallway that smelt of cigarettes and sickly sweet magic.

The same type of magic that made my own coil in disgust.

The people here were not using their magic in good ways... meaning they were just like my parents.

I would recognize this type of magic anywhere. It haunted me in my dreams and caused sour bile to rise up in my throat.

Shaking the feeling off I walked down the hallway slowly, feeling the signatures of the people that I passed, worried that there may be someone beyond these rooms that I knew.

When I reached the room at the end of the hallway I eyed the stained and torn doorway critically. The numbers on there read "*333*" and stood out to me like a bright warning sign.

In the witch community those numbers were supposed to signal that I was on the right path, that the decision ahead of me was one that would change my life, in a good way...

But I am not sure I believed it.

It was almost too good to be true.

I felt a small spike and then there was a pause before the door slowly creaked open. There was little light in the room and I could only just barely make out the shadows of a table, chair, and bed.

I took two steps in and that's when I realized there was a person sitting in the shadows. I suspected a witch, based on the way my magic reacted violently inside of me, but the signature was off...something was wrong with it.

"Glad you could make it," said a woman sitting near the corner of the room. Her face was shrouded by shadows and I watched in interest as she leaned forward, the dim light shining on her face giving me a perfect view of her twisted burned face, the entire left side of her face burned beyond recognition.

Her dark hair peeked out of her hood but that too was fried and stuck out in every which way.

The door closed behind me and I shifted on my feet.

When she turned I finally got a good look at the other side of her face and my heart stopped dead in my chest. Ice-cold fear was injected into my veins and my legs planted themselves to the cheap stained floor, barring me from any fast movements.

Xena did not die in the battle.

I swallowed thickly and looked around the room for anything to help my escape...but there wasn't even a window in this room.

Xena had somehow survived the entire ordeal and sat right in front of me. While she may not have been in perfect condition... she was *alive*.

Was Cumae trying to kill me?

"This is a mistake," I said in a grave tone. I willed my body to leave, but not even a muscle twitched.

"No mistake," she said, her voice raspy like she had been smoking for years. "Your friend reached out and I said I would help."

"I don't trust that you would want to help," I said. "You tried to *kill* us."

"No," she said and stood, her cloak falling to the ground behind her giving me a look at her entire burned left half.

I had to swallow my bile.

"I just wanted my daughter back," she said. "But I truly am not here to punish you for that. Though I will require a payment from you once my work is complete."

I took a step back with tremendous effort and a sweat broke out on my skin.

"I won't give anyone up to you," I growled.

Xena let out a harsh chuckle.

"I never said that's what I wanted," she replied.

"Then what do you want?"

I shouldn't even be considering this. I should be turning around and running back to the others, getting as far away from this psycho as possible.

But a part of me wanted to hear her out. I *needed* the help.

"I will tell you if this goes well," she said. "After all I don't even know if this is possible."

I gritted my teeth and tried to take calming breaths through my nose.

"If you won't tell me I am leaving," I insisted.

The tight cord that was holding me to my spot snapped and I

turned towards the door, but paused as soon as my hand hit the sticky doorknob.

"Do you want to die?" she asked. "Because with the way your magic feels, it seems like you don't have much longer."

Damn it all.

"How long?" I asked.

She let out a humming noise that ground on my nerves.

"Once the magic takes over I have seen people last anywhere from three months to two years, though if you have rapid signs of growth you can expect a few weeks. Those are usually the hardest for the host."

"What are the signs of a more extreme condition?"

Another pause.

"Your magic controls your every move, develops a mind of its own, its own wants and needs," she said. "Once it becomes corporeal you have little to no time left. It will come for your core."

Damn it, damn it, damn it.

"I won't allow you to hurt any of them," I vowed and turned back to her.

Even in the dim light her brown eyes shone.

"I don't have a plan to," she said.

Rosie was going to hate me.

We made such good progress and here I was confiding with the enemy that had literally tried to kill us.

And if Malik or Rae ever found out...I would be as good as dead.

But if not, and I went home *right now,* I wouldn't have long with them anyways. I would die a lonely and meaningless death, unable to live out my dreams of a happy life with them.

"Fine," I spat.

"Good, *good,*" she purred. "Now let's get started shall we? Since you seem to be in a hurry. Can't *wait* to let that little monster out."

She raised her hand, a large magic knife took shape and in my mind all I could think of was the lonely meaningless death and how that seemed to be a much better option now.

Before I could move, darkness shrouded the room and that was when I felt her lips against the shell of my ear.

"This is going to hurt," she said with a chuckle.

The last thing I felt was the knife sinking into my chest.

WANT EXCLUSIVE CONTENT?

Join my Patreon and you will get access to all stories BEFORE they are published.

If you join now you will get free stories and deleted chapters!

There is also a tier for NSFW art that is exclusive for my Patreon members

Check it out here or go to https://www.patreon.com/ellemaebooks

IF YOU LIKED THIS, PLEASE REVIEW!

Reviews really help indie authors get their books out there so, please make sure to share your thoughts!

ACKNOWLEDGMENTS

This is the FOURTH book of the Winterfell Academy series.

I cannot believe the support that y'all have given me and I am so grateful for everyone who picks up one of my books.

Thank you to my readers for believing in me and thank you to my partner for living through this stressful time with me and pushing me towards my dream.

ABOUT THE AUTHOR

Elle is a native Californian who has lived in Los Angeles for most of her life. From the very start, she has been in love with all things fantasy and reading. As soon as Elle found out that writing books could be a career, she picked up a pen and paper. While the first ones were about scorned love and missed opportunities of lunchtime love, she has grown to love the fantasy genre and looks forward to making a difference in the world with her stories.

Loved this book? Please leave a review!

For more behind the scene content, sign up for my newsletter at https://view.flodesk.com/pages/61722d0874d564fa09f4021b

 twitter.com/mae_books

 instagram.com/ellemaebooks

 goodreads.com/ellemae